THE PROTEUS CURE

D1501464

F. PAUL WILSON

AND

TRACY L. CARBONE

THE

PROTEUS
CURE

SHADOWRIDGE
PRESS

THE PROTEUS CURE

First published May 2013
by Shadowridge Press

ISBN-13: 978-0615795874
ISBN-10: 0615795870

www.shadowridgepress.com

ACKNOWLEDGEMENTS

The authors would like to offer special thanks to Dannielle Romeo for her sharp eye for the wayward word.

They would also like to thank Robert Barr of Shadowridge Press for his work in designing the book you now hold in your hands.

A NOTE TO THE READER

A while back, at a writer-reader conference, Tracy Carbone asked me about the scientific / medical feasibility of an idea she had for a medical thriller. As we discussed the biological aspects and how the idea would work into her novel, I suggested she turn her plot on its head and approach the story from the opposite direction. Many emails followed as we batted the story's throughline back and forth, hammering it into shape. I became so involved (I found myself thinking about it more than my own work in progress) that I finally suggested we write it together.

And we did.

-F. Paul Wilson

NOW

SHEILA

More rain. Would it ever stop?

Sheila chewed her lip as she maneuvered her 4Runner along the slick, twisting two-lane road from Salem, New Hampshire.

Christmas was only a few weeks away and she needed snow, white fluffy mounds of it, to breathe some spirit into her. Going holiday shopping hadn't done a thing for her enthusiasm. Crowded stores. Wet streets.

She hit a pothole, and the impact bounced her car so hard she thought for sure she'd get a flat. Her coffee splashed up out of the lid and down the side of the cup. Great.

Peace on earth, goodwill toward men . . .

Sheila wished she could find a little peace. Recently her life seemed to have become a train wreck. Things she'd taken for granted, people she'd trusted . . . her safe, sane, ordered world had taken strange turns.

A patient dead in the past week—a freak accident, they said, but a convenient one. She hadn't known her well, granted, but she'd had a face, a name . . .

If she could somehow excise the past week from her life, everything would be safe and sane again. She'd be her old workaholic self, the indefatigable Sheila Takamura, the ever-cheerful up-and-coming staff oncologist at Tethys Medical Center, going about her daily routine of curing the incurable in the clinical trial of miracle drug VG723.

But maybe it wasn't a miracle.

Or maybe miracles don't come free.

But last week had happened, and what she'd experienced had tainted her relationship with Tethys, and with its headman, Bill Gilchrist.

Bill, the gorgeous, rich mentor and a co-owner of the hospital. The man who had fed her fantasies for years. Clive Owen without the accent. She shook her head at the thought of him now.

Bill Gilchrist had fallen from grace. God, how had she been so blind? He had walked on water. Could do no wrong. "Glittered when he walked," or whatever that Richard Cory line was. Feet of clay was more like it.

Or maybe tongue of clay—discouraging her from investigating two bizarre patient anomalies.

Well she was *not* letting this go. One patient was dead and her evidence was gone, but the other was alive and kicking and demanding answers. Answers Sheila wanted as well.

She turned off the radio, leaving only the swish of the windshield wipers to distract her, and focused on her next step for diagnosing Tanesha and her strange—

Her rearview mirror brightened. Sheila glanced up and saw a car coming up fast behind her. Really stupid on this curvy road with only a metal guardrail between you and the rocky ravine below. Insane on a wet surface. Probably some teen. She remembered her attitude back in those days: immortal. Dek had felt that way too, and where was he now? Dead, leaving her a widow.

She eased up on the gas and edged to the right to allow him a little more room to get by.

She glanced at the darkness beyond the guardrail. Through the ages the river below had carved a deep pass between these hills. Scenic during the day—which explained all the high-ticket houses atop the far side—but a black pit at night.

As the headlights raced up behind her—and headlights were all she could see—she tightened her grip on the wheel and slowed even more. The near-blinding lights swerved around her rear fender and came up close beside her. Too close. She glanced over and saw a big Suburban, driven by someone shaped like a man.

Mother of God! He'd slowed to the point where he was pacing her, his front bumper a couple of feet ahead of hers. Her heart missed a beat, muscles tightened.

He passed her. Thank God. Just some nut in a hurry. Sheila took a few deep breaths, tried to lower her heart rate. Too much adrenaline. *You're okay, Sheila, you're okay.* He disappeared around the next bend.

The rhythm of the wipers gradually calmed her.

Her mind slowly drifted back to the VG723 trial. If she could only—

Out of the darkness two lights lit up her driver's side window. She screamed before the impact knocked her hands off the steering wheel, before she knew what hit her. And screamed again as she was smashed on the side a second time. The 4Runner careened over the guardrail and seemed to hang in mid air forever before plunging toward the dark river below.

Sheila felt the car crash onto the hillside with a bone-bending jar that bounced the top of her head against the ceiling. The car tilted again and rolled onto the passenger side, then onto the roof, leaving her hanging upside down in her seatbelt for an instant before the rocky ground rammed against the driver's side, slamming her head against the window, shattering it. Shards of safety glass showered around her. The car then did two more quarter rolls onto its passenger side before completing its slide to the edge of the river at the bottom of the ravine.

When finally it ground to a halt, Sheila's body weight and gravity pulled her toward the passenger seat, but her seatbelt held her painfully in place. She hovered, battered and shaken, her heart thumping against her chest wall like a trapped, frightened animal as she gasped for breath.

Still puffing, she ran her hands over her body—a bloody nose but no blazing tenderness. No broken teeth or bones. She was alive and seemingly intact. But her head . . . it seemed to be spinning.

Concussion, most likely.

Cold rain through the shattered window her splattered her face, reviving her. She was blessing the inventor of the seatbelt when the reality of what had just happened slammed into her.

No accident! The bastard had passed her and waited. Broadsided her. Tried to kill her.

Had to get out.

Sheila tried to brace herself on the steering wheel but it kept turning. Nothing to hold onto. She held her breath and pressed the release button on her seatbelt, anticipating the drop. She fell hard a couple of feet toward the passenger side of the car. Not too bad. Fighting a wave of nausea-tinged vertigo, she turned herself around and struggled upward until she could poke her head through the frame where her window had been. Steam rising from her hood wafted around her along with the odor of spilled gasoline.

She looked up toward the road for a sign that someone had seen her go over the edge and was dialing 9-1-1.

But all she saw was a big SUV parked by the guardrail . . . and a figure making its way down the slope. Not with the frantic pace of someone who'd witnessed an accident and wanted help. No, this looked like the slow, measured approach of someone who wanted to see if his efforts had been successful. She couldn't make him out, his face a dark silhouette from the SUV lights behind him, but she sensed his steady purpose: If the crash hadn't killed her, he'd do it.

But who was *he*? What enemies did she have? None really. Then reality struck her like a punch in the stomach.

Bill?

He had warned her to stop asking questions, threatened to force her to take time off, a "mental leave of sorts" if she didn't stop "obsessing about conspiracy theories." Suggested she might be paranoid and might be well-served to seek professional help. But would he actually try to kill her? God, what if he would?

Sheila grabbed for her cell phone but couldn't find it.

The smell of gas grew stronger. Had her fuel tank ruptured?

Panic spurred new strength into her, propelling her through the window frame. She crawled over the roof and staggered on rubber knees as her feet hit the ground on the far side of the car.

It struck her that the best camouflage or diversion or whatever would be a fire. It would attract attention from the houses atop the opposite slope. Her killer wouldn't be able to wait around. He'd have to run before the police arrived.

But . . . she didn't have a lighter. Damn! If only she hadn't quit smoking!

A knot formed in her chest, making it harder to catch her breath. Only one thing to do . . .

Run. Worry about identifying the stalker later. Get to safety.

Keeping low, Sheila stepped off the bank into the freezing river. At least the river was narrow and shallow here. Her vision swam and her head felt like it was going to explode. As she neared the other side, she vomited and the swirling water carried it away.

Please don't let me pass out now. Please!

The far bank was almost within reach. She'd planned to climb the slope beyond it but knew now that was impossible. She was just about spent.

How had her life come to this?

Unbidden, memories of the events of the past week began to wheel around her. She remembered when things had begun to go wrong.

Last week . . . she hadn't realized it at the time, but that was when her life started turning sour . . .

The night suddenly lit up with a thunderous roar as her car exploded.

And then her world went black.

BILL

With Elise at the mall and Robbie immersed in Call of Duty, Bill had April all to himself. The five-year old was using his multicolored Post-It notes to make a big flower on the wall of his home office. He looked up from the pile of employee reviews he needed to sign and smiled at her. Such a sweet kid. A ball of sunshine.

His desk phone rang and he picked it up. Probably Elise.

"Doctor Gilchrist?"

"Speaking."

"This is the switchboard. We have the Bradfield Police calling about Doctor Takamura."

He straightened in the chair. Sheila?

"What did they say?"

"They want to speak to someone in charge, and so I—"

"Put them through!"

A voice identified itself as Sergeant Frayne, Bradfield PD and said, *"We had an accident in the ravine outside of town. It's registered to a Sheila Ta-ka-mura—I think that's how you say it. We noticed the car had a Tethys parking permit so we assume she's one of your people."*

"Yes-yes. We have a Doctor Takamura here. Is she all right?"

"Well, we don't know for sure, but it doesn't look good."

"How can you not know?"

"There's no sign of her. It appears the car exploded on impact but we can't find her body. We feel she may have been blown into the river and swept downstream."

"Dear God!"

Weakness swept over him. He all but lost his grip on the phone.

"We're going to mount a search for her body but as I said, it doesn't look good. Do you know how we can contact her next of kin?"

April tugged at his sleeve. "Daddy, are you okay?"

He'd forgotten she was here. Damn. No, he was not okay. But he nodded and listened to the officer.

Next of kin? He didn't think Sheila had any.

"I—I don't know of any. I'm a little too upset to think right now."

"I understand, sir."

"I'll have my secretary look into it first thing tomorrow. I'll have her call you then."

Bill hung up and found April staring at him.

"Daddy?"

April looked worried. He wrapped his arms around her.

"It's all right, sweetie."

But it wasn't. Not even close.

"Are you gonna be sick?" Her lip quivered. "You look sick."

"A good friend of Daddy's got hurt and I'm very sad about it."

"Will he be okay?"

Not a "he," but Bill didn't correct her. He needed to be alone . . . just for a minute.

"Would you get Daddy a glass of cold water from the refrigerator, sweetie?"

Smiling at the responsibility she was being given, she rushed out to the kitchen. When she was gone, Bill folded his arms on his desktop and rested his forehead on them.

Sheila . . . poor Sheila. The best on his staff . . . a brilliant, caring physician, a genuinely good person . . . gone, snuffed out in the blink of an eye. The staff, the patients would be devastated. But no one more than Abra.

God, how was he going to tell her?

Had to keep this quiet until he could sit down face to face with his sister.

I'll miss her too, he thought.

But . . .

But relief tinged his grief, and he hated himself for that. Sheila was no longer a threat, would no longer be sticking her nose into places she didn't belong. The secret of VG723 would be safe. But at such a cost.

He felt something wet on the back of his wrist. He lifted his head and looked.

A tear.

THEN

__ONE__

SHEILA

Dr. Sheila Takamura snatched Sean O'Reilly's chart from the nurses' station and headed for his room. Her heels beat an echoey tattoo on the tiled floor of the lymphoma ward at Tethys Hospital. Not quite thirty-five, she had a slim, compact body, reddish blond hair, and a freckled nose.

Sheila had just got word from Bill Gilchrist that Sean had been cleared for VG723 therapy and she couldn't help smiling. So far, nine out of every ten patients who received VG723 in the clinical trial had beaten cancer. All types of cancer. Ninety percent in remission, back from the brink of death when every other therapy had failed. Remarkable results for the lucky ones who qualified for it. Sean had just got lucky.

She wished VG723 had been around when her mother had lung cancer. Gone six months after she was diagnosed. Sheila bit her lip. When would losing Mum ever stop hurting?

At least now she had Abra. Sheila smiled when she thought of the little woman who had become her surrogate mother. Abra had no children, Sheila no parents, and they both lived for Tethys. It seemed fate had brought them to each other.

Sheila heard a familiar voice as she approached the room. Paul Rosko. She smiled and listened as he read to Sean.

Paul had first shown up at Tethys seven years ago—long before

Sheila had arrived—when his six-year-old son had undergone an experimental leukemia therapy. The boy was thirteen now and cancer free. But his dad still hung around, volunteering, comforting the chemo patients. Said he owed Tethys for the miracle they'd performed on his son.

Well, he's certainly paid his debt, she thought.

Something about Paul, something in the lilt in his voice that made her smile, made everyone smile. One of those people who brought life with him wherever he went. She admired his dedication, his refusal to let people fall into the despair that pushed many over the edge. If that tenacity was needed anywhere, it was in the cancer ward. Paul made a difference . . .

She stepped through the door and found him sitting at Sean's bedside. The twenty-year-old lay propped up on his pillows, his naked scalp reflecting the overhead fluorescents, his skin so pale that it was hard to tell where Sean ended and his sheets began. Michael Stipe in whiteface.

What a contrast to the burley, dark-haired, flannel-shirted man sitting bedside. To some his size might have been intimidating, but Sheila saw him as a human Teddy bear.

"So, Professor Rosko, teaching literature again?"

Paul rose. "Oh, hi, Sheila. I wish I were a professor, but . . ."

Something in his eyes when he said that . . . something Sheila couldn't place.

"Sean, don't let him fool you," she said. "I've been a professional student most of my life and I don't know one tenth of what Paul does about literature or history. 'Professor' is well-deserved."

"No, please—"

Sean said, "Then what *do* you do, man?"

"A cable installer. Just a working stiff." He seemed to be apologizing. He gave Sheila an uncertain smile and spoke in a hacked English accent. *"I work pretty 'ard for a sufficient living."*

She knew he was quoting something but had no idea what it was.

"Beatles?" she said, tongue firmly in cheek. *"Hard Days Night?"*

Sean laughed.

"Close." Paul held up a copy of *Great Expectations.* "I've been talking to Sean about Pip. He had it tough for a long time, but he turned out all right in the end."

Sheila stepped closer to the bed.

"Funny you should be talking about *Great Expectations;* I just got word that we have some pretty great expectations for you, Sean. You've qualified for VG-seven-twenty-three."

The left side of Sean's mouth twisted. "Well, hallelujah. I've been selected by the Tethys gods to sample their elixir. I'm worthy to enter their lottery."

Earlier in her career Sheila might have asked herself why this youth was acting like a jerk. But experience had informed her. She'd offered him hope, but he'd had so many hopes dashed he'd become gun shy. He'd learned: If you don't get your hopes up, they can't be shot down.

"You were a match so you—"

"What makes me so special? We've all got the Big C."

"Seven-twenty-three isn't for everyone, Sean. You know that. It's got to be individually matched."

"The therapy uses stem cells, right? Can't they become anything, fix anyone?"

She'd wondered the same thing, many times. Why did some patients not qualify? VecGen, the company producing VG723, was secretive about the selection process—probably with good proprietary reasons. But she couldn't argue with their great results.

Males, females, blacks, whites, rich, poor, Tethys had no criteria for admission beyond the fact that the patient be eighteen or older and that all other therapies had failed. No pattern she could see to those who didn't qualify, but it appeared as if younger patients got the nod most often. She hadn't done a statistical analysis, but it seemed more people in their twenties wound up with VG723 than all other age groups combined.

Beyond the standard screening tests, VG also required current photos of each patient. A photographer shot full body views and face shots from every angle.

The heartbreak came when patients she thought would succeed didn't qualify. Like that young pre-law from Harvard. She was smart as a whip, with rich parents who begged for the VG723. God, her father was a state representative. You'd think he'd have some pull. But no match. Sweet girl. Albino. Sheila had had to watch her grow even paler as the cancer took her away. So damn frustrating, but it was out of her hands. Sheila had no say, no control. VG723 had to be tailored to the patient and the malignancy. If they couldn't make a match, it wouldn't work.

Informing the rejects usually fell to her. How she dreaded those days.

"Sean." Paul leaned over and touched the young man's foot. "Listen, when my son Coogan had leukemia, when he was in a bed like this one, he saw some of his roommates die. Good friends who didn't all come through. No, it's not fair. It sucks. But a lot *are* saved. That's what counts. Yes, I feel terrible for the others, but at the end of the day . . . well . . . " His voice caught. "I was able to take my son home and I thank God every day for that. You've got to be thankful too."

Sheila touched Paul's arm. He'd said what she felt.

"It's true, Sean. Seven-twenty-three can't save everyone, but it can save so many who'd die without it. I want you to be happy."

Sean wiped his eyes. "I *am* happy. I'm freakin' stoked. But I feel wicked guilty, okay? Katie died last week. I wanted her to get the treatment. She could have been saved."

Sheila shook her head. "Not by seven-twenty-three, Sean. They couldn't make a match. Forget the guilt, okay? You didn't take seven-twenty-three from Katie or anyone else. It simply wouldn't have helped her. But it will help you. Smile, now, okay? You're going to live."

Sean sobered. "Well, there's no guarantee."

Sheila and Paul exchanged glances.

"You're right," she said. "No promises, but seven-twenty-three has a great track record. No reason we can't add you to our successes."

A smile crept onto Sean's face. "I've got a chance," he whispered.

Then louder. "I've got a freakin chance! Do my parents know yet?"

"No, you're the first."

"I've gotta call them." He was beaming now as he turned to Paul. "Well, Prof, looks like *Classics 101* is canceled for tonight. Got about a hundred calls to make."

Sheila placed the phone on his bed and patted his hand.

"Congratulations, Sean. Come on, Paul. "

As soon as they reached the hallway, Paul threw an arm across her shoulders.

"You folks are amazing. What you do here at Tethys—"

Sheila softened at his touch. Feeling his muscular arm around her reminded her how long it had been since a man had held her. She breathed his scent, Irish Spring, just like Dek used to wear.

Paul released her. ". . . don't you think?"

Sheila stared at him. What had he said? Her mind had wandered off. He brought back feelings . . . she'd felt a *connection*.

God, what a high school thing to think.

"What?" she asked, her voice shaky.

"Don't you think it's just matter of time before Tethys wins the Nobel? They've pretty much wrapped up a cure for cancer. If that doesn't warrant a trip to Sweden, I don't know what does."

"It's not us. It's VecGen's development. We just administer it."

"So modest." He cleared his throat. "I was thinking . . . Want to go to lunch? To uh, to celebrate about Sean?"

Sheila looked at her watch. "I can't. I've got back-to-back patients till late today."

"I can hang around. Afternoon coffee?"

Sheila took a mental step back. Was he hitting on her? She'd never thought of him *that* way. Rarely thought of anyone that way. After Dek, work had become her life. But she liked Paul. Had liked him for a long time from the little she knew of him. Looked forward to seeing his smile every week.

"I don't mind waiting," Paul said. "I can bother some more patients. I'm sure someone wants to hear about Dickens." He grinned and shrugged. "Or not."

She was tempted. It was *just* coffee, not a marriage proposal.

"All right. I'd like that."

"Me too."

He held her gaze and Sheila didn't seem able to say anything else or move from the spot. But it was a good immobility. A surge of long-forgotten excitement rushed through her.

"Okay then," he said.

She broke eye contact and noticed that her heart rate had kicked up. "Three o'clock? We'll meet by the river in the parking lot. Coog wants to practice some skateboard moves. We can watch."

"Okay, see you then," she said.

"Looking forward to it."

He turned and walked down the hall. She stood for a minute, enjoying the feeling of being interested in something other than work.

Work! She needed to call a patient.

The chart was back in her office, so she put on her leather coat and gloves, and then headed outside.

Early December and unseasonably warm. By now they should have been buried in snow but the predicted high today was forty-five. She knew it was only a matter of time before they'd be into the single-digits of winter.

There's New England for you.

The clang and clatter of heavy machinery echoed through the air from the construction site of the new wing. She couldn't wait for it to be finished. No matter how much refurbishing they underwent, these old buildings were still so, well, old.

She kicked at the brown leaves as they blew into her path. A crisp morning. Tethys and its surrounding town of Bradfield sat amid rolling hills. Down the slope to her right the Copper River glistened, winding past the campus, down through the center of their little village, and on into the woods.

A month ago an Autumn-in-New England postcard. Today the trees stood bare and the massive surrounding hills blocked the sun. The grass had gone into hibernation. A clear sky today, but soon the snow would come and she'd be hurrying through a Winter-in-

New England postcard.

All the buildings at Tethys Medical Center looked the same: majestic, old, solid structures with granite block walls nearly black with age. Stately but intimidating.

All this used to be Bradfield College, a medical school built in 1890. It went under in the eighties and sat empty until Tethys Medical Center stepped in about a dozen years ago and bought it. After major renovations the Admin building kept its purpose, the men's dorm became the Tethys Cancer Center, the women's dorm the Tethys Birthing Center, a fertility clinic, the classroom building the lab. The smaller dormitories and faculty housing became homes for the employees.

Sheila had bought the gardener's home upriver. An awful nice house for a gardener: two stories, three bedrooms, roof patio . . . and for a third of what she would have paid if she'd bought off campus in overpriced Bradfield.

Bill, her boss, friend, and one of the founders, lived in the former Dean's house, a mansion overlooking the river.

Must be nice, Sheila thought. Jesus, just *look* at that house.

Even from this far, she could see Elise Gilchrist's shiny new Porsche pull into the driveway. She stiffened as the chic brunette got out of the car, arms loaded with shopping bags.

Sheila shook her head. No, I'm *not* jealous.

She turned away from the Gilchrist mansion and trudged on.

Sheila liked living in Bradfield. She'd grown up in Massachusetts, was used to the weather, wouldn't dream of leaving. This was a great town for shopping—ten miles from tax-free New Hampshire, forty miles to Boston, and only an hour to the outlet stores in Freeport, Maine. People *needed* access to L.L. Bean's winter gear if they lived around here.

A gust blew some leaves into her face. Nice. The wind puffed again but she stepped into the Admin building ahead of the leaves.

She trotted up to her third-floor office, turned on the overhead light, flung her coat on the guest chair, and sat in her rolling black leather ergonomic. She'd decorated it as an extension of her house:

White walls with the same tan curtains she'd bought for her home office.

A picture of Dek holding a model train engine smiled at her from a brass frame. She sniffed apple pie and remembered the gel candle on the side table. A comforting smell, unlike the "Summer Rain" one she'd bought a few months ago that smelled like Windex.

She grabbed Kelly Slade's chart from her desktop. Records had dropped it off because Kelly had missed her appointment today. That wasn't like her. Last week the poor woman had been virtually devastated by some truly odd symptoms. Sheila had taken pictures, ordered labs, and scheduled a follow-up for today.

She'd been a Tethys patient, another VG723 success story. For two years, no contact, then last week, presenting with those disturbing changes in her skin and hair. Sheila hadn't known what to think.

Odd she didn't make it in today.

Sheila dialed the home number from the chart. After a few rings, she got an answering machine and hung up. She couldn't find a cell number so she turned on her computer.

While she waited for it to boot up she tapped on the desk's glass top and looked around. Framed degrees and academic awards dotted the walls. Papers covered the desk. Despite her efforts, the place still didn't feel homey. Not enough color. She frowned. Have to work on that.

She reached across the desk and retrieved the clay pencil cup a patient's child had made her as a thank-you for saving her dad. She pushed back the papers and set it before her. In purple crayon it read, *Thank you, Dr. Sheila.*

It should have read *Thank you, VG723.*

For the thousandth time she wondered why 723 wasn't used on children.

Well, at least it cured their parents.

When her screen came to life she keyed in Kelly's name. Gray letters popped onto the screen: "File closed—Deceased."

Her fingers jumped off the keys. The date was two days ago. How could that be?

She put her index finger to her lips where her teeth started to tug at a nail, but she caught herself.

Bad habit.

She felt a pang as she stared at the screen.

Poor Kelly. She'd overcome so much, and now . . . gone. Doctors were supposed to be inured to death, but she sure wasn't. Not yet anyway.

No cause of death mentioned but Sheila guessed it must have been some kind of accident.

She'd presented with a fascinating syndrome. Well, fascinating to Sheila, maddening to Kelly. The distraught woman had cried for answers and Sheila hadn't had any.

She had to investigate Kelly further. She'd talk to Bill about it at lunch. Get his take.

She put on her coat on and headed back to the hospital.

TANESHA

Tanesha Green slipped off the edge of the examining table in her oversized napkin cape and stepped to the small mirror on the wall.

Lordy, how she hated looking at herself these days. Her hair, skin . . . downright scary, not to mention embarrassing what with all her friends and relations staring at her like she done it on purpose. And no matter how many times she told them it weren't none of her doing, absolutely *none*, she could tell by their eyes that they thought she was fronting, like she was trying to become some sort of Afro-Saxon.

Her hair . . . used to be so black. Black as an eight ball—and just as shiny when she fixed it up. Okay, maybe not perfect black. A touch of gray had been creeping in—after all, she was pushing forty. But now . . . mousy brown and straight as corn flax. Where'd *that* come from?

And her skin? Her lifelong shade of fresh-brewed Jamaican coffee had upped and gone. Now it was . . . she didn't know what to call it. Weak tea with four of those little creamer things thrown in. Yeah, that came close.

And it was getting worse.

Even her little Jamal was starting with the funny looks.

Something damn well had to be done. Which was why she come here again, dammit. She hated this city hospital.

Nothing here like the fancy rooms over at Tethys, but this was a lot closer. And Tethys just did cancer. This wasn't cancer. She heard a sound on the other side of the door and bustled back to the paper-covered table. But with short legs and too much belly, not easy getting herself seated again.

Damn, girl, but you're packing on the pounds.

Hell, it was all this worry. Once she got her condition fixed, she could start on a diet. Now she was just too nervous. And when she got too nervous she just ate. And ate.

Tanesha was smoothing the front of the paper cape when the door opened.

A man in a white coat stepped inside, carrying a manila folder. Tanesha had never seen him before.

"Hey, you're not Doctor Gleason."

The man smiled—not a happy smile, not by a long shot. Hardly a smile at all.

"Hey, I'm quite well aware of that."

This hatchet-faced stranger was older than Dr. Gleason by at least ten years—looked mid fifties—with graying hair, horn-rimmed glasses, and pale skin. Had that air of honkey superiority that riled Tanesha every time she faced it.

"Well then, where's Doctor Gleason? He's the one I usually see."

She knew you didn't always get the same doctor here at the public clinic, but she liked Gleason. Folks said the Penner Brigham had the best clinic in Boston, and only a short hop on the T from her place. Kind of like a lottery with which doctor you got, but if they worked here they must be good.

"Doctor Gleason is a bit under the weather, so I'm covering for him. If you wish to cancel today and make another appointment, no problem. You can stop at the desk on your way out and I'm sure they'll be happy to accommodate you."

Tanesha thought about that. She'd taken an instant dislike to this Wonder Bread with a stethoscope, but appointments here took time to get. And to tell the truth, Doc Gleason hadn't been much help. Some tests and such, but everything kept coming back normal. This one wasn't so friendly, but maybe he was smarter.

Tanesha gave a mental shrug: What she have to lose?

She sighed. "No, I guess you'll do."

"A ringing endorsement if I ever heard one."

Without another look at her he seated himself at the little desk built into the wall and opened her chart. Doc Gleason always shook her hand and acted like he was glad to see her. This cracker looked like he could care less.

"Ain't you gonna tell me your name?"

Without looking up he said, "Kaplan. Doctor Gerald Kaplan. And you, I see, are Tanesha Green." Finally he looked at her. "What can I do for you, Tanesha Green?"

She snorted. "Something more than Doc Gleason, I hope."

"That is certainly a possibility. But I'll need a little more input than 'Something more than Doc Gleason.' Could we be a little more specific?"

Lord, this was one cold-ass bastard.

She pointed to her head. "Lookit my hair. It didn't used to be like this. I used to have a full-frizz Afro. Now I gots this . . . this light brown thatch. But as if that ain't enough, my skin's going white. I been going around in circles with Doc Gleason and—"

"It's obviously some odd variant of vitiligo."

This guy sounded bored to death. Didn't even bother to get up.

Tanesha pointed to him. "That's what Doc Gleason said at first. Viti . . . viti—"

"Vitiligo. It's an autoimmune condition that causes loss of skin pigment." He frowned as he eyed her exposed arms. "But it's usually patchy. Yours appears to be unusually uniform and pervasive."

"It's all over the place too. And it ain't that viti-thing."

She saw the doctor cock his head, saw his eyebrows jump toward his hairline.

"Oh? And you received your medical degree from . . . ?"

He was steaming her, really getting her blood up. She had a mind to haul off and whack him good upside the head.

"Ain't got no medical degree, but I know I ain't got viti-whatever. First thing Doc Gleason did was send me to a skin guy. He couldn't figure it out neither, but he said it wasn't no viti-thing."

"Did he take a biopsy?"

"Supposed to but it got put off."

Kaplan frowned. "Too bad. I would have liked to have seen the result."

Yeah, he sounded real interested—about as interested as she was in watching *Seinfeld* reruns.

She grabbed her shoulder bag from behind her, fished out her driver's license, and held it out to Kaplan.

"Here. Looky this."

Kaplan didn't bother to stand, just rolled his chair toward her, took the card, and rolled back to the desk. He looked at the photo on the license, then back to her.

"You're right. A startling change."

"I been living with this skin for thirty-nine years. I know when something ain't right."

He kept shaking his head as he looked at the card, then at her, then at the card again.

Tanesha felt her patience thinning.

"Look, you gonna help me or not? I mean it's not like I like seeing doctors. I don't. I seen enough of you when I had the cancer and—"

"Cancer? Really."

Hey, all of a sudden a spark of interest. Kaplan began flipping through her chart.

"Yeah, the big C. And lemme tell you—"

"What kind of cancer, if I may be so bold to ask?"

"Colon. Started passing blood one day a couple years ago and some doctor put a tube up there for a look and said that's what I got. I don't know where it come from. Ain't no cancer in my family."

"So you received a resection followed by chemotherapy, I assume."

"Yeah. Chemo, radiation—you think all that junk's maybe got something to do with this?"

Kaplan finally hauled himself out of the chair and stepped up beside her. He bent and looked at the skin on her upper arm. Lots of skin there—too damn much. *Had* to do something about all this fat. He lifted her paper cape and looked at her back, then he poked a finger onto her hair.

He shook his head. "No, I've seen a lot of cancer survivors but never anything even remotely like this."

"'Scuse me, but just because you never seen it don't mean it ain't because of what they give me. Lemme tell you, I was sick as a dog. I wanted someone to shoot me so's I could feel better. And all for nothing."

Kaplan's eyebrows did their lift thing again. "What do you mean, 'All for nothing?' You're here now, alive and apparently well. I wouldn't call that nothing."

"Maybe you wouldn't but I would. Damn shit spread from my colon all through my liver. They said I was a goner. I was getting ready to meet the Lord up close and personal. Only then they come up with this new treatment."

"Really. And what might that be?"

"Some code name. But I'll never forget it: VG-seven-twenty-three."

His eyes got this faraway look. "Yes, codes are SOP for clinical trials. That means you were part of an experimental protocol." He shook his head. "But VG-seven-twenty-three is a new one on me, and I make a point of keeping up on these things."

"Guess you ain't as up as you think, sugar. That stuff's already a couple years old."

"Who treated you with this VG-seven-twenty-three?"

"The Tethys folks."

Kaplan started nodding. "Ah. That explains it. They play everything very, very close to the vest."

"Hey, I don't care where they plays it, long as it got me better.

They put those little stem cells in me and—"

"Wait! Stem cells?"

Something in his voice made her look closer and she saw his whitebread face got even whiter.

"Yeah, stem cells. You heard of them?"

"Yes. Cutting edge stuff."

This doc had changed. Like a different person. No more high-and-mighty honkey 'tude. Looked like a puppy who'd just heard its first roll of thunder.

"That's good. At least you know *something*. Me, I don't know what they is, but they sure as shit saved my life."

Kaplan backed toward the desk and dropped into the chair like he was drunk.

He picked up her license and started doing that look-at-the-card-then-look-at-her thing again. With each look he seemed to get older and—Tanesha wouldn't have thought it possible—paler.

"Hey, you're scaring me, doc. What's wrong?"

He stared at the license a long time before saying, "Nothing." She could barely hear him. "Nothing at all."

"Then why you so—?"

"I'm sorry," he said, popping up from his chair. "I can't help you."

"What you mean?"

He grabbed her chart and handed back her license.

"No one here can help you."

"But this here hospital is supposed to be a, watchacall, medical center, a teaching hospital—"

"Believe me, Ms. Green, this hospital has no answers for you. You need to go back to Tethys."

Now she was really spooked.

"You think it was that VG-seven-twenty-three?"

"I do."

"But you just said you didn't know nothing about it."

"No, I do know about it. Too much about it."

"But—"

"Tethys," he said, looking like an old man who's just heard his whole family got wiped out in a drive-by. "Go back to Tethys."

And then he was out the door, slamming it closed behind him.

Tanesha sat there in shock, her stomach twisting into a knot.

What just happened? One minute he's all uppity, next he's outta here.

First thing she did after tearing herself out of the stupid little cape and getting back into her blouse was pull out her cell phone. Her fingers shook as she called information for the Tethys number.

What was the name of that doctor who'd kept track of her cancer treatments? Japanese name but not a Jap. Nice lady. Nicest doctor there. Tekka . . . Takka . . . Takamura. That was it. That was who she'd ask for.

Tethys was all the way up in Bradfield, practically New Hampshire, but that was where she damn well was going.

SHEILA

Sheila walked out of a patient's room and collided with a familiar solid figure.

"Bill. I didn't see you."

He didn't step back. Neither did she. They stayed planted against each other. The feeling of his body against hers . . . damn. She hated that he was married. How the hell long before she got over this stupid schoolgirl crush?

Brilliance and dedication were reasons a plenty to find him attractive. But did he have to be so damned good looking? Mid-forties with dark hair combed back and parted high. Chiseled features . . .

Bill slid his hand to the side of her neck and down to her shoulder and gently pushed her back. But he left his hand there. He gave her an *I-want-you-too-Sheila-but-I-can't* look.

She managed to squeak out, "Time for lunch?"

He cleared his throat. "Yeah. I just swung by to get you."

"Great. Let me set this down."

She took a minute to drop off the chart and calm herself. Nothing like unrequited lust—or was it love?—to get the adrenaline going.

But how could she not be drawn to him? Beyond being gorgeous and brilliant and rich, Bill was the genesis of Tethys. The guy who saved the lives. She merely oversaw the treatments. She knew her face was beet red but couldn't do anything about it. Damn Irish genes.

They took the elevator to the first floor. When the door shut, she looked at him and he smiled. Neither said a word.

Stupid crush.

"I'm glad we're having lunch," she said. "There's a patient I want to talk to you about."

"Good." The doors slid open and they turned toward the caf. "Shoot."

"Wait till we sit down." She grinned. "You know I can't carry food and talk at the same time."

A few minutes later Sheila had her Diet Coke, BBQ soy chips, and a salad in front of her. She popped open the can and took a sip but ignored the food. Bill dug into his broccoli and ziti as she spoke.

"Last week I mentioned a patient with some unusual symptoms. Kelly Slade, remember?"

"Vaguely. As I recall, my beeper went off and I had to run."

"I just found out she's dead."

Bill's fork paused on the way to his mouth.

"Really? How come? Who told you?"

"On our computer. File closed: Deceased."

"Records is pretty efficient. How'd she die?"

"Maybe an accident. I don't know. But I so wanted to follow her case, get to the bottom of her syndrome."

"And the symptoms were . . .?"

"Sounds crazy but it was like she was turning black."

"Like gangrene black?"

"No, no nothing like that. African-American black. I knew her from her seven-twenty-three therapy. She came in the other day, her normally dirty blonde straight hair turning black and kinky, and her skin pigment darkening like a serious sun worshipper."

"I remember now. Didn't make sense."

"I know. That's why I ran so many tests."

"Anything show up?"

His tone seemed perfunctory. She hoped she wasn't boring him.

"Perfectly normal."

"So what do you think it was?"

"No idea. I took some pictures though. I can compare them to the originals taken when Kelly had her treatment here."

Bill stopped mid-chew and his face flushed. At first Sheila thought he might be choking.

Then he said, "That was a great idea." He swallowed and added, "Good thinking."

Sheila felt a flush of warmth. Bill's praise meant a lot.

"You think it could have been a reaction to the chemo?"

"No. Never heard of a reaction like that. Was the new pigment in sun-exposed areas?"

"Her entire body. She didn't have just dots or splotches. She was like a different person. I was hoping to get a paper out of it. Maybe I still can."

"If you're going to pursue it, you should request a post mortem, if there isn't one already scheduled."

"Great idea." Why hadn't she thought of that?

"If you need me to put in a call to the coroner, just let me know. I have a few connections downtown."

"Thanks. But do you have *any* theories? I mean, could it possibly be the seven-twenty-three?"

"Highly unlikely. We've had it in trials for five years. If it was to blame we'd have seen more such anomalies by now. Many more."

"That's what I thought. But *something* caused it."

"Sheila, yes—*something*, or it wouldn't have happened. But don't get your hopes up that you'll uncover some obscure etiology and get your name in *Lancet,* not without—what was her name?"

What was going on with him? She'd assumed he'd be caught up by this case.

"Kelly. Kelly Slade."

"Right. With this Kelly deceased, the chances of finding an

answer are remote. Best not to start banging your head against the wall on this. I'd hate to see you waste all that time."

"Maybe it won't be a waste of time."

He shrugged. "I hope not." Then he grinned. "So, I heard you've got a hot date this afternoon with that volunteer."

She gulped. "It's just coffee." She felt her face turning crimson. "How do you—?"

He laughed. "I happened to be nearby and heard you two. He seems like a nice guy, but a little too blue collar for someone like you."

She felt herself stiffen. Sometimes Bill could be a snob. He kept smiling though and she let it go.

"Still in a rush to get published?" He'd changed the subject again.

And how. She loved her work at Tethys but didn't want to spend the rest of her career here. She longed to teach, and to do that she needed a place on the staff and faculty of a university hospital. She loved academic medicine as much as clinical, and that way she could have it all. But to get there she had to publish. And keep on publishing.

Publish or perish.

She said, "Do you—?"

He looked at his watch. "Got to run. I have a meeting with Abra about the new wing. Construction is so far behind we might have to take legal action." He rose and grabbed his tray. "Good luck with that Schneider case."

"Slade. Her name is Slade," she called out. But he was gone.

Sheila sat staring at her food, disappointed. After a few minutes she stretched and looked at her watch. Still had a little time before she had to get back to the floors. She'd go to her office and pick up Kelly's file to review tonight.

BILL

Bill rushed into the men's room and into a gray metal stall. He leaned against the wall and tried to calm himself. Photos of Kelly Slade. Shit. Sheila was too thorough. She'd compare them to the before pictures. If she ever published them side by side . . .

He slumped onto the seat. Had to stop it before it got out of control. If the truth got out . . .

He could see it now: The police arresting him in front of his whole staff. Their eyes boring into him, accusing.

The civil suits would take every penny he had. He'd go to jail and be somebody's bitch. Elise would be left penniless, ashamed. She'd never let the kids see him again. They'd grow up never knowing the good he was doing for humanity.

Without Proteus, so many people would die who didn't have to. The generations of sick children . . .

And what would happen to Abra? Watching her dream collapse would destroy her.

He punched the wall. No. No, this is not going to happen. Bill ripped open the door and hurried out.

He had to nip this in the bud.

SHEILA

Back in her office, Sheila sifted through her desk mess for Kelly's chart.

Where was it?

I left it right here. Didn't I?

The yellow pencil cup had been pushed back among the papers, no longer set in the middle. Strange. She picked up papers and folders. Nothing. She lifted the same purple folder three times before she conceded that Kelly's file was not under it.

The charts department was supposed to retrieve only those charts in the return rack. Sheila called Records.

"Carol? It's Doctor Takamura. Did the Slade file come back to you?"

"I'll check." A minute later she came back. "Not here. It's signed out to you."

"Yes, but it disappeared from my desk."

"Barbara's doing collections today. She can be overzealous at times. The chart's probably in transit. I'll talk to her when she gets here."

"Great. Thanks."

Oh, well, she'd just look it up on the network and print out what she needed.

She tapped on her keyboard and entered "Slade, Kelly."

File closed - Deceased.

"Yeah, I know. So let's open it."

And then another message: *File Moved to Storage.*

Oh, for Christ's sake.

She dialed Bill's cell. "Hi, Bill. It's me. The computer says that Kelly's records have been moved to some other drive and I can't access them. I've never heard of that before."

"It's a new policy instituted by the IT crew," he said. "Records of deceased patients get moved onto a separate drive, specific for whatever therapy they'd received."

"Swell."

"Well, the code crunchers promise it will give us quicker access to the active files. What therapy did you say she received?"

"Seven-twenty-three."

"Well, then, she should be on the seven-twenty-three drive. I'll have the IT guys retrieve it. Might take a few days, though."

"Bummer."

"In the meantime why don't you pursue the post mortem?"

She looked up the number and called the ME. Bradfield was too small to have its own so they shared the post with Milltown. She learned that Kelly's cause of death had been a high cervical fracture from a fall at home. Her body had been released to her family and picked up by the Moscante Funeral Home.

She called Moscante.

"Hi, this is Doctor Takamura from Tethys Hospital. I'm trying to locate the body of Kelly Slade. She died two—"

"Oh, yes. Ms. Slade has a memorial service scheduled for seven P.M. tonight."

Sheila crossed her fingers. "Have you embalmed her yet?"

Please say no, please, please, please say no.

"No. We don't embalm bodies to be cremated."

"Cremated? Oh, no. When does that happen?"

"It already has. About an hour ago. A family-only ceremony."

Sheila's heart sank. Damn!

"Ms. Slade must have been quite a popular lady. You're the second doctor to call about her today."

Strange. Who else . . .?

"Did you happen to catch the other doctor's name?"

"No, I'm sorry. He didn't leave it. I remember the Caller ID said Tethys Medical Center though, just like yours does."

"Okay. Thanks for your help."

Tethys? Who else had called?

Cremated. Just great. Kelly's body in ashes, her chart in limbo, and her hospital records inaccessible. Almost as if she never existed. Sheila had the photos in her camera at home but nothing to compare them to.

So what kind of paper could she hope to end up with?

She grabbed her purse and walked back to the hospital.

Sorry, Kelly.

———···———

The afternoon sun warmed Sheila's back as she made her way down the gentle slope toward the parking lot. Any sun was good sun. She tolerated winter, but hated the cold. Naked trees depressed her. Sometimes she wished she could hibernate like a bear and wake up in the spring when everything was coming to life again.

She spotted Paul on a riverside bench watching Coogan skateboard. When he saw her he stood and waved, then held up coffee containers in each hand.

Sheila laughed and held up the pair she'd picked up at the caf.

She'd almost backed out. But . . . she'd promised. She was in no mood to be social. Between Bill's strange mood, the revelation of Kelly's death, the missing file . . .

But a promise was a promise. As for what lay ahead from this quadruple coffee, who knew?

"Looks like we're in for a caffeine overdose," she said as she reached Paul.

He grinned. "Is there such a thing?"

Not in Sheila's book.

"Ooh," she said as she recognized the containers. "Starbucks! You went all the way into town? You shouldn't have."

"I had to pick up Coog, so I stopped on the way back."

She shook her head. "After all the time he's spent here as a patient, and with all his follow-ups, you'd think he'd be sick of the place."

"Not at all. It's like his second home. And besides, he loves this parking lot. Not much flat pavement where we live, and he doesn't think he's good enough for the skateboard park—thinks he'll look like a newbie, I guess. So whenever I'm donating a day here I pick him up at school and cut him loose."

Sheila held up her two Styrofoam cups. "What do we start with—caf or Starbucks?"

"You choose."

"Let's go with Starbucks. What did you get? Anything special?"

"One's plain old coffee of the day, the other's a girlie model."

" 'Girlie model'?"

"You know: a mocha-latta-flatta something. All the women in line were ordering them."

"I'll try the girlie then."

"Deal."

He looked relieved as he handed it to her. She took a sip. Mmmm. Like liquid dessert, but with caffeine. Perfect.

An awkward silence, filled only by the construction clamor. What to say? Paul was a nice guy, sweet, good-looking, but really, what did they have in common? How much *could* they have in common? Was Bill right? Too blue collar?

"River's running high for this time of year," he said.

She nodded. "Must be all last week's rain coming out of the mountains."

This was so lame.

Okay, so they had the river in common. What else?

And then it hit her. Of course: Coog.

Sheila knew that at six Coogan Rosko had developed acute lymphocytic leukemia. ALL usually has a good prognosis in six-year olds, but Coog was an exception. It proved refractory to everything and anything oncology could throw at it.

A grim prognosis until he arrived at Tethys . . .

The doctors here had used an experimental protocol named KB26 to rein in his stampeding bone marrow and it had stayed in remission ever since.

Coog was so lucky. Shortly after his treatment, Tethys had discontinued KB26. She didn't know why but thank God he'd gotten the treatment in time.

This had occurred long before Sheila began here so she didn't know the details. But when she'd joined the staff three years ago he'd been one of the first survivors assigned to her for routine follow-up exams.

She turned as he raced by on his skateboard. He wore a helmet plus knee and elbow guards. As she watched, Coog and his skateboard lifted into the air. The board never left Coog's feet during the brief flight. Almost miraculously he landed with a clatter and rolled on.

"How does he *do* that?"

"It's called an ollie." Paul's tone held a touch of pride.

"Is that a new term for defying gravity?"

"It's all foot placement and weight shifts. He tried to explain it to me but I think he uses glue." He laughed. "I think it's impossible, but then, I don't see how jumbo jets can fly either."

She watched as Coog became airborne again, only this time the board didn't stay with him—it rotated and fell away. He landed heavily on the pavement, stumbled a few steps, then skidded to a halt.

"Missed that one," she said.

Listen to me: Mistress of the Obvious.

"Yeah, but he wasn't going for an ollie. He's been working on a kickflip—that's when you make your board do a three-sixty rotation while you're in the air and then land on it and keep rolling."

"You've really picked up the lingo."

Paul's mouth twisted. "A smidgen. It's a way to keep myself part of his life."

Part of his life . . .

Sheila liked that. Day in and day out she saw too many parents who lived on a different planet than their kids.

Coog tried another kickflip with the same result, but this time he almost fell.

"I see why you've got him padded up."

"I'd much rather have him into chess but"—he shrugged—"what can you do? I try to keep him as protected as possible, but I know it's just staving off the inevitable."

"Which is . . .?"

"Getting hurt. One of these days he's going to be out by himself and he's going to shuck his gear—'cause it's *so* not cool—and break something trying a railslide."

"Kind of fatalistic, no?"

Another shrug. "Emerson had it right when he said 'a child is a curly, dimpled lunatic.' Coog's a thirteen-year-old boy, and thirteen-year-old boys do stupid things. I know *I* did when I was thirteen. I look back and it's a miracle I survived all my hair-brained stunts."

"So," she said. "Since we're on teenage years, what about yours?"

Get him talking about himself—the favorite topic for most people. Plus she'd learn about him. All she knew was he was a blue-collar who quoted Emerson and had a cancer survivor for a son.

"Not much to tell."

She sensed a sudden wariness in Paul, as if he'd backed away a couple of steps.

"Where did you spend them?"

"Lots of places. I was what they call an Army brat—a Marine brat, actually. We never got to stay anyplace too long. Not until my father landed a steady position in Albany. I got married, Coog came along, he got leukemia, we brought him here, and here we stay."

Well, that was a condensation of a life if she'd ever heard one. But she found his reticence intriguing.

A question popped into her head. She hesitated . . .

"I've never met Coog's mother. Is she . . .?"

"Rose decided a few years ago that being a wife and a mother was holding her back—whatever that means. So she took off. Coog's contact with his mother is now an annual birthday card and a Christmas present."

"I'm sorry."

"Yeah, well . . ."

Sheila got the impression Paul would have liked to add, *I'm not*, but had held back.

"What do you think?" he said, nodding toward Coog.

She glanced up as he did a spin on his rear wheels.

"I think he's pretty good."

"No, I mean his looks. Think he looks much like me?"

Sheila watched the boy. Slim build, light brown hair, cleft chin. Coogan didn't look a bit like him. Put them side by side and you'd never guess that they were related.

Must be his mother's genes, she guessed.

But what to say?

"I can see a subtle resemblance. Why?"

"Nothing."

A father didn't ask a question like that for no reason.

He looked up at her. "Your turn. How about you? What's your life story?"

Her story? Not much to it.

She'd grown up in North Falmouth along the shore, only child in an Irish-American household thick with tobacco smoke. Smoke seemed to define her childhood. Her fondest memories involved sitting on her father's lap, breathing his cigarette smoke. Stray ashes would fall on her arms, but she hadn't minded. On play dates she'd been startled to realize that some of her friends were growing up without gray air and yellow curtains.

Both Mum and Da were gone now—lung cancer and heart disease.

But they'd lasted to see her graduate *summa* from Harvard. Straight A's since she stepped into her first classroom.

"Not nearly as interesting as yours. Kind of boring, actually."

He smiled. "We all think our own lives are prosaic."

What sort of cable installer uses a word like that?

Paul cleared his throat. "If you don't mind my asking, how does someone with reddish blond hair and such an Irish face wind up with a name like Takamura?"

Sheila was sure Paul knew the story—everyone else seemed to—but she played along.

"Easy. All you have to do is marry a Japanese guy. Dek and I met—"

Tires squealed. She jumped and turned just in time to see Coogan's body bounce off the front bumper of a Hummer. She stood frozen in horror as his body tumbled through the air in slow motion until he hit the pavement on his side and lay still.

"Jesus!"

Paul was already on his feet and running. Sheila ran too and had to dodge Coog's still-rolling skateboard.

BILL

Bill Gilchrist poured himself a couple of fingers of Jack Daniel's neat while he waited for his sister. As usual, he'd arrived early. And, as usual, Abra was already five minutes late. She always had one last thing to do that trumped being on time for their regular meetings.

Bill sipped and gave a mental shrug. He used to take it personally. Now he knew that this was simply the way she was: Abra couldn't be on time for anything. Her fertility clinic so occupied her that it shoved nearly everything else to the wayside. He admired her though. That clinic meant everything to her and to a lot a families. It didn't generate much cash flow—not with all the freebies Abra approved—but it reimbursed Tethys in ways more important than revenues.

Another sip as he looked around her living room. He needed a little ethanol when he was here. This space of hers drove him to drink. Not the décor—nondescript furniture, clearance-sale stuff. Beige carpet and dark green walls. A few framed pictures: their parents; Mama with her own mother, Grammy Hensle, long dead; Elise and Bill and the kids; and the only non-family member,

Sheila. He smiled. His reasons for bringing Sheila to Tethys may not have been the purest, but serendipity had given Abra someone to care for. She'd come alive since Sheila had joined their staff.

Then he glanced at all the terrariums. Or would that be terraria?

The terraria drove him to drink.

He didn't get a lot about his big sister but understood why she'd given him the mansion and why she'd built this sprawling ranch house near the center of the campus; just not why someone worth eight figures—*high* eight figures—would want to live like someone who made fifty thousand a year.

What he didn't get were all these terraria in her family room.

He wandered the walls, checking out the snakes and lizards and giant millipedes. He shook off a crawling sensation across his shoulders. Why surround herself with this stuff?

He stopped by one of the smaller tanks, maybe a foot high and deep, and two wide. He didn't remember this one. He leaned in closer but saw only sand, cacti, a couple of rocks, and a small hollowed-out log. Countless tiny indentations stippled the sand. But nothing moved. No sign of life. Maybe its inhabitant hadn't arrived or was napping.

He gave the glass a gentle tap—and in a blur of motion the biggest spider he'd ever seen launched itself from the hollow of the log and landed against the glass directly above his fingertip.

Bill let out a cry and lurched backward. Heart pounding, he watched the big hairy thing scrabble against the glass, as if trying to claw its way through. He glanced up to check that the terrarium cover was firmly in place.

Christ, he hated spiders. What on earth did Abra see—?

"I see you've met Blondie."

Bill recognized his sister's voice but couldn't draw his gaze from the fat, black-furred monstrosity.

"I could think of a thousand names for that thing, but Blondie isn't one of them."

"You might if you knew its specie: It's a young *theraphosa blondi*."

"You mean it's not fully grown?"

"When it's an adult its leg span will cover a dinner plate. And speaking of dinner, I'll bet it's hungry."

"What on earth does it eat?"

"I'm sorry, Bill. I didn't hear that."

Bill tore his gaze from the creature and turned to face his sister.

Abra smiled up from her wheelchair—custom built for her stature and afflictions. On those rare occasions when she was on her feet, she was only four-foot-two, so her wheelchair was child size. An adult model would have made her look like a misshapen elf.

But then, Abra would look misshapen in any chair. Thin salt-and-pepper hair cut short around a triangular face, a barrel chest and scoliotic spine that made it impossible for her to sit straight. But Abra's eyes were her most striking feature: deep blue irises surrounded by blue instead of white, a paler blue than her irises, but definitely blue, one of the hallmark traits of her syndrome.

Bill, inured to her deformities, had never overcome his awe at her intelligence. But what he admired most about Abra was her lack of self-pity despite a life spent just this side of hell.

A hundred medical procedures before her ninth birthday, but instead of wallowing in self pity or giving up, she dedicated her life to science, to curing genetic diseases. She played the hand she'd been dealt with no complaint, and played to win. Bill warmed when he saw her.

He repeated his question, enunciating carefully. Abra wore hearing aids but rarely had them properly adjusted.

Her smile broadened. A much nicer smile since she'd capped her undersized, discolored teeth.

"Oh, well, it's known as a goliath bird eater . . ."

"*Bird* eater? Oh, you're not going to—"

"Of course not. Henry will give it one of the snakes' feeder mice."

Though officially her chauffeur, sixty-year-old Henry doted on her like a child-obsessed nanny, doing everything, including feeding the pets that required live food. Abra never could bring herself to do that.

Her smile faded. "Any further word on poor Kelly Slade's condition?"

Bill took a sip of Jack and held up his glass.

"Can I fix you anything?"

"Some white wine, if you don't mind. Whatever's open."

Bill heard the whir of Abra's electric wheelchair as she followed him to the wet bar. He opened the under-counter fridge and pulled out a stoppered bottle.

"Meursault okay?"

"Fine. Anything. About the Slade girl?"

"Well . . ." Bill stalled. He plucked a glass from a rack and began to pour. "I guess you could say there's good news and bad news."

"I don't like the sound of that. What's the good news?"

Bill turned but held off handing her the glass afraid she might drop it.

"Depends on who you are. For us it's good news, for Ms. Slade it's bad: She's dead."

Abra's gnarled hands shot to her lips. "Oh dear! What happened?"

"Sheila Takamura told me today. Some sort of fall."

She shook her head. "I feel guilty for feeling so relieved."

Bill felt guilty for another reason. But it was Slade's own fault. He had met with her, begged her to let it go, did everything he could to downplay her symptoms. Told her she should be grateful to be alive and not obsess about some skin discoloration. She'd promised she'd work with him, but then he'd learned she had an appointment to see some New York specialist. Once someone else got hold of her, he and Tethys could be dead meat.

At least he'd learned in time to stop the woman. He felt bad, still did, but he'd had no choice.

He held out the wineglass, releasing it only when Abra's gnarled fingers had a firm grip on its stem.

"You've got to admit though that it's a *deus-ex* solution. Which is kind of appropriate since you said the woman was a sign from God—"

"I said *perhaps* a sign from God."

Bill remembered the fear her remark had struck into his heart. Unlike Abra he didn't agree that the public's demand for VG723 would remain high once its side effects were revealed. And even if the demand did continue they'd never get the FDA to approve it. Once they went public with the side effects, Tethys would be shut down, legal vultures would circle, and they'd be looking at huge civil suits.

Abra, however, was so sure of their treatment, she couldn't imagine anyone not wanting it. She was naïve about the public reaction and the need for regulators to regulate. He hoped he could keep her idyllic world from shattering.

"Okay, Abra. *Perhaps* a sign from God that it could be time to go public. But I'm glad we don't have to. We're not ready yet." And Bill didn't want to be ready for a long, long time, didn't want to go public until they were forced to. "I guess God didn't think so either."

"Bill," Abra said. "Her death is only *half* a solution. We both know there's another problem out there, the mirror image of Kelly Slade's, ready to surface at any moment."

Bill poured himself a little more Jack.

"That we do, that we do."

"How did this happen, Bill?"

He stiffened. "Kelly Slade's death?"

"No, no. You just said that was an accident. I meant, how did all our fail-safes, well, fail?"

Bill sighed. "No matter how carefully you plan, all it takes is a lapse by just one person to cause a major screw up. All these years . . . we're lucky it hasn't happened before."

"We're so careful selecting the recipients, matching up the donors."

"Well, it happened. One careless lab tech and the samples got switched. We've got a load of controls and this guy circumvented them all."

"But the pictures. We code the pictures and the samples. Everything is supposed to stay together."

"Supposed to, yes. But there's always human error. We have even stronger controls in place now. It won't happen again."

"What if it there are more that we don't know about.?"

"Abra, we have to go on the assumption that it was only these two cases. If there were more, we'd know. Believe me, we'd know."

Bill gulped the rest of his drink and crunched the ice. He lived with that fear everyday; he didn't need her adding to it.

"Don't tell me what to assume!" Her thin voice rose in pitch and volume. "We're talking about my life's dream and—"

"*Our* life's dream, remember?"

Didn't she understand it mattered to him too? She was the reason the whole family had slaved to develop this therapy, though for her condition they were too late. But it was his dream too, dammit. And he was putting his neck on the line to preserve it.

She calmed. "Sorry, Bill. But when I think of all the years, the endless labor, the huge hope we've poured into Proteus . . . jeopardized by one foolish mistake . . ."

"Well, if there's another mistake, it will be made by someone else. The guilty tech has been removed."

"What about your Sheila? How did she take the news? Slade was her patient, right?"

Bill couldn't help bristling. "She's not 'my Sheila' "

"What is she then?"

"A colleague. And practically your daughter."

Abra's lips curved into a coy smile. "If it weren't for Elise, she could be my sister-in-law. How many other 'colleagues' make goo-goo eyes at you?"

"Really, Abra—"

She laughed. "Only teasing, Billy."

"Why do you feel compelled to make a suggestive comment every time she's mentioned?"

"Because her infatuation is so obvious."

"It's mutual respect."

"And indebtedness. At a low point in her life you plucked her out of residency and placed her in a plum position."

Bill thought on that. Yes, that was how it looked to Abra and to Sheila. He'd done a good job masking the real reason: That he'd hired Sheila only to observe her after her husband's "untimely death." He flinched at the memory of how close Dek Takamura had come to exposing Proteus.

"You're a brilliant, good-looking man who did her a big favor. She's a young, attractive widow. A lonely widow. That's a combustible mixture."

Don't I know it, Bill thought.

But Bill did not fool around—never had and wasn't about to start now. Though he and Elise didn't always get along, they trusted each other. And Robbie and April, what would they think of him if . . .

None of that stopped the fantasies, though . . . getting Sheila's tight little body between the sheets and . . .

"I know you and Elise are having your troubles," Abra was saying.

He shook off the images of Sheila's velvet skin, her tender flesh, of touching her all over . . .

"No more than any other married couple. The friction revolves around the time I spend at home—or lack of it. I give her and the kids my every spare moment, but to her it's never enough. We'll work it out."

"I'm sure you will. But if you don't, and Sheila and you got together . . ." She winked at him. "Well, now is not a time for distractions." She sipped her wine. "Is Sheila going to pursue the Kelly Slade case?"

"She can't. I've sequestered the medical records, and the body has been cremated."

"Then she's got nothing to work with."

"Exactly."

"You know, we could just tell her what's going on. Bring her into the fold."

Bill shook his head. They'd discussed this dozens of times.

"I'd like her to be a part of this too, Abra, but it's too soon. Just trust me on the timing of this, okay?"

"It's killing me being so close to her and holding back the truth about our therapy. I just know she'd be as thrilled as we are."

Bill wasn't so sure. He thought of Sheila's photos of Slade, but no need to worry Abra with those. He'd take care of them.

"How's the fertility clinic these days?"

Abra's eyes lit. Seeing that joy always reassured Bill. It made up for all the shit he had to handle. The Tethys Birthing Center was her life.

"It's wonderful. We've got that new staining technique and can check the DNA on the embryos at the eight-cell stage."

He felt so proud of her. Most anyone else with her disease would have given up. But Abra never let her handicap hold her back. Eight thousand successful IVFs in four years with seventy-percent births. No one else had that percentage. Abra called them her "perfect little angels."

"Another drink?"

She shook her head. "Have you talked to Mama?"

"Yes. You should call her."

Abra shook her head. "Why can't she call me?"

He sipped his freshened drink and held off. Abra and Mama had had ongoing battles about the goals of Proteus. They'd both urged Abra to go wider with VG723—supply it to cancer centers all over the world, concealing their findings. Distribute millions of doses simultaneously over the course of a couple of years. Cure as many people as possible before the survivors started showing changes, before anyone figured out what was happening. Then they'd plead ignorance.

But Abra had refused to supply it to any other hospitals without full disclosure to the doctors *and* patients. Mama had raged off to Europe saying she would stay there and work on her own projects until Abra came to her senses. She'd bought controlling interest in Schelling Pharma, a failing Swiss pharmaceutical concern, and had turned it around.

Abra had felt betrayed. It wasn't that they didn't speak—nothing like that. Mama flew over for holidays and birthdays, but their close rapport had faded.

Bill called Mama frequently. But he had reason to. They were working on their own project that Abra wasn't privy to.

"You're just being spiteful, Abra. Mama's an old woman. Who knows how long before you won't be *able* to call her."

Abra laughed, not unkindly. "Don't go playing the age card. That's *her* game."

She rolled her chair to a terrarium and plucked out a small hermit crab, then returned and breathed on it.

Bill tried to ignore its presence. "It's true. Think about it."

Abra smiled as the crab crawled from its shell. She set it on her lap so it could walk. "I'm more interested in thinking about Kelly Slade's counterpart, the other switched lab sample. Kelly was only the first shoe to drop. When will we hear the second?"

"I wish I knew."

But it was coming. And he dreaded the prospect.

SHEILA

"Where's that CAT report, damn it!"

Sheila could barely contain her frustration. Tethys wasn't set up for trauma—no emergency room, plus its staff was rarely called upon for acute care. Thank God the orderlies had found a backboard with a cervical immobilizer stowed in a closet.

She had immediately taken charge, calling on the ER skills she'd learned in her moonlighting days.

Paul had wanted to lift his unconscious son in his arms and carry him, but Sheila stopped him—Coog might have a cervical fracture. So he'd knelt beside him, wringing his hands—a big bear of a man looking terribly vulnerable. A pair of orderlies transferred Coog to the board and hurried him up to a treatment room.

First she'd started an IV and began running fluids into him. Next—chest and pelvic x-rays, plus skull and cervical spine series. Thankfully the neck and skull showed no fractures, and so they took him off the board. No pelvic fracture either. The chest x-ray showed no hemo- or pnemothorax, and no air under the diaphragm. Good. That last meant no ruptured stomach or intestine. It did, however, show undisplaced fractures of three of his lower left ribs. That worried Sheila. That was spleen country. It might be ruptured.

Thus the CAT scan.

"I've got radiology on the phone," said a black nurse whose nametag read *J. Bradshaw, RN.* "It's Doctor Morten."

Sheila grabbed the receiver. "What've we got, Joe?"

"Looks good. Liver, pancreas, and retroperitoneal space all okay on the scan. Not so sure about the spleen, though. Might have a hematoma."

"But no rupture?"

"Nope. It's intact.

She breathed a sigh of relief. No surgery for Coog.

As she glanced at him, Coog's eyes fluttered open. He looked around, obviously confused. His eyes widened when he recognized his surroundings.

He stiffened. "Wha—?"

Sheila patted his arm. "It's all right, Coog. You had a little accident."

"I did?"

"Yep." She smiled and squeezed his arm. "But you're going to be fine."

Now to tell Paul the good news.

PAUL

Paul sat in the waiting room, shaking, feeling as if someone had kicked him in the chest.

Coog . . . knocked out . . . broken ribs. Thank God for Sheila. When she'd called to tell him no surgery, he'd almost lost it.

Very lucky, she'd said.

Yeah, right. Some strange kind of luck: First I almost lose him to leukemia, then this. One minute skateboarding, the next smashed on the pavement.

Paul clenched his teeth and balled his hands into fists. The chatty nurses had told him the driver was an investment counselor with a couple of Tethys doctors as clients. If Paul could get hold of that bastard—

"Mr. Rosko, can I talk to you for a minute?"

Paul looked up. A young doctor who looked about twelve was waving him to a curtained area in the hall.

As he followed Doogie Hauser, he could feel his blood pressure rising along with his anxiety. Had something gone wrong?

"Mr. Rosko . . ." Doogie said, then paused.

"What?" Paul snapped.

He'd kept his temper in check for years. Even when Rose had started screwing around on him, even then he'd kept it together. But now he could feel the rage taking over. He wanted to punch someone. Anyone.

"As you know, your son won't be needing a transfusion."

"Yes, thank God."

He realized he'd said that many times in the last hour.

"I want to keep your blood for other patients who might need it."

Paul took a breath and smiled. "Great. If Coogan doesn't need it, go ahead." Paul felt self-control returning.

"It didn't match Coogan's anyway and we don't want to waste it."

A ball of ice formed in Paul's chest.

"Not compatible? You saying he's not my son?"

Knew it!

"No, no. Nothing like that. Happens more than you expect. Nothing to concern yourself about, really."

"He's not my son," he said in a soft, calm-before-the storm voice.

"I didn't say that Mister Rosko."

"I should have known. Doesn't even look like me. Nothing like me."

He knew he was muttering like a sidewalk schizo but didn't care. A red haze filled his vision. Didn't know how much longer he could keep a lid on this.

Goddamned Rose.

Adrenaline raced through his system. He tried counting backward like he'd learned in anger management.

10 . . . 9 . . . 8 . . .

"Hey, there you are." Sheila was walking toward him with two steaming cups of coffee. "I've been looking you." She frowned. His expression no doubt told her something. "Is everything okay?"

"Ask the boy wonder," Paul said.

"What is it, Matt?"

He shrugged. "Mister Rosko's blood isn't compatible with his son's. And he just released it to the bank."

"Great."

As Matt turned and walked away, Sheila said, "Coog should be ready for visitors in about half an hour."

Paul took his coffee from Sheila. "He's not my son."

"*What?*"

"You heard him. He can't take my blood. That says it all."

Sheila put a hand on his arm. "It says nothing of the sort. It's not uncommon."

"I wish I could believe that—I *want* to believe that—but . . ."

"Come by my office tomorrow and I'll explain it to you. Right now you're too upset about the accident."

She went to put her arm on his shoulder but he shrugged her off. He saw her recoil and felt bad right away, but he hated being patronized. That wasn't what he needed. He needed to beat the shit out of someone.

"Paul, calm down." She didn't try to touch him again. "This doesn't mean anything. We can do a paternity test later okay? DNA. I'm sure he's your son. He probably just looks more like your wife than you."

"*Ex*-wife. And you know what? He doesn't. He doesn't look anything like Rose. She was a blond—very, almost-white blond hair. Only thing about her that *was* real."

Screwing around on him the whole time—even before Coog. He balled his fists, crushing the cup in a blur of anger.

"Paul?" he heard an alarmed voice say. "Are you okay?"

Who was that? Focus, Paul. Focus. 10 . . . 9 . . . 8 . . .

He saw the coffee on the floor. He saw his scalded fingers.

"Aw, jeez, I'm sorry."

He looked around for a paper towel but froze when he saw a man walking down the hall, talking on a cell pone.

Paul recognized him. The weasel-faced, Hummer-driving, son

of a bitch who'd flattened Coog while yakking on the same goddam phone, and here he was strolling along as if he hadn't nearly destroyed two lives.

The air around Paul took on a red tinge. With a strangled cry he charged. The guy never saw it coming. Paul shoved him against the wall, then pushed him to the floor. He ripped the cell phone free and poised it over the bastard's mouth.

"You like this thing? You like talking when you should be watching out for kids? How about I shove it down your goddamn throat!"

He raised the phone above the terrified face, winding up to smash in a few of the guy's pretty caps—

"Paul, no!" Sheila yelled.

Paul heard her and stopped. He didn't know how, but he stopped.

He felt arms pull him off. Big arms. Security guards surrounded him. Where the hell had they come from?

They lifted him to his feet.

"He's all right," Sheila said. "His son was just hit by a car. By that driver. He's not thinking clearly."

They let him go.

He shook himself and looked at the shocked driver still cowering on the floor.

No blood. Thank God Sheila had stopped him in time.

He closed his eyes. It had passed. Now he was shaking.

Sheila guided him to a chair in the waiting room. She wiped the coffee off his hands. He felt numb.

"Why don't I get you a tranquilizer? It will help. It's been a hell of a day for you. Anyone would flip out." She smiled. "I know you would have stopped before you hurt him. Right?"

If she only knew.

He glanced at her. Was that a trace of fear in her eyes? Fear *for* him, or fear *of* him? A world of difference. He liked Sheila—a lot. Looking at her, talking to her . . . had he just screwed that up?

"I'm okay now. I really don't like to take pills."

"Okay. You want a new coffee?"

"No, I'm revved enough. I'm really sorry you had to see me like that."

She swatted her hand at the air. "That's nothing. You think I've never seen a parent go nuts? Happens all the time."

He hedged but finally admitted, "I've had my doubts for a while about Coog being my son."

"Do you really think he's not yours?"

"He used to look just like me. Same round face, same dark hair. A mini-me. That's what the old photos show. But nowadays . . ." He shook his head. "You've seen him."

"Lots of children change as they mature."

"Yeah, well, when he got sick, Rose couldn't deal with it. She stayed away from the hospital as much as she could. I was all he had. He was all I had. I didn't realize until then how much he meant to me. I was with him day and night, treatment after treatment. They told me he was going to die and you know what I did?"

She shook her head.

"I went out and bought him spelling flashcards. I wasn't going to let him just lie there and wait for death. It's like that book, *On the Beach* by Nevil Shute. Ever read that?"

She shook her head again.

"All the countries blew each other up and the radiation killed everyone. Except in Australia. It was far enough away so they didn't get sick for a while. They knew they'd die once the dust blew their way but they just kept on living their lives. They planted gardens and went to school and worked. They refused to lie down and wait for death. Because what kind of life is that?

"So I bought him flashcards. We did spelling and writing and some math. I wasn't going to give into death. Not in front of him. I'd go in the men's room and cry my eyes out, because I knew the end was coming. But I kept making him live like he was going to be around forever."

"And he did live," she said.

"Yeah. He lived. Tethys stepped in with their miracle. Soon after that, Rose left us. So he's all I've got. I don't have the big life-altering job you do. I wish I did. I'm just a cable guy. I've made my whole life about that kid in there." He pointed down the hall. "If Coogan's not really my son, I have nothing."

"No, you still have a son. Remember, you're all he has too. If he used to be a mini-you, then inside he still is. I really wouldn't worry about your paternity, Paul. I'm sure he's yours. We'll run some tests, though. Okay?"

He held her hand. A bold move, but he meant it as a friendly gesture. Just a friend. He squeezed.

"Thank you so much. I don't usually babble on like this, and I hardly know you. Sorry I got all emotional. You must think I'm a wimp."

She turned his hand over with her thin, manicured fingers.

"With hands like these? Nothing wimpy here." She rubbed his hand with her thumb. "Ready to see him?"

"You bet."

They got up and started walking. She led the way.

Quite a woman. He hoped, prayed, that she was right about Coogan. The DNA would prove it. He'd just have to keep his fingers crossed.

KAPLAN

Gerald Kaplan knew he was rip-roaring drunk. He sat on his tan recliner on his tan rug in his stupid neutral-colored living room. Except for the big, flat-screen TV, not one extravagance. Place had no character. Just like him. Mister Invisible. Except he had made the biggest medical discovery of all time! Of *all* time. Wished he hadn't. It was blowing up in his face. Damn. He stared up at the stucco ceiling to stabilize himself, keep the room still.

Hardly ever drank, and hadn't been drunk since college. But tonight . . . exception. Big-time exception.

Trouble was, the only booze in the house was scotch. Didn't like scotch. Tasted medicinal. Kept it around for company. But he'd forced some down tonight. Hell, he'd forced down lots.

Didn't help in the way he'd hoped. No surprise about the queasy stomach. Couldn't walk straight, couldn't see straight. But he hadn't been able to pickle his brain enough to blot out the memory of that lady in the examining room this morning, that Tanesha Green.

Poor woman.

Still felt the shock of seeing her bizarre pigment changes, hearing of her experimental cancer therapy, and knowing in a frightening and infuriating epiphany what had happened, and what was taking place inside her.

All because he, Gerald Kaplan, M-freaking-D, Ph-goddamn-D, had developed the stem-cell therapy that had cured her. All by himself. No help from anyone, thank you very much. His own stinkin' lab. Those were the days. A private lab, employees, a wife . . . things had been pretty damn good for Jerry Kaplan. Yeah, he'd been Jerry back then. Pulled out all the stops. Big house, a Porsche . . . he researched so many hours that his wife "had to seek out affection." He banged down his glass. Fuck her. Seek out affection. Hah!

"I've been living just fine without affection since you left, Loretta!"

Whoa, he'd made himself dizzy.

The therapy. He'd found venture capital and then he was even richer. But then the shit hit the fan. Loretta left him, then the disturbing side effects in the KB26 clinical trials. Similar to the side effects Tanesha Green was experiencing. He ran test after test. Conclusion: Yes it cured the incurable but it could be devastating to the human genome.

So he pulled it from trials. Then the money dried up and next thing he was working in a city clinic. But he had picked himself up over the years, got into a group practice. He'd thought his therapy dead, gone, erased from the face of the Earth. No harm done.

Obviously not.

Someone had stolen it, *looted* it.

He didn't know who that someone was, but he was pretty damn sure of the middlemen.

Had their number. Thank God he'd looked it up earlier. No way he could have found it in his present state.

He was going to call them. Goddamn call the scheming, no-conscience bastards right now and tell them that the chickens are coming home to roost and that the inevitable global opprobrium and financial ruin to follow will be but a fraction of what they deserve.

He reached for the phone but his hand stopped halfway.

Those same chickens would roost on him too. Yeah, he'd abandoned the therapy as soon as he knew its side effects, but he'd been the innovator. His name was on the patent.

No.

He withdrew his hand. No call.

The gun he kept in the closet for emergencies—maybe that was his best way out. Turn them in, then blow his brains out. But he felt too woozy to haul himself off the couch.

Scared too. Too scared to kill himself or turn anyone in.

Best to keep his head down, and make plans to leave, disappear. Maybe even pray . . . pray that he wouldn't be dragged into the coming shit storm.

Gerald sobbed.

If only they'd left it alone, no one ever would have known.

He grieved for the poor, poor woman who had no idea what lay ahead of her.

ABRA

Abra watched Billy drive away. He was tipsy but it was only a quarter of a mile home. Still, she wished he hadn't drunk so much. Abra sighed. She wished a lot of things.

Like this problem with the VG723 swap. Kelly Slade's symptoms might well bring Tethys tumbling down despite what Billy had said. "Under control," he'd insisted, but she knew he sometimes skewed the truth to protect her. Heart of gold. Such a good boy.

She remembered how bleak life had been before he was born. So lonely. The broken bones and the pain, those she could handle—but the loneliness . . . sitting on piles of pillows with her dolls . . . never allowed to play with other kids. She was like a China doll, Mama said, and if she ever played rough she'd smash like a teacup.

Someone might fall on you and you might die. Then we won't have a little girl anymore.

A long, painful, lonely childhood until, when she was eleven, dear Billy was born.

She squinted into the distance until she saw his car pull safely into his driveway and his garage. He'd made it home safe and now she could relax.

SHEILA

Sheila was used to long work days but this had been a doozy. The great news about Sean, the terrible news about Kelly, Bill's mood, the "date" with Paul, Coogan getting hit . . . and then the ER and Paul's fit about his paternity.

God, what a day.

She managed to wash her face, brush her teeth, and stumble toward her bed. She stripped off her clothes, threw them on the floor, then donned one of Dek's old sweatshirts. Within minutes she felt sleep pulling her into its embrace . . .

What was that?

She popped her eyes open and looked around. Nothing. The moon shone bright through the skylight and lit up the room. Empty. The noise had come from downstairs . . . a soft sound, but one that didn't belong, something that had set off her internal alarm and roused her.

Was someone in the house? She sat up in bed and tried to catch her breath. Listening.

But then no more sounds. No footsteps, no creaking floors. A full five minutes went by. Still nothing.

Did she imagine the whole thing?

She lay back and stared at the ceiling, listening. Nothing. Only her rapid heartbeat.

Slam!

The kitchen door shut. No mistaking that noise. She grabbed the cordless phone to call 9-1-1 but stopped. Tethys security would be quicker. They patrolled all night and could be here within seconds.

She dialed the main number, hit 4 for security, then 1 for emergency.

Shen Li, the chief of security for Tethys, answered.

"Thank God you're there, Mr. Li. This is Sheila Takamura from the gardener's house. I heard someone in my house. I think he left but I don't know. Please come over."

"I am nearby, Doctor Takamura. Making rounds. I will be right there. No more sounds?"

"I don't know. No sounds, but maybe he's hiding. I'm afraid to leave my room."

"I am approaching front of your house now. I hang up and call you back after I search outside. You stay in room."

Sheila already felt better and held the cordless to her like a security blanket.

Minutes later Li called back. "All clear outside. I will search inside. Kitchen door is unlocked. Am coming in."

Unlocked? Then someone had been here. Could still be here. Sheila huddled deeper under her blankets.

"All clear down here, Doctor," he called up to her. "May this one come up for search?"

"Well, I didn't hear anyone come up the stairs."

"He could go up while you asleep. Maybe he very quiet. I come up?"

God, he was right. The burglar could be hiding anywhere. Right in this room, even. She fished her jeans off the floor and turned on the light.

"Come on up."

Shen Li appeared in her doorway. He nodded hello but said nothing. He had a strange presence. His manner was humble and deferential, though his compact frame was thickly muscled. And his eyes . . . his onyx eyes were arresting in the most literal sense: They stopped people in their tracks.

Li checked all the upstairs bedrooms and closets in minutes.

"All safe here too. No prowler. No danger here tonight."

"Thank you. I guess I was just being paranoid."

"No, someone *was* here. Door unlocked, branches in bush broken. Not paranoid. But he gone now. Anything missing?"

She walked downstairs and started looking around. "My laptop. Oh, no. All my stuff was on that."

Well, at least they'd left the PC. She scanned the rest of her home office, then walked into the kitchen.

"My purse! Oh damn, it was right here on the table."

"You have lot of cash in wallet?"

"I think about fifty dollars. But my camera was in it. I need that camera. I had pictures on it I can't get back."

"Life you cannot get back. Camera is replaceable, no?"

"You're right, of course." He had a wonderful way of putting things in perspective. "Thank you."

"Most likely man who want money for drugs take your things but I will call police and take care of this. They investigate. What was value of items?"

"I guess about $2500. I can file a claim with my house insurance."

He nodded. "Good night then. I bring police papers to you tomorrow for signing. You rest now, Doctor Sheila. This one will keep eye on your house, make sure no one comes back."

"Thank you again."

She led him out, turned the deadbolt and went upstairs. She turned on her bedroom light, took off her jeans, and stared at the ceiling, listening.

" 'You rest now, Doctor Sheila,' " she said in Li's accent. " 'This one will keep eye on your house.' "

She smiled and suddenly her exhaustion outweighed her fear.

TWO

SHEILA

Sheila awoke early and downed two cups of coffee before she headed to her office.

When she got in she called her bank and all the credit card companies. She walked over to get a new Photo ID. Luckily her image was stored in they system. The way she looked today her photo would have been a mess.

The business done, she called Abra to see if she was free for lunch.

The phone rattled as Abra said she was doing some work in her clinic today and couldn't get away.

"How about dinner?" Abra offered. Rattle, rattle.

Sheila wanted to see her sooner. She needed to talk to someone and get this all off her chest.

"What if I pick us up lunch from the caf and bring it to the clinic?"

Abra thanked her and said she'd see her at twelve on the dot. Sheila didn't need Abra's order. She knew it by heart: a BLT with mayo on whole wheat bread, ruffled chips on the side, and a can of Sprite.

Sheila loved going to the fertility clinic. Seeing those women, so anxious and depressed when they walked in and so happy when they left. Walls of pictures of their infants lined the halls. Each photo tangible proof of the ability of medicine, and specifically Tethys, to perform miracles.

When she hung up, the phone rattled a little more. She shook it.

What was that? A loose wire?

The sound seemed to be coming from the mouthpiece. She unscrewed it and a little black disk fell out. Her first thought was that something had broken off. Then it occurred to her that it looked like an electronic bug. She smiled at the thought.

Who'd want to bug me?

Then she noticed the adhesive coating on the surface. She'd never seen one in real life but had watched enough detective shows to know that bugs were usually stuck in out-of-the-way places.

Like inside a phone . . .

Oh my God. The break in. And now a bug. Her chest tightened and she felt pressure behind her eyes. Her heart pounded. Who would want to bug me?

She bolted from her chair and ran downstairs.

BILL

Bill pulled into the Tethys lot, smiling. Last night had gone down perfectly. Had to hand it to Shen, the man knew his stuff. Made enough noise to awaken Sheila but not terrify her. Alarm her just enough to call security. And he snagged her camera.

Now they could drop the Kelly incident and move on. And who knew? The way things were going, maybe the other woman who received the errant VG723 would never surface.

Yes, it was shaping up to be a great day.

He walked into his office and was surprised to see Sheila. She was holding out her hand and looking angry.

"Look at this!"

He repressed a gasp when she dropped a bug into his hand. He had to fake looking puzzled, but no problem looking shocked. When he'd hired Sheila, he'd had her office wired for audio and visual surveillance. He'd needed to monitor her, make sure her husband hadn't told her about his investigation of Tethys before Shen had silenced him. How the hell had she found it?

"What is it?"

"A bug—an electronic bug! In my phone! What's going on, Bill?"

He held it closer pretending to examine it.

"Are you sure? I've never seen one."

"Me either until now. It was in the mouthpiece of my office phone."

"This is crazy!"

He put the bug on his desk and hung up his coat.

"Bill, it's got me spooked. Who'd be listening in on me? And last night someone broke into my house."

"I heard about that. Shen called me first thing this morning. He said they took your purse and laptop."

"Along with my camera. So much for Kelly's pictures."

"Are you all right? You weren't hurt?"

"It was while I was sleeping. They took my things and left. It was scary, Bill. I feel violated."

Such a typical female term.

"Sheila, there's no need to get dramatic. Robberies happen all the time. I'm sure it was random."

"A robbery where they take my laptop and camera, and the next day this?" She pointed to the bug. "It's not random—that's a pattern. But why me?"

What to say? How to explain it? Next time Shen had better use a stronger adhesive.

Then he had an idea.

"I'll bet dollars to doughnuts it was VecGen's competition, GenEon. They've been snooping into VecGen's secrets for years."

GenEon didn't go near oncology but he had read an article about their being accused of corporate espionage. And they were in the stem cell field.

"You think? And they're watching me?"

"I'll bet they've bugged a lot of phones. Looking for corporate secrets. Did you have any patient files on your laptop?"

"Yeah, some, but Dave Ellis in IT encrypted my hard drive so if anyone stole it they couldn't access my files. It's technology from the Navy. At least that's what he told me."

Bill picked up the bug. "Look, I'll call Shen and have him do a sweep of all the offices."

"Do you think they'll come back?"

"Doubt it—not with Shen keeping an eye out. We'll get rid of all the bugs and whoever it was will go away." Bill was thrilled she seemed to be buying this. "Do you need the day off? After last night you must be exhausted."

"No, I'm okay. I'll turn in early tonight."

Good girl, he thought.

"I'm meeting Abra for lunch. That'll bolster my spirits."

Oh, hell. How was he going to explain the bug to Abra? Well, he'd give her the GenEon story too. She'd have no way to disprove it. Shen would do a sweep, pretend to find and remove half a dozen others, and that would be the end of it. And during the sweep he'd replace Sheila's in a new location with a lot more glue.

"It's a stroke of luck you found this. Who knows how long it's been going on? I'll get Shen on it right away."

Sheila got up and walked out.

So much for a calm, smooth, easy morning.

TANESHA

Tanesha Green looked around.

Well, here she was again, back in an examining room. Second one in two days. Why did they all look alike? Did doctors all order their rooms from some catalog?

They all *had* to order these dumb-ass paper capes from the same place.

Tanesha dried her sweaty palms on the cape. Lordy she was nervous. That quack at the Penner clinic had her running scared. The way he'd washed his hands of her like . . . like Pontius Pilate. Did he think she was a lost cause?

Worry wouldn't go away and had kept her up all night. If she didn't find an answer soon—

The door opened and Tanesha almost puddled up and bawled as Dr. Takamura stepped in. At last, a friendly face.

She remembered how gentle and caring she'd been back in the VG723 days, treating her like a real person, not some number. Everything here was numbers—numbered people getting numbered treatments. But Doc Takamura had been different.

"Tanesha?" she said, frowning and knitting her brows as she looked down at the chart and up again. "You look . . ."

"Different?" Tanesha bit back a sob. "I know. That's why I'm here."

Dr. Takamura didn't look any different though. Didn't look a minute older than back when Tanesha was taking the cancer cure. Same reddish blond hair, same bright blue eyes and freckled nose, same slim body—Tanesha would kill for that body. Or would have before her skin and hair had started changing. Now she'd keep the blubber—she'd *love* the blubber if she could just get back to her old self.

"I . . . I . . ."

The look on Dr. Takamura's face made Tanesha's heart stumble. Her expression reminded her of that Dr. Kaplan.

"What's wrong? Why you lookin' me like that?"

"Because . . ." She stepped closer and touched Tanesha's hair, then her skin. "Your skin's half a dozen tones lighter."

"Tell me about it."

"And your hair . . ."

"Is coming in straight and light brown. I knows all that. What I don't know is why. *That's* what I needs to know." She felt a tear roll down her cheek. "I'm scared, doc. Really scared. I don't know what's happening to me."

Now the locked-up sob broke free. Tanesha squeezed her eyes shut to hold off a complete meltdown. She felt a hand on her shoulder and looked up to see Dr. Takamura staring into her eyes.

"We'll lick this, Tanesha," she said, her voice soft but firm. "But first we have to find out what's causing it. When we know that, we can start working on returning you to normal."

Tanesha grabbed her hand and squeezed. "I knew you'd help. What's happening to me?"

Dr. Takamura shook her head. "I don't know."

That didn't sound so good. Tanesha felt her faint hope fading.

"Girl, you saying you ain't never seen nothin' like me before?"

"As a matter of fact I have. Just recently."

Tanesha could've started bawling again. She wasn't the only one.

"What was wrong?"

Dr. Takamura looked away. "I didn't get a chance to work her up."

"But you gonna work _me_ up, right?"

She smiled. "Six ways from Sunday. We'll start with blood tests, then I'm sending you to Doctor Haskins."

"Who's he?"

"A dermatologist."

"Hope he better than the one I been to."

"He's tops. He's going to look you over, then take a skin biopsy and do a hair analysis. First we find out what's going wrong—the changes in the tissues that are making this happen. Then we find out why. Once we know the what and the why, we can start figuring out _how_ to fix it."

Tanesha sobbed again. Couldn't help it.

"Oh, Lordy, I sure hope you right. 'Cause if you ain't, I don't know what I'll do. I'm so sick of them strange looks people give me, I don't want to go out. And even little Jamal's starting to look at me like I ain't his mother no more. He don't understand—shit, _I_ don't understand—and I think he's as scared as me. Maybe more."

Dr. Takamura touched her arm again. "I'm not promising a solution, Tanesha. I want to be clear on that. But I'll use everything modern medicine has to offer to find an answer for you."

"Can't ask for more than that, I guess." She paused. "You think this was caused by my cancer medicine?"

Dr. Takamura blinked. "What makes you think that?"

"The doctor I saw yesterday—"

"Who?"

"At the Penner clinic. Real piece of work. All the personality of a collard green. Maybe less. Anyway, he's looking me over, and as soon as he hears I had cancer therapy, he gets all shook up and says I gots to get back to Tethys."

"He probably wasn't familiar with the therapy and thought your immune system might be compromised."

"You wanna say that in English?"

She smiled. "What's important is that he sent you to the right place."

Tanesha sensed something bothering Dr. Takamura.

"But you didn't answer my question, doc: Could this be from the treatment?"

She shrugged. "I don't know. But that's one of the things I'll be looking into."

"This other patient—she get the same cancer treatment as me?"

Another head shake. "I can't discuss other patients—privacy, you know."

Dr. Takamura seemed to be plenty worried, about more than privacy, but Tanesha let it go. She trusted this lady. Had to. She had no one else.

SHEILA

Sheila wished she'd seen Tanesha before lunch so she could have told Abra. She'd told her all about the bug and Paul, but this was big. Exciting. Abra would have to wait, but not Bill. As soon as she finished her round of appointments, Sheila headed for Bill's office, walking at top speed. It took all her reserve to keep from running.

Two patients with pigment changes—radical, pervasive changes. Hair too—not only color but texture as well. And both treated with VG723. There *had* to be a connection.

She pulled open the door to the clinic building and found herself facing a wall of rain. What had begun as a light mid-morning drizzle had graduated to a full-scale deluge. And her umbrella was in her car.

Damn.

Well, she'd just have to get wet. This couldn't wait. She had to tell Bill. And a phone call wasn't going to do it. This was face-to-face stuff.

Wait—the tunnels.

She passed the elevator and pushed through the stairwell door to its right. Two flights down, through another door, and she was in the tunnel system.

The underground network that crisscrossed the campus had been dug back in the nineteenth century when this had been Bradfield College. The granite blocks forming the walls, floors, and arched ceilings gave the tunnels a chill, dungeony feel.

Sheila wondered what it had been like down here before electricity. What had folks used to see? Torches? Kerosene lamps? Must have been dark and foreboding. Now, with fluorescent light boxes strung along the ceilings, they were anything but.

Light alone couldn't dissipate the damp chill, however. Nor keep out the trickles that seeped through from above.

Sheila rarely came down here, so she had to pause to orient herself. The Admin building was to her right, and then left. They needed signs down here. Take a wrong turn and you could wind up in one of the unrefurbished dead-ends.

She maintained a hurried walk, nodding and smiling to other Tethys staff members taking advantage of the shelter.

She was glad to see them. After last night, the last place she wanted to be alone was in these eerie tunnels.

Reaching the Admin stairs, she ran up to the first floor, down the hall, and pushed through a door emblazoned with *William P. Gilchrist, Jr. MD.*

"Is he in?"

Marge, his secretary, looked startled by Sheila's precipitous entrance.

"Yes, but he's on a call."

"Thanks."

Sheila stepped through the inner door into Bill's sanctum without waiting to be announced. He had the phone to his ear but smiled and gestured to the settee. Sheila felt too wired to sit, so she wandered the room.

She loved this office and hoped to have one just like it someday.

The big windows with their diamond-shaped panes of leaded glass, the richly paneled walls, the hardwood floor, the stone fireplace that had been converted to gas. It used to belong to the dean of Bradfield.

She'd been here numerous times but never tired of inspecting the photo-bedizened walls. Bill had been everywhere and seemed to know everybody. He had framed photos of himself with politicos—President Bush, Senator Kerry, Kofi Annan, among others—and celebrities—everyone from Bono to Arnold Schwarzenegger. Salted among the photos were award plaques from the American Society of Clinical Oncology, the American Society of Pediatric Hematology / Oncology, the Massachusetts Society of Clinical Oncology, plus a host of cancer advocacy groups.

She studied his smiling face under a ten-gallon Stetson as he shook hands with Imus at his ranch for kids with cancer. The same smile that had pulled her back into the light from the darkest moment of her life.

She remembered that time . . . she'd never forget.

Her mother had recently died, only a year after Da. Sheila's pregnancy had helped her deal with her grief and she'd begun applying for positions at cancer centers. Then the call came that Dek was DOA after his accident. She'd miscarried the very next day. She'd had the D&C and then gone to pick out Dek's casket.

The back-to-back losses were more than she could handle and she'd begun to sleepwalk through life. Job interviews but no one called back. Why would they? Who'd want to hire a zombie?

Bill was the only one who'd asked her what was wrong. She remembered his words to the letter.

"I look at you and I look at your record and I see two different people. Am I missing something?"

First she'd been amazed that someone in his position not only met with her personally, but then had the insight to see how emotionally raw she was. It was as if he knew all of her sorrows and cared enough to ask about them. She'd trusted him instantly; breaking down, she told him everything.

He'd listened patiently, then shocked her by offering a one-year trial on the spot. She'd also have free access to the psychiatrists and psychotherapists on staff to help her get back on track. A dream come true. If she proved herself, she'd be offered a long-range contract; if not, well, then . . .

Sheila had planned to make full use of the shrinks, but then she'd met Abra. The seemingly debilitated woman's indefatigable drive and courage motivated Sheila to pour out her heart. Losing Dek was a near mortal blow, but the miscarriage had all but put her over the edge. And she'd never told anyone, so had no one to console her. But Abra had listened. She always listened.

And when Abra talked, it was never about herself. The fertility clinic was everything. Most of the women they saw there, Abra told her, either couldn't conceive or had miscarried several times. One in five pregnancies ended in miscarriage she'd said, but that didn't make it less emotionally devastating. There's no greater disappointment, Abra had said as she patted her hand. Just like Mum used to do.

Abra now let her come into the clinic and hold the newborns whenever she wanted. And she assured Sheila if and when the time came, Abra would make sure Sheila had a successful pregnancy.

Sheila knew she filled a void in Abra's life too. Abra had never had a lover, much less a daughter. Theirs became the perfect symbiotic relationship.

Her companionship and Sheila's work proved to be all the therapy she needed. The patients on the oncology unit, whose problems were so much worse than hers, healed her perspective. She became fully functioning.

And she owed that to Bill. In so many ways he had saved her life. God knew what would have happened if he hadn't thrown her a lifeline. She would always revere him for that.

A handsome, brilliant man with a heart. You didn't find one of those very often. If he weren't married . . . but he was.

She still felt an aching void where Dek had lived. If the child had survived, at least something of him would remain. But she'd learned to compartmentalize it. At least during the day. Nights were the worst. When the lights went out and she lay alone, thoughts of Dek and what their child would have been hovered around the bed like ghosts.

She turned as she heard Bill hang up. He leaned back in his green leather chair and looked at her from the far side of his huge mahogany desk.

"What's up, Sheila?"

She stepped to the edge of the desk, trying to rein in her excitement and sound professional.

"You'll never guess who walked into my exam room today."

He smiled. "Brad Pitt?"

"No! Remember Kelly Slade? We talked about her yesterday—the woman with the hair and pigment changes?"

Bill's smile faded a bit. "Of course. But I thought she—had an accident."

"She did, but I've just found another one."

He frowned. "Another . . .?"

"Another patient with pervasive pigment changes."

"Who is she?"

She couldn't contain her excitement.

"Name's Tanesha Green, only she's the exact opposite of Kelly. Instead of a white woman turning brown, this lady's a thirty-nine-year-old African-American who looks like she's turning Caucasian!"

Bill shook his head. "How can that . . .?"

"That's what *I* want to know. And here's the kicker: Just like Kelly, she was treated with VG-seven-twenty-three. There's *got* to be a connection!"

She grinned but it faltered when she saw Bill's mood change.

"Wait a sec, wait a sec," he said, raising his hands. "Don't go off half cocked. Sit down please." His voice shifted to a disappointed tone. "*Post hoc ergo propter hoc?* Not what I'd expect from someone scientifically trained."

He was right of course. Just because Event A preceded Event B didn't mean that A had *caused* B. But . . .

"Seven-twenty-three is something these two have in common."

"Okay, I understand the thrill of finding something new, but step back for a wider perspective. These two women may have many things in common that you don't know about—exposure to toxins, for one. You'll have to background that. But from where I sit, I see something very important that they *don't* have in common."

"What?"

"A *syndrome*: One is losing pigment while the other is—or rather, was—gaining it. You've got two different problems here, Sheila."

Okay, on the surface, she had to agree.

"But still, I sense a connection."

He shrugged. "Instinct is wonderful, and shouldn't be ignored. But instinct isn't enough. You need a pattern, you need evidence of replication. I shouldn't have to explain the scientific method to you. What you have is an observation of pigment changes in two seven-twenty-three patients. So you've come up with a hypothesis: VG-seven-twenty-three *caused* those pigment changes. But all hypotheses need to be tested. How can you do that?"

The answer was obvious.

"Find more cases."

"Exactly." He tapped a few buttons on his keyboard, then rose from his chair and swiveled it toward her. "Sit here."

"Why?"

"We're going to see if we can find more pigment changes."

After hesitating a heartbeat, she walked around the desk and sat in his chair. The seat was still warm. On any other chair that would have put her off, but this was Bill Gilchrist's seat.

He moved behind to hover over her right shoulder.

"Click the *Global Search* button."

Sheila frowned. "Global Search? I don't have anything like that."

"Only two people do: Abra and yours truly. It allows access to the entire system—the records of every patient who's ever been treated at Tethys."

Sheila was impressed. "Super. An all-access pass."

"You could call it that."

"Some research tool."

"One that could easily be misused. I've already entered my password. Go ahead."

Sheila clicked and up popped a dialog box.

"Now what?"

"Type in 'vg723' plus 'pigment' plus 'change' and let's see what we get."

She did. "*552 VG723 files found*" popped onto the screen.

"Five-fifty-two?" she said. "I had no idea."

"The trial was well underway when you joined us."

She watched a blinking magnifying-glass icon meander about the screen until a dozen or so names popped up, Kelly Slade's among them.

"Aha!"

Bill leaned closer over her shoulder, close enough to identify his aftershave—Woods. She found the aroma almost intoxicating.

"Okay. Start going through them and see what we've got."

The search engine impressed her, bold-facing the key words wherever they appeared. As she scanned the files one at a time, her disappointment grew. The incidences of pigment changes in VG723 patients appeared limited to nevi, scar tissue, and nail beds. Nothing but Kelly's mentioned a pervasive change.

"Damn."

He rested a hand on her shoulder. She liked the sensation.

"Looks like you'll need a new hypothesis."

"But—"

"But what? Hundreds of seven-twenty-three patients, and only one match."

"Two if you count Tanesha. I haven't entered her data yet."

"What's her last name again?"

"Green. Tanesha Green."

"Whatever. Do you see how important it is not to jump to conclusions? Implicating seven-twenty-three in these two rare syndromes could harm the clinical trial. I hope you haven't mentioned this to anyone."

"Me? No. But Tanesha brought it up to me."

She felt Bill's grip tighten on her shoulder, then relax. He released her and moved away.

"Did she now?" he said in a low voice.

Sheila rotated the chair and saw him staring out the window, his back to her.

"Something wrong?" She rubbed her shoulders, doubting he realized how hard he had squeezed.

"Not yet." He turned to face her, his expression grim. "But there could be. How convinced was this Tanesha Green that seven-twenty-three was at the root of her problem?"

"Not convinced at all. She just asked the question. And I think it's a natural question. I mean, the major event in her life these past few years was a miracle therapy. Now there's another major change in her body and she's wondering if the two are related."

Bill's gaze locked onto her. "Sheila, I'm making it your job to put an end to such wondering."

Shocked, she blurted, "B-but why?"

"Because it's groundless—you've seen that for yourself." His face reddened and a vein bulged on his forehead. "But that doesn't mean it can't harm the clinical trial. If she starts blathering to the world that seven-twenty-three is turning her Caucasian or some such nonsense, God knows what damage she could do."

Sheila was baffled.

"How?"

"By making other seven-twenty-three patients paranoid. Soon they'll start questioning every mole, every splotch of color—*Was that there before? I never noticed it. I wonder if it's that medication they gave me.* As soon as that starts, the lawyers will come sniffing around. Before you know it, VecGen and Tethys will be chin deep in a host of frivolous suits. We're on the brink of a cure for cancer, Sheila. A *cure.*"

Though it was cold in his office, Bill was sweating. He wiped his brow with his cuff.

"But it's VecGen's product, not ours." Unease made her voice barely audible. "Anyway, what if it's a delayed reaction? What if the other patients simply haven't shown symptoms yet, or theirs aren't as severe as these two? If nothing else, we're obligated to report our findings to VecGen."

"God, Sheila. They are not *our* findings. They're *your* findings, and I don't agree with them. Read my lips. There is *no* connection.

Don't ruin a good thing here because you're anxious to get your name in print."

She flinched. He may as well have slapped her across the face.

He paused. "It *is* VecGen's product, but we've been overseeing the clinical trial—*we're* the ones who put it into the folks who become plaintiffs." He glared at her. "Do you understand now?"

Sheila felt like crying. How dare he think she was only pursuing this to get published. What a crass, know-it-all, arrogant—

And all that aside, she didn't want to believe that formerly terminal patients would sue the very people who'd saved their lives. But who was she kidding? This was twenty-first century America—everyone's a victim, anything for a buck, devil take the hindmost.

Then a thought struck her.

"But wait. As you just proved, there's no connection. They can't win."

Bill shook his head and threw his hands up.

"Even if you're the victor in one of these suits, you lose."

"I don't—"

"Legal expenses, for one," he said. "Victorious or not, frivolous suit or not, VecGen and Tethys will have to defend themselves—our overpriced lawyers against their ambulance chasers. But that's only the most obvious cost. The real damage will be if seven-twenty-three becomes stigmatized. Think of the people who'll shy away from it, people who could be helped. And here's an even worse scenario."

Sheila couldn't imagine it.

"What?"

"VecGen discontinuing VG-seven-twenty-three because it simply isn't worth it."

"They wouldn't."

"Really? It wouldn't be the first time a company has backed away from a useful drug. Why do you think we had that fifty-million-dose shortage of flu vaccine back in oh-four? Because not one American company would produce it, and still won't produce an injectable. It's costly, time consuming, and they got fed up with being sued every time someone had a reaction. So they said to hell with it and concentrated on other areas." He rubbed his eyes. "Thankfully we have that new Swiss company picking up the slack."

"So what should I do?"

"You investigate Tanesha Green's syndrome, but in the meantime you disabuse her of the idea that it could be in any way, shape, or form connected to seven-twenty-three. We *must* keep its reputation pristine."

Sheila had never seen Bill so fiercely demanding. She felt her stomach knot.

"I'll do everything I can."

He gave her a half-hearted smile. "I know you will." He glanced at his watch. "I'm supposed to meet with Abra shortly. Keep me informed on this, Sheila."

Half dazed, she rose and headed for the door. As she walked out she thought about how Bill had asked her, *Who is she?* when she'd told him about the new patient. But she hadn't mentioned the sex. How had Bill known?

You're being paranoid, Sheila. Probably just a lucky guess. The first had been female so he'd assumed the second was too.

That had to be it.

Sheila made a beeline for her office. Tethys was depending on her to keep it from being sued. Not a responsibility that should be hers, but she'd do her best.

And the best way would be to find the cause of Tanesha's syndrome and prove beyond doubt that it had no link to VG723.

She just hoped she was up to it. She never wanted to see Bill that angry again. But despite Bill's opinion, two such cases did warrant investigation.

BILL

"Drinking so early in the day?" Abra said with her pursed-lipped smile as she rolled into her family room wearing her usual dark-colored dress slacks and a neutral blouse. Her critters heard the hum of her chair and scurried and slithered to the fronts of their tanks. She ran her hand along the terraria until she reached Bill.

He rarely drank before five, but he'd scheduled a short afternoon, so he'd treated himself. He *needed* a drink right now. Not for the usual reason, either. The damn menagerie of snakes and spiders didn't faze him today. Couldn't. Not after what Sheila Takamura had set on his plate.

He turned to his sister. "It's been a bad day."

She took a breath and held it as she closed her eyes. When she released it she looked at him.

"Sheila told me she found a bug in her office. Was that your doing?"

He didn't respond.

"Honestly, Billy, I know you're infatuated with Sheila, but don't you think it's a little obsessive to bug her phone? If you want her, then leave Elise and pursue her. But don't play these games. It's unbecoming."

Bill sighed with relief. He wanted to laugh but didn't. Abra thinking the bug was about his stalking Sheila was perfect. One little lecture and he was off the hook.

"I'm sorry. You're right. I installed it a long time ago. I haven't listened in ages."

"And the break-in at her house? Her camera, laptop, and purse stolen. Was that your doing?"

Bill looked at the floor. Damn.

"I had to get the pictures of Kelly."

"Did you have to take her laptop as well, and her purse? She had to call all over the place and get everything cancelled."

"If I just took her camera it would have been obvious."

"Billy, it's a felony to break into a house. Why take that risk?"

"I didn't. I sent Shen in."

"What on Earth were you thinking? Why put Shen at risk like that? He's a good man. That's very unfair. Very, very unfair."

Abra looked through him and Bill wanted to hide under a couch. Her disapproval felt like a whiplashing.

"I was just protecting Proteus. I—"

She put her hand up. "I don't want to hear it. Do what you

will to steer her away, but no more cloak and dagger. See that this doesn't happen again. No more bugs."

He nodded. She made him feel like a little boy.

"Or teasing her if she wants to go on dates. I heard about your blue collar comment."

Bill's face reddened. She had him there. Was there anything Sheila *didn't* tell Abra?

"I'm sorry. You're right. I respect Sheila as a co-worker. That's as far as it will go. I'll let her live her life."

Abra smiled and nodded. "Good boy."

Was it over? Was she done dumping on him? He'd tell what he had been holding back. That would get the attention off him.

"Abra, my snooping on Sheila is the least of our concerns."

She clenched her chair. "What do you mean?"

"The other shoe has dropped."

"Why didn't you tell me as soon as you got here?"

"You were too busy being my older sister, running me through the ringer."

"What happened?"

"Tanesha Green, the woman who got the other sample, came in. And guess who saw her."

Abra closed her eyes and shook her head. "Of all the gin joints in all the towns in all the world, she walks into mine." She sighed. "The poor woman . . . Tanesha . . . what she must be going through. We'll have to find a way to compensate her."

"We saved her life, didn't we?"

"Yes, but—well, Tanesha Green ending up in Sheila's office really muddies the waters. It makes it a lot harder to cover up." Abra surprised him by striking her armrest with a tiny gnarled fist. "How does that happen? Two people out there who could bring Proteus down in flames and both show up in the same doctor's office. How does that *happen*?"

She struck her armrest again.

Bill couldn't help smiling—just a little. "Five years ago you'd have broken a few metacarpals doing that."

"What?" Then she looked at her hand. "Oh. Yes, my bones

are stronger these days, stronger than at any time in my life." She shook herself. "But that's not important. *How?*"

Bill sipped his drink. "Not so unlikely when you think about it. Sheila is one of our staff oncologists. The two women in question were patients here. Sheila is not only a skilled doc, but she cares. Patients love her. Put all that together and it's not such a stretch that both women turned to Doctor Takamura when their skin and hair began doing strange things."

"I suppose not." Abra shook her head and shifted her twisted, withered body in her wheelchair. "But this has complicated an already precarious situation."

"Au contraire," Bill said. "Instead of juggling two curious physicians, we can devote our efforts and attention to just one—one who happens to be right under our roof. It could be worse."

Abra was nodding. "I see what you mean. Yes, I suppose it could be very much worse. Sheila is an ally."

"I hope so."

"What?" Abra tapped her hearing aid.

"Nothing. The fact that this is an isolated incident—one that will never occur again, I pray—means that she will find no pattern, and thus have no trail to follow. I ran her through the database and showed her that her two cases are anomalies."

"But what if she should stumble upon the truth?"

"She won't."

"You don't know that, Bill. What if she does? I think we should simply tell her everything now. Wouldn't that be easier? If she finds out on her own—"

"I'll see to it that she never gets that far. If she starts getting close, I'll find ways to keep her so busy she won't have time for extracurricular investigations."

"I don't want to see her overworked. I'd rather bring her in."

"Abra, it's too soon. If it comes down to losing Proteus and Tethys or losing Sheila, you know we'll have to let Sheila go."

Tears started to form in Abra's eyes. Bill had been placating her with the idea of eventually bringing Sheila in, but too much was at stake. She'd never embrace it the way they did.

"It will never come to that, so don't worry. I'm sorry I upset you. I'll steer Sheila away from this and things can return to normal. Okay?"

She nodded. "I am trusting you to make sure she doesn't get too close to the truth. If she does, I'm telling her everything. I'm not losing her."

Her look drove the point home. Stop Sheila from learning too much, or let her in and risk having the Proteus Cure fall apart around them. And it *would* fall apart. Miss Straight-and-Narrow did not have the vision to accept Proteus.

"Very well, Abra," Bill said, grimacing. He hated fighting with her. "I'll take care of it. She won't find out."

Shen had placed a new bug in Sheila's office. Bill had kept a close eye on Sheila since the day she started and wasn't about to stop now. She hadn't discovered how VG723 really worked, or its side effects. With continued surveillance he could keep her from discovering anything in the future.

ABRA

Abra sighed as she watched her little brother leave.

Billy, Billy, Billy, what are we going to do?

He swore he had the situation under control, but did he? Drinking a lot lately, and his hands shook. What was going on that he wasn't telling? The poor boy always put so much pressure on himself.

She knew he kept things from her, to let her concentrate on the clinic, but she so hoped he knew what he was doing.

Nothing to do except pray and hope Billy could keep it all quiet. They had all worked so hard, Billy, Mama, Daddy—God rest his soul—and her to make the Proteus therapy a reality so that no one would have to endure what she did.

Abra recalled how half her childhood seemed to have been spent in hospital rooms. Drab, gray walls . . . smells of medicine . . . cold sheets. The memories felt as crippling as her disease. She'd been nine years old when she finally learned to pronounce her disease: Osteogenesis imperfecta . . . a genetic defect that interfered with collagen production, leaving her bones like glass.

That had been the year of her worst Christmas ever. She remembered falling down the stairs Christmas morning and awakening in the hospital. But never before had she felt so much pain.

The rods were to blame. She'd heard about them for years. Someday, Mama had said, they might put pipes in her bones to make them stronger. She'd made it seem easy, like getting a pair of glasses. A good thing, she'd said, so Abra wouldn't snap all the time.

But Mama had fibbed, never said it would be agony. No one even asked Abra about it. Just rammed them in without telling her.

And when the painkillers wore off, she'd felt as if her body were on fire. Screaming and screaming and the nurses giving her more morphine.

No one should have to suffer like that. And Abra knew that no one would have to if Proteus could be kept alive. But Bill and she both knew that this situation with Kelly Slade and Tanesha was a potential catastrophe. She prayed trouble could be averted. If not, their dream might well be over before they could achieve all the good they'd hoped for. A cure for so many illnesses. Such a tragedy if all the needy people never got their chance.

Like her niece April . . .

BILL

Bill, Elise, and Robbie took off their coats and settled into the folding chairs ringing the thick blue mat. Bill sniffed the air: cider and sugar cookies. Crayon and glitter pictures covered the walls. Abra sat a few rows up in her wheelchair. Today was April's gymnastics recital. Bradfield Gymnastics and Dance hosted a Christmastime event so the kids could show how hard they'd worked. Everyone laughed when the kindergartners pranced out onto the mat wearing brown velvet bodysuits, antlers, and red rubber noses. "Rudolph the Red-Nosed Reindeer" played in the background.

They did jumping jacks in a circle, then dropped to the ground and did somersaults, a tangled mess of little arms and legs. Bill and the other parents applauded. The kids preened.

"April Gilchrist doing a cartwheel," the teacher announced.

Dark-haired, blue-eyed April stepped forward, found her family, and smiled. She gave Bill a thumbs-up and his heart swelled. Her chest rose and fell quickly and evenly. What a relief. She ran and made almost a full cartwheel. Damn good for a five-year old.

"Very good, April. Now let's have Laura Flanagan."

April waved into the video camera Elise was aiming her way.

He watched April return to her friends, giddy. A picture of health.

Thanks to me.

His joy in seeing her reminded him of the anguish he'd felt six years ago when the results of Elise's intrauterine tests came back. Abra, her expression grim, had taken him aside and told him.

"Bill, the baby has the F508 mutation. Cystic Fibrosis."

He'd collapsed into a chair and cried. Really cried, no holds barred. Elise would never have an abortion. She'd had two miscarriages since Robbie already, and pinned all her hopes on this pregnancy. This one was "her little miracle," as she said so often.

Abra had pulled his chin up to face her. "Billy, you listen to me. This doesn't have to happen."

"Abra, I can't—she won't give up the baby."

"She doesn't have to, Billy. We've got Proteus. We can fix her."

"But . . ."

"Just because we don't use it on children anymore doesn't mean we can't make an exception. As soon as she's born, we'll treat her. And no one will ever know."

"But if we use it, she won't—."

"Don't say it, Billy. Don't *ever* say it." She put her finger to his lips. "It doesn't matter. The side effects will far outweigh the kind of life she'll have if we stand idly by."

And so they told Elise the results were perfectly normal and she was thrilled. Four months later, Bill whisked April away from the nursery and he and Abra treated her with VG723. Now they had a perfect and healthy little girl. Adorable.

God he was glad. Side effects be damned. Abra was right. They didn't matter. His angel was healthy. Nothing more important than that.

He threw his arm around Elise and squeezed, unable to contain his joy. "Isn't she great?"

Elise smiled. "She's our little miracle."

Yes, our little miracle.

Elise had no idea how true that was.

SHEILA

Sheila checked the ultrasound to confirm the placement of Sean's PICC line: perfect location. The VG723 would infuse directly into his central circulation.

"Okay, Sean. You're ready for your first dose."

The too-pale boy on the pale sheets looked up at her. "Tell me again how this VG-stuff works."

She'd already explained it twice. Sean was no dummy, but he couldn't seem to grasp how a bunch of stem cells would cure him. Sheila couldn't blame him. The radical concept was shrouded in proprietary secrecy.

"Okay. You know what a stem cell is, right?"

He nodded. "Special cells that can turn into any other kind of cell in the body."

Simplistic and overgeneralized, but close enough.

"Remember the bone-marrow biopsy we did last week?"

"I've lost count of how many I've had, but yeah, I remember it."

"Well, VecGen took the blood stem cells we found there, cultured them, then modified them into omnipotential stems."

That was the big mystery: How VecGen turned marrow stems into omnipotential stems—the equivalent of embryonic stem cells.

"Then the virus, right?"

"Right. They embed a virus into the stem's cellular membrane."

Sean shook his head. "*That's* the part that creeps me out. Someone shooting me up with a virus . . ."

"It sounds crazy, I know, but viral vectors have been used for gene and tumor therapy since the nineties. So that in itself isn't new. What VecGen has done is embed a modified adenovirus—modified to render it innocuous—into the surface of these stem cells to act as a guidance system."

"Like a Tomahawk missile."

"More like a heat-seeking missile. Adenoviruses are attracted to multiplying cells, and right now the most rapidly multiplying cells in your body belong to the lymphoma."

"So when the virus latches onto a lymphoma cell, it drags the stem cell with it."

"Right. Thousands and thousands of them. And once they reach those hot spots, the stem cells do what they do best: Multiply and change into whatever tissue they happen to be in contact with. If the tumor's in a lymph node, they infiltrate the mass and become lymph cells—normal, non-cancerous lymph cells. When they arrive at one of those metastases in your liver, they'll infiltrate the met and start becoming normal liver cells."

"Yeah, but the tumors are still there."

"Not for long. Stem cells multiply very quickly, even faster than malignant cells. The special stems strangle the tumor by commandeering its blood supply and crowding out its cells. And they go on doing this until every cancer cell in your body has been killed."

"And then where do they go?"

"Well, once they undergo mitosis—that's what we call it when a cell splits—"

Sean made a face. "I'm no bio major, but I know *that*."

"Good. With mitosis they lose their viral guidance system and so become regular old stem cells."

Sean mulled this for a few seconds, then frowned. "So why can't VecGen do that for everyone?"

"I'm not sure. They keep certain aspects of the process under wraps—don't want anyone stealing their secrets." And as the bug in her office proved, someone was indeed after their secrets. "But I imagine it has to do with whether or not they can embed the vector virus. If your stem cells reject the virus, they won't have a guidance system, and you're out of luck."

Sean smiled. "I'm a laid-back kinda guy. Gotta figure my stem cells are too. I'm guaranteed a cure, right?"

Sheila had to be honest.

"Rarely there's an immune reaction to seven-twenty-three—the patient's defense system doesn't recognize the modified stems and attacks them as invaders. They never get to where they're supposed to go. No cure."

Sean's smile lost some of its shine. "Let's hope my immune system is laid back too."

"I'm sure it is."

Sheila turned to go.

"One more thing," Sean said. "It's named VG-seven-twenty-three, does that mean there were seven hundred and twenty-two failures before it?"

Sheila winced. "Gee, I hope not." Then she smiled. "Seriously, VecGen spent years developing it, testing it first on rats and such, then moving to primates, and now, finally, humans."

He held up a pair of crossed fingers. "It'll work for me."

Sheila laughed and headed for the door. "That's the spirit."

God, she loved this job.

———···———

Sheila rarely looked at her appointment schedule, so was surprised to see Paul Rosko waiting for her in examining room three.

"Paul? What are you doing here? Is something wrong? Is Coogan—?"

"Coog's doing fine. I'm the one who's a wreck."

"Sick?"

She seated herself on the room's wheeled stool, shifted into her physician mindset—not always easy when there's a relationship outside the examining room—and looked up at him. He didn't look sick.

"Physically I'm fine but this paternity thing—it's driving me nuts."

"Why?"

He seemed surprised by the question.

"How else can you react when the boy you've believed was your son, who you've raised as your son, turns out to be someone else's. It's . . . it's devastating."

"Who says he's someone else's?"

"The blood test! The doctor told me he's O-negative. I'm A-positive. I couldn't donate blood to him, and a father's blood should be compatible with his son's."

"Not necessarily. Sometimes neither parent can donate. Did he have a bone marrow transplant?"

"It didn't work but yes he had one. Before the KB26."

"Well, even without a transplant, sometimes parents can't donate blood."

Paul's brow wrinkled. "Yesterday you said you'd explain that. I *need* that explanation."

"Okay. Here's how it goes. Your blood type consists of two genetic components: one from your mother and one from your father. You could have A-positive from your father and O-neg from your mother. That's your genotype. But since type O is non-reactive, your phenotype—how the genes are expressed—is A-positive. When it comes to you being a father, however, you can donate only one of those two alleles to your child. Which one he gets is up for grabs. Coog could have received your O-negative half. What was your wife's—?"

"Ex-wife."

"What was her blood type?"

"I haven't the foggiest."

"Okay, let's say she was B-positive / O-neg. That would give Coog a chance of four configurations: A-O, B-O, A-B, and O-O. In the last case, Coog would be O-O-neg, known as the universal donor. But as a recipient he could be given only O-O-neg blood. Any other type would cause a transfusion reaction. He'd be ineligible to receive blood from either his A parent or his B parent. The same would hold if he'd turned out AB."

Paul chewed on that, then looked her in the eye.

"Then I guess only a paternity test will settle it."

"But I just explained—"

"Sheila, I love that kid and nothing will ever change that. But I want proof he's mine."

"Why?"

"I didn't come to you so you could play Socrates, Sheila. I need help."

Seeing anger flaring in his eyes, she raised her hands and said, "Paul, I want you to look at the big picture. The result of a paternity test, no matter which way it goes, won't change Coog. He'll be the same as he ever was, the same boy you say you love."

"I don't just *say* it—I *mean* it."

"I'm sure you do. But think: Even though the test won't change Coog, a negative-paternity result will alter a crucial part of his life."

Paul looked down. "You mean the way I'll look at him."

"Exactly. And you don't strike me as a man who's adept at hiding his feelings. Coog is going to sense a change in you, sense something's wrong. You're the most important person in his life, Paul. If he senses rejection from you, what's that going to do to him?"

"Since I'm already looking at him and wondering, I can't see that a test will change much. It's eating me up, Sheila. Eating me alive. I've got to know."

She sighed. She could tell he was bound and determined.

"Okay. I'm advising against it, but if that's what you want, that's what we'll do. I'll take a swab of your cheek now and get one from Coogan later today. Painless and quick. Where can we get hold of your wi—ex-wife?"

"Rose? Why?"

"We need a sample of her DNA."

Paul winced. "I haven't a clue where she is."

Sheila tried to hide her relief.

"Well, then, we're up the creek. We need samples from Coog, you and your ex to get a definitive answer."

Paul punched his thigh. "Damn!"

He looked so tortured. Her heart went out to him but she reined it back. Had to stay in doctor mode, had to keep professional distance.

"I'm sorry, Paul, but maybe it's for the best."

He sighed. "Yeah, maybe you're right. I—" He stiffened and looked at her. "What about HLA and histocompatibility reports? Will they help?"

Where had he learned about that?

"Yes. I'm sure they would, but—"

"I've got those. Rose and I were screened when they were looking for a donor for Coog's bone marrow transplant." He frowned. "I wasn't eligible, of course. Should have known then . . ."

"I told you, parents frequently don't match." But it was no use. He wouldn't rest until he saw it in black and white. "You still have the reports?"

He gave her a sheepish smile. "I'm a pack rat. Never throw anything away. I know where they are. Just get Coog's DNA. I'll bring the reports."

Oh, hell.

"Well, I guess if you bring them in . . ."

He hopped off the table. "I'll have them to you tonight. Tomorrow latest." He grabbed her shoulders and gave her a peck on the cheek. "You're a lifesaver, Sheila!"

She hoped he felt that way after the results came in.

SHEN

Li Shen knelt on the living room carpet and played with his son's foam blocks, carefully stacking one atop another as he built a spindly tower. Fai knelt on the far side, dark eyes wide as he watched, waiting for his moment. Only two years old but already bilingual. Often he would confuse his English and Mandarin, sometimes with hilarious results.

Finally, when the tower passed the two-foot level, Fai could wait no longer. He sprang forward, swinging his arms like a miniature Godzilla and demolishing the tower. Then he looked at his father and laughed.

"Do 'gain!"

Shen grinned at this little person he loved more than life itself and said, "But every time I do, you knock it down!"

That, of course, was the whole point.

"Do 'gain!"

"Okay, but this time don't knock it down."

Fai didn't reply, simply sat back on his haunches and waited, readying to strike again.

"Let Daddy rest and let *Ma* try," Jing said, dropping down beside them.

Jing was as beautiful and graceful as her name. Shen rubbed a thin arm and stroked the glossy black hair of the only person he loved more than Fai.

"That's all right," he said. "You get to play with him all day."

"Then we'll do it together."

As she started on a new tower, the phone rang.

Shen rose before Jing could move. He wanted to get a beer from the refrigerator anyway. His gaze lingered on his wife and son, his heart swelling. But it sank when he saw the phone's caller-ID screen. He hesitated, then picked up on the third ring.

"Shen," said a too familiar voice. "I'm on my way to your place. Meet me out front in about five minutes."

"Yes, doctor."

He turned and gazed across his toy-strewn living room.

"I must meet with Doctor Gilchrist."

"But you just got home," Jing said in their native *Hanyu*. "Now you have to go back?"

"No. He is driving by."

She shot to her feet. "He is coming here? But I have not prepared enough dinner! What will I—?"

"We will talk in his car."

"In his car? Isn't that strange?"

"He did not say why, but it is surely a security matter."

"Could he not talk on the phone?"

Shen shrugged.

Jing pouted. "He should let you have your time with your family."

"He is brother to *Jiù-zhù-zhě*. And without *Jiù-zhù-zhě* I would have no family."

Jing bowed her head. "Yes. That is so."

Indeed so, Shen thought.

He was Shen Li here—he still found it odd that Americans put their given name first—back home he had been Li Shen, second in command of elite security answering only to the Party's Central Committee. He had been trained in a thousand ways to kill, and from time to time had been called upon to use those skills. Always he had obeyed without question.

Born during the Cultural Revolution, Shen had been raised to revere the CPC. He had demonstrated many times that the Party could always count on him, and had trusted that he would always be able to count on the Party.

How wrong.

When Jing fell sick, Shen learned his true value. The doctors removed her cancerous ovary but would do nothing more. Chemotherapy was reserved for a select few, and Shen was not in that number. He offered to pay, to give all he owned for his wonderful Jing, but the Party was deaf to his pleas.

Desperate, he converted everything to gold, stole a government boat, and set out with Jing for Taiwan. The Taiwanese Navy picked them up halfway across. To embarrass the PRC, the Taiwan government trumpeted Jing's plight to the world, saying *they* would treat the poor woman. But privately they informed Shen that the delay since diagnosis had allowed the cancer to spread. Jing would die within the year.

Shen had sunk into despair. No one could offer Jing a shred of hope. Yes, she could start chemotherapy, but the chance of success was almost nil, so why make her spend her remaining time feeling sick and weak.

And then, from the United States . . . a call.

An American woman named Abra Gilchrist had read about Jing's plight and offered an experimental therapy. She flew Shen and Jing here, to Tethys, where a miracle treatment cured her.

Cured!

Shen still could hardly believe it. His Jing, so pale and drawn and hollow-cheeked then, had returned to her former round and healthy self within a year. Her name meant "sparkling," and indeed she sparkled again.

He met many times with the poor rich woman—rich in dollars but poor with her terrible body—who wanted only to heal. That was her dream, she had told Shen: To heal the world . . . one person at a time.

He came to call her *Jiù-zhù-zhě*: Savior.

She had instructed her brother to help Shen find work. When Dr. Gilchrist learned of Shen's past, he offered a job in the foundation's security department. Shen worked hard on his shifts and studied English in his off hours. He advanced quickly, and when, years ago, Dr. Gilchrist had asked him to remove a problem, he'd hesitated. He had left that life behind. But it was for *Jiù-zhù-zhě*, Dr. Gilchrist said. And it would only be just that once. For this deed, Shen was promoted to chief of security.

And then another miracle: Fai.

Not only had his beloved wife returned to him, but she had given him a son.

All because of *Jiù-zhù-zhě*.

Shen would do anything—*anything*—for *Jiù-zhù-zhě*.

Earlier this week her brother had called upon him once again. Shen hadn't wanted to but, as with the last time, *Jiù-zhù-zhě*'s dream depended on it. So he had done it. No death this time. Just a break in. No one hurt.

He hoped this meeting with Dr. Gilchrist would not involve an assassination. He was no longer the man who had worked for the Party. He was a father now, with a son to think of, and he wanted Fai to have the future Shen never could have dreamed of.

He shrugged into a black leather coat and stepped onto his front porch. At the curb he turned and looked at his house. A three-bedroom ranch, fourteen hundred feet of space. Small by American standards, but a palace compared to the cramped apartment he and Jing had shared back in Beijing. And he owned not one car, but two. His television provided hundreds of channels—hundreds!—and he could watch any he wished, even the ones that spoke against or made fun of the government. Unthinkable back home.

No. Not back home. China was forever in his past. This wondrous land was his home. His forever home.

At least so he hoped. Shen was not yet a citizen. He studied for the exam in his spare moments and would be ready soon. But not if linked to a crime. Especially murder. He would be imprisoned or, worse, deported with Jing and Fai along with him. Back to China . . . to face the fury of the Party.

As he blew warmth into his hands, he heard a car and saw two headlights approaching. A black Mercedes pulled up. Shen opened the door and slipped into the passenger seat.

Dr. Gilchrist, wrapped in a dark blue overcoat, offered his gloved hand.

"Shen. Good to see you."

Shen shook his hand and nodded. "How may this one help you, sir?"

"We have another problem, similar to the last."

Shen's heart sank. A refusal rose to his lips—but he held back. If this was for *Jiù-zhù-zhě* . . . for her dream.

He kept his voice even. "Most unfortunate."

"Yes, it is."

Shen tightened his fists as his fragment of hope faded.

"What does *Jiù-zhù-zhě* wish?"

"My sister's concerns involve two people. One is a former patient. My sister wishes to be more circumspect this time. She wants surveillance and nothing more."

Shen released a breath. He wondered what it would be like to have a god to thank. The Cultural Revolution had condemned belief in any god. The Party was all the god a comrade needed. So now he thanked the stars.

Only surveillance. That he could do.

"Very well."

"We need to keep track of her movements. My sister doesn't care what stores she goes to, what friends she visits. Her only concern is if she should consult a doctor other than Doctor Takamura."

"That will require extra man—"

"No." Dr. Gilchrist waved his hand between them. "No one else can be involved. Only you."

"But how can this one watch twenty-four hours a day?"

Shen needed a way out. He had done surveillance for the Party and found it a soul-deadening waste. And then he had an idea.

"If patient make doctor's appointment she will do by phone. If we tap phone, we know. The other way we not know until she goes to doctor."

Dr. Gilchrist rubbed his chin as he stared through the windshield. Shen was about to add to his suggestion when the doctor turned to him and smiled.

"Great idea, Shen. I knew you'd be a valuable asset."

Shen basked in his approval, for he was speaking for his sister, *Jiù-zhù-zhě*.

"I shall place tap tomorrow night."

"Excellent." He dug a slip of paper out of his coat pocket and handed it across. "Here's the address."

And now the hard question. "And if this woman decide to see other doctor? What do then?"

Dr. Gilchrist looked down. "Then she must be removed."

May it not happen, Shen thought.

Then he said, "You say two people?"

"The other is Doctor Takamura."

Shen choked, trying to hide his inner turmoil. Dr. Sheila . . . everyone liked her. Shen too. She had a smile for everyone, including him.

He remembered her husband, Hideki Takamura, an investigator for the JCAHO, who had discovered a connection between Tethys and VecGen and was about to reveal his findings. Dr. Gilchrist said that if they lost their accreditation, it would be the end of Tethys, the end of their ability to help people like Jing. An end even to *Jiù-zhù-zhě*.

And so Shen had loosened the bolts on the front wheel of Takamura's motorcycle, while it was parked at his office. When the man reached the right speed, he lost control and smashed into oncoming traffic. An unfortunate accident.

That had been in the days before fatherhood. Shen had been

different then. And he had not given the man or his fate a second thought until Doctor Takamura joined Tethys's staff. He recognized the name, and soon learned that he had killed her husband.

Even then he had not felt too bad. She was young and smart and pretty. She would find herself another man, perhaps one even better.

But as he'd grown to know Dr. Sheila, he saw the emptiness in her life, a void created by her husband's death, and it saddened him.

But his sadness expanded, ballooned when he learned that he had created a double void in her life: She had been pregnant when her husband was killed, and had miscarried the next day. He had caused that miscarriage. He had killed Dr. Sheila's baby.

What would her life be like now if she had not lost that child? Wouldn't she find the same joy in him or her that Shen found in Fai?

"What wrong has she done?"

"Nothing yet, but she's straying into dangerous territory. She's got to be stopped."

Shen closed his eyes and stifled a moan.

Stopped . . .

Kill Dr. Sheila . . . just as he had killed her husband because he too had "strayed into dangerous territory."

The brother had hired Dr. Sheila so he could keep an eye on her. In addition to routine monitoring, her work phone had been hooked to a voice-activated recorder, her office was watched on video, and Shen had installed spyware on her computer so the brother could see what files she accessed. Shen had monitored her for years but she kept her nose to her work. No suspicious calls, no sign that she knew about her husband's discovery.

But now Dr. Gilchrist said she had to be stopped.

"Doctor Sheila?" Shen said, hoping for a different answer. "I must stop her?"

Dr. Gilchrist's gaze faltered. He turned and stared through the windshield again.

"No one can be allowed to threaten my sister's dream. No one."

PAUL

Paul sat down at his computer with a bottle of beer. He turned on the banker's lamp and stared at the dark screen. Two nights ago he'd left the protagonist in his novel, Grisbe, on page 220, hanging in a precarious situation.

Paul had started novels before—lots of them—but always with invented characters plunked into fictional settings. That was how he thought writing fiction worked. He tried to copy his idols, John Irving, Charles Dickens, Wally Lamb. But his work always sounded forced, even to him. His characters seemed cardboard-flat, living in manufactured situations. Paul beat himself up with criticism. He'd finally decided he simply didn't have what it took and threw away all the old partial manuscripts.

But a few months ago he started a new book. The hell with it, he'd decided. He was going to write a gritty, semi-true account of a part of his life he wished had never happened. No Beverly Hills setting with a Brad Pitt type as the lead. But reality, starring Paul Rosko. Or rather, Jim Grisbe. Ever since that decision to write from his heart, the novel had become an obsession. Each night when Coogan went to bed, Paul slipped into their den and poured out his heart, his memories. What a release.

After a day like today he needed a release. But too much was going on now to escape into fiction. Coogan was still in the hospital and Paul needed to find those old medical records. Tonight Grisbe would have to wait.

He descended to the basement and knelt on the dusty floor. Under a naked sixty-watt bulb he started sifting through a large plastic storage bin, kept tightly lidded to protect the papers from the damp.

Years ago he'd planned to finish the basement, but after the divorce it seemed a waste. Lots of things had seemed like a waste then. So the space had become a repository for whatever overflowed from upstairs. That included Paul's free weights and punching bags, set up at the other end of the space. Paul found something cleansing in sweating and making his muscles ache.

Right now he felt an ache in his throat as he sifted through the boxes stacked in the container. The history of Coog's life. A life that almost ended yesterday.

Some boxes held the good years—the baby records, the first drawings, the homemade Santa Clauses, Easter Bunnies, and Halloween ghosts. And the photos. Good God, he'd taken so many shots of that boy, all preserved in albums.

He opened one with *YEAR 4* Sharpie-printed on the cover and scanned the photos, shaking his head at shots of him together with little Coog. They'd looked so much alike back then. What had happened? When had Coog developed that cleft in his chin? Where had that come from?

He moved on to the bad years: two boxes of medical records, hospital bills, doctor reports . . . the detritus of a desperate battle.

And somewhere in that mess lay Rose's histocompatibility results.

Took him an hour and a half, but he finally found Rose's printout. And his too. As he hefted the two reports he remembered Sheila's warning.

Even though the test won't change Coog, a negative-paternity result will alter a crucially important part of his life.

Will I be different? Will I be hurting Coog?

He put down the reports and walked over to his workout area. He pulled on a pair of Everlast gloves, stepped up to the speed bag, and began working it.

He moved to the heavy bag and began punching away. No fine rhythm here, just brute force, pounding jabs, uppercuts, and roundhouse rights and lefts until his arms ached.

And by the time he'd finished and stood there bathed in sweat and gasping, he'd made up his mind.

He had to know.

__THREE__

SHEILA

The first thing Sheila had seen in the morning's emails was a note from Hal Silberman, wanting to talk to her.

Yes!

She made a beeline for his office. "No need to tell me who this is about," she said on entering. "Tanesha Green, right?"

"Right." He pointed to the only other chair in his cramped office. "Have a seat."

Hal didn't match his office. He was trim, always perfectly groomed, and obsessively neat; Sheila had never seen him without a bow tie. His office, on the other hand, looked like a paper-recycling center.

Tanesha was scheduled for her follow-up soon and Sheila wanted to offer her *some* encouragement. But she didn't see that happening.

The extensive labs—she'd put a *stat* on the orders—showed nothing. Sheila had done the usual profiles, plus more esoteric tests to tease out some rare variant of one of the connective tissue diseases or evidence of an autoimmune disorder. But every result fell within the normal range. The woman was—to borrow a phrase from her residency—disgustingly healthy.

Jim Haskins's dermatology consultation yesterday was equally helpful—as in, not at all. He'd called to say how fascinating she was but his diagnosis was a figurative head scratch. He recommended a number of blood tests—all of which Sheila had already ordered—and deferred a diagnosis until he'd seen the path reports on the biopsies he'd performed.

That was where Hal Silberman, Tethys's dermatopathologist, came in. Hal said, "I wish I could add to what's in there, but . . ."

"What do the slides show?" Sheila said.

"She has some melanocytes that are producing the expected amount of melanin for a dark-pigmented person, but in among them are cells that are producing much less. So even though she appears to be suffering a general loss of pigment in the macroview, histologically it's spotty."

"Not a vitiligo variant, then?"

"No. Not mycosis fungoides, either. She's got these normal-looking cells that have simply cut back their melanin production."

"Ever seen anything like it?"

He shook his head. "Never. I searched through a number of sources and couldn't find a thing that resembled her slides."

"Any guesses as to etiology?"

"Off the top of my head I'd say that inhibition of tyrosinase activity is somehow involved, but don't ask me how."

Sheila knew that tyrosinase stimulated melanin production. Drop activity to zero and the result was an albino.

"So all the cells are producing melanin, just in different quantities."

He nodded. "Right. Which implies that inhibition is originating locally, at the cellular level. Because a systemic process would cause more uniform changes."

"Okay. But what about the hair changes? I knew Tanesha from her VG-seven-twenty-three therapy for colon cancer. She was an overweight, very dark-skinned African-American woman. The Tanesha I saw this week has changed into a hefty Jodi Foster. Light skin, straight light brown hair at the roots, but with the kinky black hair at the ends."

"That's another one for the books." He rubbed his jaw. "Her follicles have changed shape and so, consequently, has her hair. The older portions of her strands are flattened, just as you'd expect in the woolly hair of a typical African. The portions nearest the scalp are oval in cross-section—typical of Caucasians. And the cortices of the newer segments contain less melanin."

That explained *how* Tanesha's hair was changing from kinky black to smooth brown. But not *why*.

"I'm going to send slides to all the big centers and I'm arranging a scanning EMG of her follicles. Maybe we'll get a hit."

"Any chance her chemotherapy could be responsible?"

"Hadn't thought of it. Why, are there other cases?"

"Two weeks ago, a Caucasian women who had the same therapy with the opposite problem. She died accidentally before I could look into it."

He smiled. "Never rule anything out. That's my policy. I'll research it with that slant, maybe check with the doctor who sent her back here. I'm sure his name is in the file somewhere."

Finally someone responsive to her theory.

"So you think there's a possibility the changes could be from the chemo? From VecGen's therapy?"

"You never know. Certainly a possibility. Whatever happens, Sheila," he said, "don't lose track of this lady. I'd like to do another biopsy next week and compare slides."

Sheila left. Silberman didn't dismiss a link the way Bill did. *Certainly a possibility.* If Hal found a link, Bill would have to take him seriously. This guy had worked for Tethys since it opened its doors. Slides to all the major cancer centers. He guy didn't fool around. Sheila felt better already. Between Hal and her, they'd find out the truth.

PAUL

"Now," Paul said, "let's take a look at the goateed gent in the first panel on the next page."

He sat at Coog's bedside. His boy looked pale this morning, but not nearly as pale as when he'd had leukemia. Stronger than yesterday, and he was eating a regular diet, but still had an IV running. The nurse said she expected Dr. Brody, the internist overseeing his care, to order the IV pulled and discharge him when he made his morning rounds.

Paul refocused his attention to the matter at hand: He and Coog each held a copy of *The League of Extraordinary Gentlemen*.

A comic book, Paul thought. No, check that: a graphic novel.

He'd never dreamed he'd be reading and discussing such a thing—and with his son of all people. But he'd come to regard this as an extraordinary work of popular fiction. He hoped that by pointing out the literary references in the comic he could induce Coog to check out the originals. Anything to divert him from those damn videogames.

Paul had tried to get into the games with Coog but all too quickly learned that he lacked the reflexes, the manual dexterity, and—most important of all—the patience. One day it had taken everything he had to keep from ramming the damn controller through the screen.

Coog shifted in his bed and winced.

"The ribs?"

Coog nodded. "They're not so bad if I stay still, but rolling over is the pits."

"Want me to have them give you a pain pill?"

He shook his head. "Nah."

Paul smiled. "Think they'd give me one?"

Coog laughed and grabbed his side. "Don't make me laugh! Please! It kills."

The boy's pain subsided and he went back to flipping the pages.

"I never knew all this stuff was in here." He looked up at Paul and smiled. "It's so cool, Dad!"

Dad . . .

Despite all Sheila's caveats, he had to know. He'd never been one to take things on faith. He knew he had a lot of St. Thomas in him, had to stick his finger into the wounds, confirm the gap in the flesh, feel the congealed blood.

Learn what's real and then deal with it: That was the way he lived. He couldn't stand being in limbo.

That was why he'd dropped of the HLA reports at her office this morning. Soon he'd know—

"Are you mad at me?"

Coog's voice snapped him back.

Paul forced a smile. "No. Why would I be mad at you?"

"Because of the accident?"

"That wasn't your fault."

"Yeah, but I should have seen him coming."

"And I should have insisted you go to the skateboard park."

On reflection, Paul had realized that he had to shoulder some of the blame. Yes, the guy in the Hummer should have been going slower and paying attention instead of yammering on his cell phone, but Coog should not have been skateboarding in a parking lot. Paul had to take full responsibility for that. It had seemed harmless then, but it was a dumb thing to allow. He'd somehow assumed that if he was there watching, everything would be okay.

Wrong.

The memory of Coog's skinny, angular body sprawled unmoving on the asphalt would stick with Paul the rest of his life.

"You *sure* you're not mad?" Coog said.

"Positive. Why do you keep asking? Am I acting mad?"

"Well . . ." he twisted his mouth to the side, a tic Paul found endearing. "Maybe not mad. But different."

Different . . .

The word sucker-punched him.

Was his relationship with Coog changing already—even before the results? Was he unconsciously distancing himself?

No. He couldn't allow that. Biological son or not, this blessed boy was at a critical stage. Feeling rejected by his father . . . who knew what that could do?

Paul hid his turmoil.

"Maybe I'm suffering some residual shock because I almost lost you. You're all I've got, Coog. If . . ."

The swelling lump in his throat choked off the rest.

He couldn't jeopardize moments like this. The mere possibility was unbearable. He'd tell Sheila to cancel the paternity test.

He looked at Coog's smiling face. This boy was his son. He couldn't allow some lab test to change that.

SHEILA

Sheila's shift was nearly over and she was signing off on the last of her charts. She heard two of the nurses talking and laughing, discussing their plans for the evening. They were going to see a Johnny Depp movie. Simple, but at least they had somewhere to go. And after the last few days, she needed a quiet night alone, but it seemed quiet nights alone were all she ever had.

She heard Randy the orderly call someone. She leaned in to hear.

"I've got a gig tonight. Can you make it? Great, bring friends. Lots of friends. It's gonna be a great time." He hung up.

She studied the tall, longhaired man, his wavy locks tied in a ponytail. She'd heard him talk about the metal band he played in part time and wondered why everyone else seemed to have outside lives except her? At the end of her shifts all she could imagine was going home and putting her feet up. Once in a while she visited Abra, but that was more a mother-daughter thing. No friends her own age, no men calling. Work had become her life. It had been that way since Dek died. There never seemed time for anything or anyone else.

One of her dad's favorite songs echoed back to her. *Don't get around much anymore . . .*

Ain't that the truth.

As she headed for the parking lot, she felt a little jealous that all these people were going out while she'd be home alone. Again. Spending her night re-watching *You've Got Mail* or *As Good As It Gets*. Or going to Abra's and re-watching *Casablanca* or *The Maltese Falcon*.

Her life: She worked and she went home, worked and went home. And it wasn't so bad, really.

She reached her 4Runner and had just started it up when she saw a familiar figure waving.

Paul.

She turned and watched him hurry down the walk from the

hospital wing carrying a skateboard. She cringed recalling Coogan's accident.

She pointed to it. "Don't tell me you're—"

He laughed as he stopped. "Not a chance. This wound up in the lost and found and Coog wanted it back. Not that he'll be on it any time soon."

"I hope not."

"How's Coog doing?"

"Great. Doctor Brody's discharging him today. Hurts all over, especially those broken ribs, but otherwise . . . it's like a miracle."

She hesitated. Here was why doctors were advised not to treat family members or friends. Narrowing the distance between physician and patient could lead to major mishaps—like missing or delaying a diagnosis because you don't want to *believe* it's that diagnosis—or minor predicaments like being the bearer of bad news to someone with whom you have more than just a professional relationship.

Sheila faced that with Paul.

As an oncologist here, she never had to tell anyone that they had cancer—they all knew that before they passed through the gate. But she'd had to tell too many that she could offer them no hope. The experienced oncologists had warned her about becoming emotionally involved. A high percentage of her patients were going to die no matter what she did.

So far she'd failed to develop that hard shell. She hated to think that one day she'd be viewing her patients as tumors, or problems to be solved, rather than as people. But she supposed it was inevitable. Allowing yourself to care, and then failing people you care about, dashing their hopes, numbering their days . . . she'd have to build that shell or go mad.

And now she had bad news for Paul. But at least not cancer.

Sheila shut off her car and stepped out. Paul leaned against Hank Belson's silver Jaguar in the neighboring space. He folded his arms. His eyes locked onto hers.

"I'm glad I caught you. I wanted to talk to you about that paternity test."

Here we go.

She said, "The results—"

He waved a hand. "I know they're not back yet. I just wanted to tell you to cancel it."

Sheila blinked, startled.

"What changed your mind?"

He shrugged. "Like you said, finding out may change me. It would change *something*. I realized it doesn't matter. So, thanks but no thanks. Please cancel the test."

What a wonderful man, she thought. Why aren't there more like him?

Yet she wished he weren't quite so wonderful, because what she knew would rattle his world to its foundations.

Her heart urged her to shred the results, but she knew the billing department's computer had already charged Paul's insurance company for the test; the company would soon send him an EOB and then he'd want to know what she was hiding.

Better to deal with this now than later.

"The results came in this morning."

His eyes widened. "So soon?"

"It wouldn't be so quick if we were dealing with a commercial lab, but we do our own."

Paul had dropped off the HLA reports and she'd delivered them to the lab. This afternoon's printout had confirmed Paul's fears and added a result she'd never anticipated. Something he should know.

Paul stood up with closed fists and a wide stance, as if readying for a punch.

"And?"

"I thought you didn't want to know."

He stood silent. Finally he spoke.

"I didn't. And I could have got by with only Rose knowing the truth. But now it's all down in black and white. *You* know. So I've got to know too."

"You're sure?"

He nodded.

The results she'd printed out had shocked and baffled her. Still did. But one thing was certain.

"The results are negative for paternity."

Another frozen pause, then . . .

"Negative . . . that means I'm not . . ." his Adam's apple bobbed ". . . not Coog's father?"

God, she hated this.

"I'm afraid so."

In a flash Paul whirled and slammed his fist against the Jag.

"Whore!"

Sheila stepped back, shocked by his ferocity. Shocked too by the dent he'd made in the front fender.

As the car alarm began to beep and whistle and wail, Paul looked at her. Her throat tightened at the infinite hurt in his eyes.

"Sorry," he said over the racket. "But I guess that's what I get for marrying a . . ."

He balled his fists again, but this time he closed his eyes and stood statue still. He seemed to be counting.

"A whore?" Sheila said. "I'm not so sure."

He opened his eyes and looked at her.

"You have a better term? We'd been married one year—*one year!*—when she conceived Coog. What do you call a woman who cuckolds her husband during their first year together?"

"You don't have all the facts."

"Which are?"

She'd have to shout to be heard above this racket, and she didn't want to do that.

"Let's go to my office. I have all the data there. Some of it you might need to see to believe."

Some of it she still didn't believe. Or want to.

BILL

Bill sat in the dimly lit room and peered at the ten-inch black-and-white screen that showed Sheila Takamura at her keyboard. The tape was less than an hour old.

He'd had about half the offices—his own excluded, of course—wired for visual monitoring, usually from an overhead light fixture. He couldn't be too careful. When he'd installed the surveillance in Sheila's office he figured he may as well expand it to other offices to keep an eye on everyone. Never know who she'd talk to. All the feeds ended in this tiny basement room under the Admin building where every imaginable electronic device lined the walls. Only he and Shen had the key.

Bill had been leery at first about allowing Shen access, but the man was loyal to a fault and never asked the obvious question as to why "*Jiù-zhù-zhě*" deemed all this espionage necessary.

Except his dear "*Jiù-zhù-zhě*" didn't know a thing about it.

Both he and Shen knew why Sheila needed extra watching, and exactly what to look out for. Since Shen and Abra had no direct contact except at the annual holiday party, it was safe to let Shen assume that Abra had ordered this.

Even through the high-angle, low-resolution lens Sheila stirred Bill. If he had something like this set up in her bedroom he could—

He gave himself a mental slap. Cool it. She made him feel like a horny high school kid. He had to get over this. And he'd tried. He'd sworn he'd never act on these feelings, but seeing her every day, hearing her voice, her intelligence, her devotion to her calling, to Tethys . . . it wasn't easy.

But I can dream, can't I?

Her closeness to Abra, getting to know her through Abra's stories about her, only made it worse. Especially compared to the incessant strife with Elise these days.

He kept pressing the button but couldn't get the spyware to work. Shen usually operated the system for him but Bill wanted to do this alone, needed to see what she was up to without Shen's prying eyes. He pressed another key and lines of type cascaded the length of the monitor.

She read her mail, then visited Amazon to order a gift certificate, then updated chart files.

Good girl, Sheila. Keeping your nose clean.

Bill had seen her leave twenty minutes ago and she wasn't expected back for the rest of the day.

You need to get a life, Sheila, he thought. Better learn to put some distance between yourself and this place or Tethys will eat you alive.

Bill turned off the tape and hit the rewind button. But as he turned to go, movement on the screen caught his eye. She was back. Odd. He hit record.

Curious, he leaned closer to watch. Bill saw a familiar-looking man enter behind her.

What was this?

SHEILA

"I don't understand why you're being coy," Paul said as he shut the door behind him. "Why not just come out and tell me?"

Good question, Sheila thought.

"Maybe because I feel I'll need hard copy to back me up." She moved behind her desk and removed the file with the printouts from a side drawer. "And maybe because I feel it might be a good idea to have you seated when you hear this."

Paul's expression slackened as he eased himself into a chair.

"What is it? What's going on?"

She dropped into her own chair and spread the reports on her desktop.

"Coogan's DNA came back."

"I know that. I'm not his father, so you said. You had to drag me in here to—?"

"Just listen. I knew about the KB26 treatment Coogan received of course. You also told me Coogan had a marrow transplant before he came to Tethys. Once I heard that, I wasn't too worried about the fact your blood didn't match."

"Why?"

"The marrow transplant he had pre-Tethys was what we call an allogeneic transplant. Meaning his marrow was donated from someone else."

"A stranger."

She nodded. "Hematopoietic or blood-forming stem cells are immature cells that can mature into blood cells. These stem cells are found in the bone marrow and some other places. That's what he received. In Coogan's bone marrow transplant, the doctors killed off all his marrow with chemo or radiation. Those donated cells were then injected into his veins. The marrow, or stem cells, migrated into the long bones of his body. The donor's blood type and genetic material became Coogan's blood type and genetic material."

"His blood and DNA changed?"

"Only the DNA in his blood and maybe the type. I don't know what he had before. Anyway, I wasn't surprised that his blood wasn't compatible with yours. That alone didn't mean much, so I took a swab from Coogan's cheek and extracted the DNA."

Paul leaned back and sighed. "And?"

God, here it comes. "I'm sorry, Paul but not only are you not his father, but Rose is not his mother."

Paul bounded out of the chair. "But that can't be!"

"There's no way around it, Paul."

He paced before her desk.

"But how?"

"She didn't have in vitro fertilization, did she?"

"Hell, no. We did it the old-fashioned way." Then he stopped and pressed his hands against his temples. "Oh, God! Switched at birth! I've heard of it but never dreamed—"

Just what Sheila had been thinking.

"It's rare, Paul, but it happens."

He resumed his pacing, waving his arms as he moved.

"But that means . . . that means that somewhere out there is a thirteen-year-old boy who could be my son!"

"That's true. And if you were harder on your ex than she deserved—if she hadn't been cheating before Coog—then *that* boy most likely *is* your son."

He stopped his pacing and sighed. "Yeah, well, maybe so. No question that she cheated later on, but maybe not back then. Maybe only after Coog." He shook his head. "Switched at birth . . . . I still can't believe it. Neither Rose nor I ever left the hospital, and when she was discharged, we took him with us. I saw the way the nursery kept tabs on the babies, checking Coog's wristband against Rose's every time they brought him in for feeding."

"Maybe between the delivery room and the nursery . . .?"

He shook his head. "I was *in* the delivery room. I saw them clean him up, watched as they footprinted him."

"Do you still have the prints? Maybe we could do a comparison?"

He shook his head. "No, Rose took his baby book." His desperation filled the room.

"Paul," Sheila said softly. "The footprints wouldn't matter anyway. The DNA says it all."

"No. You don't get it. I feel it in my gut, damn it. There's got to be another explanation."

Sheila shrugged. She wished there were.

BILL

Bill's knees felt rubbery. This couldn't be happening. Jesus God—

Paul Rosko. That goddamned volunteer. First coffee with Sheila, now this.

He rewound the tape to the beginning. He needed to hear something again.

"I knew about the KB26 treatment Coogan received of course."

No-no-no-no-no!

Coogan? Was that what she'd called him? That was the name of his son—the one run down in the parking lot.

Before rushing upstairs to his own office, Bill reset the system. He didn't dare miss one thing that went on in Sheila's office.

At his desk he dried his sweaty palms on his pants legs and entered "Rosko, Coogan" into the search box. He prayed he had the spelling right. And if so, he prayed harder for a null result from the search.

Apparently God was not listening, because a second later a file popped onto the screen: *Coogan Paul Rosko.*

The most recent entry involved his accident. He knew about that.

He felt relieved until he scanned through all the other entries. The dates were from six years ago . . .

No, don't let this be true.

But it was.

No!" He pounded his fist on his desktop. "Damn it to hell!"

His secretary stuck her head through the doorway.

"Doctor Gilchrist? Is anything wrong?"

"Nothing, Marge." He waved her off. "Everything's fine."

Like hell.

When she was gone he leaned back in his leather chair and glared at the screen.

The files confirmed it: Coogan Rosko had had leukemia. Tethys had cured him with the KB26 protocol.

KB26 . . . the precursor to VG723.

Bill rubbed his eyes. Could it get any worse? Could it get any goddamn worse?

And how the hell was he going to tell Abra?

PAUL

Paul had been sweating all day. Thirty degrees out, but his shirt clung to him. His hands were shaking. He looked at Coog, lying on the couch, watching TV. Days ago he had viewed the handsome light-brown-haired boy with the cleft chin and widow's peak— no one in the family had one of those—and thought that Coog couldn't possibly be his. And now that the evidence proved it, Paul found himself doing a one-eighty and insisting he *was* his son.

Without a doubt, Sheila said, Coog was someone else's kid. Wasn't that what he'd expected? It wasn't what he hoped, that's for sure. He had hoped she'd come back and say the DNA matched, that it was just a fluke Coog looked different. No such luck.

The boy with piercing blue eyes and the perfect movie-star teeth. Both he and Rose had needed braces, but not Coog. Pre-orthodontia, Paul had had a huge gap between his front teeth, à la David Letterman. Coog had that gap when he was six. But then it went away. Weird. The dentist was surprised but said you never knew with teeth.

Lucky kid, Paul thought. Good looking kid. Too good looking for Rose and him.

So why now . . . now that he knew that Coogan was not his

child, not even Rose's child, did he have this compulsion to push the other way?

Because he had to know if a child he had fathered was out there in the world.

"Hey, Dad, you okay? You don't look so hot. Well, actually you do look hot. You're all sweaty. What's up with that? Sick?"

Paul forced a smile. Even if Coog didn't look like a Rosko, this definitely was the baby he had seen delivered. He knew it. Paul had been with him since the minute he was born. The test was wrong. Had to be.

Otherwise, he'd know a gap-tooth, dark-haired kid was wandering around out there, or maybe a blond boy with a bad temper and maybe Rose's predisposition for depression.

But as he answered Coog he prayed to any god who would listen: Please let him really be mine.

"It . . . it just knocked me for a loop, seeing you in the hospital again."

"Me too. I always thought if I died, it would be the leukemia, but when I saw that Hummer heading for me, I thought I was a goner."

"Me too, kid. Me too."

He hugged the boy he prayed was his son.

BILL

"I've got more bad news," Bill said.

He paced Abra's family room, too wired to sit, too queasy to drink. Bad enough to have Abra's eyes bore into him, but these damn lizards and spiders seemed to be watching him too. He looked at Abra.

She wrung her gnarled hands. "What now? Tell me."

"We've got the father of a KB-twenty-six patient sniffing around."

Abra looked up at him. "Is that all? We knew that might happen. We even have a contingency plan in place, remember?"

"Some plan. We just shrug and say, 'Sorry we can't explain it.

And what does it matter in the long run? Your child is alive and cancer free, isn't he?' "

"You seemed to like it when we cooked it up."

"I know, I know. I just never . . ." He didn't know how to tell her.

"Never what?"

"I never imagined that the father would consult the very doctor who is investigating a pair of seven-twenty-three catastrophes."

Abra's hand shot to her mouth. "Dear God! Not Sheila!"

"Yes. Sheila. That kid that got hit by the Hummer—"

"The son of that volunteer she likes," Abra said.

"She 'likes' him?"

Bill took a deep breath. Had to get over his obsession with Sheila.

Abra nodded.

"Well, that's not all," he said. "The two of them are going to put everything together."

"You don't know that."

"I do. It's not a matter of if—it's a matter of when."

Abra closed her eyes. "How can this be? It's almost as if fate is turning against us. We've perfected the technique, we're building the genome base at VecGen. Proteus is a reality. And now this." She opened her eyes. "Remember what I said about this being a sign that the time to tell the world has come?"

"It's not the time to tell *anyone!* We're not ready yet!"

Would she ever get it? The world would *never* be ready, would never accept what Proteus offered, never accept the price of curing so many diseases. People were stubborn and afraid. Stupid. She thought the public would embrace Proteus with joy. Sure. With the same joy the Palestinians accepted the Israelis.

He and Mama knew the only way to get Proteus into the population was without their knowing. He'd humored Abra with the promise of going public, because she needed the dream of recognition, of gratitude from the masses. But not Bill. And certainly not Mama. It wasn't about the glory, but about the cure. Over Bill's dead body would the public ever be aware of what was really going on.

"Well not everyone," Abra said. "But it's time to tell Sheila."

He so wished he could be candid with his sister about the true plan. But that wasn't an option. At least Bill now had an excuse for not telling Sheila.

"It's no longer just Sheila, it's this Rosko guy. If we tell her, she tells him, he files a suit, and God knows what follows!"

He saw Abra's startled expression and realized he was shouting. He had to stop her talk of going public or telling anyone, even her beloved Sheila. If anyone knew, it would demolish his and Mama's plan.

She stared up at him. "Then what are we going to do?"

"I don't know."

And he didn't. At all costs he wanted to protect Sheila. For himself and for Abra.

For now he'd wait. And watch. Watch very carefully.

__FOUR__

Paul

Paul wondered if he'd ever sleep again.

He glanced at the glowing numerals on the computer monitor: 5:15. He'd dozed off after the Letterman monologue but found himself wide awake half an hour later. After that he'd done endless tossing and turning. At 4:30 he finally conceded that sleep was not on his agenda and set to work on his novel.

He'd smiled as soon as the Word document opened.

There you are, Grisbe. Good to have you back.

Grisbe was still stuck there on page 220, his life hanging in the balance until Paul could find a way to help him.

Paul cracked his knuckles and set to work. His fingers danced across the keys but then stopped. He read the two poorly written paragraphs.

Ugh.

He deleted them and wrote a new one. Still no good.

Delete city.

He hit save—not that he he'd changed anything—and shut down the computer. His mind was not on Grisbe now, but on Coogan.

Should he try to contact Rose and—if she gave a damn—begin the search for their real son? The thought of his real child out there in the world with strangers . . . maybe being abused . . . it made him ill. Switched at birth . . .

He banged on the keyboard and got up. He wished he'd never opened this damn paternity Pandora's box.

So get over it, he told himself, and move on. Pretend you never ran the test. But if there's another kid out there—no, just get over it.

He remembered a time almost a decade and a half ago when he figured he was set. He'd written off his dream of a teaching career, but he had a wife he loved, a wonderful son, a house, and a steady job. No, he wasn't teaching, but he had just about everything a man could ask for.

And now? He still had the house and the job, but no wife and a son who wasn't his son.

Coog's leukemia had started it all.

It began as aches and pains. Coogan complaining that his legs hurt and his pediatrician writing it off at first as "growing pains." But when Coog had started bruising all over—far more than expected even for a rough-and-tumble six-year old—Rose worried people would think she was beating him. A blood count revealed the awful truth.

The shock of the diagnosis, the terror about the outcome, the numbing possibility of losing his dear boy, the agony of all the failed therapies—the memories hit Paul like a hard right, spinning the room about him. He and Rosie had been close then, the closest they'd ever be. All that time spent with their arms wrapped around each other in hospital waiting rooms. And Coogan had been a carbon copy of Paul then.

And if he wasn't biologically his, well, Paul had lived the lion's share of his life hiding the truth about his past, worried each passing day someone would find out, condemn him. Just call me Jay Gatsby. Worked for him. For a while at least.

He walked by Coogan's room, peeked in on the sleeping boy, so sorry he had asked for the truth in the first place.

Paul walked into his own room, flopped on his bed, and recited the Fitzgerald line. "And so we beat on, boats against the current, borne back ceaselessly into the past."

————■■■————

ABRA

If Abra had the strength, she'd work in the clinic full time. But no matter how strong her will, her damaged body restricted her activity. Inside she felt so alive and energetic, but her skeleton had broken and healed so many times it was a wonder she was alive.

But whenever she entered the Birthing Center and rolled down the long hallways, she felt renewed. The total now came to 8,172 births, all thanks to Tethys. Most doctors called themselves successful if they saved one life. Abra Gilchrist helped create brand-new lives everyday.

She didn't know the exact figure of the babies her parents had damaged, but she doubted she'd surpassed it. Not yet. But she would. If not from the clinic, then certainly with VG723.

It was quiet this early in the morning. The birthing area was always busy, but on this floor, where they performed IVFs, she could be alone until 8:30. She gazed again at the walls of photos. So many healthy babies.

She shook her head, recalling the night she discovered the awful truth about her parents' fortune, the night she knew she'd devote her life working to reverse what they'd done.

It had been the night of her graduation from MIT. She'd had a little too much to drink and had wandered into a closet she had no business being in. She'd found a journal written by her mother back in the days when Abra was a child and they all still lived in Germany. And in that journal she'd found the source of her family's enormous wealth.

Her parents both worked for a company named Chemie Grünenthal and had invested heavily in its stock. The shares soared during the 1950s with the runaway success of its new product, Contergan. The journal said that even though her father had seen early reports and had questions and doubts about the drug's safety in pregnant mothers, he'd said nothing.

Her parents sold their shares before the news of all the deformities hit.

Contergan was a brand of thalidomide.

The source of their riches had created thousands of infants with deformed arms and legs. Little flippers. Babies with flippers. That was the big project Mama and Dad had worked on. That was what had made them rich.

And her too.

She'd read the journal over and over, searching for redemption in the pages, something to justify what they did. She found nothing.

They'd known.

"Abra? Are you okay?"

Abra looked up and saw Marlene, one of the IVF nurses. "Yes. Just daydreaming."

"You look a little pale."

"I'm fine. Just haven't had my coffee yet. I'll be in my office if anyone needs me."

She rolled her electric wheelchair down the hall, her twisted hands shaking.

I'll make up for it. Truly, I will.

TANESHA

"Come on, Jamal," Tanesha said. "Time to get you to the bus stop."

The seven-year old hung back, eyes on the floor. He was set to go—knit cap, jeans, scuffed hightops, and his blue Pats jacket—a gift from his no-account deadbeat dad on one of his whenever-he-feels-like-it visits. The boy won't hardly take it off. Damn near sleeps in it.

"Jamal! Move or you'll miss the bus!"

Eyes still on the floor, he mumbled something that sounded like, "Don't wanna go."

Tanesha put her hands on her hips—a stance she'd picked up from her own mother back in Mississippi—and gave him a hard look.

"Since when you don't wanna go to school?"

"Since now."

"Somebody beating on you? That it? That how you got that bump on your face?"

He'd come home yesterday with a bruised cheek. Said he fell on the playground, but Tanesha wondered now if that was true.

"No."

"Don't you be afraid, Jamal. You tell me who it is and I'll put a hurt on him. On his momma too, I have to."

Finally he looked at her. "Ain't nobody beatin' on me, Mom. They's makin' funna me."

"Making fun of you? Why on earth—?"

"They just are. Can I go by myself?"

"Where?"

"To the bus stop."

Jamal's words set off a faint alarm in Tanesha, so faint that she wasn't sure why it was ringing.

"Now why you want to do that?"

His eyes started checking out the floor again. "I just do. Can I? Please?"

"No. You too young."

"It's just down the corner."

Making fun of him . . . not wanting her to take him to the corner . . . she didn't want to see the picture she sensed forming.

"You tell me why they making fun of you. What they saying to you?"

He sobbed and kept his head down.

"They say you tryin' to be white." He raised his tear-rimmed eyes toward her. "Why you doin' that, Mom?"

Tanesha closed her eyes and swayed. Oh, no. Please Lord . . .

She went down on one knee before him and gripped his shoulders. She felt her own voice on the verge of breaking but she kept a grip.

"Jamal, I ain't tryin' nothin'. It's just happening. I been to a doctor and she's gonna help me."

Tears started sliding down Jamal's cheeks.

"Jerome call you Michelle Jackson, so I hit him!" He rubbed his bruised cheek. "He hit me back."

Oh Lord, oh Lord, oh Lord. Michelle Jackson! And Jamal getting hurt defending her.

Tanesha had been so worried about her condition that she'd forgot about how it might be affecting her little boy. Her heart went out to him.

"Listen, Jamal, you just tell them it's a medical condition and—"

"Jerome say that what Michael Jackson said and nobody believed him neither. So can I please, please go down the corner by myself? *Please?*"

She wanted to say, You're breaking my heart, child. You know that?

But poor Jamal . . . he was only seven and didn't know how to handle this sort of thing. Lord, Tanesha didn't know how to handle it neither.

She forced a smile as she hauled herself back to her feet.

"Okay, Jamal. You can go."

It near killed her to see his shoulders slump with relief.

"But I'll be watching," she said as he wiped his eyes on his sleeve. "And if anybody gives you trouble you just ignore them, okay? Just remember that old saying: Sticks and stones can break my bones but names'll never hurt me."

But that old saying was wrong. Michelle Jackson . . . Lord, how that hurt.

As Jamal started toward the door Tanesha straightened his coat and hat.

"You have a good day at school now, hear?"

As he nodded and hurried out to the sidewalk, Tanesha closed the door till it was barely an inch from the jamb. She watched through the narrow opening. She broke down and started bawling.

She had a follow-up appointment with Dr. Takamura tomorrow. If that girl didn't have some good news, Tanesha didn't know what she'd do. Maybe jump off a bridge.

SHEILA

Sheila found a welcoming committee of one waiting by her Tethys parking space: Paul Rosko pacing the curb, wearing jeans, a windbreaker, and a troubled expression.

"Paul?" she said as she got out. "What are you doing here so early?"

"Waiting for you.

"Something wrong?"

"Could the test be wrong?"

"No. DNA is never wrong."

He started pacing again. "You think the KB26 could have changed his DNA?"

"His blood DNA, maybe. But not the tissue and that's what we checked. I'm sorry, Paul. I know it's hard but you'll have to accept the results."

"I'm telling you, he's changed right in front of my eyes. *Something is rotten in the state of Denmark* and I'm going to find out what."

Another literary reference. What was that? *Hamlet?*

He walked off in a huff toward the far end of the parking lot.

Sheila watched him go, struck by his intensity, his unshakable certainty. But it didn't matter how certain he was, DNA didn't lie.

But as she hurried through the chill air toward the Admin building, she wondered how to prove that to Paul. He was bullheaded, but no dummy. His education might have been limited to high school—she assumed a cable installer wouldn't have progressed much beyond that—but he was undoubtedly smart, and extremely well read. One of those intellectual diamonds in the rough who, for one reason or another—maybe family finances— hadn't fulfilled his academic potential.

Despite Paul's emotional volatility, Sheila found herself drawn to him. She couldn't say why or how, but she sensed a core of secret pain hidden deep within him. The healer in her reached out to that.

The first thing she did in her office was light up the computer. While it ran through its boot-up, she poured some bottled water into her Keurig single-cup coffee maker, popped in a Cool Beans Midnight Blend pod, and turned it on. By the time she'd hung up her coat and straightened her wind-ruffled hair, both coffee and computer were ready.

Okay, she thought as she slid into her chair, first I'll pull up Coog's record. Then go from there. But her search for "Rosko, Coogan" came up with only her own notes for his regular follow-up care. She modified the search with "+hospital" but came up with nothing but his recent trauma admission. Same with "+inpatient."

Odd. He'd been a cancer inpatient here. Why weren't his—?

Oh, right. Archived, no doubt. Just like Kelly Slade's. And speaking of Kelly Slade . . .

A search for "Slade, Kelly" also returned null.

Not that Kelly was all that important now. But Coog . . . she wanted to straighten out Paul in regard to the DNA. Neither KB26 nor anything else had changed Coogan's DNA no matter how much Paul wished it were so.

BILL

Bill visited the security room to check Sheila's activity for the day.

Shen had programmed the spyware to notify him if certain words were being searched. That list got longer every day. A flashing icon alerted him that Rosko and Slade searches had been on her agenda today.

Oh hell. *Rosko, Coogan,* looking for hospital and inpatient records.

Bill didn't have to wonder what she'd found. He'd erased everything in the file and then archived the empty folder. Even if she did manage to get hold of the folder, she'd find nothing.

He might have to find a way to explain that, but he'd worry if and when the time came.

She'd also searched for Slade.

Was she going to keep pushing and pushing until she'd backed him into a corner? The possibility made his stomach clench.

He made sure the video system was set to record and then left the room.

SHEILA

Sheila's office phone rang. "Hello?"

"Hi, Sheila. Paul Rosko."

She smiled. "Hi. You okay?"

"Listen, your hospital takes credit cards right?"

"Yes but any expenses from Coogan's accident will be covered by the driver of the Hummer or his insurance."

"It's not about that. I want a new DNA test."

Why did he need to hear again that his son wasn't his? "Paul, DNA tests are never wrong. They hold up in court. People are executed based on the submission of DNA evidence. I'm sorry again, but they're conclusive."

"Sheila." His voice lowered. Softened. Was he ready to explode or had he finally conceded his position? "Please. I don't want Coogan to know and if I go somewhere else and they test him again he'll grow suspicious. Please just do this for me. I know the insurance won't pay for this twice and I don't have much cash lying around but I have a Visa."

For anyone else she would have said I'm sorry again or issued a lecture. But she felt his desperation. Wanted as badly as he did to find something other than what they did.

But that wouldn't happen. Still, if the results of this test would bring him closure, she'd do it.

"Okay."

"Really? Okay?"

She could hear him smile over the phone. If this brought him peace, one way or the other—

"Bring him back here so I can take another sample and label it myself."

"Thank you. Thank you so much. I'll be there in a half hour." He hung up.

If she asked the lab to rerun it because of a potential error, there would be no charge. Paul Rosko would have enough to deal with when the new results came in without incurring debt.

Sheila wondered about KB26. Seven years ago Coog had been cured by it. She knew the name but wasn't familiar with that protocol; it had been discontinued years before her arrival.

But if it had cured Coog, why wasn't it still in use?

She turned to her computer. A search for "KB26" yielded a host of hits. But only within a two-year span. The most recent were six years old. She clicked on those and found mostly notes about completion of therapy on a variety of patients. But then she came across one that mentioned KB26 being withdrawn by its manufacturer. No reason given.

So she searched "KB26 +adverse" and got a fair number of hits. She scanned through a dozen or so but found that all mentions of "adverse" were found in sentences like, "no adverse reaction."

She leaned back in her chair. How odd. A successful cancer therapy with no adverse reactions was worth millions—hundreds of millions. Why withdraw it?

Sheila had more questions than answers.

BILL

All of the moisture in Bill's mouth seemed to have transferred to his palms.

He flicked his gaze from the video screen to the remote monitor. She was looking up KB26! Worse, she was going to run another DNA probe on the Rosko kid's tissue! Next thing Diane Sawyer or Katie Couric would be interviewing Rosko about how his child was switched at birth. There'd be an investigation. And it would all lead back to Tethys. This was a catastrophe in the making, the beginning of the end of Tethys and all of his and Mama's plans.

He could see millions suffering needlessly. Orphaned children whose parents could have been saved. Genetic mutations increasing with each generation. The cost of healthcare doubling, tripling over the next fifty years, crippling the economy.

And of course, his life would be over—imprisoned forever. A cockroach for a pet, and nothing but dreams of what could have been.

There had to be a way to fix this. If he stayed calm he'd find it.

Perhaps the KB26 problem wasn't the awful threat he'd first thought. Years ago he'd seen to it that all details and references to the exact nature of the therapy had been expunged from the files. He'd held back from wiping all KB26 references from the medical records of the kids who'd received it because those charts were, in a very real sense, legal documents.

So Sheila would find nothing in the Tethys computer. And any search in the real world would lead to blind alleys and dead ends.

The DNA test, though . . . what could he do about that?

He had to stop Sheila without resorting to Shen. He didn't want her to end up like Kelly Slade.

And then in a flash he had it: the perfect solution. And like so many perfect solutions, as simple as it was elegant. He clicked a series of numbers into his computer and waited. The KB drive opened and he put in yet another password. There they were. He typed in Coogan's name and a serial number came up. Bill wrote it down and logged off the computer. He had a call to make. He could do this without Mama's permission but she hated being out of the loop.

SHEILA

After half an hour of plowing through the KB26 hits on the Tethys system, Sheila switched to the Internet. She found nothing beyond a few mentions in personal web sites and Facebook thanking God and Tethys and whoever developed KB26 for curing them or someone in their family.

Whoever developed KB26 . . .

Good question. Who *had* developed it?

But Sheila could find no trace of its origin.

Frustrated, she turned away from the computer and reached for the patient files she'd planned to read over. Might as well return them if they were going to remain unread. They were gone.

Oh God, not again.

She sifted through everything on the desk. Damn. Where had she last seen them? But she drew a blank. Her memory was shot to hell lately.

Corporate espionage? Were they now taking her files? No. Couldn't be. Stop it, Sheila. You're making yourself crazy. Take a deep breath.

But it didn't calm her. Her hands were shaking, her heart pounding, and she was afraid. She was *not* being paranoid. Her files were gone. All of them and they'd been right on her—

Out of the corner of her eye she spotted her bag. There they were. Tucked in the bag. That's right. She *hadn't* taken them out.

Mother of God, I am losing it.

She shut off her computer, grabbed her bag, and left.

When she reached Bill's office, Marge was nowhere in sight. Sheila breezed past her desk and was about to push on Bill's door when she heard his voice through the opening. He sounded agitated.

"—problems are not going to work themselves out," he was saying.

He paused but Sheila heard no reply. Must be on the phone. She might have stepped inside anyway if not for his exasperated tone.

"Right," he went on. "That's why I need to play fireman and stay on top of things."

Another listening pause, then . . .

"Believe me, I don't like taking liberties with someone's privacy either, but all of Proteus could be on the line here. It's why we keep them here. Just for such an occasion."

A pause . . .

"Well, if you know of a more ethically pure way to protect it, tell me now."

Another pause . . .

"I didn't think so. So until we come up with something better, this is what we're left with. Okay?"

Sheila flinched when she heard the receiver slam onto its cradle.

She decided her questions could wait until he calmed down. Besides, she had to get back to her office to meet Paul and get a new sample from Coogan.

As she walked away she pondered what she'd heard. Who had he been talking to? And "Proteus"—what was that? She'd never heard of it.

She'd check back with Bill tomorrow.

But tonight . . . tonight she'd take a break do some Christmas shopping. Why not that mall in Salem? Shopping always took her mind off her problems. She'd feel much more relaxed tomorrow.

NOW

FIVE

SHEILA

. . . voices . . .

Sheila opened here eyes . . . where was she? Cold and wet, she knew that, but where? She lifted her head and was poked by dozens of small branches.

Slowly it filtered back to her . . . being run off the road, the crash, wading into the river, the explosion.

She didn't remember crawling out of the water and into this knot of thick underbrush, but she must have.

She curled into a shivering knot as her consciousness wavered again. Had to sit still . . . utterly still . . . barely breathing. This was like a nightmare. Huddled in these bushes hiding from someone out to kill her.

She held her breath as she saw a flashlight swinging back and forth on the far side of the river. Then her attention was drawn to the flashing lights on the road atop the ravine.

Police? The police were here.

She crawled out of the underbrush.

"Help!" Her voice sounded like a croak. "Over here! Help!"

———•••———

Sheila sat in the back of the squad car and shivered despite the blanket around her and the heater blowing on high. The cops had demanded a Breathalyzer test, which of course she'd passed.

A sergeant named Frayne was driving back to the station.

"Taykamaya. How'd a redheaded little wisp of thing like you get a name like that? Never seen freckles on a Chinese person before. You sure your name ain't Finnegan or Casey?"

She didn't know if he was trying to lighten things up or just being obnoxious.

"Takamura. It's Japanese, not Chinese," she said. "It's my married name and I don't think being run off the road is anything to joke about."

"Sure you weren't on your cell phone and lost control?"

Sheila lost it then. Still soaking wet, chilled and shivering, so scared she could barely think, and this dick head doubted her?

"I did *not* lose control, goddammit! I was T-boned twice—not once, *twice*—by a dark suburban! Someone tried to kill me!"

"Okay, okay, ma'am. I'm sorry. We'll do everything we can. I'll take you back to the station, get a full statement, and get you some hot tea and a blanket, okay? And we'll arrange to have a cruiser watch your house after you go home."

Sheila leaned back. That outburst had dispelled her lingering adrenaline. Her mind gradually shifted into shock mode, quarantining some of the fear.

"We'll check the ravine and the woods thoroughly come daybreak," the cop said.

Fine, but what good would that do? Her car was a charred, crumpled mess and the rain would wash away any trace of evidence.

Then the question with no answer: "Is there anyone we should call for you?"

Who *could* she call?

Not Bill. What if he had something to do with this? And not Abra. What if she knew something too? Paul? She didn't know him well enough for a desperate call like this. And certainly not in the middle of the night.

She had no one else. A tear rolled down her cheek. Husband dead . . . folks gone . . .

No. No one to call.

No one to lean on. Just herself. *Alone again, naturally.* The Gilbert O'Sullivan song went through her head as it often did. Change the title Gil. Call it Sheila's theme.

————**:::**————

Home again.

After several hours and three cups of hot tea at the police station, they'd driven Sheila to the cottage and left her. She'd taken a hot shower, put on flannel PJs, and crawled into bed.

And here she huddled under the covers, tense, unable to sleep, listening to every sound, scared, chilled to the core, and more lonely then she had ever felt in her life.

Where do I go from here? What do I do?

The police thought she was crazy.

Hell, if the situation was reversed, I'd probably think the same.

A part of her wanted to run away—as fast and as far as possible. Something so appealing about that. She'd have no trouble finding a position, especially after the glowing recommendation she'd receive from Bill—he wouldn't dare give her anything less.

But another part of her said she had to stay.

She'd been giving patients this therapy and if there was something wrong with it . . .

She felt her face redden with anger. If she was giving them something harmful, something Bill knew about—

Maybe Bill was keeping it from VecGen. If that were the case, she'd tell them herself. Send them a report.

She covered her face and the tears overflowed. She didn't want to believe it could have been Bill. But who else had a reason for wanting her out of the picture?

Sun-Tzu or somebody had said: Keep your friends close, and your enemies closer. That was what Sheila would do. Keep Bill close until she found out what he was hiding.

And he *was* hiding something. Someone doesn't try to kill you if you're barking up the wrong tree.

Sheila would stay and see this through.

SIX

SHEILA

Sheila walked to Tethys.

Sometime today she was going to have to rent a car, but the rain had stopped and the cold morning air had been a tonic. She arrived at Admin before sunrise. Why not? Sleep hadn't been an option. How do you sleep after someone deliberately runs you off the road?

Another thing that had kept her awake was Bill.

He'd mentioned a VecGen competitor spying. What if *he* was the spy, getting secrets for the competitor? No, that didn't wash. As a spy he would have encouraged her to pursue the Slade and Green cases so he could steal her findings.

All right, what if he was secretly working for VecGen? When he'd come down on her about Tanesha, he was doing more than following protocol. Almost as if he had a vested interest in VG723's success and couldn't let it fail, no matter who or what she presented.

Well, the hell with him. She didn't care what he had going with VecGen, he had an ethical obligation to pursue these cases. And if he wouldn't, she'd do it alone.

She shook her head. But Bill wouldn't try to kill her, would he?

That certainly hadn't been him driving the SUV. She'd seen only a silhouette, but it had been smaller than Bill. Still, somehow, some way, she sensed he was involved.

During her long, sleepless night she'd come up with a plan. She'd test Bill. Better to know than to keep looking over her shoulder.

She settled herself in her office and watched the lot. She knew Bill's routine: coffee at home, then straight to his office to catch up on emails and voicemails, then over to the caf for more coffee.

Shortly after sunrise he arrived and entered the building.

Now . . . the moment of truth.

No one except the police knew about last night. It had happened too late for today's paper. Probably show up tomorrow in the police blotter, but that would be about it.

If involved, Bill would know about the attempt on her life. His reaction when she told him would confirm or deny her suspicions. She hated the thought, but she expected confirmation.

His outer door stood open, as did the inner. She paused, shaking inside. She was far from recovered, and this test was making her even shakier.

She stepped past Marge's desk and knocked on the inner doorframe.

Bill looked up from his desk and shot to his feet, hands against his face as if frozen into a parody of *The Scream*.

"Sheila! Dear God! It's you! You—you're alive!"

Oh, no. This confirmed it: It *was* him.

She forced herself to speak. "Of course I'm alive. What did you—?"

"But the police called last night and said you'd been killed in a car crash!"

Had they? She could check on that.

He rushed from behind his desk and threw his arms around her. "I'm so glad they were wrong!"

Her body stayed rigid. "You mean everyone thinks I'm dead?"

Bill shook his head. "I haven't had a chance to tell anyone except Elise. I was going to keep a lid on it until I could tell Abra myself." He let out a long, slow breath. "Now I won't have to."

For an instant Sheila sensed that he might be more relieved

about not having to break the news to his sister than her being alive.

He backed off to arms' length. "But good Lord, how on Earth did it happen?"

"Someone tried to kill me last night, Bill." Damn the catch in her voice. "He drove me off the road on the way home from Salem."

"*What?*" His eyes widened.

"The car flipped over and rolled into the ravine and exploded."

His face registered shocked concern as he gripped her upper arms.

"My God! The police told me about the crash and explosion but nothing about—are you all right? What a terrible thing! But what makes you think—?"

"He rammed me *twice*, Bill. I got away—just barely."

Bill's jaw dropped as all the color drained from his face.

"You're . . . you're kidding, right?"

"No, Bill, I'm not. Someone wants me dead. Who can it be, Bill? Who wants me dead?"

Watching him gape and run a shaking hand through his hair as his face grew even paler, Sheila felt a burst of relief.

Popping eyes and a shocked, horrified expression could be faked. Shaking hands too. But going white involved blood draining from the facial capillaries . . . no way he could fake that.

"I . . . I don't know," he whispered. "I can't imagine." The color was still gone from his face.

Bill was genuinely shocked. So she'd been wrong: He wasn't involved. At least not with the attempt on her life.

Disappointment tinged her relief. She hadn't wanted Bill to be involved, but knowing he wasn't left her even more frightened.

What had she ever done to make someone want to kill her?

"Could it be whoever bugged my phone? I mean, something's going on here. A break-in, a bug, an attempt on my life. Someone thinks I know something but, Jesus, I don't. If it's a competitor, then why aren't they after you?" She saw him flinch. "If anyone knows anything it's you and Abra. Not me."

He put his arms around her again.

"We'll figure it out, Sheila. Please don't worry. We'll make sure you're safe now."

She pushed him away. "Bill, that's not going to help. We need to figure this out. It all started when I approached you about Kelly's case. I think someone at VecGen is trying to stop me from finding something out."

She stared him down. By "someone" she meant him.

"Sheila, I swear to you, I know nothing about this. VecGen is a small outfit. They aren't some huge Silicon Valley tech firm with billions of dollars in resources. I was wrong the other day when I suggested corporate espionage. I talked to Shen about the bugs and he did find several, but know what? He said they weren't done professionally. He also said they were probably there for a long time. They weren't even transmitting—too old. Some former employee probably placed them to eavesdrop, and then left. And as far as your break-in, the police told me they think it was a random burglary for drug money. I'll bet your laptop or camera will show up in a pawn shop any day."

Didn't he get it?

"Bill, someone tried to *kill* me."

"I know it seems that way, Sheila, but who would want to kill you? There has to be another explanation. I don't know what happened but I just thank God, you're okay." He shook his head. "I almost passed out when you told me. I thought I was going to be sick."

No lie there: she'd sensed genuine shock.

"You know, we've got lot of sickos out there and you're an attractive woman. Someone could have followed you from Salem. Were you at the mall?"

She nodded.

"What if some nutcase spotted you getting into your car in the lot and got some crazy idea in his head. I bet the police find him."

She so wanted to believe him. Needed to. Maybe he was right. There were other explanations.

But what about the connection between Kelly's and Tanesha's symptoms?

Yeah, he might be steering her away from investigating the cases to protect VecGen, but what if there was no big conspiracy? What if she was just having a freaking bad week?

She fought off the tears as long as she could but then broke down and crumbled in his arms.

BILL

Bill paced the monitoring room while he waited for Shen. Not easy to do in the tiny space. Two steps this way, then turn and two steps back. But he couldn't sit still.

As soon as he'd ushered Sheila out he'd put in an urgent call to Shen to meet him here.

Someone tried to kill me last night . . .

It could only be Shen. But what the hell was he up to? Acting on his own? What was he *thinking?*

And if he'd succeeded? Abra would have been crushed . . . inconsolable.

He'd tried to get Sheila to take the day off, but she'd refused. She said she needed to work. He understood that.

Bill heard the latch turn and then Shen appeared.

"You wanted to see me, sir?"

Yes, he wanted to see him. Also wanted to take a swing at him but knew that would be dangerous. No question who'd come out worse.

So he held his temper and steadied his voice. "Shut the door behind you, please."

When Shen complied, Bill stepped closer and got in his face. He lowered his voice to a harsh whisper.

"Are you out of your mind, Shen? What were you thinking?"

The man's dark eyes showed confusion. "This one does not understand, sir."

"Sheila—Doctor Takamura. It was you who ran her off the road last night, wasn't it? You tried to kill her."

"Try, sir?" She is alive?"

"Yes she's alive. Marched into my office bruised but safe and sound. No thanks to you."

Shen lowered his head. "I am ashamed that I failed in my mission, but I—"

"Your *mission?* Where in heaven and earth did you get the idea that you were supposed to do that?"

Shen looked back up at him. "Why, from you, sir."

"Me? When? I never told you—"

"In your car. You tell this one that Doctor Sheila 'got to be stopped.' Those your exact words, sir."

Dear God. But he'd never meant . . . never dreamed that Shen would take it the way he had.

"Shen, I didn't mean *stop* in the sense of her life. I meant stop her nosing around where she shouldn't. That was to be my problem, not yours."

Shen dropped into one of the chairs and covered his eyes.

"What's wrong?"

Shen kept his head down. His voice shook. "I am glad I failed, sir. I did not wish to kill her."

Seeing emotion leaking from this man's impenetrable façade shocked Bill.

Shen looked up, his expression unsure. "She is a good woman."

Sheila was indeed a good woman.

"She's not out of the woods. This isn't a reprieve. More like probation. She's under watch."

"This one is most sorry, sir."

"I know you meant well, but . . . what's done is done. We're both glad she's still alive and I want you to take over monitoring her here. Are we clear on that? Monitoring, that's all."

"Yessir. She will not be harmed."

"I'm not saying it will never come down to that, but only if there's no other way."

SHEILA

Sheila's stomach plummeted when she walked into the examining room and found Tanesha sitting on the table and dabbing at her teary eyes with the corner of her paper cape.

"I hope you got good news for me, doc." She frowned. "And what happen your face?"

Oh, the scratches from the underbrush. She'd forgotten about them.

Sheila forced a smile. "Chased my hat into a pricker bush." She patted her arm. "Give me a moment to check the reports."

All show, of course. She sensed a new fragility in Tanesha. She needed a way to give her the bad news—or rather, the non-news—without sending her into a tailspin.

"Well?"

Sheila looked up to find Tanesha staring at her. The hope in her tear-reddened eyes tore at her.

Okay, she thought, translating Hal Silberman's dermatopathology into RealPeoplese. Here goes.

"We've determined that some of your cells—many of your cells—have cut back their production of melanin."

"What's melanin?"

"The pigment that darkens your skin."

Tanesha snorted. "Shit! I coulda told you that! Tell me something I *don't* know. Like *why* they cut back and *what* we do about it."

"We don't know why, Tanesha. Not yet."

She sobbed and covered her face with her hands. "You promised!"

"I'm not through yet. We've only just begun to fight."

"What you mean 'we'? I don't see your skin changin' color. And hell with that '*begun* to fight' shit. I need help *now!*"

"Tanesha, you have to realize that you've got a unique, complex problem that can't be solved in a week."

"So all these tests was a waste of time—that what you tellin' me?"

"Not at all. We know a lot of things that it's not."

"What good is that?"

"Look. You know who Thomas Edison is, right?"

Tanesha made a face. "Course I do. You think I'm stupid?"

"No, of course not. When he was trying to invent the light bulb he tried a thousand different filaments and every one burned out. So when a reporter asked him if he was discouraged, he said, 'Of course not. I now know a thousand things that won't work.' "

"Girl, what's that got to do with me? I ain't no light bulb! And a light bulb ain't got a kid that don't want to be seen with her!"

Her face screwed up and she started to cry again. Her sobs, and the realization of what this poor woman must be going through, broke Sheila's heart.

She rose and laid an arm across Tanesha's quaking shoulders.

"We'll beat this, Tanesha, but this sort of investigation takes time. The pathologist is running more tests on your hair follicles, and since this may be some rare genetic fluke, I'm going to arrange some DNA testing."

Tanesha wiped her eyes and looked at her. "What that gonna show?"

Sheila smiled. "If I knew that, I wouldn't need to run the tests, would I?"

"Guess not."

"But it's going to require more skin biopsies. You up for that?"

"Anything, doc. Just tell me when and where."

"Great. I'll make the arrangements and give you a call."

"Don't be too long. I don't know how much more of this I can take."

"I'll make it my first priority."

Right along with her other first priorities: Coog's tests, a sit-down with Bill, seeing outpatients, and monitoring in-house chemo.

"I think it's gonna turn out to be that treatment I had. You know, the VG thing. I think it changed me inside."

Sheila stared, startled. This was the second time Tanesha had brought this up. Bill had warned that she might latch onto VG723 as a cause and go after Tethys and VecGen. Paul had asked her the same thing yesterday.

Coog's KB26 had been a stem-cell-based therapy, just like Tanesha's VG723. What if there was a connection?

Could it be . . .?

She'd better check out some specs on VecGen and VG723.

Maybe she could ask them if they'd seen anything like this before.

Till then, she'd have to do what Bill said.

"I'm sorry, Tanesha. It's highly unlikely that your treatment caused this problem. But we'll figure it out. Don't worry."

Tanesha tried to smile as Sheila left the examining room. Sheila tried too. Poor woman.

TANESHA

As Tanesha walked toward her beat up, paint-chipped '95 Dodge Neon, she promised herself she was going to make it to the car before she started blubbering. Damn if she wasn't feeling like swallowing some killer pills right now. She looked down at her ugly honkey hands and her eyes filled up. Her stocky legs shuffled along fast as they'd go. She just knew she could make it the few more feet to the car.

"Miss Green!" a man shouted.

Tanesha turned around to see a good-looking, dark-haired guy. He was hurrying toward her, his coat blowing around.

"Miss Green, could I have a word with you?"

She stopped and he caught up with her.

"Who you?"

He smiled. "Thank you for stopping." He put his hand out. "I'm Doctor Gilchrist. I head up Tethys. Doctor Takamura said you'd been in a couple of times and I'd like to talk to you for few minutes if you don't mind."

She shook his hand. Strong handshake.

"I don't mind."

And she didn't. If he headed up Tethys, then maybe he'd have some answers.

"Good. Would you like to go out for a coffee or something?"

That got her hackles up. Why not right here, unless it was bad news? She sure as shit wasn't driving all the way to Starbucks and putting up with the stares to hear no death sentence.

"Start talkin'. I'm listenin'."

She folded her arms. She'd read once that in body language that meant *Don't bullshit me. I don't trust you.*

"All right then. Well, I just want to let you know that Tethys will find the answer to what's happened to you. It may take a while but we will find it. You have my word."

"Doctor Takamura already told me that. You got something new?"

"No, but, well, I just think if you look at this from the right perspective and—"

"And what perspective is that, mister?"

Her arms were folded tight now, which wasn't easy with this big belly.

The doc looked a little less cocksure now.

"The perspective that . . ." He cleared his throat. "That you're alive. Sure your skin has changed but you're still you underneath. Your skin is healthy and uniform. It's not like you're covered with tumors or ulcers or burns. It could be a lot worse, you know."

Tanesha glared at him, getting madder by the second, but he just kept talking.

"And your cancer is gone. Forever. You're cured. And you'll live a long life and be around to raise your son—"

"That's it! No one says nothin' 'bout my son, you no good snake honkey bastard!" She reached out and grabbed him by the arm, digging her too-pale fingers into his wrist. "You know what? Lookin' like I do, I don't *want* to live a long life. I want to curl up and just die right here and now. It could be worse, my ass! You try facing your kid when he don't want nothin' to do with you."

She could see by the look in his eyes he was done talking so she let go.

"That what you wanted to tell me? You come runnin' after me to tell me I should be happy? Tell you what, I give you till my appointment next week to get some answers or I'm callin' Doctor Phil, *The View*, and Oprah. We'll see what *they* think of your damn *perspective*."

She turned around and walked. Didn't look back, just opened her car door, started it up after a few tries, and took off.

Snake bastard.

———···———

SHEILA

Bill had said he could meet with her, but it would have to be in his office—a working lunch of sorts. He said he was waiting for a fax that required an immediate response.

Sheila played waitress. Why not? She'd asked for the meeting. She brought a tray from the caf: turkey club for Bill, vegetable lasagna for her.

She was stiff from the accident and muscles she'd only seen in textbooks were killing her. Carrying the tray was no easy feat, but this would be the first lunch they'd ever eaten in private. She noticed how he closed the door behind her as she brought in the tray. She hoped this wouldn't be awkward.

The desk would serve as a barrier of sorts. Lately he'd made her uneasy. He used to be the center of her fantasies, but lately they were starting to flow elsewhere. To the man Bill had described as "blue collar." Last night, when she'd been scared and lonely, she'd found herself wishing Paul were there, not Bill.

"Now," Bill said around a bite from his sandwich, "what's on your mind?"

Besides the fact that every muscle in my body feels like it went through a meat grinder and my life is in danger? Had he forgotten everything?

At least he seemed to have recovered from yesterday's phone snit over the mysterious Proteus and was the same old even-tempered, mild-mannered Bill she knew.

"I went to look up someone's record, a patient who received KB-twenty-six, and his past record came up blank."

Bill held up a finger. "Let me guess: He was here more than five years ago."

"How did you know?"

"That's when we had a system crash." He waved his hand. "A host of records sailed into the ether."

"Everything?"

"No. We had almost everything backed up. Almost, but not all. We won't make that mistake again. Who was the patient?"

"Coogan Rosko."

"Oh, the boy who was hit in the parking lot."

Sheila was surprised that Bill would remember.

"Right. Well, I treated him in the ER and got curious about KB-twenty-six since I don't know much about it. Can't seem to find any information on that either."

"Why would you want to? It's dead and gone."

"But it was a stem-cell-based therapy like seven-twenty-three, right?"

Bill nodded. "It was sporadically successful, but not enough to continue in trial. The Rosko boy was lucky."

"I'd still like to learn some details." She saw his lips pursing for a *Why?* so she hurried on before he could voice it. "Who supplied it?"

"A company called Kaplan Biologicals."

"Which is where?"

"Nowhere. Gone. Finis. Kaput. When KB-twenty-six proved not to be the blockbuster it had been touted to be, Kaplan Biologicals went under and its founder, Gerald Kaplan, a brilliant researcher, was left with nothing. I offered him a post here but he refused it."

"Do you know where I can find him?"

He shook his head. "Haven't a clue."

Damn.

Bill said, "I must say I'm baffled by all this interest in a defunct therapy."

Sheila hesitated. She wasn't sure how he'd react to what she was about to broach.

"Well, remember how I was wondering if there was any connection between seven-twenty-three and the changes in Kelly Slade and Tanesha Green?"

He nodded. "I also remember instructing you not to breathe a word of that to anyone else."

"And I haven't. But Tanesha Green asked me about it again this morning. She seems convinced seven-twenty-three is behind her hair and skin changes."

"I trust you disabused her of that notion."

"Seems I've been doing a lot of disabusing these past few days."

Bill leaned forward. "Someone else?"

"Paul Rosko. His son's DNA doesn't match his and he refuses to believe it. Yesterday he asked me if KB-twenty-six could have changed him."

Bill's lips tightened into a straight line. "He signed a consent acknowledging that KB-twenty-six was an experimental therapy and that its side effects were unknown. If he's looking for a malpractice angle, he's out of luck."

Sheila was taken aback.

"He's too grateful to Tethys. I can't imagine that's even crossed his mind."

"Well, imagine it. And get used to imagining it, Sheila. America has become Victimland. Gratitude and fairness go out the window when the almighty buck rears its ugly head. The odds of a jackpot in the malpractice lottery are infinitely better than in Powerball."

"He wouldn't—"

"He's a man whose wife screwed around on him and now he's looking for a lightning rod for his anger. Tethys makes a convenient target."

Bill's vehemence shocked her. He was making this personal. Abra was right. He was jealous of Paul. Maybe that explained his cold attitude. Sheila found herself on Paul's side here. His concern was for Coog, not cash.

To hide her discomfort, she took a bite of her lasagna. Cold. She swallowed the clump and put her fork down. Something he'd said bothered her.

"How do you know so much about Paul Rosko?"

"Hmmm? Oh, well, you don't think I'd give someone access to our campus without a thorough vetting, do you?"

But to know his ex-wife cheated on him? Pretty thorough background check on a volunteer.

"And on the subject of litigation," he added, "watch out for Tanesha Green. If you don't handle her better she'll be looking for a payday at the Foundation's expense as well."

Sheila didn't know what to say. She'd never seen him like this.

"What?" he asked, staring at her.

"I—"

Just then the fax machine beside his desk began to ring, then purr as it printed. Bill lifted the first sheet from the tray.

"Finally!" He looked a Sheila. "Excuse me while I read these over."

"No problem." She wanted out of here. "I've got to run myself."

God, so self-centered. Why hadn't she ever noticed it before? Not once had he mentioned the attack or asked how she was doing.

She left her tray and hurried out.

Paul

"Hey, that's me."

Paul looked up to see Coog standing beside him, looking over his shoulder. He'd been so engrossed he hadn't heard him enter.

"Yep. That's you."

But was it?

He'd been sitting here in the family room, sifting through shoeboxes stuffed with Coog's childhood photos. He and Rose had exposed a _lot_ of film during his early years. The photo chronicle abruptly halted around age six. Neither of them had wanted photos of their son wasting away. A year after his cure they picked up again—nowhere near the number as in his early years—but he was in shots of family gatherings, and Paul had taken a fair number of him playing for his middle school basketball team.

The Coogan Rosko before the illness, and for a couple years after, looked the same—thinner post cancer, of course, but still the same.

Around age nine, Coog began to change. Nothing obvious. Paul hadn't noticed it then. But now, because he was looking for it, he had no doubt.

The change in his build, from stocky—like Paul—to lanky could be blamed at first on the weight he'd lost during his sickness. But he'd never gained it back. Instead he'd begun to stretch. Okay. It happens. So far no problem.

But then his face had begun to change. Elongating, and developing a cleft chin. He was already five-ten with plenty of time for more growth. Strange but still not alarming.

But the hair . . . how could anyone explain the way it had changed from thick, near black, and wavy like Paul's, to thin, straight, and light brown?

"Man," Coog said. "Look at me as a kid and look at me now. Who'd guess this guy"—he tapped Paul's recent photo of him making a foul shot, then tapped his five-year-old self playing with his Hot Wheels—"came from this shrimp."

Paul felt as if he'd been kicked. Out of the mouths of babes . . .

"Who indeed?" he managed to say.

He didn't dare look at Coog for fear of giving away his inner turmoil.

After a few heartbeats Coog said, "What are you mad at me for, Dad?"

"I'm not, Coog." Now he could look at him. "Really I'm not. I told you that in the hospital."

"Then how come we never do anything together? We used to do lots of stuff and now you just sit around. You hardly talk to me." His lower lip quivered. "What did I *do*?"

Paul rose and wrapped him in a bear hug.

"You didn't do a thing, Coog. Not a damn thing. I've just been preoccupied, that's all."

Coog backed a step away. Fear shone in his eyes.

"Does this have anything to do with that test?"

Oh, shit.

"Not at all. Doctor Takamura and I gave it to you straight: The test results from last week were inconclusive. They just need to rerun it. That's all."

"If there was something wrong, you'd tell me, right?"

"Of course I would. You're not a little kid anymore."

That seemed to buck him up, driving the fear from his eyes.

Paul gave him a gentle punch on the shoulder. "Why don't we go to a movie?"

"You kidding? On a weekday afternoon?"

"Why not? You're out of school, I'm off work. We'll buy popcorn and Sour Patch Kids and sit with the old folks."

He smiled. "Okay. Cool."

"Check online for what's playing. Find some action flick where you have to check your brains at the door."

"What if it's R?"

"Hey. You're with an adult. Besides, you see worse gore on your videogames."

"All *right!*"

"You pick the movie. And after I've done a little workout, we'll head out."

Heavy-bag time. Until he got the new results he'd be a ticking bomb. Paul needed to hit something. Hit it hard. And often.

SHEILA

Sheila's phone rang: Bill.

"Before you hang up on me, please listen. I want to apologize for my behavior at lunch. It was inexcusable."

He certainly had upset her, but hearing him contrite and apologetic was making her even more uncomfortable. Cranky was one thing, but lately he was vicious. And too defensive about Tanesha and Kelly for her still to believe there was no connection to VG723. She had hit a nerve. Maybe he wasn't behind that attempt on her life, but he was hiding something.

"Look, you don't have to—"

"I do. The JCAHO has been nit-picking me to distraction in the accreditation renewal process. It's not an excuse—there is no excuse—but I offer it as an explanation of sorts."

That brought her up short. The JCAHO . . . the Joint Committee on Accreditation of Healthcare Organizations. Dek had worked for them as an investigator who looked for conflicts of interest and made sure everything was on the up and up. He'd been working for them when he'd . . .

"Bill, You don't have to explain. I know you're being pulled in a thousand different directions. A person can take only so much."

Like having your house broken into and almost getting killed . . .

She was losing patience with Bill's self-absorption but didn't want to show her fading respect.

"Yes, well, my plate may be pretty full, but that's no excuse for the way I treated you. Can you forgive me?"

"Everybody has a bad day." Did that sound convincing?

"And about KB-twenty-six—go ahead and look into it. Investigate until you're satisfied. If you need any help, just call me and I'll do whatever I can."

That was a switch.

"But I'll have to ask you to do it on your own time."

"Of course."

"And please, don't make a habit of stat DNA probes."

"How did you know about that?"

"Hmm? Oh, well, whenever a stat request shakes up something as fragile as the DNA schedule, I'm informed."

"Sorry."

He laughed. "I'm the one apologizing today. This one made it through but next time you'll have to get in line."

"I promise."

"Whoops. Got another call. See you tomorrow?"

"Sure."

She left. Bill said it had made it through which meant it was complete. The hardcopy report could take hours, maybe even a day to reach her. But the test result would hit the server as soon the lab finished running it.

She turned to her computer and accessed her patient log, entering "Rosko, Coogan." All his labs since the accident popped up.

And here it was: Rosko, Coogan: Biological mother, Coogan, Rose; Biological father, Coogan, Paul.

Holy shit. She leaned back. Unbelievable.

Paul had been right.

The bad news was that Tethys lab had made a huge error. Inexcusable. She'd have to file a report.

But first to tell Paul the good news. She looked up his number and dialed, but got his machine.

Disappointment wafted through her. She'd looked forward to hearing his voice. It was oddly comforting.

She shook off the warm feeling and got down to framing a message. She'd always been wary—even before the HIPPA Nazis invaded medical care—of leaving medical information on an answering machine. But if she could couch it in terms that would be meaningful to Paul yet meaningless to a stranger . . .

"Paul. This is Sheila. You were right. The old test was incorrect. The new test confirmed what you'd hoped. Call me if you have any questions."

She hung up and swiveled back and forth in her chair. Sheila was thrilled for Paul but also deeply disturbed. A lab error this big couldn't be dismissed. She'd have to file an incident report.

PAUL

They returned when they returned from the latest Vin Diesel actionfest and Coog headed toward his room.

"Thanks for the movie, Dad. Vin Diesel is so jacked. Think I could ever build myself up like that?"

"Not playing videogames."

He laughed. "Maybe I'll start working out with you."

"Now's as good a time as any."

"Nah. The ribs remember? "

"Okay, you're off the hook."

Then the boy was around the corner and out of sight.

Paul noticed the blinking light on the answering machine and hit the play button. He pumped a fist as Sheila's voice told him there'd been a lab error and the retest confirmed Paul's paternity. He hit the replay button. As he listened again he found some relief, but nowhere near what he'd hoped for.

Lab error . . . okay. But photo error? No way. Not the photos he had of one kid metamorphosing into another. Almost as if the leukemia had been some sort of chrysalis: the Coog who had entered wasn't the Coog who had emerged.

He picked up the receiver and dialed Sheila's extension. When she picked up he said, "Hi, Sheila. It's Paul. Thanks for the good news. I'd like to buy you a drink."

She laughed. "That's not necessary. I just wish we hadn't had to repeat the test in the first place."

"Coffee then? I need to show you something."

"What?"

If he told her it was photos of Coog growing up, would she beg off? It sure as hell didn't sound too exciting. But if he played coy . . .

"Seeing will be believing."

Another laugh. "Come *on.*"

"When do you get off?"

"I was just getting ready to leave."

"Meet me downtown at Covington's. That way I can have a beer and you can have coffee. Although you may want something stronger after you see what I have to show you."

Would that set the hook?

"Now I'm intrigued. I can be there in ten minutes."

"Perfect. See you then."

He hung up and hurried downstairs to the photo box.

BILL

"Covington's?" Bill said, more to himself than to Shen who stood stiffly opposite his desk. "Not exactly a trysting place. What did he want to show her?"

Shen had brought him the day's logs of Sheila's computer activity and phone calls. Nothing much of interest except for this last call.

He shook his head. Almost blew it at lunch. Tanesha Green and Paul Rosko . . . he could see the malpractice summonses being delivered. And then Sheila wanting to probe into KB26 . . . too much. It had terrified him.

After Sheila had fled his office he realized that he had to stay close to her, retain her confidence. If he set up roadblocks, she'd become suspicious. On the other hand, if he gave her the green light and offered to help, she'd keep him in the loop. And that way he could steer her away from what might be trouble.

After all, with the new DNA results, what did he have to worry about?

They showed Coogan as Paul's offspring this time around.

When Coogan came to Tethys as a sick child, they'd taken blood and tissue samples and frozen them just for such an occasion. Mama's idea. Always thinking ahead. Rosko and Sheila would be satisfied with the results and stop pursuing KB26. And even if, for God knew what reason, she still wanted to research KB26, there was nothing to find. If she was able to access the FDA filings documenting Kaplan Biologicals' KB26 primate trials, she'd see nothing but good results.

Finally Bill had put an end to this.

But Paul Rosko was still sniffing around—in more ways than one.

Bill would have to do something about him. First step would be learning about him. All he knew now was from eavesdropping. Despite what he'd told Sheila, he hadn't done any backgrounding. Never occurred to him as he was just a volunteer.

Tethys used a security consulting firm to background every employee before hiring. He'd give them Rosko's name along with any other data available. He seemed like an everyday working stiff, but you never knew.

Right now, though, what was Rosko so anxious to show Sheila?

He looked up at Shen. "Head down to Covington's and see what Rosko is up to."

"Pardon, sir, but is difficult for this one to go unnoticed."

"Do what you can. If they spot you, say hello and pretend to be waiting for takeout. But learn something."

Shen turned to go, then turned back. "Wish to mention that Doctor Sheila call Doctor Silberman about Tanesha Green."

Well, that figured. Hal would be looking at the biopsy slides. No risk there.

"What was said?"

"She want to know when he expect report on Tanesha Green slides he send out."

"Sent out? When?"

"He not say."

This was bad.

SHEILA

Sheila smiled when she saw Paul through the door of Covington's. But his jaw dropped as he neared her.

He touched her face. "What the hell happened to you?"

"A car accident."

"When?"

"Last night. Let's go sit down and we'll talk about it."

She glanced around. No one seemed to be paying them any attention. She'd kept careful watch driving, especially in her rearview, and felt sure no one had followed her. Well, pretty sure.

God, she hated this.

"I've never been here," Sheila said as she slid onto the bench opposite him.

Paul was dressed in his usual lumberjack ensemble of jeans and plaid flannel shirt. He'd picked out a booth near the rear. Except for a gaggle of early drinkers at the bar, Covington's—a locally owned Applebee's / TGIF wannabe—was pretty much deserted. Come five o'clock that would change.

She glanced around, taking in the décor: a faux Tiffany lamp hung over each table; movie posters, old photographs of the Red Sox and the old Bradfield football team graced the walls amid scatterings of Americana—Ameri-kitsch was more like it.

All so normal . . . all so unlike her life lately.

"It's Coog's favorite place. Loves the burgers."

"Then you should have brought him."

Paul shook his head. "Not this time. I wouldn't want him to see what I have to show you. But first, tell me about this *accident.*"

She glanced around, then leaned toward him. "I think someone tried to kill me."

Paul sat back and stared. He was about to speak when a perky young waitress stopped by. Paul ordered a draft of Bass, Sheila an iced tea.

When they were alone again, he said, "Are you serious?"

She nodded and told him what had happened.

"Sheila, what is it you're not telling me? I know something's up with Coogan, but there's got to be something else."

"There've been other things."

"Like what?"

"Someone broke into my house and then I found a bug in my office. I shouldn't tell you that because I don't want to start rumors of some kind of conspiracy at the hospital, but God, it does seem like something's going on, doesn't it?"

"Of course. Anyone would think that."

"Bill had such good explanations, but if you could see how upset he's been whenever I mention—"

"Mention what?"

"Patient information I can't discuss, but it's something I'm working on and none of this started until I began digging into it."

"So you think it's the head of Tethys trying to kill you? Doctor Gilchrist?"

She shook her head. "Don't think it didn't cross my mind, but you should have seen his face when I went in this morning. He was shocked, really, truly shocked, when I told him."

"You can fake shock."

"You can't make yourself go white as a ghost. I'm positive he knew nothing about last night's car crash. But still, there's something going on with him. I don't know what, but, well, I've known him for years and really look up to him. His sister has become like my adopted mother. I just don't feel like I can trust him anymore."

Paul reached over and held her hand and she felt her heart melting. She so needed someone she could trust right now.

"You can trust me. I'll help you. We'll do this together."

Together. There was a word she missed.

She nodded and managed a small smile. "But I can't say much about the other stuff I'm looking into. Privacy laws. And it's unrelated."

"For the record, I think someone did try to kill you. And despite the relationship you have with this Bill, he knows about it. And I'll bet dollars to doughnuts the bug and the theft were related. We'll need to watch your back, Sheila."

We. He had said "we."

"You think I'm still in danger?"

"Until they catch whoever drove that other car, yes, you are in danger."

"But why? I don't know anything."

She looked over her shoulder. Everyone looked safe but how could she really tell?

"Could be someone's afraid of what you *might* dig up." Paul pulled a stack of photos from his breast pocket and laid one on the table before her. "Coog at three."

She saw a chubby little guy that she never would have recognized as the boy she'd seen skateboarding last week.

Then another photo next to the first. Looked like a mini Paul.

"Coog at four."

And so on. Snapping them down like a blackjack dealer, Paul placed them one after another, announcing Coog's age with each. In the end, twelve photos, one for each of the last ten years of his life except age six—left as an empty space—lay before her like a Tarot array.

He tapped the empty spot in the middle.

"That was the year of his leukemia. Look at how he was developing before, then at what he's become."

Puzzled, Sheila studied the display. She soon saw what Paul was getting at. The post-leukemia boy didn't look anything like the pre-leukemia toddler.

Sheila shrugged. "Quite a change. But kids do change as they grow up. Adolescent growth spurts can wreak all sorts of havoc."

"Does their hair change?"

"Sometimes. And so does the hair pattern on their scalp."

"You mean they can develop a widow's peak where they never had one before?"

"Maybe."

"How about color and texture?" He tugged at his own thick, dark brown hair. "Can it go from this bear pelt to that?" He tapped the latest photo.

Coog's hair had gone from an exact match of Paul's to a finer, thinner, lighter brown.

Odd. Very odd. Something like—

Oh, God! Kelly and Tanesha! Their hair had changed too.

At least Coog's skin had remained the same.

"And here's the kicker," Paul said. "I didn't see it until I started arranging these in chronological order." He tapped one of the earlier shots. "This is his kindergarten photo. What color eyes do you see?"

Sheila squinted. "Brown."

"Now take a look at the latest."

She did—

And saw blue . . . Coog's eyes were now Paul Newman blue . . .

Something cold crawled through her gut.

She shifted her gaze back and forth between the photos, but the evidence was undeniable.

"I'm seeing but not believing."

Paul's expression was grim. "Believe it. I've heard of a baby's blue eyes turning brown, but not a grown boy's brown eyes turning blue. Have you?"

Sheila shook her head. "No. Can't happen. Blue is a recessive trait. Brown always wins in the phenotype."

The waitress returned then with their drinks.

She saw the pictures and smiled. "Cute kids."

Sheila took a sip of her iced tea and wished it were a Cosmo.

"Let me ask you," Paul said when the waitress was gone. "When a brown-eyed kid becomes blue-eyed, doesn't that indicate a change in his genes?"

Sheila didn't answer. Too many thoughts colliding. Change in genotype—a new set of genes would explain what Tanesha was experiencing. And what had happened to Kelly . . . and to Coog . . .

Finally she found her voice. "But it's impossible."

"Impossible?" An edge crept into Paul's voice. "Hey, it's staring you right in the face, Sheila. Don't say 'impossible' until you can come up with another explanation."

Could it be? All three cases had one thing in common: cancer therapy. And not just cancer therapy, the same _kind_ of cancer therapy.

Stem cells . . . administered by Tethys.

"I feel it in my gut, Sheila." His clenched fists bracketed his beer. "That therapy, that KB-twenty-six changed Coog's genes."

"But that's im—" She caught herself in time. An automatic response. She couldn't help it. "Look, if KB-twenty-six changed genotypes, wouldn't there be a parade of parents dragging their kids back to Tethys demanding an explanation?"

"Maybe there will be, maybe not. Maybe the parents just haven't noticed yet. The changes are so gradual, maybe they'll never notice. I'll bet none of those fathers discovered that they were married to a cheating wife. If I didn't know what I know about Rose, I'd be blowing off Coog's changes. You can make up a million reasons. But not when you've been cuckolded. Makes you wonder if the infidelity you know about was the only time. Add to that a son who looks nothing like you, you can't help start wondering."

"But the DNA—"

"A lab test. Letters on paper. Letters that seem to change the more you look into this." He swept a hand over the photos. "Here's the real truth." He sighed. "Look, Sheila, I don't believe it myself—I don't want to believe it—but it's there. The boy after KB-twenty-six isn't the boy before KB-twenty-six. He's my boy and I'm goddamned grateful for that. But they changed something inside of him. Changed him into someone else and I want to know why."

And so do I, she thought, then stiffened.

How many people knew about Kelly, Tanesha, and Coog? How many people could connect them? Only one.

Me.

And maybe Bill.

And her missing photos of Kelly . . . the stolen camera.

Of *course* it was all connected. God, she was so stupid. Whoever bugged her office must have heard her talk about the pictures of Kelly. Damn! If it wasn't Bill—and she couldn't rule out his involvement as much as she'd like to—then who?

She seemed to be the nexus of too many tough questions . . . questions someone might not want answered. And one sure way to keep them unanswered was to remove the questioner.

But who could she go to? The cops? It was all so flimsy. They already seemed to think she was a little nuts.

Maybe she was. Last night already seemed like a dream. If not for the wrecked car and her scratched-up face, she'd wonder if it really happened.

And Kelly's death . . . she couldn't help wondering now if it really was an accident.

No-no-no. Don't go there. If someone were killing everyone talking down VG723, Tanesha Green would not be walking around. So as long as Tanesha stayed healthy—

"Where did Tethys get the KB-twenty-six?" Paul said.

Sheila shook herself out of her ramblings and gave him a short version of what Bill had told her.

Paul leaned back. "Out of business, dead and gone. I wonder."

"Well, Gerald Kaplan might still be around. Let's see."

She pulled out her Blackberry and turned it on. She made a wireless connection to the Internet and then to the state's online directory of licensed physicians. She entered "Kaplan" and the little screen filled with hits. But only one Gerald.

"Hey. He practices in Salem—in a multi-specialty group. If he's on today, maybe we can catch him."

"Salem, New Hampshire or Mass?"

"Mass."

She dialed the number and found herself talking to a receptionist at Rolling Hills Medical Associates.

Yes, Dr. Kaplan was in today but leaving soon. Last appointment at 5:30.

"This is Doctor Sheila Takamura. I can be there in half an hour. I'd like to consult with him about a mutual patient."

The receptionist said she would pass that on.

Sheila slid out of her seat and reached for her coat.

"Come on."

———•••———

They were fifteen minutes late.

Sheila hurried up the front walk toward the two-story glass-and-steel building that housed Rolling Hills Medical Group.

"I hope he's still here."

Rush hour traffic heading south had been a bit slow but once they got into Salem the streets were clogged. The witch town always had tourists driving too slowly, peering at the witches as they walked down the street in black robes or at the House of the Seven Gables. They'd taken Paul's navy blue Explorer and he'd muttered frustration at the other drivers and had all but fogged the windows as they'd crawled along.

Paul paced her. "He'll wait, won't he? I mean, as a professional courtesy?"

Sheila shrugged. "He doesn't know me and if he has somewhere else to go, he'll go. This was arranged on the fly without consulting him."

A thin, pale, sharp-featured man stepped through the doors and approached them. He had graying hair and horn-rimmed glasses, and was tucked into a blue stadium coat that looked too big for him. He made no eye contact as he passed.

Sheila hoped he wasn't Kaplan. She was tempted to ask him but his remote demeanor made her hesitate, and then he was past.

Paul held the front door for her—a gentlemanly gesture she always appreciated. Once inside she bustled across the marble floor to the central desk where three women manned the phones. The middle one looked up.

"Can I help you?"

"I'm Doctor Takamura. I called earlier about meeting with Doctor Kaplan. Is he—?"

"Oh, you just missed him. Didn't you see him on your way in?"

"We've never met. The man in the blue coat?"

"That's him." Her tone told Sheila that Dr. Kaplan was not one of her favorites. "He waited a few minutes, then told me to have you call him tomorrow."

Paul was already heading back toward the entrance.

Sheila followed at a half trot as he hurried toward the parking lot. Kaplan pulled his dark gray SUV out of a reserved space and headed for the street.

"Maybe we can catch him."

"We can talk to him tomorrow," Sheila said.

"We're going after him. I want to hear what he has to say *now*."

HAL

Hal Silberman whistled while he walked to his car. He'd had some time to read over Tanesha Green's file and was intrigued. Her before-and-after pictures had blown him away. He hadn't seen any changes that dramatic since, well, since that KB26 case a bunch of years back. Nothing as drastic as a race change but that guy went from being a redhead with green eyes to a person with black hair and brown eyes. He looked Greek when he came into Hal's office. What was it? Six, seven years ago? Hard to say. Before he could do the proper workups on that guy, he went out and contracted HIV.

After that, the patient said he didn't care anymore how he looked. He committed suicide about a year later. Hal had wanted to examine him further, dig deeper into the case. But without patient cooperation there was nothing he could do.

Now, with Tanesha Green, here was a similar situation; plus Sheila said there had been another one. Two woman changing races, complete hair and pigment changes. He hadn't made the connection to the old KB26 patient until after Sheila left, when he looked at the pictures. Sheila had tried to tell him but he had no idea it was so extreme. He had to call the doctor she saw last at her clinic and ask about her history the last couple of years. Tanesha hadn't done her follow ups at Tethys, which was too bad. Would have made things a lot easier.

"Hal!" He looked up as he neared his car.

"Hi, Bill. How are you?"

"Great, great. What's new?"

The head man was being unusually friendly.

"Not much. Finally over the divorce and now I'm dating again. Not such a bad life. Brenda's coming tonight. Twenty-three-year-old Brenda from Starlight Donuts."

Hal's heart pounded when he thought of her. So far the only date they had was a concert she wanted to attend. He hoped like hell she wasn't using him. She had seen his Jag in the drive-thru and her eyes lit up. Well, tonight would be the test. She said she would *probably* come over and that was good enough for him. Keeping his fingers crossed she'd show.

"She's coming to my place tonight. I'm making a special dinner for her. My first attempt at gourmet cooking. chicken Marsala."

Hal smiled, counting the minutes till eight o'clock.

"Dating huh? Lucky stiff. Well, I won't keep you. I just wanted to touch base on the Green case. I'm following her with Sheila."

Hal welcomed the opportunity to discuss this with Bill.

"Here let me set my things in the car. I want to show you something."

They walked to Hal's car together. He put everything but the file on the seat. He opened it and pointed.

"Look at this. Green is turning white. These pictures are from last week."

"Wow."

"Here's the thing, Bill. Sheila said she had another patient, a white turning black."

"The Slade woman. But she died."

"I know, but remember that redheaded kid, seven years ago or so?"

"No."

"Sure you do. I asked you about it. A KB-twenty-six patient, got Leukemia in his early twenties. Got KB and was cured. He came in a couple of years later, completely changed. Even his eye color was different."

"Oh yes, now I remember. He was a drug addict though, as I recall. You thought maybe the drugs caused his change."

"No, I never I assumed that. I wasn't sure—"

"Yes, you did. He contracted HIV from IV drug use. You concluded it was most likely some experimental street drug causing the changes. But after he got AIDS he refused more tests."

"His condition never escalated to full-blown AIDS. He

committed suicide long before that. But you're right, he did refuse more tests and later died. I never was able to conclude anything either way. At the time I questioned if the KB-twenty-six could have been responsible."

"But he died and you were never sure."

Boy did this sound like someone trying to cover his ass. "No, I was never sure."

Bill looked satisfied. Time to shatter that.

"Never sure on that one but Green here is another case. Pervasive pigment and hair changes down to the cellular level. I've sent some reports and slides to all the big centers to see if any of those folks have seen anything like this. And it's stem cell therapy again. Maybe Sheila's right. Could be a connection. I think it's worth pursing."

Bill sighed, leaned back on Hal's car. He started sweating. Opened his overcoat and loosened his tie.

"You okay?"

Bill didn't speak. Closed his eyes and leaned for a good couple of minutes. Finally, "You might be onto something Hal. It's great you're on top of it. When Sheila mentioned it, I was leery. She has a tendency to jump into things with both feet, but you . . . If you think there's a connection, there may be. Any way I can help?"

That was a quick turnaround. Hal was glad he saw the light.

"No, I think I'm good. It's out of my hands until the folks get back to me. Sheila ran some more tests and Green's coming back for another biopsy next week. I'm kind of excited actually."

"Excited!" Bill's face reddened. "Excited? Are you crazy? Excited that you might have found a flaw in the perfect cancer therapy? Do you have any idea how quickly this whole program could be shut down? What kind of scrutiny—?"

"No, of course not." Hal looked around. No one else around to hear Bill yelling, thank God. "I was just thinking that if there's a way to change hair and eye and skin color on command with no other side effects, well, it might be something people would be interested in. An unintended but beneficial side effect. Like plastic surgery without the risk of anesthesia and infection. Big market out there for people who want to change themselves."

Bill seemed to relax. "Right. Hadn't thought of that. Sorry, just a little sensitive when it comes to VG-seven-twenty-three."

Hal patted his back. "No problem. Don't worry. I won't say a word to anyone till I know something for sure."

"I appreciate it. So when did you send the slides out?"

"Just now. Dropped in the outbox in the clinic."

"Good. Hopefully we'll hear something soon. I'll let you get to your date."

"Thanks, Bill. Good seeing you again."

"You too, Hal."

Hal watched Bill walk away. He certainly was sensitive about VG723 therapy. Hal never knew why the KB26 trial ended. Had to be some kind of glitch and now Bill was worried VG723 would meet the same fate.

Oh, well. Off to the specialty grocery store to pick up the ingredients. He was going all out on fancy mushrooms for the chicken Marsala. He looked at his watch. Two more hours till Brenda came over. He got excited just thinking about the night ahead of him.

SHEILA

After a few minutes of watchful cruising, Paul pointed ahead. "Got him. Easy to spot a Navigator, just a little bit smaller than an aircraft carrier."

The trip turned out to be a short one: To Marblehead where Kaplan pulled into the driveway of a small Victorian cottage a few blocks after they passed the ocean. Paul pulled in right behind him.

"I'll do the talking," she said.

Kaplan was standing by the open door of his car, watching them with a concerned look.

"Doctor Kaplan?" she called. "I'm Doctor Takamura. I'd like to talk to you."

His features relaxed somewhat. "I passed you outside the office. From your name I'd expected—"

"Someone Japanese, I know. Happens all the time." She stopped half a dozen feet away. She knew Paul was right behind her and she didn't want their presence to seem threatening. "Can we have a few minutes of your time?"

"What's this about? The receptionist said something about a mutual patient. I really can't discuss—"

"I'm not looking to discuss specifics. I . . ."

She hesitated not knowing if this was the man they were looking for. She'd have to ask him flat out. A bluff.

"I really want to discuss your old company, Kaplan Biologicals—specifically KB-twenty-six."

Something flitted across his features. Sheila couldn't be sure, but she thought it might be fear.

He cleared his throat. "The company is ancient history. I don't care to discuss it."

So . . . he *was* the right Dr. Kaplan.

As he slammed his car door and turned away, Sheila said, "I can understand that, sir. But I work at the Tethys Center where we're using another stem-cell therapy, and I was hoping—"

He turned back to her. Interested.

"Tethys? Can you prove that?"

She fished out her ID badge and showed it to him.

He nodded as his watery blue eyes fixed on her through his thick lenses. "I can give you a few minutes. I'll answer some of your questions if you'll answer a few of mine. Deal?"

Odd . . . but Sheila returned his nod.

"Deal."

He looked past her at Paul.

"And who is this?"

Paul gave his name, then added, "An interested party."

Kaplan waved them to follow him.

BILL

Bill took Shen's call.

"Very sorry, doctor, but this one has nothing to report."

"Couldn't get close enough?"

"Covington's very empty. Follow them to Salem where they go

into building. Was almost seen when they come out right away and drive off."

"What building? Give me the address."

He'd check it out later.

"Where'd they go then?"

After a heartbeat's hesitation, "This one is shamed to report that I could not follow. Traffic trap me at red light and by time I am through, they are not in sight. Could not find them."

Damn it to hell! Where were they? What were they up to?

"Just as well. I—my sister has something else for you to do."

SHEILA

They ended up at the dining room table—Paul and Sheila on one side, Kaplan on the other—with their coats hung on the backs of their chairs. He didn't offer coffee or anything else.

The house amazed Sheila. Not a single personal touch in the rooms she could see. Not a photo, not a painting. Nothing. As if no one lived here.

"All right," Kaplan said, glancing at his watch. "I can give you fifteen minutes. What do you want to know?"

Sheila cleared her throat. Where to begin?

"I'm having difficulty learning much about KB-twenty-six."

"Why should you care?"

She cocked her head toward Paul. "Mister Rosko's son was successfully treated with it."

He swiveled his gaze to Paul. "He's still well, I trust?"

Paul nodded. "Yes, and no."

Kaplan turned back to Sheila and she found it odd that he didn't ask Paul what he meant.

"What exactly was KB-twenty-six? I know it was stem-cell based, but . . ."

"I've got time only for a thumbnail version. I found a way to make blood stem cells antigenically neutral. The advantage is obvious, I should think."

Sheila nodded and turned to Paul. "If you can sidestep a systemic reaction, the donor won't need to be a close HLA match." Back to

Kaplan: "But how—?"

Kaplan shook his head. "That's intellectual property. But it went beyond donor HLA. These stem cells were grown in cultures. I'd done away with the *need* for a donor."

Sheila blinked. "And you're not sharing it with the world?"

Kaplan's gaze wandered to the tabletop. "I tried, but it was only sporadically successful—not enough to make wider use feasible."

"But still—"

"When my backers learned that it wasn't going to be the home run they'd anticipated, they pulled the financial plug." Bitterness sharpened his tone. "With no product and no backing, Kaplan Biologicals had to go chapter seven."

Sheila said, "I'm sorry." And she was. "Who's got the patient records?"

He shrugged. "Whoever bought the assets. But as usual, to safeguard patient privacy, we were never given names—just numbers. Just as experimental therapies are numbered."

"The experimental records then?"

"Whoever bought the computers. The backers locked me out—bastards. Impounded everything—office equipment, lab fixtures. Everything. I never got a chance to wipe my hard drives—but I'd used 128-bit encryption on the files as I went along."

"Why would you want to wipe the drives? You said KB-twenty-six wasn't financially feasible."

He tapped his forehead. "What's mine stays mine."

"But it would seem to have so much potential. Why didn't you pursue it with Tethys?"

He frowned. "Tethys? Why would I go there?"

"Well, Doctor Gilchrist offered you a position. I'd think you'd—"

"He did no such thing. I tried to get in touch with him on another matter and he never even returned my calls."

Sheila felt a ripple of shock. Bill had been very clear about that.

I offered him a post with Tethys.

Something was very wrong here, but she couldn't let it distract her. One last question:

"Who were your backers?"

"A pack of sharks that called themselves Innovation Ventures. Cared only for the almighty buck." Kaplan leaned forward. "Now, as agreed, time for a bit of turnaround: Tell me about this VG-seven-twenty-three."

"How do you know about that?"

"Through pure luck. You mentioned it's stem-cell based. What else can you tell me?"

"Not a lot, I'm afraid. They keep the details close to the vest."

"They? They who?"

"A company called VecGen."

"Never heard of it."

"It's small—probably a lot like yours was."

"Yes . . . *was*." He sighed. "KB-twenty-six was delivered into the marrow space to treat leukemia. But VG-seven-twenty-three is used for other cancers, correct?"

"Who told you that?"

"A former Tethys patient. But how are the stem cells delivered to the tumor?"

Sheila hesitated, not wanting to say too much. But then she remembered that VecGen's technique had been published elsewhere.

"They attach a viral vector."

His eyes took on a faraway look as he rubbed his chin. "I see, I see. Clever." He refocused on Sheila. "Do they treat children as well as adults?"

Sheila shook her head. "No children. Which is a shame. I don't understand why—"

"No," Kaplan said. "You wouldn't."

Sheila glanced at him. "And you would?"

He shook his head. His melancholy mood had vanished. Instead he looked . . . furious.

"What about the selection process? What are their criteria?"

"God only knows. They photograph all the applicants but I'm sure their looks have no bearing on their acceptance. I think it's to monitor the demographics."

Paul spoke for the first time since they'd sat down. "Can we get back to KB-twenty-six?"

Kaplan gave him a steely stare. "I can't see that there's anything left to say."

"How about kids changing?"

Sheila sensed Kaplan stiffen as his hard look faded to wary.

"What are you talking about?"

Paul tossed the photos on the table.

"I'm talking about a kid's hair color changing, about brown eyes turning blue!"

Kaplan shot to his feet. "This discussion is over."

"No!" Paul jabbed a finger at him. "Not till I get some answers."

Kaplan pulled out his cell phone.

"If the two of you aren't out of here in one minute, I'm dialing the police."

Sheila tugged at Paul's sleeve.

"Let's not get the police involved. If he won't tell us, we'll find out another way. We'll dig it up"—she leveled a hard stare at Kaplan—"and then we'll be back."

Paul leaned across the table. "What are you hiding, you son of a bitch? _What?_"

He snatched the photos from the table and strode for the door.

Sheila hadn't taken her eyes off Kaplan. "To be continued, doctor."

And then she followed Paul outside.

KAPLAN

Gerald watched them get into the SUV and drive away. When they were out of sight he stepped to the liquor cabinet, poured himself a Scotch. Took a gulp and felt the burn. He was getting to enjoy the sensation. Enjoying it too much, perhaps.

But booze was no solution.

What a fool he'd been to think this would go away.

He walked into the kitchen pantry and slid a flat box off the top shelf. He opened it and stared at the loaded .40 caliber Glock.

He didn't know if he could stand exposure. He might have to

take another way out.

SHEN

He looked at his watch. Time for another unpleasant chore. Dr. Gilchrist said Dr. Silberman was about to cause a lot of trouble for Tethys. Mailing Tethys secrets to other hospitals. Shen did not believe this because he had known Dr. Silberman for so long, and trusted him. So after talking to Dr. Gilchrist he checked the Tethys mail bin. There were the packages. Inside them, letters from Dr. Silberman. The letters did not say anything Shen understood, but each contained slides. That was where the secrets were, Shen knew.

Dr. Gilchrist said it was best if the *Jiù-zhù-zhě* did not know about this. To know such a good and trusted doctor was a spy would upset her. Shen agreed. She was a fragile woman.

Shen remembered what they did to spies back in China. If he punished Dr. Silberman in that manner, it would not look like an accident. Too bad. Spies did not deserve easy deaths. He patted his pocket to make sure the mushrooms were still there. The crinkle of the package confirmed. It would be a slow death, but untraceable. Not torture but almost bad enough for his crime.

SHEILA

They were almost back to Bradfield before Paul seemed himself again.

"Sorry, Sheila. I wish I were better company but . . ." He shook his head.

Sheila understood. Frustration gnawed at her too.

"At least we didn't come away completely empty handed. We know he's hiding something."

"Yeah, but what?"

"We can check with the bankruptcy trustee. The court always appoints one."

"I can't see Kaplan telling us who he is."

"We don't need him. It's public record. Get me to a computer and I'll find him in no time."

"We can go to my place and—" He caught himself and gave her a shy smile. "Hey, don't worry. Coog is there."

She returned his smile. "What, me worry?"

PAUL

Paul had almost laughed out loud at Coog's expression when he saw his father and his doctor walk into the house together.

Paul wondered what he'd been thinking, asking her back here. The place was a mess. Usually he kept it fairly neat. Some clutter was okay, but too much got on his nerves. With all that had been going on he'd been too distracted to notice.

He began buzzing around, picking up newspapers, magazines, sneakers . . .

Sheila laughed. "You don't have to do that. You should see my place."

He'd like to do just that—and soon—but didn't say so. Not with his son standing there.

Coog adapted quickly—he adored Sheila—and within minutes they were chatting away.

"Something to drink?" Paul said. "I've got cold Bass and a warm bottle of Chardonnay somewhere in the basement."

"I'll take a Bass."

"Me too," said Coog with a grin.

Paul laughed. "As if!" He pointed to the fridge. "But you can do the honors while I unload my pockets." Then a glance at Sheila. "Be right back."

He hurried into the bedroom and emptied the photos into a drawer. He didn't want Coog to see them and start wondering what they'd been up to. With those stowed away, he headed back to the kitchen and found Sheila sipping a bottle of dark amber ale.

"Oh, drink from the bottle, Paul. It's better that way."

"A woman who understands beer." He popped open his own bottle.

"Where's your computer?"

"In the spare bedroom," Paul said.

"What kind of hook up?"

He spread his arms. "Hey, I'm the cable guy."

She laughed. "Please don't say that. I saw the movie and, well, all I can say is, please don't say that."

In the spare bedroom, she seated herself before the already running computer.

"Hey, what's this?" She pointed to an icon marked by a book. It said "novel."

Paul sucked in his breath. Well, what harm would it do to tell her?

"I'm writing a book."

"Really?"

She seemed impressed. Imagine that—impressing her.

He laughed. "So the shortcut says."

"Have you written other books? Are you published?"

"I've started several but only get about halfway and they end up in the Recycle Bin; but this one might have a fighting chance."

"Huh. Who knew?" She smiled at him. "What's it about?"

That he couldn't tell her.

"I'd rather not say just yet. I'm not sure where it's going."

Lie. He knew exactly where it was going.

"Fair enough. Can I read it when it's done?"

Hell, if he didn't get poor Grisbe off page 220, it would never be done.

"Sure."

She had the cursor hovering over the icon, and he could tell her finger was itching to press it.

He leaned over and put his hand over hers, moving the cursor onto the Explorer icon.

"The best place to go, I think, is Google."

He double clicked.

"Just tell me the title to hold me over. Please?"

He left his hand on hers another second, then gave it a squeeze. The title wouldn't give too much away.

"The Four Walls of Jim Grisbe."

Coog had followed them. "What're you looking for?"

Paul was glad to get her off the novel but hesitated with Coogan.

He could *not* let the boy know that what they were researching was all about him.

"We're looking up a defunct company," Sheila said. "It went out of business years ago—chapter seven and all that—and we want a little more information."

"Oh," Coog said, deadpan. "That sounds reeeeeally interesting. I hope you don't mind if I watch some TV."

"Sure you don't want to stay?" Paul said.

"I'd love to, Dad, but there's a show I want to see."

"Which one?"

"The Discovery Channel has a special on arranging your sock drawer."

He gave Coog a friendly slap on the back as he headed for the hall.

Sheila looked up at Paul. "Amazing how truth works."

Not as amazing as you, Paul thought.

"Okay." She turned back to the screen and began hitting the keyboard. "Real quick, before we get to Kaplan Biologicals, I want to check out another company."

She typed in VecGen.

"Does that have something to do with this?"

"No," she said. "Just something I'm checking for one of my patients. It's the company that developed VG-seven-twenty-three. I might contact them."

Her fingers flew across the keys, then stopped.

"Hmmm."

"What?"

"It says here that VecGen started up six years ago—a year after Kaplan Biologicals went under."

"And?"

She took a deep breath. "Maybe just coincidence. But the VG-seven-twenty-three clinical trial began five years ago. That means VecGen developed it within a year of startup. Awfully quick."

"Maybe they had it in development before incorporating."

"Yeah, maybe."

She took her pen and scrawled something on a sticky pad. Paul tried but couldn't decipher it.

She looked up and smiled. "It's VecGen's address and phone number."

He picked up the sheet and squinted at it.

"If you say so."

She poised her fingers on the keys. "Now, let's see about Kaplan Biologicals."

Google wasn't a lot of help.

"Okay, let's try some other places."

"Another search engine?"

"No. There are websites out there that give you a surprising amount of information on individuals and companies."

"What about privacy laws?"

"You'd be amazed what you can dig up with very little effort. You just have to know where to look."

"And how is it you know where to look? Is there something you're not telling me? Are you some sort of hacker?"

Sheila laughed. "No, nothing like that. I knew someone who was an investigator at his job and was privy to an amazing array of information. He showed me websites and techniques to get around almost all attempts at privacy. It's scary knowing how unsafe our information is, but in this case, it's a good thing."

She began keying in URLs and zipping through screen after screen at warp 7. Wasn't she afraid of missing something important? Paul wondered how she could she absorb anything at that pace.

Then again, to be the kind of doctor she was, she probably had to be able to sift through huge amounts of data at breakneck speed.

Paul felt he should be watching the monitor, but the images flashing across the screen made him a little dizzy. So he let his gaze drift to the nape of her neck. She had her wonderful strawberry blond hair clipped up in the back and he found the downy skin and stray strands there mesmerizing. He wanted to press his lips against that neck and—

"Here we go," Sheila said. "Got it. The court-appointed trustee for the Kaplan Biologicals bankruptcy was one Alfred T. George, Esquire. Office in Manchester—Mass." She smiled up at him.

"Guess where we're going tomorrow morning."

Paul couldn't help it. He kissed those upturned lips and found them soft, moist and . . . yielding. She was returning the kiss!

He pulled away.

"Sorry. I don't know what I was thinking. I—"

Sheila rose and faced him.

"I kind of liked that."

They kissed again, and Sheila pressed against him, and he could have stayed like that all night. But then he remembered—

"Coog."

She took half a step back.

"Yes, Coog. But there'll be other times, won't there?"

Paul felt as if someone had opened a bottle of champagne in his chest.

"If I have anything to say about it there most certainly will."

Lots of other times.

HAL

Hal Silberman had never been this sick in his life. Brenda had failed to show up for their date so he'd eaten alone—two helpings of chicken Marsala. And he'd been violently ill ever since. Salmonella from the chicken? Maybe a rogue in that container of pre-sliced mushrooms he'd bought. He remembered a couple of mouthfuls tasting kind of funky.

Explosive diarrhea with vomiting. At first they took turns debilitating him, but then they became simultaneous. He'd sat at the toilet defecating while throwing up in his chrome trashcan. After a few hours, his rectum started bleeding. By two o'clock in the morning he was vomiting blood and too weak to make it to a phone to call for help. He lay curled up on the floor of the bathroom.

By late morning he was shivering, too weak to sit on the toilet. Too weak to lift his head out of his bloody vomit. He fell asleep thinking of Tanesha Green. As soon as he was better, he had to sit down with Sheila and compare notes. There was a connection between KB26 and VG723. The more he thought of it, the more certain he was.

__SEVEN__

SHEN

"Candy?"

Shen stirred. He loved Fai, but longed to sleep just once until the alarm went off. It seemed Fai never slept. He often woke up before six in the morning and turned on the TV without waking anyone. Unless they locked him in his room there was nothing they could do, except make sure the house was safe. No sharp corners, locks on the cabinets and doors, covers on the outlets.

"Candy?" Shen heard the crinkle of paper and looked over to the boy standing beside his bed.

He gasped and jumped from the bed, then snatched the package from Fai's hand and inspected it carefully. Still tightly wrapped in tape. Shen looked back at Jing who was still asleep. He shut the door and scooped up his son, then ran him into the living room.

Fai began to cry. "Pa, give candy."

Shen unlatched the snack drawer and handed him a chocolate bar. Anything to keep him quiet.

He sat his son on the couch and hugged him hard. "Pa loves you." He hugged him again but the boy just squirmed, trying to see the TV.

Fai had dug into Shen's pocket and found the rest of the poison mushrooms. The ones used to poison Dr. Silberman. He'd thought it was candy. Shen's eyes welled with tears just thinking of it. *Fai almost ate the mushrooms.* Shen clenched the package so hard in his hand that his nails dug into his flesh and made his palms bleed.

What have I done?

Shen looked at his boy, so innocent. So full of life. And he could have died.

Because of his father's chosen profession.

No more killing. No more.

"Fai, Pa has to do some business. You watch TV. If you need anything you go see your Ma." He patted him on the head and walked into his bedroom.

"Jing. I have to go out and do something important. Fai is in the living room. You sleep some more. It's still very early."

She smiled and nodded.

Shen grabbed a large plastic trash bag from under the kitchen sink and tossed the mushroom package into it, then headed for the garage.

He unlocked his fireproof cabinet. Seeing the contents with new eyes was a slap in the face. This arsenal filled Shen with shame.

He was no better than the murdering monsters from which he had run. He always had been, and still was, nothing more than a hired killer. He pretended to have left that life in China, but he hadn't. And his son had almost died because of it.

He picked up his brass knuckles and nunchuks and dropped them in the bag.

Fai almost died.

He grabbed the knife his father had given him when he turned thirteen. The shiny steel showed him the reflection of a murderer. His father had taught him the art of killing. He would not teach the same lessons to his boy. He turned the knife away, unable to look any longer at his own face. He dropped the knife in the bag.

Tears fell down his face. He swept all the bottles and packages on the top shelf into the bag. Poisons.

What kind of father am I? What kind of human am I?

When the cabinet was empty, he tied up the bag, grabbed his shovel, and drove to the local hiking trail. No one was there in the winter. He drove around the lake and up the big hill to the old fort. He took out the shovel and dug a deep hole. Deep enough for a grave. Ceremoniously, he lowered the bag. Li Shen did not deserve to live. If it weren't for Jing and Fai, he would jump into the grave as well and take his own life. But he had an obligation to take care of them and love them.

Within a half hour he had replaced the dirt and covered it with twigs and wet leaves. He felt relieved to truly be changing his life. No matter what the consequences, he would never kill again.

SHEILA

Sheila thought about Paul while depositing a chart onto the desk.

His kissing her last night had knocked her off balance. But in a good way. Not a wake-up call—more like a wake-up jolt. Lit a flame in her. She was eager to see him. In twenty minutes he was picking her up at her house. She couldn't help smiling as she pressed the down button on the elevator.

She realized how much she missed being part of someone's team, the other half of a couple.

And what about her own life? How could she be thinking romance when she was in someone's crosshairs?

If nothing else, thoughts of him offered a safe harbor from obsessing on the awful possibilities.

"Sheila?"

Ellen Bascomb, director of the center's blood bank, bustled toward her. At five-two, and just shy of two-hundred pounds, bustle was the best she could do.

Sheila knew what this was about and did not want to deal with it today.

Should have taken the stairs, she thought.

"Hi, Ellen, I—"

"I wish you'd come to me before filing that incident report."

Here we go.

"I had no choice. You know that."

"We do *not* err in our DNA tests. It simply doesn't happen."

Sheila could feel her Irish rising. Didn't need this today.

"Your lab's error had someone thinking he wasn't the father of his child. He was convinced his son was switched at birth. Do you have any idea what kind of anguish that caused him?"

Ellen cast her eyes down.

"If that's not an error, Ellen, tell me what is."

The little woman lost some of her steam. But not all.

"We've got so many safeguards in place, damn it. It couldn't happen."

"But it did. I had to report it."

Ellen sighed. "I know that. I just wish we still had that sample."

Sheila knew that they followed the typical lab policy of discarding samples after five days unless instructed otherwise.

"I labeled the second sample myself, handed it to your tech personally, to Jenny, and it showed a completely different result than the first one."

Ellen shook her head. "Weird shit going on down there lately."

"Such as?"

"Well, that screw-up, for one." She looked at Sheila sheepishly. "Jenny temporarily lost the sample you gave her." Sheila felt herself redden with rage. Ellen reached for her arm. "But she found it of course. Obviously. Jenny said she's sure she racked it but then it was nowhere to be found. Then there it was again, a few hours later, on the rack. I don't understand it. I've got a tight staff, they're dedicated . . ." She shrugged.

"No system is foolproof."

"You don't believe me." She looked hurt. Not defensive, just hurt.

The elevator doors opened and Sheila fairly leaped to escape.

"Gotta go. Don't worry. I'm sure it won't happen again."

She meant that. Ellen was tops.

So how come her department screwed up?

PAUL

Paul pulled up to Sheila's house and smiled. Quaint. Not a word he used often, but it fit. Early New England. Light gray, weathered shingles, white shutters on all the windows. He imagined yellow tulips sprouting in the spring. The dormant lawn looked well tended. He figured Tethys mowed it for her. They gave their employees a lot of perks.

Sheila stepped out of the house before he shut off his car. Too bad. He was hoping to see the inside, check out her bedroom. He laughed to himself. Maybe she was a little out of his league, but he could hope. Anyway, he had some big issues at hand.

"Hi," she said when she reached the car.

"Hey. Did you eat yet?"

"No, just coffee." She opened her door and got in. "I thought maybe we could pick something along the way."

"No need. I've got two Starbucks real coffees, not the dessert kind for wimps, and two scones."

Sheila reached for the small brown bag. "You wouldn't happen to have a maple scone in here . . ."

Paul grinned. "Yep. Two of them. I went out on a limb, assuming everyone likes them as much as I do."

"Like? I *love* these. It's the only kind I like enough to justify the calories. Thanks."

"It's the only kind worth buying." He winked and put the car in drive, balancing his own scone on his lap. "We should reach Manchester in about forty minutes if we don't encounter much school-bus residua."

Sheila munched a bite of walnuts and maple icing.

"That's some vocabulary, Paul."

He grinned. "You sure this is okay with your boss?"

"Absolutely. Made morning rounds and don't have outpatients until two-o'clock. I normally catch up on my charts during this stretch, but they can wait."

"I really appreciate this."

She seemed flustered by his gratitude. "De nada."

He pointed. "So, cute little house you have there. Cozy."

She smiled. "I like it. Love it, really. All those years living in dorms or apartments makes you really appreciate having your own house."

"So this is your first?"

"Uh-huh. Why?"

Paul was surprised. He had started his grownup life so much younger. This was his fourth house if you counted that condo. And here was Sheila, only a little younger than he, never married, no kids, first house.

Wait. Right before Coogan got hit . . .

"Sorry to jump around but I just remembered the conversation we were having right before Coog's accident. You were just about to explain your last name."

"Look, shouldn't we first talk about what we're going to say to this trustee?"

She was stalling. He didn't want to talk about his life either but hoped she'd reveal a little about herself.

"We have plenty of time. Come on, tell me about you. It will get my mind off the paternity thing."

"All right. Maiden name was Donnelly. Both parents Irish. They died years ago. And I married a nice Japanese boy right out of college. Hideki Takamura. Everyone just called him Dek."

Paul watched her smile as she recalled what he could tell was a happy time.

"We had our future all planned out. He'd get a job then I'd finish med school. I'd go into a residency, complete it, and then we'd have two little Amer-Asian children, a boy and a girl. Dek Jr., and Mary after my grandmother."

She paused, smiling. He wondered what else she was remembering.

"We were right on track. I was completing a great residency at BU Medical Center. Dek worked for JCAHO, a government body that approves hospitals and nursing homes. He was gearing up for a promotion and was knee deep in an investigation. Some kind of conflict of interest. Not sure what, exactly, but Dek was excited. He said as soon as he sent in his report, he knew he'd get promoted. We were both thrilled. It was like things couldn't get any better."

Paul smiled along with her. He was a little jealous. He remembered when he had felt that kind of boundless enthusiasm. When life couldn't get any better. Lucky girl. Perfect life, compared to what he'd gone through.

"And then it was all over. Dek was dead. I was working over at BU when I got the call. His motorcycle had skidded off the road and he was gone."

"I'm so sorry."

He'd never dreamed she was a widow.

She kept talking, as if she needed to keep going. "I was destroyed. I wasn't raised in a very emotional home. My parents weren't demonstrative or affectionate. You were always supposed to hold everything close to the breast. 'Never let 'em see you cry,' " she said in a harsh Irish accent.

Paul was stunned. He'd been raised that way too. He'd seen her as Snow White, Pollyanna. Perfect, sunny, and happy all the time. He'd envisioned her singing as she did house work. And now to hear all this . . .

Maybe she wasn't out of his league. Maybe she *would* understand his circumstances . . . accept him and his past. Even if the Kaplan trustee couldn't help, this talk was making the drive worthwhile.

"I was good about holding things in. Very good. Mum died of lung cancer and Da of heart disease a year apart. Damn chain-smoking. Thank you, Philip Morris. They made it to my graduation from medical school. They were so proud. At least they saw that. Then they were gone. I had to deal with their deaths and keep up with my residency, but I held it together."

He could see Sheila clenching her jaw, reliving the sadness.

"I managed by clinging to Dek with everything I had. He *was* everything I had. Training and Dek. They were my life. When he died, it was too much. I fell apart. I looked fine, but inside I felt like I'd died too."

Paul swallowed hard. He knew exactly how that felt, to watch everything in your life fall apart, and then to try to go on. The world expected it.

Easier said than done. If anyone knew that, Paul did.

He reached over and touched her hand, squeezed it, gently. She squeezed back. Paul thanked God he didn't drive a standard and could hold her hand as long as she'd let him.

"Bill Gilchrist saved me. Head of the whole hospital and he interviewed me personally. He was the only one who understood what was wrong, but he hired me anyway. He gave me a lot of leeway those first few months. Really took me under his wing."

What chance did he have? A cable installer who reads books to terminal patients, writes unpublished novels, and lives on the Milltown border in a tired colonial?

She said, "Bill Gilchrist . . . I was so intimidated back then, and now . . . he's just a regular person after all."

Sheila took a deep breath let it out. He could hear the whoosh, feel her grip relax. She took back her hand and wiped her eyes.

"I'm sorry. I can't believe I just dumped all that on you. I didn't mean to. I just—you're a good listener."

"Well, I've only seen you at work. I wondered about the rest of your life, your past mostly. Now I know."

"Now you know." She nodded. "Okay, your turn. Let's hear your past. Hope it's sunnier than mine."

If only his were one tenth as sunny. But now was not the time.

He saw the sign for Manchester.

"Hey look, we're here."

That was close.

SHEILA

Paul parked in front of a white shingled house that sported a navy blue wooden swinging sign. Gold letters read *Alfred B. George, Attorney at Law.*

"Here's the place. He'd better be more helpful than that idiot Kaplan."

Sheila grimaced. "We can only hope."

They walked up the wooden steps. Sheila noticed that all the houses on the street looked old but well preserved. Painted wooden shingles, white trim, shutters. A seaside Stepford village.

"Come on, let's go meet this guy."

Alfred B. George had an appropriate name. Seeing him, Sheila guessed he'd been a nerdy know-it-all kid who'd remained that way when he grew up. Skinny and balding, he wore a light blue button-down shirt with a plain navy blue tie, and spoke in a whine.

"Have a seat please. Hmm, let's not waste any time. You called about Kaplan Biologicals?" He looked at his watch and tapped his pen on his desk. Mont Blanc. Tap-tap-tap. "Is that correct?"

"Yes." Sheila saw he was in a hurry. "We want to know who bought the assets."

"Lee T. Swann."

"Who?"

Alfred B. George pointed to a piece of paper.

"Right here. Lee T. Swann. He bought all the assets. That's what you wanted to know, that's what I got for you. If you want a list of all the creditors who didn't get paid, I can get you that. But you specifically asked for the name of the party who purchased the assets of Kaplan Biologicals."

Sheila and Paul looked at each other.

"Yes," Paul said. "That's all we need. What was his name again?"

"Lee T. Swann. Two N's. Want his address?"

Paul scribbled down the name and poised his pen. "Yes, please."

"160 Milk Street, Suite two-five-seven, Boston 02109." Alfred B. George rose. "Will that be all? I hate to rush but I've got clients waiting."

Sheila could see Paul's face redden and concluded that one of his anger triggers had been pulled.

"That's all, Mister George," she said. "Thank you so much for your time." She hoped he noted the sarcasm.

"My time, yes," he said as Paul and Sheila rose. "My time will cost one hundred dollars."

Paul scowled. "One hundred—? We were here only five minutes."

"I bill at two hundred an hour. It took me nearly a half hour to research this and see you." He looked at his watch. "Twenty-seven minutes exactly. That rounds to half an hour."

"That's fine, Mister George." Sheila pulled out a check. "I'll pay it. Thank you for the information."

"Sheila, you can't pay. This is my problem."

"I may yet get a paper out of this. Consider it a research expense."

She slipped the lawyer the check and they left.

"That was quick and painless," Sheila said. "Now what?"

"Now we go visit Mister Swann and ask him what the hell is going on. I'm happy to see where he's located."

"Why is that?"

"There's this great sub shop near there. It's not a classy place by any means but you've got to try it. After we see Swann, we'll grab three subs. I'll bring one home for Coog."

"I usually try to eat healthy but if it's such a special place, I suppose I can bend."

"You won't be sorry."

"Do they have eggplant parm subs?"

He grinned. "I should have known you'd ask that. It's amazing how alike we are. Of course they have eggplant parm. It's the only one worth getting."

As they got back into Paul's Explorer, Sheila looked over at him. He was cute in an L.L. Bean-ad kind of way. Not dashing like Bill. Not *GQ*. But solid. A man with substance.

"Okay," she said. "Your turn to talk about yourself." Seeing his hands tighten on the wheel, she added, "I don't mean the big heart-wrenching events, just some little things. Where you went to school or what you wanted to be when you grew up. That kind of stuff."

"Okay. That I can do."

Good. The combination of the sugar, caffeine, and his promise to divulge some of his past stirred up a strange feeling. She felt like a teenage girl who suddenly discovers that she likes her best friend as more than a friend, likes him "that way."

"I always wanted to be a teacher," he said. "A high school English teacher. Not a very high aspiration, some might say, but I couldn't imagine anything more rewarding than talking about books all day, and teaching kids about them. Books can bring the world to your doorstep, you know?"

Sheila nodded tentatively. She'd learned almost everything she knew from textbooks but sensed he meant literature.

"One story can change someone's whole life. You see a kid who's ready to commit suicide and then she reads *The Diary of Anne Frank*, and all of sudden her life isn't so bad. Saved. Look at *Romeo and Juliet*. Do you have any idea how many times that story has been retold in different ways?"

Sheila nodded. "Perhaps too many."

He looked at her and smiled. "Yeah. Perhaps. But I've always loved books. I guess I wanted to share that. When I was little, books were my best friends. I was a lonely kid but I had my books, my storytellers, each one of the authors reaching out to tell me something about life. That was how I felt.

"My father was in the military. We'd move as soon as I'd hook up with new friends, or at least that's how it seemed. I have a little brother who had no problem with moving all the time. He thought it was an adventure. I hated it. I was a shy little kid."

Sheila laughed. "It's so funny to hear you say that. I would never have pegged you as shy. You seem more a rough-and-tumble type. The way you attacked the guy in the Hummer and punched that car the other day, you strike me more as more of a Heathcliff than a Walter Mitty. And before you give me credit for reading *Wuthering Heights*, I didn't. I saw the movie."

"Heathcliff was a sensitive guy too. He simply hid it by being tough." Paul gave a short, harsh laugh. "Like me. Been there, done that. You talked about your parents making you hold in your emotions. How do you think it was to be raised by a Marine? Anger was acceptable, sadness was not. Weakness too was verboten. The only thing Dad encouraged was fighting. Creep. But I had my books. They were my hidden indulgence and he was none the wiser."

"He encouraged fighting? Did he hit you?"

"Of course he hit me. He figured if he batted me around enough it would make me tough. Got news for you, if a kid is crying and you hit him, it makes him cry more."

"Didn't your mother stop him?"

"She was raised by a Marine herself and married Dear Old Dad when she was young. Went along with everything he did. She was soft with me when he wasn't around but would never publicly defy him. Bob, my brother, he ate it up. He was just like Dad. Creep junior. He rarely got hit."

Paul stopped talking and stared in his rearview mirror. It seemed he was recalling a bad memory that he wanted to keep to himself.

"Look in your sideview mirror. Don't turn around, just look. See that silver Honda a few cars back?"

Sheila looked. "I guess so. I see silver. I can't tell the make."

"It's a Honda Accord. I think it's following us. It got on the highway when we did. I swear it's been behind us since Manchester."

Normally she would have laughed, said he was being paranoid. But now . . .

She scrunched down in her seat. "Who's driving it?"

"Can't tell. Too far away and the windows are shaded. Let's slow down and see what happens." Paul slowed to fifty and eased into the right lane. The Honda slowed as well. Finally Paul pulled onto the shoulder.

"What are you doing?" she cried. "Don't stop! What if he wants to kill us?"

"If he wanted us dead, we'd be dead already. This guy is fishing, trying to see where we're going, what we're doing, what we know."

Sheila and Paul sat and watched the Honda cruise past them. Her stomach churned the maple scone.

"Now what?"

Paul hit the gas and they started moving again.

"Now he's in front where we can watch him. If he really was following us, and I'm not being paranoid, he'll stay just in front. He can track us from there."

"How do we know it's not someone who's just going to Boston like half the other people on this road?"

"I'm not taking any chances."

Paul swerved the wheel and abruptly took the next exit. As they went into the turn Sheila saw the Honda's brake lights go on. He *was* watching them.

Paul shot her a glance. "Believe me now?"

Sheila nodded. "I wish I didn't."

"It's okay, we'll go the back roads. He'll never find us."

Sheila stuck her fingertip in her mouth and started chewing on the nail. There was a time to kick bad habits and this wasn't it.

Paul took her hand and eased it away from her mouth.

"You're not in this alone. I'm here. Don't worry."

She looked at him, his image blurred from tears. "Thank you."

For a few minutes they rode in silence, Sheila focusing all her attention on the rearview. The Honda was nowhere in sight, but that didn't lessen her fear.

"You okay over there?"

"I think so," she said, trying to keep the quiver from her voice. "Why don't you finish your story? That'll get my mind off things." She saw Paul stiffen. "You were talking about your childhood."

He half-grinned. "I'd rather be tailed by a mystery man than talk about that, but for you, I'll do it." He sighed. "Where was I? Oh, yeah. By the time I reached high school, I'd been to six different schools and was a ball of repressed emotions. The only one Dad approved of was anger so I focused all my energy there. It was how I had been conditioned. I was ready to explode."

Paul swallowed hard. Sheila saw his jaw clench. She reached for his hand. Warm and rough, like the rest of his exterior. He gave her hand a squeeze.

"Mom bought me a punching bag and that helped a lot. Then she encouraged me to join the wrestling team. Great outlet. With all my rage, I was damn good at it. Next to going out and killing people for the government, a/k/a soldier, which is what my dad had planned for me, this was the next best way to blow off steam. I won all kinds of trophies and Dad couldn't have been happier."

"Were you happy?"

"I was. But I had no intention of joining any branch of the military. I planned to go to college for English and become a teacher. With all the moving around we did, I knew I might not qualify for an academic scholarship, but maybe for wrestling. I couldn't wait till the day when I could tell Dad that I was going to college to teach a whole new generation of little sissies. That's what he called me. I knew he'd flip out but there'd be nothing he could do. I even considered joining The Peace Corps just to piss him off."

Sheila smiled. "I've heard lots of people join just for that reason. Spite."

Paul laughed. "Well, at first it went just like I wanted. I got a full ride at Bridgewater State College right here in Mass. Not Ivy League, but they have a good teaching program. When I told Dad he went nuts. Almost broke my jaw. But it was worth it to say, 'I'm an adult now, and I'll do whatever I want.' "

She cringed. She had never been hit. Never even spanked. Couldn't imagine it.

Bastard, she thought.

"Good for you. I don't know if I would have turned out so well. So you did go to college then? I know you must have."

"Well, there's more to it but enough for now. Suffice to say, I did go, but then my life fell apart because of something stupid. And then came Rose, then Coogan. And now here I am—or rather, here we are."

He was still holding her hand.

He'd said plenty for one day, she thought. More than she'd expected. For someone who'd lived through such abuse, he seemed almost unscathed. Smart and handsome . . .

"I'm glad you told me this. Now I don't feel like the only one who got her heart dragged through the mud."

"Most people get their hearts shredded at some point. It's all about how they put them back together. Some never do. They just leave them in pieces."

What a guy, Sheila though. Besides Dek, most of the sensitive guys she'd ever known were gay. This one was not only straight, but sexy. This guy was, in a very real sense, something else. Nothing she would have thought she was looking for, but exactly what she needed. He had opened some long-closed doors in her.

Paul slowed the car.

"What is it?"

"Swann is supposed to be at 160 Milk Street but that says *Mailboxes and More*. This can't be right."

"Well, pull over and we'll ask inside. Maybe suite two-five-seven is upstairs."

Paul parallel parked the SUV seemingly without effort. Sheila was impressed. With all her achievements, she couldn't parallel park to save her life.

"Why don't I talk to the clerk?"

He nodded with a tight smile.

A young girl with pink hair, too much black eye makeup, and piercings through her lips and eyebrows sat at the counter reading Nietzsche's *Beyond Good and Evil*. When she saw them she stuck a black painted fingernail in her page.

"Can I help you?"

She had a sweet smile and a pretty face. Sheila never understood why so many kids felt a need to deface their natural beauty.

"Yes, we were given this address as someone's office. Does a Lee Swann work here?"

"No, sorry." She cocked her head.

"Do you have any offices upstairs?"

"Just a hair salon."

"But we were given this address . . . suite two-five-seven."

She laughed. "Lots of people do that—call their mailbox a suite. Makes them seem more important."

"Yeah," Paul said in a low voice. "Weird. Why am I not surprised?"

When they were back on the sidewalk, he said, "I can't believe it. If this was legitimate, why would he give the lawyer a mail drop as an address?"

"I don't know. I'll check the Internet later and see what I can find on Mister Lee T. Swann. And I *will* find something."

He managed a smile and kissed her cheek. "Promise?"

She touched the spot, imprinting the memory warmth of his lips on her cheek. She was starting to fall for this guy. And that was not such a bad thing.

"Promise."

"And now how about a sub at Capone's?

Sheila was about to say yes when she saw a silver Honda turn at the next corner. She could have sworn the driver was watching them as he passed out of sight.

The same car that had followed them? No way to be sure, but her stomach turned.

"I . . . I'm not hungry."

BILL

Henry brought in cucumber sandwiches for Abra and a ham and Swiss on rye with a pickle for Bill.

"Drink, sir?"

Bill looked at Abra's pictures and was struck by one of Robbie and April taken at Christmas last year. They'd grown so much since then, and he'd barely been around to see them. Before long their childhoods would be gone. Elise was right—too much time spent at Tethys. Lately, he felt suffocated. Too many loose ends that he was expected to tie together. Too many fires to put out.

Damn it, he'd given everything, everything to Proteus and to this hospital, but didn't know how much longer he could keep it up. Right now there was too much at stake, too much that could fall apart; he couldn't let his guard down for a minute.

But when would it stop? When would he ever be able to relax?

"Drink, sir?" Henry touched his shoulder.

Bill was dying for a dose of Jack but needed to go back to work after lunch. He opted for Henry's special iced tea. He then turned to his sister.

"So they're off track then?" Abra said, holding the tiny sandwich in her tiny twisted hand.

"Yes. Sheila found KB-twenty-six on her own. At first I panicked, thinking it would be a disaster, but it's perfect. If I keep pointing her to it, what can she possibly find? Kaplan can't tell her anything—it would be self immolation. He may be burned out, but he won't push himself over the edge."

"He's had a difficult time since the failure of his company."

Good old Abra, Bill thought. Always feeling sorry for people. Even the wrong ones.

"Whatever, Kaplan is a dead end. He can't tell them about

where his company's assets went because he doesn't know. Kaplan Biologicals is dead and gone without a trace."

"You're sure?"

"Very sure. I took care of it myself."

Abra looked at him doubtfully. "It's easy enough to find who bought the assets. It's public record. If Sheila gets close, Billy, I want to be the one to tell her."

He usually let her pull the older sister routine, but not this time.

Bill didn't mention that Sheila reran the DNA, or that he'd switched the sample. He shielded Abra whenever possible.

Sometimes he felt like a traitor to his sister, working so closely with Mama in Switzerland, keeping Abra on a need-to-know basis. But he had no choice. *He* was the one Mama trusted to keep it all together, at any cost. Not Abra.

"It's all taken care of. She won't find out a thing."

He had this under control. Why couldn't Abra accept that? Paul and Sheila would run in circles and get tired. And despite Tanesha's threats, she wouldn't be a factor. He hated bloodshed but Tanesha was the last piece and then their lives could go back to normal.

"Well, I trust you, Billy." Abra smiled at him and wheeled herself over to the couch. "What would I do without you?"

She patted his hand and he felt his heart swell.

He *did* do good work. And Sheila and Rosko *would* reach a dead end and give up. They'd have no other options.

But he'd keep an eye on them to make sure.

He looked back at the family picture over the mantle. Work could wait. His kids couldn't.

———···———

"Daddy!" April yelled as he walked into the playroom.

She had morning kindergarten and had been home a couple hours. Her dark hair was braided and her blues shone with delighted surprise. She didn't often see her Daddy at this time of day. She and Nanny Maureen were playing a letter game.

April showed him a white card with "qu" on it.

"Nanny's teaching me about q today. Can't use q without u. Ever. Queen, quiet, quality." She took a little bow.

He clapped. "That's wonderful, April. Thanks, Maureen."

The shy, blond, British girl offered a crooked-tooth smile. She never talked much to him but the kids adored her. April said she was a chatterbox when the grown ups weren't around.

"Daddy really missed you kids today so I thought we'd pick up Robbie from school and go see a movie."

"Yay!"

"Go get your coat."

April ran to get her shoes and jacket while Bill told Nanny Maureen to relay their whereabouts to Elise when she got home from her exercise class.

He buckled his daughter into her booster seat then drove to Robbie's school. Bill felt buoyant. He couldn't wait to see Robbie's surprise. Seeing his father shouldn't be such a monumental thing, but Bill had been too absent a parent.

He went into the principal's office and told them his son had a doctor's appointment. Minutes later Robbie came down.

"Dad, what are you doing here? Is Mom okay?"

"You've got a doctor's appointment, Robbie," April said, giving him an obvious wink.

"No I don't."

"Robbieeeee." She pulled his arm and kept winking her eye.

They got outside and she said, "Daddy's taking us to the movies for a surprise because he misses us."

"Really?"

Bill smiled. "Yup. Just us. No reason except that I wanted to see you guys. I even skipped an important meeting. You up for a movie? Tons of candy and overly buttered popcorn? Those big blue slushes?"

April jumped up and down and Robbie grinned, his equivalent of extreme excitement.

"You rock, Dad."

Bill hugged him and kissed the top of his head. "*You* rock."

He opened the car door and ushered them in.

"I have no idea what's playing or when but if there's nothing for a while we'll get ice cream and play some video games at the theater. Sound good?"

They gave him high fives and started chanting, "Daddy rocks, Daddy rocks!"

As he drove by Tethys, unavoidable to get to the highway, he hesitated. If it weren't for this place, and its fruits, April wouldn't be the energetic kid she was now. Despite his complaints about the pressure, he loved that he had been able to cure his daughter, could cure others. Maybe he was obsessed with work but anyone who did what he did would be. Saving a life was the greatest thing anyone could do. If Sheila didn't stop sniffing around, if she got too close to the truth, well . . .

Didn't matter what he'd told Abra. No way in hell was he letting all this fall apart because one woman wouldn't leave well enough alone.

Bill looked in the mirror, gave his son a wave and released the brake pedal he hadn't realized he'd pressed.

He told himself to forget Tethys. Today was all about his kids.

ABRA

Billy seemed so sure these little bumps in the process were nearly over that Abra decided not to spend any more time worrying about them. He was competent to take care of matters. When he'd left, Abra logged into her computer to see what the Tethys Foundation could help with today.

She read through her email requests. So many people suffering. She wished she could help everyone, but how much could only one person do? She was already spending Tethys's profits to help as many people as she could.

Next to giving people babies, this was her most fulfilling mission.

She had an appointment in a few minutes with a desperate woman. Abra didn't know what she wanted or why it couldn't be handled over the phone, but she'd insisted. Abra was achy today and didn't want to venture out so she told the woman to come here and she'd see what she could do.

In the meantime she replied to a missionary about a severely deformed child he'd found in the jungles of Zambia. The girl needed extensive plastic surgery to correct a hideously deformed face.

She typed an email: *Bring her to the Floating Hospital in Boston and tell them to send me the bill. If you need help with transport, we'll take care of her.*

Abra also approved funds for an MRI machine at a strapped hospital in Bolivia, and some electric wheelchairs for Belize City. She copied her accountant on all.

Funds . . . she had all she needed to pursue Proteus, and plenty left over. All because she listened to that young broker, Ernest Tinsdale, who'd urged her on a winter day back in eighty-six to buy Microsoft. As that stock soared and split again and again, she made Ernest her financial advisor. For the last twenty years she'd listened to him and his advice had been flawless.

She'd made great strides in balancing the thalidomide scales. Improved so many lives. Surely that helped atone for the sins of her parents. She had long since forgiven them, and wondered now if, in the idealism of her youth, she'd treated them too harshly.

Images of the thalidomide babies flashed through her head . . . no, she had not treated them too harshly at all.

She rolled away from her desk and wheeled herself to the family room. Exactly on time, the doorbell rang. She pressed a button on her remote and the double doors swung inward.

A young woman in her early twenties, with lifeless brown hair, battle-fatigued eyes, and a ragged coat, walked in with a little boy. Even before the child took off his Scooby Doo ski hat and exposed his bald head, Abra knew. The pale face, and the wide, haunted eyes were testament to what he'd gone through, and why they had come.

Leukemia.

Tethys used to treat children, used to cure Leukemia, but no more.

This meeting could lead only to heartache, but she saw no way out of it now. They walked over to Abra and the child stared at her.

"Stop it, Ben. " The mother nudged him, then looked at Abra. "I'm sorry. We didn't know you were . . ."

"In a wheelchair? We all have our troubles. Please sit."

The mother and son huddled on the huge couch. Ben, fascinated by all the cages, kept trying to get up. The woman restrained him, grabbed his hand.

"Go ahead," Abra said. "Look at all the creatures while I talk to your mother. They can't get out or hurt you."

He smiled and ran to the terraria.

It must be like a zoo to him, Abra thought, glad for the distraction. She knew what his mother would ask and dreaded the answer she'd have to give.

"I'm Emma Smallwood. That's Ben."

"Abra. I'm Abra. How can I help you?"

Tears filled the woman's eyes. "He's dying," she said softly.

Emma pulled a strand of hair with her hand and brushed it on her lips. A nervous habit. Abra had seen so much death. It was never easy. And losing children . . . nothing worse.

"Leukemia?"

Abra gripped her wheelchair as the boy ran his hands along the glass of the cages, filled with wonder at her lizards and spiders.

"They say there's nothing anyone can do. But I heard about your program, your success with hopeless cases. I was hoping we could try it."

Little Ben was suffering. Wasn't that the point of Proteus, to end this kind of pain? Prevent anyone from going through what she had?

Abra began to shake her head.

"No!" The woman twisted her hair frantically. "Please don't say no. I don't have any money and my doctor said my insurance is tapped out, but I'll do anything. Please. I could work here, be your housekeeper. Anything. Please."

The strand of hair poised by her lips, waiting for an answer.

"It's not that. We'd give it to you if it would help but we can't use it on children. Only adults."

Abra hated that restriction but it was the caveat of Proteus. Never used on children during the trials. But weren't they the ones they most wanted to help?

"Why not? I don't care about side effects. It doesn't matter. I just don't want to lose my boy." Tears rolled down her cheeks.

Abra glanced over at the boy, smiling as he gingerly touched the glass. He was intrigued by her tortoise and thankfully not paying attention to their conversation.

"We can't. It won't work on children." The lie made her grip her chair. "I'm sorry. It just wouldn't be effective."

It pained Abra to look into the woman's eyes and sentence her son to death. VG723 could cure Ben, give him a long, healthy life, create a bloodline of healthy people. But she couldn't say that.

Giving it to children would lead inevitably to questions . . . unanswerable questions that would lead to investigations. And then Proteus would be finished.

No, this child would have to die.

"I'm sorry. We cannot help you. But why don't you take him to Disney World? We'll pay for it."

"Disney World! Goddamn Disney World? That's it?" The woman stood, tugging incessantly at her hair, brushing it against her cheek. "What good will that do?"

"It will make Ben happy. I'll get you a private flight, the best hotel, admission to the parks, a driver . . . everything you need. Stay as long as you like." Abra looked down, breaking the eye contact. "It's all I can do. I'm sorry."

Damn Mickey Mouse! She was throwing the boy to the white-cell wolves, yet what else could she do?

"I don't want to go Disney World!" the mother shouted.

"I do," Ben whispered in the shadow of his mother's scream. "It's all right, Mom. I know I'm going to die. But I really would like to go. I can tell the kids in Heaven all about it."

Silence from the adults.

Abra opened her mouth, tempted to say the hell with it. Save the child. Make the mother sign a confidentiality agreement. No one would have to know.

She wiped her eyes with her twisted hands.

No! She couldn't risk it. Couldn't. Not for just one boy. Someday

Proteus would save millions of children, but not this boy. Not now

What must he think about her, this tiny broken woman offering him a trip in exchange for his life? She couldn't bring herself to look at Emma.

Abra knew Ben would probably come home wearing a Mickey Mouse T-shirt in a coffin.

"Please, Mama," he said. "Please can we go?" His dull eyes showed a spark. "Please?"

The mother gave a weary nod. "Yes, Ben. We'll go. We'll go today. Right away. And you'll have more fun than you ever had in your whole life."

Emma seemed to have aged since she came in. Tethys had been her last hope, and now that hope was gone.

Abra showed them out and left a message for Billy to make the arrangements.

"God bless that little boy—and forgive me for what I had to do."

But what about her? Would God bless her for Proteus, or damn her?

Abra wondered if hell could be any worse than this afternoon.

BILL

Bill and the kids walked out of the movie, talking about their favorite parts. April was running around Robbie, singing the theme song. Just seeing her with such lung capacity thrilled Bill. His little miracle.

Whenever he saw her it affirmed the choices he'd made. Sure, he'd love to come home every day, share dinner with them, watch TV, ask them about school. On weekends go camping with them or to ball games. But if he'd done all that, April would be a different child. A very sick child.

If he could have told Elise, then she wouldn't nag him so. Then she'd understand.

But he'd never tell her. Because then she'd be like all others. Asking, "Why is her blood different from ours? Where did that nose come from?" or about other superficial traits. Who cared?

At the end of the day, if the kid you gave birth to or fathered was healthy and happy with no physical suffering, who wouldn't opt for that?

These thoughts prompted him to turn on his cell phone and check his voicemail. He stiffened when he heard Abra's message. He called her right away.

"Abra, what is it? I didn't understand your message. Please stop crying, just tell me."

Bill handed the kids a handful of quarters and told them to play some games. He felt like someone had sucker punched him in the gut as Abra told him about the little boy.

Why did *he* always have to be the strong one? Just once, why couldn't she be the heavy? The one to do the dirty work? Because she couldn't. Wasn't in her. Saying no tore her apart. That was why she was pushing for public disclosure, to help more people.

"Abra, you did what you had to do, so please calm down. I'll go see them right now and take care of it . . . send them to Florida."

He hung up. Killing a child. That's what this amounted to. Looking that little boy and his mother in the face and then refusing to help. Killing him.

April giggled on a carousel horse. Such a picture of health. He pictured the little boy. It wasn't fair. Someday this wouldn't be an issue, but for now he had to deal with the harsh realities of the clinical trial.

"Come on kids, Daddy has to go back to work. It's an emergency."

Robbie walked over with his sister who got off the sculpted horse.

"But you said we were going for dinner at the Roadhouse with Mom remember?"

This was what it always boiled down to. Quality time with his kids, or saving lives.

———■■■———

Bill introduced himself to the mother and son.

"I'm Ben," the boy said and put out his pale hand to shake Bill's. "Thanks, Doctor Gilchrist."

Thanks for what? Letting you die when I could easily help?

Marge sat at her desk, teary eyed. "Bill, Abra said to set them up for Disney. I made some calls and booked them a flight for tonight."

"Thank you, Marge."

"I bought Disney Park Hopper passes and tickets to Universal and put them in a hotel where everything's included. Oh, and a rental car."

He nodded to Marge and then asked Emma, "Is there anyone else you'd like to bring?"

Ben jumped up but Emma pulled him back.

"No, we're fine." She didn't look fine. She was having her life ripped out too. "You've already been very generous. I could never afford to—"

Bill crouched before the boy. "What were you going to say, Ben?"

"My sister. I can't go without my little sister, Amy. She's only four."

Bill had to wipe the tears from his own eyes. "Marge?" His voice cracked. "Can you get Amy on that flight too? Oh and plenty of spending money so they can do whatever they want."

He was amazed Abra had been able to turn them away. She had more resolve than he'd given her credit for.

"Thank you," the woman said, twirling her hair and wiping her eyes.

Bill wondered how April would carry on if she lost her older brother.

"Emma, Ben looks a little dehydrated. I'd like to just give him some fluids, keep him here a few hours. He'll be better able to travel then. Why don't you give Marge your daughter's information, then go home and pack and get your little girl. You can go to the airport from here."

She nodded but couldn't speak.

"Come on, Ben, let's get you ready to fly."

Ben had a lilt in his step, the only one now who was happy.

Bill led the boy down the hall and through the tunnels to the hospital. He set him up in a private room and then went into an empty restroom to call Abra.

She answered in a sleepy voice.

He said, "Abra, I can't do it. Go to the lab and grab me a brown-haired, blue-eyed, Caucasian stem. His mother thinks we're rehydrating him so we've got just a few hours. When he begins to improve, she'll assume it was a miracle brought on by his joy."

"But we decided—"

"I know, but I can't look in that kid's eyes and write him off. No one will know. I need you down at the hospital to help me."

She hung up without saying anything. Bill had to smile.

This was why Sheila *had* to stop, why he had to make her drop it. Even if he had to kill her with his bare hands.

SHEILA

There, Sheila thought as she surveyed her front room. Ready.

She should have been ready for a nap, considering the amount of sleep she'd had, but was too wired to be tired.

Lust.

It had kept her tossing and turning all night. How long had it been?

Too long. Not since Dek. This longing to touch Paul gave her a light, frothy feeling. She'd lusted for Bill in a way, but that was different. She'd never lain awake nights thinking of touching unattainable Bill.

But Paul . . . the other day when he had kissed her . . . if Coog hadn't been in the house, who knew what might have happened? Something long-buried had started bubbling. She might have lost it . . . ripped his clothes off . . .

She sighed and mentally threw cold water on her face.

If nothing else, lust trumped paranoia hands down, pushing her fears to the periphery.

She'd have liked to have seen Paul first thing this morning, but he'd wanted some father-son time with Coogan. So she invited him over for dinner and some Internet surfing. She didn't actually tell him she was going to *cook* him dinner, so she didn't feel guilty about ordering from Joseph's

Serving takeout was for Paul's own good. Anyone would prefer Joseph's cooking to hers.

The official reason for his visit might be more detective work, this time trying to find Lee Swann. But she figured they both knew it could be something more. God, she hoped so.

She'd spent most of the day cleaning her house and setting candles. Nothing more romantic than candlelight.

She looked at her watch. Paul would be walking in soon. She ran and checked herself in the bathroom mirror.

———···———

When she heard Paul's car pulling in, she started toward the door but stopped, forcing herself to wait until he knocked. An eternity. Finally . . .

"Hi, Paul. Come on in."

He wore a brown crew neck sweater, cotton, not wool. Not itchy. It looked soft and she had to restrain herself from reaching out to touch it.

"Hey, Sheila. Nice place. You look nice too. That color is good on you."

Sheila smiled, glad she opted for the green blouse. "Want a tour?"

"Sure. Here, I brought some wine. I wasn't sure what you were making so I brought a bottle of red and one of white."

"It's Italian food. Actually, Joseph's restaurant made it. I just need to cook the ravioli and heat the sauce." She struck a dramatic pose with the back of a hand against her forehead. "A daunting task, but I'll endure."

"I love Joseph's. Ever had their lobster ravioli?"

Sheila smirked. This was too perfect. "It's the main course."

"A woman after my own heart. Okay, let's see this place."

She walked him around the open kitchen / living room area. She had white appliances but vowed to buy all stainless steel as soon as the student loans were paid off. As if. How old would she be when that happened?

She reached for his hand, planning to walk him upstairs, but stopped herself. The way she was feeling she knew they might just jump into bed. Better leave upstairs for later.

"Here's the plan," she said. "We'll have some wine and dinner, then look up Swann on the computer and see what we can find."

Paul nodded. "Sounds great." He brushed her face with the side of his hand and looked into her eyes. "But what do we do after that?"

She smiled. "I'm sure we can think of something."

By seven they were finishing their Tiramisu. Two glasses of wine had relaxed Sheila.

She reached over and touched his hand. "Why don't you go over and boot up my computer while I get these dishes."

"I'll get the dishes."

"Hey, I invited you. When I come to your house you can do the dishes."

Paul rose and turned on the computer while Sheila loaded the dishwasher. Minutes later she logged onto the Internet. Paul pulled up a kitchen chair and sat beside her.

She said, "This site, CEOexpress.com, searches for company execs. If Swann bought up all the assets, he's probably the head of something."

She typed in his name and waited.

No results found.

Undaunted, she said, "That's all right, I've got lots of sites to try. I'll look up his personal information. We can track him down and speak to him if he's local."

The screen read, "Did you mean Lynn Swan?"

"That's the football player, right? From the seventies?"

"Yeah. Steelers. I doubt he's our guy."

"Let's check out some media searches. Bizjournals.com should yield something."

Sheila scanned field to field, unable to believe nothing was coming up.

"Besides the football hero, there's no one out there named Swann who's done anything newsworthy. Where the heck is this guy? Let me try virtualchase.com."

She waited, flying through screen after useless screen.

"Here. In the public records search. I've got his purchase of the Kaplan assets, but we already knew that. It lists that same damn address on Milk Street."

She checked the handwritten list of snoop sites Dek had made for her years ago. Some no longer valid but most still up. She squinted to see the pencil-written notes on the yellow lined paper.

"This is stretching but let me try crimetime.com."

"What's that?"

"It will show if he's ever been convicted of anything." Though she was looking at the screen, she noticed Paul stiffen out of the corner of her eye. "What?"

"I doubt he's ever been arrested. Come on, that would have shown up somewhere else."

"Maybe not. There are still other sites, but let's just go with this one. Maybe he's locked up right now. It happens."

No results found.

Paul rose and turned away. "Okay, that's enough searching. We can't find him."

She wondered why he was so eager to stop when she still had half a page of sites left.

"Well, there others," she said, "but you might be right. Something should have turned up somewhere by now. Crimetime. com is fun though. Every once in a while I'll look up the names of old boyfriends or rivals, hoping to see they've landed in jail. We could look up Rose—just for kicks."

Paul shook his head. "There's nothing fun about jail, Sheila."

"Paul, I'm just searching the net. Of course crime isn't fun. You're right. I'm sorry. But don't you wonder where Rose is?"

"No, and I don't want to know."

"Okay." She sat and looked at him, trying to figure out the sudden cold tone. To lighten things up she said, "Well here, we'll type in your name on Crimetime, see if you've—"

Without warning Paul spun her chair and kissed her hard on the mouth.

"Forget the Internet." He began kissing her neck, raising gooseflesh all over her. "Show me the upstairs instead."

Breathless, she rose and started toward the stairs as he continued to kiss her. They didn't make it to the bedroom. Barely made it as far as the living room couch. Paul kissed the base of her throat and started to unbutton her blouse. She reached down to his jeans and the feel of the hard bulge within sent a wave of heat through her. It had been too long. She fumbled for the zipper but found only buttons. She *hated* button flies.

"Paul, you have to help me with these. I can't manage with one hand."

By now he was on top of her. She glanced to the window and noticed her curtains were drawn. Good. She smiled when she saw all the candles. But there was too much light. She wanted this to be perfect.

"Wait. Let me shut off the lights. I want just candlelight."

"I'll get them, you stay right here."

He carefully rose and reached for the wall switch. His other hand worked on his pants, then he took off his sweater. The sight of his chiseled stomach and chest sent a delicious tingle through her pelvis. Her heart was taching like mad. He was so arousing in the candlelight.

He smiled and crawled back on top of her. "I've been dreaming about this. You have no idea how I've wanted you."

"Oh, I think I do. I think we've been having the same dreams."

He managed another two buttons on her blouse and Sheila was squirming in anticipation. His stubble against her neck shot electricity though her.

Then the phone rang. Paul stopped and raised his head.

"Let the machine get it," she pleaded.

He started kissing her again as the outgoing message came on. Sheila heard her own recorded voice, and then Coogan's.

"Dad, dad are you there?" He sounded desperate.

Paul jumped up and tried to find the cordless. It wasn't in its cradle so he turned on the lights as Sheila ran for the kitchen phone.

"Dad, someone was outside, looking in our window. I think he's trying to break in. Dad? You there?"

Sheila handed Paul the phone.

"I'm here, Coog. Take it easy." Paul's voice had turned cold. Sheila could see he was shaking. "Are you okay? Where is he now? Okay, calm down. You call nine-one-one and I'll be there in five minutes. Got that? Nine-one-one, then me, okay? And don't move. I love you too, buddy." He hung up and turned to her. "Sheila, I have to go."

"Want me to come?"

"No, you stay here." He looked her in the eyes. "You understand, right?"

"Absolutely."

He tried a smile but she could see he wanted to be home now.

"Call me as soon as you know anything, okay?" she called after him just before the storm door closed.

Sheila watched him race off, then shut the inner door, sat on her couch, and let her jumping insides calm. The unfulfilled passion left her feeling chilled and jumpy. It had to be the same for Paul.

Poor guy. With everything else going on—his worries about paternity and the changes in Coog, plus their dead-end investigation—the last thing he needed was someone trying to break into his house.

She stiffened, remembering her own break-in. Was this connected?

Suddenly the glow of the candles wasn't enough. She hurried through the house turning on all the lights.

PAUL

Paul called Coog as he backed out of Sheila's driveway.

"Everything okay?"

"Yeah. I called the police. They said they'd send someone over."

"Good. I'm on my way. Stay on the phone while I drive."

Paul could feel the rage growing as he raced along residential streets at speeds he knew were unsafe. Some perv, some would-be burglar, some son of a bitch could still be outside the house.

His rage approached murderous when he came up behind a panel truck doing the speed limit. High beams and honking couldn't get the turtle to pull over. Paul pounded on his steering wheel and screamed for it to get out of his way until he found an opening and swerved past.

The guy honked and high-beamed in retaliation but Paul didn't give a shit.

He beat the police to his house. He pulled in and ran to the door. It opened before he could knock.

"Dad! I—"

Paul wanted to wrap him in his arms but knew Coog considered himself too old for that. Not cool.

"You okay?"

"Yeah, I'm fine. Sorry for dragging you home but—"

"Hey, you need me, you call me, and I'm there. 'Nuff said?"

Coog smiled and nodded.

Paul stepped back off the steps.

"You stay here. I'm going to look around."

A look of concern flashed across Coog's face. "Hey, that's what the cops are for, Dad."

"Yeah, well, I don't see any at the moment, so I'll have to make do."

He returned to his car and hit the garage door remote. Inside, he looked around and saw the Louisville Slugger he'd bought last summer. In warmer weather he used it to hit pop flies to Coog. He grabbed it and hefted it.

You'll do, he thought.

With the bat on his shoulder he began roaming the yard, searching the shadows. When he found no one, he began to relax. And that opened the door to thoughts about where he and Sheila had been headed a few moments ago. His groin ached. So close, so—

"Freeze!"

Paul whirled and was blinded by a flashlight directed at his eyes. He couldn't see who was holding it but spotted a police car at the curb.

He said, "I'm Paul Rosko, officer. I live here."

"We'll see about that."

A window opened and Coog shouted, "Hey, that's my dad!"

The flashlight beam lowered to the grass.

"Let's move around to the front," the cop said.

He waited for Paul to pass, then followed him. "Your name, officer?"

A kid—probably hadn't reached his mid-twenties yet—in a gray uniform.

"Evers, sir."

"Well, Officer Evers, I appreciate your coming. I just got here myself."

The beam played over the bat in Paul's hand.

"And what were you planning to do with that, Mr. Rosko?"

"Don't know exactly. Maybe hit a home run or two if the opportunity presented itself."

"Bad move, sir."

"And why is that? A guy sneaks into my yard, scares my kid—"

"If he's outside your house and you hurt him, you're the one that winds up in handcuffs. Then he finds a lawyer and sues you for every penny you're worth."

"Some legal system."

"Better than most. I'll need to come inside and take your son's statement."

"You have to?"

Paul didn't like the idea of a cop in his house or being mentioned on a police report, but saw no way around it.

Evers nodded. "Afraid so."

Paul sighed and turned toward the house. "Okay. Let's get it over with."

EIGHT

PAUL

Paul found a visitor parking space near the front entrance to the VecGen building. He turned off the engine and sat a moment, giving himself a pep talk.

"You're going to *be* calm and *stay* calm. You won't expect to learn anything because they're not going to tell you a damn thing. You will act deranged but you will *not* lose your temper."

He'd dreamed up this little fishing expedition last night while thinking about the mysterious Lee T. Swann. What if Swann had sold the Kaplan Biologicals assets to VecGen? It made sense in the timeline. VecGen starts up a year after Kaplan goes under, and comes out with a therapy very similar to KB26.

Coincidence? Maybe. G. K. Chesterton called coincidences spiritual puns. Paul didn't sense anything spiritual about VecGen.

He'd bounced it off Sheila this morning. She'd been intrigued by the theory but thought the trip was a waste of time: If VecGen was secretive with the doctors using its VG723, they'd hardly open up to a man coming in off the street.

Paul had no delusions about that. He was out to stir up the animals—clank a steel bar against their corporate cage and see who responded and how. Sheila couldn't get away—initiating new courses of therapy this morning—and Paul didn't want to wait. He figured he'd be more effective as a solo anyway.

He'd called and told the receptionist that he was experiencing "serious side effects" from VG723 therapy and wanted to speak to someone in charge—today. As expected, they'd referred him back to his oncologist, but he wasn't having any of that. He wanted— demanded—to see "the Head Man." Well, that wasn't going to happen either. But he kept hammering away at the poor woman until—after putting him on hold four times—she finally told him she was referring him to the public relations office. He screamed that he didn't want some flack, he wanted the Head Man or, at the very least, a scientist.

No use. He was switched. So Paul badgered the unfortunate PR underling who took his call until—only twice on hold this time—he was granted a meeting with Arnold Brown, head of the department.

Well, it was a start.

VecGen occupied a long, one-story building on Canal Street in Milltown. It looked more like a brick-fronted warehouse or a widget factory than the home of a cutting-edge research firm. Weren't these little companies always trying to attract capital? This didn't have the look to spur investors to reach for their wallets. Why weren't they out on the 128 strip with the other biotech companies?

Convenient that it was in Milltown. Another coincidence? Or had it set up here to be close to Tethys?

He pushed open the glass front door and stepped up to the reception desk.

"Hi, I'm Paul Rosko. I have an appointment with Mister Brown."

The young, pretty woman with curly dark hair became flustered.

"Oh, yes. Mr. Rosko. We spoke before and—"

"Was that you? I'm sorry if I was rude. I'm just upset—terribly upset."

"I understand. But I . . . I'm sorry to inform you that Mr. Brown had to go out to an important meeting."

"*What*?" Paul didn't have to feign outrage. "He's not here? You mean I drove all the way out here for *nothing?*"

It hadn't been all that far, but no reason for her to know that.

"I'm sorry, Mr. Rosko. He said he'd see you some other time but—"

"Then I'll see Swann!"

"Who?"

"Lee T. Swann. You know him, don't you?"

She shook her head. "I'm sorry, I've never heard of him."

The woman jumped as Paul banged his fist on her desk. He'd expected to be stonewalled but this was the metaphorical finger. Damn these sons of—

Be calm . . . be cool. 10 . . . 9 . . . 8 . . .

He let out a breath. He believed that she'd never heard of Swann.

"Okay, then, who *can* I talk to?"

"I'll call legal. Maybe someone there can help."

She hit a couple of buttons. As she started a hurried conversation in a low voice, Paul looked around. He saw a couple of guys in white labcoats amble down the hall to his right and step through the front door. Cigarette break.

He shook his head. Biotech researchers should know better.

The receptionist cringed as she hung up and turned to him.

"Everybody is busy. I think you'll just have to reschedule."

Paul could see that he was frightening her. He hadn't intended that. Wasn't her fault. The cowards in the back offices had left her on the front line to take his fire.

But he had to keep up the unstable act, even though it was becoming less and less of an act.

"You tell them for me—" He pointed to the pad on her desk. "Write this down. You tell them that their VG-seven-twenty-three therapy has made my body change—my hair, my eyes, lots of things. I'm becoming somebody else! And you tell them I want to know why. I've already sent a letter to the FDA, so don't try any funny stuff. Anything happens to me, the feds are on notice!"

With that he turned and stomped back outside.

But he was smiling by the time he reached his car.

That ought to shake things up.

BILL

Bill sat at his desk, swiveling back and forth and thinking about Sheila, wondering how she'd spent her weekend. He hoped it was shopping or the movies.

What would I do without you? Abra had said.

If she only knew what he'd done for her lately . . .

A chime drew his attention to his monitor. An alert icon flashed. He didn't have to open it to know what it was. After all, he'd set it up himself. It would read *Make the call.* He'd programmed it to remind him every Monday, Wednesday, and Friday to call the answering machine at Innovation Ventures.

Never in the six years since he'd set it up had anyone left a message. And that was good.

But he checked it religiously three times a week. He hit *9* on his office fax's speed dialer without bothering to pick up the receiver. He'd set the answering machine to pick up after four rings unless it had a message; then it picked up after two. Bill's routine was to listen until the third ring, then hang up.

One ringy-dingy, he thought. Two ringy-dingies. Three—

"You have one new—"

Bill almost fell out his chair as he snatched up the receiver.

"—message."

A message. What was the access code, damn it? It had been so long. He remembered it had to be four digits—

His birthdate—his old standby. He punched in 1-1-3-0 and heard a hesitant voice come on the line.

"Is there a Mr. Swann there? This is Jason Fredericks from legal at VecGen. I have instructions to call this number in the event of any trouble down here. Well, it seems we had an incident this morning. A man came in with some wild story about VG-seven-twenty-three changing him into someone else."

Oh, God. Oh, dear God.

"He's obviously deranged but he seemed to be talking litigation. And he asked for you by name."

What? What?

"His name, by the way—at least the name he gave—was Paul Rosko. I'm at extension two-two-three if you need to get back to me."

A disembodied voice came on with a menu of options. Bill hit *3* to erase, then leaned back.

Paul Rosko . . . Goddamnit!

Every time he turned around, his name popped up. His kid had the KB26 therapy, not VG723, so what was he doing at VecGen?

Then it hit him. Sheila. She must be feeding him information about VG723. Bill slammed his fists on the desk. Shit!

So, she hadn't really believed all his explanations, hadn't accepted there was no link between her patients' changes and the VG723. And now she'd made the connection between Rosko's kid and the KB26 . . . put it all together. She couldn't contact anyone about KB26, so she'd sent that hairy buffoon Rosko to VecGen to bully his way around.

No . . . ease up. If they knew anything, they wouldn't waste their time at VecGen. They'd have already gone to the police. Or FDA. Or JCAHO. They had nothing.

So calm down.

Sheila suspected a connection because KB26 and VG723 were both stem-cell therapies administered at Tethys. Recipients of each had exhibited inexplicable changes in appearance.

But Rosko's kid had the "correct" DNA type now, so they wouldn't suspect that it was changed.

He took a deep breath. They were fishing, that was all.

Rosko was a known quantity. Not as known as Bill would have liked—he'd yet to receive the background check—but at least he knew who he was dealing with. And Sheila . . . she was always right under his thumb. And Abra's. She was easy.

Nosing around what was happening to Tanesha Green was just what Sheila was supposed to do. The woman had come to her and, like the dedicated healer she was, Sheila was trying help her. Just doing some extra work, that was all. It wouldn't lead anywhere.

Bill smiled and opened his Rolodex. Bembridge Security. Time to see what skeletons they'd found in Rosko's closet.

Yes, soon, things would go back to normal. Once Tanesha's case was closed . . .

Tanesha . . . he turned to his computer and searched for Tanesha Green to see if she'd had another visit with Sheila.

No. The latest notes in her file were from last week. Good. At least—

Bill stiffened in his chair when he saw the next hit from the search: Tanesha Green was scheduled for skin and scalp biopsies for DNA analysis. Tomorrow.

Shit! The probe would yield results that could start a scandal all over the bioscience world.

Okay. Be calm—*calm*, damnit!

He leaned his elbows on his desktop and cradled his head in his hands. Splitting headache. He cudgeled his brain for an answer but came up with only one way out. One he did not want to take.

He'd have to call Shen.

ABRA

Abra Gilchrist opened an envelope. Yet another plea for help. This one for extra flu vaccine for rural parts of Appalachia that were missed by the government due to another shortage. It was still early enough to do some good. Those poor people were sick year round. Someone had volunteered to deliver and administer the vaccine, so how could she say no to providing it?

She smiled as the sun caught the edge of her letter opener. She held it closer. "Love, Lee Swann." Lee, her childhood nickname for her little brother Billy. And Swann, their inside joke. Someday they would turn all the ugly ducklings into swans.

Not much else to smile about. Her chest still ached where she'd had her sternotomy. It had been a choice between opening her undersized chest or letting her heart crowd out her lungs. Not much of a choice. The pain never seemed to stop.

How many broken bones? She'd lost count. How many surgeries? Too many. Waking up from anesthesia was always scary. Every time. She doubted Bill and Mama had much compassion for each new procedure. They probably assumed it was a walk in the park by now. But it wasn't. Fresh incisions, fresh pain. It never got easier.

Sheila always offered her sympathy. But Abra couldn't burden her with her aches and pains. Had to appear strong for Sheila. It was what mothers did. Or maternal figures, as it were. She knew the girl looked up to her and relied on her strength, so she was obliged to be strong.

Speaking of mothers, Abra had broken down and called Mama in Switzerland. If Mohammed won't come to the mountain . . .

Abra didn't understand Mama. And apparently, Mama didn't understand her. They'd had a falling out over the pace of Proteus. Mama wanted a much more aggressive approach; Abra insisted on slow and easy. The conflict grew so contentious that it threatened Proteus itself.

Finally Mama had stormed off, saying she wanted no more to do with anything connected with Tethys.

Things had remained a little tense since then, but time was a healer. Mama's resurrection of Schelling Pharma was going well.

Still . . . she could have so much greater impact on health and humanity if she had stayed with Tethys.

She called her again. Mama wasn't in, so Abra left a message with her secretary.

She wished she could get more involved in Mama's day-to-day work. See her new lab, see firsthand what she was working on. But flying wasn't easy for Abra.

Billy was always flying out there. He got to work with Mama. He even helped with her marketing campaigns for their vaccine line.

She had to smile. Still the jealous older sister.

Maybe in the spring she'd fly out and see the new lab. It was less risky now that her fracture rate was down. Her bones were growing stronger. Not straighter or longer, but tougher. They no longer broke like glass.

Yes, in the spring, she'd bite the bullet and join her mother in the lab. Perhaps help her with whatever she was working on these days. Flu vaccine was valuable in its way, but nowhere near as noble or potent as Proteus.

———•••———

SHEN

Jing answered the phone. She spoke a few words, then turned to Shen with her hand over the mouthpiece.

"It's Doctor Gilchrist for you—again. Why doesn't he leave you alone?"

Shen could not answer that. He had to keep Jing in the dark.

He took the phone from her and said, "Yes, sir?"

"Shen, I'm outside your house. We need to talk."

"Yes, sir. I'll be right out."

He hung up and went to the closet for his jacket.

"Where are you going?" Jing said as she balanced Fai on a slender hip.

"A meeting. He is outside."

"Why so secret all the time?"

"I will know that when I speak to him."

Shen walked outside and slipped into the passenger seat.

"We have a problem, Shen," he said as he put the car in gear.

Shen nodded and held his breath.

"We have another serious threat to my sister's dream."

Shen's heart sank.

"As serious as the one before?"

"More so. *Jiù-zhù-zhě* has tried to avoid this, but there is no other way."

He had no wish to be impertinent, but had to ask.

"You have tried everything, sir?"

"Everything."

"Who is this threat? Not Doctor Sheila?"

"No, not Doctor Sheila. Tanesha Green. You tapped her phone. She's scheduled for biopsies tomorrow at eleven A.M. She must not keep that appointment. She must not keep any appointment ever again."

Shen sat silent. He did not want this. He felt as if the jaws of a trap were slamming closed on his life.

"I would rather not."

"What?"

"Shen would rather not kill anyone else. I have a son now and a new life in the United States. I cannot live the life I did in China. I am sorry, but no."

Shen hated to disrespect his boss, but he had promised this to himself, for Jing and Fai.

"But Shen, I—my sister needs this. You wouldn't have this new life you speak of if it weren't for my sister and me, right?"

Shen slowly nodded. "This is correct."

"Then please, Shen, please, one last thing for her. Once Tanesha is out of the equation, everything will return to normal."

The doctor had promised this before. But Shen had already killed Dr. Sheila's husband. Also he had made Dr. Silberman deathly ill. And it was not back to normal. He had to know that if the situation took a bad turn he could run away with his family and start another new life. He had some money saved, but not enough.

"This one need three tickets for family to—" he had not come prepared but he had to say something. He thought of a movies he had recently seen, *The Firm*—"to Jamaica. And fifty thousand dollars in an account there in my name."

Dr. Gilchrist's jaw dropped. "Fifty thousand dollars? Shen, I can't get that kind of money."

Shen stared at him, waiting. He could see in Dr. Gilchrist's eyes that he *could* get the money, so he sat silent, waiting.

"Shen, please."

"Doctor Gilchrist, you are protecting your family and your dream; I must protect mine. I do not wish to leave my home or Tethys. I will do as you command, but I need a refuge if things *not* return to normal."

The doctor's face reddened until Shen thought he would explode. Then his color faded.

"Fine, Shen. If that's how it has to be, I'm sure my sister won't mind. I'll work out the details with you later. For now, let me tell you about your job."

"Thank you, Doctor Gilchrist. We shake on it."

Shen extended his hand. Dr. Gilchrist was a man of his word and if he took his hand, it would be a deal. The doctor hesitated but finally shook Shen's hand. A contract.

"Let's move on now. We don't have much time. The problem with this job is you must make it look much different than what happened to the Slade woman. If Tanesha Green dies of a broken neck, or even a car accident, the wrong questions will be asked by the wrong people. You must find another way."

Shen knew of another way but did not want to speak of it. The right mixture of certain herbs—herbs he could find in Chinatown—would do the job.

"It will be done."

Shen looked straight ahead and thought of all the people he had killed in China at the Party's behest. He had never counted them, but there were many.

He sighed. Would one more make so big a difference?

Bill

Bile had crept up into Bill's throat the whole time Shen was delivering his demands. It took every bit of his willpower to remain calm. Or pretend to. As soon as Bill dropped off Shen and turned the corner, he slammed on his brakes, shoved open his door, and vomited onto the pavement.

He looked down at his tie. An Armani, his favorite. Puke all over it. Another wonderful day in the life of Bill Gilchrist.

Bill took it off and set it on the passenger seat. Clenched the wheel of the idling car.

He didn't care that Shen wanted money. Hell, why shouldn't he get paid extra for killing people? But that much cash would leave a paper trail. And if Shen fled the country with his family, that meant he, Bill, would be left holding the bag. With Shen gone, who else would be blamed?

William Gilchrist, head of the Tethys Corporation, indicted for murder . . . probably be convicted too.

Bill pounded the steering wheel with his fists. Fuck! Fuck! Fuck!

This was not going to happen. He was *not* going down for this. No one was. Shen was going to eliminate Tanesha, and Sheila and

Rosko were going to get off his goddamn back.

And everything *was* going to go back to goddamn normal. And Abra would never find out.

Bill drove as quickly as he could back to Tethys. His hands shook as tears welled. Things had to return to normal. They just had to. He *couldn't* let Abra or his kids down. He could not go to jail.

He wiped his eyes and thanked God for the lock on his office door. If ever he needed to drown himself in a bottle of Jack it was now.

__NINE__

TANESHA

Tanesha was just heading for the shower when the front doorbell stopped her.

Who could that be? she thought, reversing direction. Not Jamal—she'd watched him get on the bus and drive away.

She peeked through the keyhole and saw a Chinese guy standing on her front stoop. He was thin with a shaved head and his eyes were eight-ball black.

She wasn't about to open the door to no stranger. Tanesha Green wasn't born yesterday.

"What you want?" She said as she leaned close to the jamb.

"Mrs. Green," he said softly. "I am from Tethys."

She could barely hear him.

"Tethys? I'm goin' there at eleven. What you doin' here?"

"They did not tell you? Your appointment canceled."

"Canceled? What you talkin' 'bout?"

"No need for biopsy. Doctor Sheila Takamura send me. Just swab of mouth for DNA. It will do same thing."

"Oh, right. Like I'm gonna let you come in here and stick something in my mouth."

"I stay out here, give you swab. You rub inside mouth, give back, and I go."

Tanesha thought about that. This was good news in a way. She hadn't been looking forward to going all the way up to Bradfield to have someone cut on her for a few minutes, then come back home again.

But no way was she letting this guy in, even though she could probably whup his skinny ass with one hand tied behind her back. She spotted her chain lock dangling beside the door and hooked it into the track. She opened the door but she stayed back out of reach. And stick her hand out the door? Not hardly. Let him stick his in here.

"You hand that swab through the door."

"Yes, ma'am."

He pulled a small case from his pocket, opened it and snapped on a plastic glove. He took test tube and a paper-wrapped swab from the case, peeled the wrapper then handed the swab through the opening. Tanesha snatched it from his fingers and backed further away.

"Just rub cotton tip on inside of cheek," he told her. "Twirl as you rub."

She did as he said. It tasted kind of funny but it wasn't in there long. When she finished she handed it back.

"That's it?" she said.

"That is all." He stuck the swab into the test tube and gave her a little bow. "I hope you will believe that I am sorry for you."

"I don't need you feelin' sorry for me."

"You shall be free of your problems. May your soul find peace."

Tanesha closed the door. What a weirdo. *May your soul find peace?* What up with that?

A squeezy feeling hit her chest about half way across the living room. Another two steps and it became a pain, a feeling like she was being crushed between two trucks. She turned and started toward the phone to call Tethys. She tried to call for help but couldn't take a breath. She dropped to her knees and that hurt, but not as much as her chest. She reached out, got her hand on the phone.

Black spots began floating in her vision.

Lord, just let me have one breath so I can dial.

She hit the ON switch but as she began thumbing 9-1-1, the

pressure increased and the black spots became spreading splotches, running together, blotting out everything.

KAPLAN

"Doctor Kaplan?"

Gerald stopped halfway through the reception area and turned at the sound of the woman's voice. He groaned when he saw that Japanese doctor—she had a long name he couldn't remember.

"Don't waste you time or your breath," he told her. "I've said all I care to."

Her scary boyfriend came up behind her and said, "We can continue it out here or in your waiting room. I have a very loud voice."

A lot of anger in that man. Gerald didn't want to call his bluff. He wouldn't care if the lumberjack screamed his head off at the Penner, but not here in the medical group's waiting room. He glanced at his watch.

"I can give you ten minutes, no more."

The woman nodded. Takamura—that was her name. "That should do it."

He led them to his consultation room where he seated himself behind the desk but did not offer them chairs. He didn't want them getting comfortable.

"Very well, what is it this time?"

Dr. Takamura said, "Do you know anyone named Lee Swann?"

"No. Should I?"

She looked disappointed. "He bought the assets of Kaplan Biologicals."

Gerald straightened in his chair. "He did? Who is he?"

"We were hoping you'd know."

"No idea. Who gave you his name?"

"I know where to look. Besides, it's a matter of public record."

He slumped back. "What does it matter? It's over, done, finished."

For him maybe. For KB. But his therapy lived on.

"Maybe not. I think he sold KB-twenty-six to VecGen."

Just what he'd been thinking. But he wanted no connection to VecGen.

"KB-twenty-six never used a viral vector."

"Didn't have to," she said. "Its use was limited to leukemia. It was introduced directly into the marrow space. VG-seven-twenty-three is used to treat a variety of tumors. But I think there's a connection."

Don't go there, he thought. Please don't go there.

"Kaplan Biologicals is dead," he said, "and—"

"Why is it dead? Who killed it?"

"My backers—Innovation Ventures." The name was bitter on his tongue. "They liked to refer to the company as 'IV'—infusing capital into worthy ventures. Get it? Clever?" Their expressions said they didn't think so either. "Anyway, they pulled the plug when they saw that KB-twenty-six wasn't going to be the cash cow they'd anticipated." He shook his head. "But why do you care?"

The big man stepped closer to the desk.

"Because of the changes in my son—I told you about them last week. We can't look at KB-twenty-six, but if it's the forerunner of VG-seven-twenty-three . . ."

A question sprang to mind. Did he dare ask it?

"Did your son exhibit changes in his tissue DNA?"

The consultation room went as silent as interstellar space.

"We—" Dr. Takamura swallowed as if her saliva had vanished. "We thought so at first, but retest showed it was the same as before."

Interesting. How could it?

Gerald restricted his response to a nod and one word. "Good."

"Why did you ask that?" the man said. Gerald saw his hands bunch into white-knuckled fists. "What do you know?"

"Nothing. Just idle curiosity." Gerald fixed his gaze on Dr. Takamura. "And you? Is your interest scientific or in this man here?"

He saw her redden. Gotcha.

"I have a patient who's experiencing changes that parallel those of Mr. Rosko's son. We're combining our efforts."

"Tell me about her."

"A Negro woman developing Caucasian features."

"That patient wouldn't happen to be named Green, would she?"

Her eyes widened. "How do you know?"

He allowed a smile. "I sent her to you. What have you learned?"

"Not much yet. But she's scheduled for more biopsies and some DNA tests this morning. That should point us in the right direction."

Oh, it will, he thought with a sinking feeling.

He quelled the rush of anxiety. The only way to link Kaplan Biologicals to VecGen was the mysterious Mr. Swann. Since Swann would be downwind when the shit hit the VecGen fan, he might want to remain mysterious.

But all that aside, Gerald's curiosity had been piqued. He hesitated, wondering if he should push this line a little further, then decided to go for it.

"Is there a Caucasian patient at Tethys with complementary changes?"

Another widening of her eyes. "Yes! How can you know that?"

Easy when you have certain facts at your disposal.

"Have you biopsied her?"

Dr. Takamura's face fell. "No. She died of a fall at home and the family cremated her body before I could arrange a post."

Gerald hid his elation. This was good news for all concerned. Now, if Tanesha Green would be so kind as to step out in front of a bus . . .

"Most unfortunate." Gerald glanced at his watch. "I have patients waiting. I've told you all I know and I hope not to see either of you ever again."

"What are you hiding?" the man said.

Dr. Takamura opened the door and took his arm, pulling him toward it.

"Come on, Paul. That's not going to help."

His voice rose as he stopped in the doorway and pointed a finger at Gerald.

"You're hiding something, Kaplan. I'm going to find out what it is, and when I do, you're through!"

SHEILA

"Sorry about that," Paul said as they walked toward the parking lot.

"It's all right." Sheila pulled her coat closer around her. God, the wind was cold. Gray rain clouds lidded the sky. "That man definitely knows more than he's saying."

"Damn right. Coog's altered tissue DNA—he didn't pull that out of thin air."

Sheila agreed. But the retest had come back correct.

So why this uneasiness creeping through her? She tried to shake it off.

"Let's concentrate on Innovation Ventures."

Paul sighed. "I suppose we should. I guess that's our next look-up. Maybe we can get some answers from them."

Like last time, Sheila had made morning rounds early and didn't have to be back on duty until two. Paul had picked her up in the Tethys lot and they'd headed for Salem. The downside of her schedule today was that she wouldn't get off until eight. So now looked like the perfect time to hunt down Innovation Ventures.

"Your place is closer," she said. "Let's get there and start searching."

She had another reason for choosing Paul's. Coog was still home from school and that would keep them on their best behavior. Since their close encounter, whenever Sheila was alone with Paul the throbbing between her legs distracted her. Good ol' lust. Today, though, she needed to stay focused.

At Paul's place, he made coffee while she began the search. Coog's interest flagged after a few minutes and he wandered off.

Innovation Ventures turned out to be almost as elusive as Lee T. Swann. But its name did pop up in articles on a number of biotech startups. For the hell of it, she linked IV with VecGen and . . .

"Well, will you look at that," Paul said as he leaned over her shoulder, distracting her with his Irish Spring aura. "IV pulls the plug on Kaplan and then funds VecGen to do basically the same thing. That make sense to you?"

Sheila shook her head both to say no and to clear it. She really wanted to kiss him. She couldn't remember the last time she felt this swept away with wanting someone. She finally answered.

"It might if we had the whole picture. We need more info."

Silence . . . then an idea.

"What if I call Innovation saying I'm doing an article for a financial journal? Maybe I can squeeze a little something out of them."

Paul smiled. "What've we got to lose?"

Sheila got the phone number and address on the Yahoo Yellow Pages. Just a few towns over, in Andover. Coincidence?

After four rings an answering machine picked up. A creaky female voice said, *"Leave a message after the beep."*

Sheila hung up.

"Just an answering machine, and no mention of the company."

"Maybe they're out of business."

"If so, why are they paying a phone bill?" She looked up at Paul. "Short drive. Want to take a look?"

He shrugged. "Probably a waste of time, but sure, why not?"

———···———

The address turned out to be a two-story Dutch colonial box with an adjacent ten-space parking lot, nearly full.

Paul pulled into one of the spaces, "Not exactly the kind of place I'd expect a venture capital company to call home."

Sheila had to agree. Far from shabby, but it could have used some sprucing up. She pulled out the mini-recorder she'd borrowed from Paul.

"Time to get into character."

She and Paul had discussed this on the way over and decided she'd go in alone, pretending to be a reporter doing a series for

Biocentury Publications, which published newsletters on biotechs and venture capital firms.

She walked up to the front entrance where she stopped to read the directory: a real estate broker, a dentist, an accountant, and Innovation Ventures.

Inside she saw *Innovation Ventures* printed in some sort of digital font on the first door to the left. She gripped the doorknob, then hesitated.

Sheila took a deep breath and turned the knob.

Locked.

So she knocked. And knocked again. Then a third time. No answer.

What sort of business wasn't open at ten-thirty on a weekday morning?

She headed back to Paul and the car.

"That was quick," he said. "They shoot you down?"

She shook her head. "Nobody home."

His eyebrows rose. "Really?" He stepped out of the car. "Something's not kosher here. First floor?"

She nodded. "On the other side."

"Let's go take a look."

"The door's locked, Paul."

He smiled. "I mean the windows."

He started walking toward the building.

"I don't know if that's such a good idea."

"Why not?"

"What if we get caught?"

"Doing what? Not as if we're going to break in or anything. We're just looking to see if anybody's home."

Sheila followed him to the far side where he pushed aside some overgrown yews and peered in the window. Sheila did her own peering—around. She couldn't get over the feeling of being watched, but saw no one.

After a moment Paul turned to her. "See for yourself."

She stepped through the branches and cupped her hands against the glass for a look. The blinds were down but not completely drawn.

She saw an expanse of empty, carpeted floor, bare of furniture except for a chair and single desk. And on that, an answering machine.

She backed away. "I don't get it. It looks like they're out of business."

"That it does. But if so, why keep paying rent on office space you're not using? It doesn't add up."

A lot of things didn't add up. Especially Kaplan mentioning Coog's changed DNA on that test.

"Take me back to Tethys, will you? I've got a few things I need to look into before I start seeing patients."

———···———

"Ellen?" Sheila said as she knocked on the doorframe of the laboratory director's office.

Ellen looked up from her desk. Her short stature and rotund figure made her look like an overweight child sitting at an adult table.

"Oh." No smile. "Sheila."

The room temperature seemed to drop ten degrees.

Sheila stepped in without waiting to be asked.

"You know that incident report I filed?"

"How can I forget?"

Ellen wouldn't have Coog's original sample—it was long gone—but . . .

"Do you still have the follow-up sample?"

"I know we do. It's passed its five-day mark but I'm holding onto it."

Thank God.

Ellen looked down at her desk. "I . . . I retested it myself."

"And?"

"Still Paul Rosko's son."

"Could I have a look at it?"

Ellen looked up again. "Why?"

"I just want to look it over. Okay?"

Ellen's expression turned puzzled. She looked as if she was going to make a comment, but shrugged instead.

"Check with Amisha out there."

Sheila tracked down Amisha, a lithe Indian woman wearing a white lab coat over a red-and-yellow sari. She readily found the sample.

"Here it is," she said as she placed the tube in Sheila's hand.

Sheila turned it over to check the label. Her blood froze. She'd labeled the tube herself.

But this wasn't her handwriting.

As the shock wore off she strained to understand . . . why would somebody relabel Coogan's sample? Unless . . .

No. Unthinkable. But she had to know.

"Amisha? Dr. Bascomb mentioned a missing sample last week."

"But I found it," she said in melodic tones.

Could someone have switched Coogan's sample?

Yes, they could have.

But where could they find a sample that would show him as the child of Paul and Rose?

From Coogan. Before the therapy. Someone saved some of his old tissue because they knew . . .

Coogan's DNA—just like his eyes and hair and face—*had* changed after his KB26 treatment.

And someone wanted to keep that a secret.

But who would have had a sample of Coogan's before KB?

Kaplan? He'd mentioned it this morning. He'd suspected it or why would he have asked? But he couldn't have made the switch. He'd only been provided control numbers, no patient IDs. Anyway an outsider couldn't just waltz in here and start fiddling with the samples.

One of the techs?

No motive.

Bill. She'd thought it odd that he'd known about Coogan's DNA probe. Could he . . .?

"Has Doctor Gilchrist visited the lab lately?"

Amisha shook her head. "Not on my shift."

She had to get out of here. But first . . . just to be extra sure, she popped her head back through Ellen's doorway.

"Had any visits from Bill Gilchrist recently?"

Ellen shook her head. "Not personally, but someone on the late shift mentioned he'd been down here nosing around."

The back of her neck crawled. "When?"

"Last week." Her tone turned frosty. "Anything else?"

Speechless, Sheila turned and walked away, trying not to stagger.

Bill . . . somehow, some way, Bill had been involved all along.

She had to get back to her office . . . lock herself in so she could be alone and think. The one thing she wanted to do—get another sample from Coog and bring it to an outside lab for processing—was out of the question. Because she couldn't do it without telling Paul. Who knew what he'd do? If she told him that she suspected someone of falsifying Coog's results . . . he was already a ticking timebomb.

No, she had to find another way. One that didn't involve Paul.

SHEILA

Out of habit, the first thing Sheila did when she reached her office was check her voicemail. She found a message from Bill.

"Sheila? Bill. Meet late afternoon? Call me."

How could she sit across from him without his sensing something wrong? It was all circumstantial, yes, but the pieces fit together too well. And what if he asked how her investigation was going? What's new with Tanesha? No, she'd have to make up an excuse and hope she didn't sound phony.

With a shaking finger she punched in his extension. Marge picked up and told her he was out.

Thank you, God.

She left her regrets. Tied up. Sorry. She'd take a raincheck.

Marge said it would have to be next week then, as Bill was leaving for Switzerland on business.

Sheila was shaking when she hung up. Switzerland. Good. Having him away would make her feel a lot safer. She didn't trust him anymore.

She needed evidence. All she had at this point was speculation.

She headed for the clinic where Tanesha Green would be waiting . . . but wasn't. So Sheila waited. Half an hour late. Then an hour. With any other patient, she wouldn't have worried. But Tanesha was not only a sick patient with an undiagnosed problem, she was evidence.

Sweating now, Sheila dialed the woman's phone number. This wasn't like Tanesha. She was concerned, wanted answers, and wanted them now. No way she'd skip out on a biopsy.

"Hello?" said a woman's voice.

"Tanesha, this is Doctor Takamura. I just spoke to—"

"This ain't Tanesha. This her sister." Mean Aunt T, no doubt.

"Oh, sorry. You sound alike. Can I speak—?"

"Tanesha's dead."

A wave of shock slammed through Sheila.

"Wh-what? How?"

"Heart attack."

"When?"

"Last night. She dialed nine-one-one but by time they got here she was just about gone. They kept her going till they got her to the 'mergency room, but then she was done for. After twenty minutes, she was gone. They couldn't bring her back."

Sheila sat stunned. How could this be?

"You said you was her doctor?" the sister said.

"What? Yes."

"Then how come you didn't see this comin'?"

Good question. Tanesha had been overweight, but her blood pressure had been good and her cholesterol only borderline high. She'd never had a single cardiac-related complaint. But then, angina in women is often silent.

"She never gave me any reason to suspect a heart problem. She came to me about her skin and hair."

"_That_ what killed Tanesha—all her stressin' 'bout her skin. Her wires was pulled as tight as tight can be. They finally broke."

Sheila felt dazed. She'd known it had to be something serious to make Tanesha miss her biopsies, but never dreamed it would be—

"Where was she taken?"

"What?"

"The funeral home. I want to ask them about the autopsy. Where—?"

"She gone to Landy's but ain't gonna be no one filletin' my sister open like a fish. I seen that on TV and it ain't gonna happen."

"But don't you want to know what—?"

"What killed her? Don't need her all cut open to know that. Heard it from the doctor hisself. Her heart."

"But if we can get biopsies of her skin and hair—"

"What for? She way past carin' now."

"But we can find out—"

"Too late. You doctors shoulda already found out. Maybe she still be alive now if you had. You ain't cuttin' on my sister. She suffered enough."

And then a click as the connection was broken.

Sheila had failed little Jamal Green. Broken her promise. Now he'd have to go live with mean Aunt T.

Numb, Sheila missed the first time she tried to replace her receiver on its cradle. The second attempt made it.

She called the ER in the Penner Clinic in Boston. It took a few minutes but she finally located the doctor who had worked on Tanesha. He was a resident and working round the clock so she wasn't surprised to find him there. After some explaining, he opened up.

"She was a grossly obese, thirty-nine-year-old African American. She had abnormal cardiograms and her blood showed an acute myocardial infarction. She went into cardiac arrest and we couldn't revive her."

"But her skin and hair? Didn't you find the way she looked odd?"

She heard him sigh. "Listen this is the ER. She was having a heart attack and she died. It was clear what caused it. Her appearance was extraneous."

"But I've been working with her on some medical problems—"

"Heart related?"

"No. Cosmetic. But I was hoping to get some tissue samples—"

"Then I'm sorry. Can't help you. We offered the family an autopsy but they refused. Sorry we can't aid you in making Ms. Green your guinea pig but—"

She hung up. He didn't understand. How could he?

What was happening? She hit a wall every way she turned. First Kelly Slade's broken neck, now this. If Tanesha had died in some sort of accident, she'd be running to the police. But how to prove foul play on someone who appeared to die of natural causes? How to prove anything at all?

Goosebumps stood up on her arms and she rubbed them hard, but they didn't go away. This sick scared feeling never seemed to go away.

Both her VG723 cases had died. Directly or indirectly people who posed a threat to the VG723 therapy had been eliminated. And she was the last threat left. A chill went up her spine. And how long would she be left, now that everyone involved—

Wait. Hal Silberman! He'd agreed there was a link. Yes! She'd go see him. He'd know what to do.

She started walking toward the lab and remembered the rain. Great. The tunnels again. She wanted to call Paul and tell him about Tanesha but didn't want to risk being overheard here.

Sheila took a quick look over her shoulder. All clear. She shuffled down the stairs to the tunnels.

PAUL

"Paul?"

"Sheila, hi."

"Listen, I need you."

"What going on? Where are you?" He heard the sound of a radio and windshield wipers.

"I'm driving. Tanesha's dead."

"Jesus. How? Don't tell me it was another car accident."

"No. She had a heart attack but it seems awfully coincidental."

"Yeah it does. Aren't you supposed to be at work?"

"I got Liz Keene to cover. I traded her some hours tomorrow. I went to talk to Hal Silberman, the dermatopathologist, remember him?"

"Yeah. What did he say?"

"He hasn't been to work all week. He has some kind of stomach bug."

"You think Bill did something?"

"No, I'm sure he's just sick, but I need to talk to him. I'm going to his house."

"I'm going with you. Kelly's dead, Tanesha's dead. Who do you think is next on the list? No way I'm letting you go there alone." He heard a horn blare. "What was that?"

"I-I almost hit someone. Okay. Meet me there. I'll wait for you before I go in. Here's the address."

He hated leaving Coogan alone but there wasn't time to take him anywhere. It was still light. He'd be fine. Paul got the address from Sheila, handed Coog the cordless phone and a can of Coke, and ran out the door into the freezing rain.

SHEILA

As soon as she and Paul got close to Hal's front door, Sheila knew something was wrong. It was daytime but the sky was dark from the rain. All Hal's lights were off. She rang the doorbell several times but no one answered.

"Can you get us in?"

"There might be an alarm."

"I don't care. We may need the police or an ambulance anyway."

He leaned to the door and grabbed the handle. She guessed it was to check out what kind of lock he had. He smiled and turned the knob. "Huh. Not locked. Didn't anticipate that."

The minute they walked in, foul odors assailed them. Blood, urine, and feces. But not the smell of death, thank God. At least not old death. She followed the stench to a bathroom. Hal lay in a pool of bodily fluids. She touched his face. Burning up.

"Hal, can you hear me?" She tried a few more times. "He's alive, but barely. Call 9-1-1," she said to Paul.

Whatever was wrong with him appeared to be natural. No wounds so far as she could see. Not appendicitis with all this bloody diarrhea. Campylobacter? Salmonella? E-Coli? Hard to say.

He must have suffered the last few days. Poor guy. If this was food poisoning, whatever did this to him was already long out of his system. Most likely he'd never know what caused it. If he lived.

She wet a towel and placed it on his forehead. If he died, then they would be at a standstill with their investigation. Anything Hal was going to tell her about KB26 and VG723 would be sealed up forever within him.

Sheila wet another towel and wiped Hal's face and hands.

Paul gagged in the other room. The smell bothered her too but Hal was a friend. She couldn't just walk in the other room and leave him. Anyway, her own clothes were covered now too. She probably smelled as bad as he did.

"Sheila?"

Paul stood in the doorway, a paper towel over his nose. "You all right?"

She nodded. "But he's not. Could be botulism or any of a number of things. The lab will figure it out. I just hope we got here in time. What are you holding?"

"I thought you might want to change your clothes after they take him so I went into his room. I was going to get you a shirt, maybe some sweat pants if I could find them. I know I shouldn't be going through his things—"

"But you don't have any clothes. That looks like a file."

He held it out to her. "It's a copy of Tanesha's file. It was on his bed, open. He must have been reading it."

"I gave him a copy to look through."

"Look at this though." She reached for it but he pulled back. "Don't touch it. Just look."

If she were him, she'd be leery of her contaminated hands too.

Sheila leaned up as much as she could from her seated-on-the-floor-with-a-dying-man-on-her-lap position.

Written in blue ink were the words, *"Changing the world. One person at a time."* It was underlined over and over again.

"It's Tethys Medical Center's slogan." Sheila didn't see the significance. That phrase was printed on every piece of stationary at work, on her pay stub, on the marble and brass plaque at the main gate.

"Think about it, Sheila. It's what they're doing. Changing people. Not just curing. Changing. The world. One person at a time."

Sirens and then the doorbell interrupted them. Then squeaky wet boots on the tile floor of the bathroom. Paramedics lifted Hal off Sheila.

She shifted into doctor mode, assisting the paramedics. But she couldn't stop seeing the words in her mind, underlined hard in what must be Hal's writing. He was trying to tell her something. But goddammit she didn't understand. She needed him to wake up and explain. None of the other VG723 survivors had complained about transformations, so what did it mean? If the others looked the same on the outside, then how were they being changed?

TEN

SHEILA

Paul called Sheila the next morning to invite her over for dinner and a movie. Coog would be over at a friend's house watching a *Lord of the Rings* marathon, he said. By the dusky sound of his voice, Sheila knew they wouldn't be watching any movie. They'd be lucky if they got to eat dinner.

A sex date.

God, she needed something like that. She felt so jumpy and uneasy. She needed a break, a blast of physical and emotional release, someone to cling to. Every trip to the store was white knuckled, every time the phone rang, she jumped.

Sheila smiled as she stood at the nurses' station, just thinking about making love again made her feel so alive.

It had been ages. After Dek there had been that one guy, that one time. From that support group for widowed people. Horrible. He wasn't even cute. He went at it too fast. One minute dinner, the next she was in this stranger's bed, having sex and telling herself it was important to move on with her life. Right after he filled his condom, she ran out of his apartment crying. What a mess. She shuddered thinking about it.

She was on the brink of having an orgasm just thinking about touching Paul. Maybe it was her age or the span between encounters. Maybe it was just that Paul was such a man's man. She was zoning out, thinking about what to wear, how she'd stop at the mall, Victoria's Secret—

"Don't forget you're on tonight," said a female voice.

She looked and saw Liz Keene, a fellow doctor.

"Me? Where?"

She smiled. "Here. You're covering for me tonight, remember?"

Mother of God, she'd forgotten. Liz's little girl, Sammy, was scheduled for a tonsillectomy in Boston this afternoon and she wanted to be home with her tonight. Sheila couldn't very well back out now.

"Oh, yeah. Right." Despite her sinking heart she forced a smile. "Glad you reminded me. Good luck to Sammy."

Gotta get coverage, she thought.

She started calling, but it was too short notice—everyone had plans.

It seemed as if fate were keeping Paul and her apart. She'd have to call and put it off for yet another night.

Wait. Who said it had to be night?

Not quite believing she was doing this, she picked up the phone to call Paul. She'd tell him dinner was off but how about a late lunch—say, about two?

————■■■————

Sheila jittered with anticipation. Two o'clock had arrived. She prayed this came off the way she hoped. Paul would think it was an innocent late lunch and nothing more. No one ever expected sweet little Sheila to do anything spontaneous or seductive.

When he arrived in her office she met him at the door. As he kissed her cheek she reached behind him and shut it. Then locked it.

"What's this all about?" he said.

She knew from the look in his eyes that he had a pretty good idea.

"I'm hungry," she said casually. "You?"

She could see his breath catch as he answered her. "Yes. Very."

He leaned in and kissed her on the mouth. Perfect—so soft, just enough. Not chaste . . . and he didn't ram his tongue down her throat. Just enough to tease her. Make her want it. She kissed him harder, a little more tongue.

She started feeling dizzy. Why? She'd never gotten dizzy before. Certainly not from a kiss.

He must have sensed it because she felt those big, strong arms tighten around her. Irish Spring and fuzzy flannel covering a broad hairy chest. Heathcliff on the moor. He kissed her cheek and her lips, his stubble chafing her face. The rough skin made her want him more.

He looked at her. "I don't see a bed in here."

Sheila felt short of breath. How could she be so excited from a kiss? This was nuts.

He whispered in her ear. "Don't forget to breathe."

She nodded and took a deep breath. Her head started to clear—until he pulled away her collar and nibbled her neck.

With her arm she knocked all the files off her desk. She heard the pencil cup fall and saw the pens scatter on the floor.

She gestured toward the desk. "Will this do?"

Paul lifted her with seemingly no effort and lay her down, started kissing her again, unbuttoning her blouse. She tried to help but he grabbed her hand and held it firm over her head, pinning her to the desk. With his other hand he took off her blouse.

This is what she had needed for years, she realized. To be ravaged. Everything in her life was so damn regimented. She was in charge of everything she did, everything that happened. But not now. She was held down, her skin scraped because of Paul's noon shadow. He had thrown her blouse on the floor and started to undo her slacks. And her hand was held firm.

She couldn't get away if she wanted. And she didn't. The proverbial wild horses couldn't drag her away. She leaned up to kiss him again, his lips teasing her, the tiniest taste of tongue, just enough to make her yearn for more.

All his motions so smooth and rough at the same time. Sheila started getting dizzy again, started shaking. Never had she been so excited. She was ready to climax and she was still partially dressed.

Then he was on top of her. It happened quickly. His pants long gone, her panties off . . . and in one quick motion her bra came unlatched. He smiled at her trembling body, arching up toward his. He sucked on her nipples and she swung between feeling like a frightened schoolgirl and a red-light-district pro.

Paul looked down at her. "Don't forget to breathe. You have to breathe."

She took a few quick breaths, "Please, please," but she didn't have to say anything else. Paul held her arms over her head and pushed his way in slowly. Too slowly as far as Sheila was concerned.

She looked at him. No words. For once, not a single word in her head. Just feeling. Pulsating, aching to be filled, wet . . . feeling stretched and satisfied and ravaged and . . . he thrust in deeper and she had to stifle a scream. She remembered she was in her office.

"Are you okay?" he whispered. "Did that hurt?"

She couldn't talk. Was beyond anything as civilized as speech. He brought her to a state of flat-out animal hunger. Words would ruin it. She shook her head and pushed herself onto him harder.

He bit into her neck and after that all was an ecstatic blur.

SHEN

"Turn it off!" Dr. Gilchrist said.

Startled by the raw emotion in his voice, Shen looked up and found that the doctor had turned away. He stood rigid, head thrown back, arms straight against his sides, hands in tight fists.

"Sir?"

"Off, goddamn it! *Off.*"

Shen shut down the visual and audio feeds from Dr. Sheila's office.

Dr. Gilchrist was obviously shocked. Shen too. But he hadn't wanted to turn away. Here was an unsuspected side of the proper Dr. Sheila. Who would have dreamed she possessed such a wonderful body, curving and swelling in all the right places? She had hid it well within her loose clothing and even looser lab coat. And who would have dreamed she was a woman of such passion . . .

It made Shen want to rush home to Jing and ease the throbbing hardness behind his fly, make her moan with pleasure like Dr. Sheila.

"The bitch!" Dr. Gilchrist said. He turned toward Shen with teeth bared like a wolf. "Pretending to be pure as driven snow but . . . this . . . to think . . . in the office . . ."

He seemed to run out of words, or lose the ability to speak.

Why so upset? This surely was not the first time someone had had sex in a Tethys office. But then he saw the hurt mixing with the rage in Dr. Gilchrist's eyes and he knew.

Dr. Gilchrist was in love with her.

Shen found that more shocking than Dr. Sheila's lust. Dr. Gilchrist was always so in control, seemingly above the petty needs of common people. And yet here he was, raging like a betrayed lover.

Lover . . . Shen wondered if the two doctors at one time had had an affair.

But no. Shen sensed that Dr. Gilchrist had loved her from afar, had admired her, placed her on a pedestal.

And now . . . to see this . . .

"What should I do, sir?"

Dr. Gilchrist calmed himself—Shen sensed it took much effort—and fixed his gaze on the blank screen.

"Continue to monitor her phone and computer. Erase the recording and when they've . . . when they've finished, resume AV monitoring."

"Yessir."

"I'll be in my office." Dr. Gilchrist still looked shaken. "Keep me informed of any new developments."

"Of course."

As Dr. Gilchrist left the tiny room, Shen thought about erasing the recording. Yes, he would do it. But not yet. He wished to watch it again.

KAPLAN

"One last thing before you go."

Gerald Kaplan looked up at the clerk—a young black woman

in a green skirt and blouse—and concealed his annoyance. He was only scheduled till three today and he wasn't staying late. Whatever "last thing" she had, she'd better be quick about it. He'd put in his hours, now he wanted to go home.

It had been raining steadily all day and the parking lot was flooded. The longer he stayed, the deeper it would get. "What is it?"

"A chart. You were the last to see her, so you need to sign off on her."

"What's the story?"

The clerk shrugged. "Dead. That's all I know."

Gerald looked at the name. Icy shock stabbed him. *Tanesha Green*.

He flipped open the chart and looked at the typed note pasted inside the front cover: *Deceased. Cardiac arrest.* The time of death, the names of the hospital and the doctor who pronounced her were listed below.

He closed the chart and leaned back, chilled yet sweating. Takamura had told him that the first patient showing pigment changes had died in some sort of accident—a fall at home. And now that woman's counterpart was dead too.

Coincidence? If so, it was damn convenient for the folks producing VG723.

Try as he might, Gerald could not escape the conclusion that someone was covering tracks. An outlandish idea, wacky, absurd, and yet . . .

Let's just say it's true, he thought. Who would it be?

Not the Tethys crew—they were an altruistic bunch. They'd never kill anybody to hide a secret, no matter how dangerous. But he couldn't say the same about VecGen. For all he knew it could be a money-laundering front for organized crime.

Now *there* was a thought.

Any way about it, Takamura and that Rosko goon had better watch out. They were loose ends.

Gerald bolted upright in his chair.

And so am I!

What if there really were people out there covering their tracks? How long before they decided he was too much of a liability?

How else to explain the two oh-so-convenient deaths?

Yes, it could all be coincidence, but why take chances? He'd been looking for an excuse to get away for a while. This could be it. Claim a family emergency, and disappear.

Not forever. He'd keep watch. And if nothing happened to Takamura or Rosko, he'd come back.

But if something did happen . . .

He wondered if he needed a license to practice medicine in Honduras or Ecuador.

He checked his watch. The bank was still open. Time to put it all into traveler's checks.

But before he disappeared maybe he'd throw some gas on the fire—then see if anyone showed up to put it out.

SHEILA

Sheila sat on the floor in the corner of her office, snuggled in Paul's arms. The corner provided a haven. She was still naked, but Paul had draped his sweater over them, covering what he could.

She smiled at him. "I'm still dizzy. I've never gotten so dizzy from sex."

Paul returned her smile. "I've never made someone dizzy before. You seemed really excited. Unless you're a good actress."

"No act, believe me. I was out of control."

"In a good way. A very good way." He stroked her hair. "What a fabulous surprise. I thought I was just coming here for lunch."

Sheila laughed. "It's been such a long time since I've done anything with anyone. Hanging around with you just pushed me over the edge. I haven't been able to stop thinking about you." Ooh, that might scare him. "I mean, I couldn't stop thinking of having you. Of you having me."

She giggled and turned red.

"I know what you mean. I haven't been able to get anything done at home. I can't sleep. It's a good thing I'm off work or I might have wired somebody's cable up to a gas range." He tapped her nose. "Can't think of anything but you."

"I hadn't planned for it to be so . . . well, you know. I wanted it to be candlelight and, jeez, at least a bed, but I just couldn't wait anymore."

"Hey, no apologies. That was . . . I hate the word, but that was incredible."

"Yeah," she sighed.

She closed her eyes and leaned against his shoulder. Not only was the sex great but she felt so comfortable with him. No embarrassment, no remorse. Just . . . good.

"We could do it again, you know," Paul said. "Just to make sure you weren't faking."

He kissed her lips. Her heartbeat picked up tempo. Twice in her office . . . did she dare?

Her phone rang and answered her question.

As Sheila reached for it, Paul grabbed her arm.

"Let it ring."

She sighed. "I wish I could, but in my business you don't ignore pages and phone calls."

She picked up the receiver. "Doctor Takamura."

"If you recognize my voice, don't say my name. Do you know who I am?"

Sheila knew instantly that it was Kaplan. "Yes."

"Good. Meet me at the place where we first spoke if you want the answers to your questions—all your questions."

Was he for real?

"Can't you tell me now?"

"Over the phone? Not likely."

"Okay then, when?"

"A-S-A-P. In two hours I'll be on my way to the airport and you'll have missed your chance."

He hung up.

"Don't tell me," Paul said. "You've got an emergency."

"Not the kind you think. That was Doctor Kaplan."

Sheila gave him the gist of the call.

"He didn't want you to say his name or where you were supposed to meet him. Sounds like he knows something."

Paul grabbed his shorts and began stepping into them. "We'd better get going. It's raining pretty hard out there so the traffic might be slow.

"He didn't say anything about you."

"Maybe not, but if you think you're going out there alone, forget it.

He had a point. She was half dressed when she remembered.

"Oh, no! I'm on till eight tonight!"

"Get someone to cover for you."

"I can't. I'm covering someone's shift as it is. Damn!"

"Try. Call in some favors. We can't miss out on this."

BILL

Marge's voice blared through the intercom: "Mr. Li on two."

Bill didn't want to speak to anyone, especially someone who had been witness to Sheila's wanton display. Bad enough that he'd been subjected to it, but to think that another man had been privy as well . . .

Almost unbearable.

Sheila . . . flesh bared . . . legs spread . . . allowing—no, *inviting* that cretinous beast Rosko into her.

Bill had wanted to vomit. Still felt queasy. He'd just learned the truth about Rosko from the security company. If Sheila knew she'd never have let him near her. Well, he'd make sure she knew real soon.

But still . . . such lascivious carrying on right here on the Tethys campus. Never in a million years would he have imagined—

"Doctor Gilchrist?" Marge again.

"I've got it." He reached for the phone. "Yes, Shen?"

"Doctor Sheila receive call from man who did not give name, but after call she say it was someone named Doctor Kaplan."

Kaplan! Jesus God! Not Kaplan! How the hell did she find him?

"What . . . what did he want?"

"He say to meet him and he would answer all their questions."

Bill closed his eyes as he stifled a groan. It was all coming apart.

"Where are they meeting?"

"He say in place where they first speak. No more."

Did Kaplan suspect a phone tap?

"Shen, I want you to trace that call and—"

"Did, sir. It come from Boston—from Penner Brigham Hospital."

Damn. Useless. The place was huge.

"All right, then. Follow them. Call me when you find out where they're meeting. This man Kaplan is a terrible threat to my sister's dream."

"Yessir."

As he hung up, Bill felt his insides coiling into knots.

Was Kaplan insane? Anything he revealed would turn around and bite him as well. What was he thinking?

PAUL

"A dark and stormy night," Paul muttered as he pulled into Kaplan's driveway. "Well, almost night."

He turned off the engine and sat. Alone. Sheila hadn't been able to find coverage.

Thoughts of their lovemaking had kept him warm all the way to Marblehead—God, what a woman—but now that he was here . . .

Sheila had written down a number of questions and he was to call her with the answers so that she could ask follow-ups.

Paul hoped he was up to it. He had no grounding in medicine. It was such a wide, arcane field—and growing wider and more arcane every minute—that he felt daunted by the prospect of making sense of whatever Kaplan had to say.

He glanced at his watch: 4:20. The days were getting short fast.

Kaplan looked surprised when he answered Paul's knock.

"I don't recall inviting you."

"Doctor Takamura couldn't get away. I'm here in her stead."

"Sorry." He started to close the door. "I'll only talk to—"

In a burst of anger Paul slammed his hand against the door, knocking it open. He stepped in and faced the cowering Kaplan.

"I have a list of questions for you to answer, and I intend to hold you to your word."

He closed the door behind him.

"I-I'll call the police!"

"I think not. Paul pointed to a chair. "Sit down."

Kaplan dropped onto a sofa. Paul positioned an armchair opposite him and pulled out Sheila's list.

"Okay. First thing she wants to know—"

"I'll tell this my way, if you don't mind."

Paul looked at him. Kaplan had regrouped and replenished his vinegar.

Paul nodded. "Okay. Go."

Kaplan leaned forward, hands clasped atop his knees.

"I'll skip the scientific details. You wouldn't understand them and they're not germane to the big story." He cleared his throat. "It all started ten years ago when I was heading up a research team working with embryonic stem-cells. I'd had some luck with cloning an antigenically neutral strain."

"KB-twenty-six."

"Not yet. I was still a long way from KB-twenty-six. I needed money for development. I applied for grants from NIH, NAS, anyone else connected to the government who had dollars to give away; I applied to universities and foundations—ironically, the Tethys Foundation turned me down. I got offers but only small amounts. Nowhere near what I needed. And then out of the blue this venture capital company contacts me and says they'll underwrite whatever I need."

"Innovation Ventures."

"Exactly. I thought they were the greatest—then. True to their word they funded me to the max. And that allowed me to develop a strain of embryonic stem cells that might offer a last-resort hope to people with refractive leukemia. So I started primate trials." He looked at Paul. "You following me?"

Paul nodded. No problem. Pretty straightforward so far.

"You mean monkeys and such."

"Exactly. And the primate trials were a roaring success. So I applied for and received the go-ahead from the FDA for clinical trials. The ink on the approval was hardly dry when Tethys came knocking on the door to run the trial."

"*Now* KB-twenty-six comes in."

"Right—as does your son and a host of other refractive leukemias."

Paul remembered the bright summer day Rose and he drove Coogan through the Tethys front gate—and the forlorn hope that this time something would work. KB26 was new and experimental, but they didn't care. They'd tried everything and had nowhere else to go. Coog was on his last legs. If he didn't respond to *something*, they'd be burying him before Christmas.

"It saved my son Coogan's life," Paul said. "I'll be eternally grateful for that, but—"

Kaplan grimaced. "There's always a 'but,' isn't there."

"Afraid so. And my 'but' is that KB-twenty-six changed him." Paul held up a hand as he saw Kaplan's mouth begin to open. "I know what you're going to say. Just like Sheila you're going to tell me it's impossible. I have no scientific proof, but that's what I feel, that's what I *know* on some deep, fundamental level."

"I wasn't going to contradict you. I was going to tell you that you're right. KB-twenty-six cured most of its recipients, but it made startling, unforeseen changes in some of the survivors." He looked down at his hands. "The curse of unintended consequences."

Paul knotted his fists. He'd been right . . . all along he'd been right.

"Tell me about it."

Kaplan sighed. "All the KB-twenty-six stem cells were embryonic and all O-negative."

"Coogan is O-neg."

Kaplan nodded. "Of course he is. All the recipients are. They changed to that type if they didn't have it before. But let's get back to the unintended consequences. We assumed that, like the primates, the human recipients would change to O-neg. No big deal. Happens in some bone marrow transplants and the important thing was that all the survivors were alive and cancer free. We'd achieved the intended consequence." He leaned back. "Then other changes came to the fore."

Paul nodded. "In hair and such."

"Right." Kaplan sighed. "Not in all the kids. And the parents weren't complaining—their kids hadn't had *any* hair during previous chemotherapies, and post-chemo changes in hair color and texture aren't uncommon. They couldn't care less. But I could. The changes worried me. So I did a full chromosomal analysis on the three children with the most obvious changes."

Kaplan hesitated, and Paul didn't prompt him.

Because suddenly he wished he were somewhere else, wished some*one* else was sitting here. For though he knew what Kaplan was going to say, knew that it would only confirm his suspicions, he didn't want to hear it.

Yet knew he must.

"And?"

"They all had the same DNA. Not just in their blood but in their tissues as well. Biologically and genetically, your son is not your son."

BILL

Bill was readying to leave his office when the phone rang. Marge had gone for the day. He glanced at the blinking button. His first instinct was to ignore it. Whatever it was could wait.

Unless it was Shen.

He picked up and heard the Asian voice that was becoming too familiar.

"I have followed the man, sir. He is visiting other man in Marblehead."

"Can you get close enough to hear what they're talking about?"

"Hard to hear in rain, but I press ear to window and hear man say talk of something called 'KB-twenty-six.' Is this of help?"

Help? Dear God, no. Anything *but* help.

Bill couldn't fathom it. Kaplan was tying a noose around his own neck. Had he completely lost it?

He tugged at his hair, wanted to pull it out. What to do? He had to silence Kaplan—and Rosko too, now that he knew. But how? He couldn't have Shen eliminate both of them. That would raise far too many questions.

Had to be a way . . . had to be—

And then he remembered the background report and what it contained about Rosko. An idea began to form.

"Shen, these two are a threat to everything. When I tell you about Rosko, you'll agree he has to be stopped. And there's a way to take care of both of them in one fell swoop."

"I do not understand 'one fell swoop' but I do understand what you will want from me."

"Good. I—"

"A hundred thousand dollars."

"What?"

"A hundred thousand dollars and I listen to one-fell-swoop plan."

"That's double what I paid last time!"

Shen didn't answer, just waited.

He's blackmailing me. But what other options do I have?

"Fine. A hundred thousand. Listen. Here's what I want you to do . . ."

PAUL

Paul shook his head. Kaplan had said it. No going back now.

"But how?"

"The donor stem cells moved out of the marrow and into the general cell population."

Paul was following. "But we all have stem cells, right?"

"Yes. We all start out as one cell, then two, then four, and so on in a geometric progression. The early cells are stem cells—that means unspecialized but with the potential to change, to differentiate into any of the various tissues and organs that make up a human being. That's what we mean by 'omnipotential.' All your organs started out as stem cells, but just because you're fully formed doesn't mean their work is done. They keep multiplying and replacing damaged cells in various organs throughout the body. They're the basis of tissue regeneration."

Paul was beginning to see. "The KB-twenty-six cells took over regeneration duties from the recipient's own stem cells?"

"Exactly."

"But how come that doesn't happen with a bone marrow graft? That's a form of stem-cell therapy, right?"

Kaplan's eyebrows rose. "You're more medically informed than I thought."

Paul didn't tell him that he was repeating what Sheila had told him.

"Whatever. Marrow recipients don't morph into their donors. How come those cells don't go out and take over?"

"Because they're semi-specialized—they're *blood* stems. They create blood cells. KB-twenty-six was a modified strain of omnipotential *embryonic* cells that have the capacity to change into any type of cell in the body. The process I used to make them antigenically neutral—so the recipient's immune system wouldn't attack them as invaders—apparently wrought other changes. The KB-twenty-six cells were aggressive multipliers. Wherever tissue regeneration was needed, they pushed their way in and did the work."

"I don't—"

"The new cells, carrying their own DNA, dominated. They took over everything. Your son is not who he was before the KB-twenty-six therapy."

Paul felt queasy. That was what had been going on in Coog all these years. It wasn't in his head. He *had* changed.

"How come that didn't happen in the primates?"

"It might have, but we didn't keep them around long enough. We sacrificed them for autopsy. Everything looked fine."

"Why didn't you tell anybody?" Paul said, fighting a flare of anger. "If I'd known back then—"

"What? What would you have done?"

"I don't know."

"Well, I do. You would have sued me. Not immediately, but once you got over the thrill of having him alive and well, you'd start thinking about how he was becoming less and less the child you'd fathered, and how, by the time he fathered his own kids, there'd be very little of you left in him. Your grandchildren would be as genetically related to you as your next-door neighbor's. *Then* you'd call a lawyer."

Paul couldn't see himself in that scenario, but he could easily imagine others doing just that.

"Still, you should have told us."

"To what end? The process is irreversible."

"Then why are you telling me now?"

Kaplan's gaze shifted. "To clear my conscience. I did the right thing, the ethical thing by halting the trial. I wanted to go public with the rest, but I couldn't. I just . . . couldn't."

Paul didn't know whether to believe him or not.

"You said it's irreversible. But that doesn't mean it's unstoppable."

"No, it doesn't. And I might have been able to find a way to stop it, but I was never given the opportunity. When I stopped the clinical trial my backers howled. But I held firm: No more KB-twenty-six until I'd found a way to prevent the cells from taking over. The result? They yanked their financial rug out from under me. You know the rest: bankruptcy, no more Kaplan Biologicals."

"Do you know anything about Innovation Ventures these days?"

Kaplan shook his head. "No, and I don't want to."

"Then you don't know that they funded VecGen's startup."

Kaplan looked as if he'd been slapped. "The bastards! When I pulled KB-twenty-six, they pulled the plug on me and locked me out. They must have gone through my computers and dug out my method for modifying the stem cells."

"But why then would they allow this Lee Swann to buy up the assets?"

"Probably just a front man. They wanted me to think that Kaplan Biologicals was history, dead and gone, and KB-twenty-six with it. But they used my processes and procedures to start VecGen."

It didn't hold together for Paul.

"But . . . if they ferreted out your secrets, then they'd also know about the genetic changes. Why would they risk the suits, the public outcry?"

"They must have stem cells from a collection of genomes, and they try to match the source phenotype as closely as possible to the recipient—hair, eyes, complexion, general features."

Paul wasn't buying this.

"But there's no such thing as a perfect match. People would have to notice changes after a while."

"Not necessarily. An adult's bone structure—the skeleton, shape of the head, facial features—are all pretty well set. Match hair and eye color, skin tone, and so on, and no one will ever be wiser. But in a child it is a different story."

Paul nodded. "Because they're still developing. That's why VecGen won't treat kids."

"Exactly. But they screwed up in the case of Tanesha Green and that other patient Doctor Takamura mentioned. When she confirmed my guess that another patient was having changes the opposite of Tanesha Green, my suspicions were confirmed. Obviously someone fumbled and the stem samples got switched: the black genotype meant for Green wound up in a white woman, and a white genotype wound up in Green. Thus the hair and skin changes, which were only the beginning."

"Why them first?"

"Because skin and hair follicles have a high cell turnover. That's where the phenotype of the invading genotype would make its first appearance."

"But what about memories. The brain is a tissue. Wouldn't it be replaced? My son—what's left of him—still remembers things from his early childhood. Wouldn't memories be lost?"

Kaplan shook his head. "Your neurons stop reproducing shortly after birth. They make new connections all the time, but when they die they're not replaced. The supporting tissues around them will be replaced, but you've still got the same neurons you were born with. So in the sense of shared experiences, your son is still your son. But in every other sense . . ." He shrugged.

Paul leaned back, dazed. "It's like science fiction, like—like *Invasion of the Body Snatchers* or mad scientists creating a master race."

"Except that I understand they're treating all races."

"Right. Then what's the rationale?" Paul didn't get it. He shook his head. "Whatever the purpose, the project is doomed. Sooner or later more people are going to notice too many changes and start asking questions."

"You mean like Tanesha Green and her counterpart?"

"Yes. And then the whole house of cards comes tumbling down."

"Not if the complainers are silenced."

Paul stared at him. "Jesus! You don't think—?"

Kaplan shrugged. "The two people who could bring down the VecGen house of cards died within a week or so of each other. Make of that what you will. I know it frightens me. I'm also someone who could expose them. That's why I'm getting out of town. Tonight."

Two deaths that Kaplan knew about. But what about the attempt on Sheila's life?

Kaplan leaned forward. "Two threats are dead, and one—yours truly—is disappearing for a while. That leaves three loose ends: you, your son, and your lady friend."

"But we're not involved."

"Of course you are. Coogan is evidence, and Doctor Takamura— she knows too much. And now so do you."

Paul felt the muscles at the back of his neck begin to bunch. Coog . . . Sheila . . . in danger?

Kaplan sighed. "I'm not taking any chances. Neither should you. Play it safe: Stop nosing around, stop pushing this inquiry into your son's changes. Be happy he's alive and well and get on with your life."

Paul shook his head. "I don't think I can do that. Sheila won't stop until she's got all the answers."

"You *have* all the answers. I just gave them to you."

"Won't be enough. Sheila will want to blow the whistle. And she will."

Kaplan smiled. "That was what I figured."

And suddenly it was all clear.

"*That's* why you've told me all this! You want Sheila and me to act as lightning rods! You know we won't let it rest, so you run off with your tail between your legs and wait to see if anything happens to us!"

Paul wanted to smash a fist into the center of Kaplan's marshmallow face.

Kaplan must have read that because he scooted farther away on the couch.

"No-no. You've got it wrong. I'm giving you the facts because you deserve to know. What you do with them is your business."

Paul shot to his feet. He told himself *Don't lose it, don't lose it,* but his fuse was lit and burning fast.

"If you'd done due diligence there'd be no foreign DNA taking over my son's body, or anybody else's."

"They didn't give me the chance. At least your boy's alive!"

"*Someone's* alive, but he's no longer the child I fathered. He's someone else. The boy I fathered is as good as *dead!*" He jabbed a finger at Kaplan's frightened face. "And *you* killed him!"

Paul knew he was feeling too crazy to allow himself within reach of Kaplan, so he backed away. Couldn't touch Kaplan, but he had to break something, anything.

His chair. He picked it up and hurled it at the nearest wall, gouging the paint where it struck.

"If anything happens to Coog or Sheila," he said as he stormed toward the door, "I'll find you and I'll—" Don't say it, he thought. Don't. "You'll be to blame!"

"No," he heard Kaplan say. "*You'll* be to blame."

———···———

Paul's wipers beat at top speed but still it was hard to see. Damn rain. Enough already. He sped through a huge puddle. Thoughts raged—not simply with anger, but he felt so damn confused.

You'll be to blame . . .

Kaplan's parting words kept hammering at him.

What if he was right? If someone from VecGen was eliminating anyone who threatened VG723? It seemed so insane, yet those two women—who had no doubt become mosaics just like the KB26 kids—were both dead.

Would telling Sheila what Kaplan had said put her in more danger?

These killers knew that Kaplan was in on their secrets, but probably thought self-preservation would keep him quiet. They couldn't know that Kaplan had spilled the whole story, so if Paul kept quiet, Coog, Sheila, and he might stay out of harm's way.

If they stopped nosing around.

But the whole idea rankled him. Here, only hours after sharing such intimate moments with Sheila, he was considering betraying their budding bond of trust. Didn't seem right.

His cell rang. He recognized his home number and opened the line.

"Dad?"

"Yeah, Coog. Why aren't you at Tommy's?"

"He got sick so I didn't go."

"Why didn't you tell—?"

"Dad, I thought I heard someone in the garage."

Shit.

"Is the door to the garage still locked?"

"Yeah. Should I call the cops?"

"No. I'm just a few blocks away. Hang on. Be there in two minutes."

Paul felt an icy blanket settle over him. Was Coog imagining things or did they have another prowler? Kaplan's story made him fear the latter.

His free hand tightened on the wheel as he goosed the SUVs' speed.

KAPLAN

Gerald had just started packing the second suitcase when he heard a noise toward the rear of the house, then a flow of cool air around his ankles.

An open window?

Heart pounding, he snatched his pistol from where he'd left it on the bed.

Earlier he'd moved the Glock from the kitchen to the upstairs bedroom while he was packing. He'd told himself he was overreacting, but now he was glad. In a few hours he'd be far away, but until then he was taking no chances.

He hefted it and worked the slide to chamber a round. He'd taken it out to a firing range a few times to become familiar with it. After all, what good was a weapon you didn't know how to use? He'd proved to be a terrible shot, but home defense didn't require marksmanship. Anything that happened would be within a few feet. Just point and pull the trigger.

He prayed he wouldn't have to, but if it meant his life he wouldn't hesitate.

"Hello?" he called as he stepped into the hall. "I've got a gun!"

God, that sounded stupid, but he imagined that half the effectiveness of the weapon lay in your enemy's awareness that you had it.

He checked the three bedrooms on the upper floor, then headed downstairs, moving slowly but stepping heavily to announce his descent. He didn't want to surprise anyone.

"I'm coming down. And I've got a forty-caliber Glock ready to fire."

He turned on all the lights and did a thorough search, room by room.

No sign of anyone. He was alone. As usual.

He rushed back upstairs to finish packing. The sooner out of here the better.

He tossed the Glock on the bed. He wished he could take it with him, but no way on a plane.

PAUL

Paul found no sign that anyone had been in the garage. As for around the house, the rain made a reconnoiter unfeasible.

Now he sat and stared at his phone. He owed Sheila a call. Even if he hadn't gone to see Kaplan, he'd be expected to call. He wanted to call but . . .

She'd ask a thousand questions and he didn't know what to tell her. The truth would play right into Kaplan's scheme—set her charging about and acting as a lightning rod. A lie . . . he hated the idea of lying to her.

But he had to call and say *something*.

And then it hit him: Sheila was still at the hospital. He could call her home phone and leave a message. Great. Make contact and duck questions—at least until tomorrow.

He punched in her number. He'd tell her about the wonder of this afternoon and how lucky he felt—all true—then say something about Kaplan changing his mind about spilling the beans. He was no help . . . see you tomorrow . . .

That would work. He hoped.

KAPLAN

Gerald had to sit on the second suitcase to close it.

He checked his watch. The cab should be here soon. His flight to Florida left in two hours and he wanted to get to Logan with time to spare.

He groaned with the weight of the suitcase as he lifted and lugged it downstairs to the front door. As he set it on the floor he sensed that he wasn't alone.

He turned and gasped at the sight of a soaked Asian man. His eyes were cold and black, his expression almost sad, but the baseball bat clutched in his gloved hands sent a spasm of fear through Gerald's gut.

He reached for his pistol but it was still upstairs.

"Who—?"

"I am very sorry for you," he said as he lifted the bat.

Gerald opened his mouth to scream, raised an arm to ward off the blow, shifted his weight away to leap aside, but too late. The impact against his skull rocked him to his toes. The world went white as he slammed back against the door. His legs turned to water and he slid toward the floor.

He heard the voice say, "May your soul find the peace it deserves," and then he felt another, crunching impact on the top of his head.

After that, Gerald Kaplan felt no more.

—ELEVEN—

PAUL

Paul was sitting in the kitchen when the doorbell rang.

He'd spent the morning agonizing over what to tell Sheila. She'd called three times already but he'd let the answering machine take it. Finally he'd decided to come clean and tell her. She deserved to know.

The doorbell again. The clock on the kitchen wall said just a little past ten and Coog was still asleep. Who'd come knocking on a weekday morning? Jehovah's Witnesses? He hoped not.

Paul took his coffee with him as he headed for the front door. His heart tripped a beat when he pulled it open and saw the men on his front stoop.

One was a uniformed cop. Paul recognized him: Evers, who'd shown up in response to Coog's 9-1-1. The second, although dressed in a suit and an overcoat, had cop written all over him. Rain splashed them but Paul didn't invite them in.

They made him uneasy. *More* than uneasy—scared. What was going on?

"Officer Evers," he said. "Did my son call you again last night?"

He'd told Coog not to call, but . . .

Evers looked puzzled. "A nine-one-one? If he did, someone else must have taken it. Another prowler?"

Paul nodded. "Thought he heard someone in the garage. But I got home a few minutes later and couldn't find anyone."

"We're here on another matter, Mister Rosko." Evers cocked his head at the second man, mid-fifties and tired looking. Willy Loman at the end of the line. "This is Detective Winters from Marblehead PD. He's got some questions."

Marblehead? The word set off an alarm in his head.

He took a sip of coffee to hide his confusion. He sensed he'd better tread carefully here.

"I hope you don't mind my asking," Paul said, "but why is a detective from Marblehead standing on my front step?"

Winters cleared his throat and wiped water from his face. "Do you know a Doctor Gerald Kaplan?" The detective's voice was unexpectedly soft.

He sensed what was coming.

"Yes, but not well. We've only met a couple of times."

"Are you aware that he was murdered last night?"

Paul lost his grip on his coffee cup, caught it before it hit the floor, spilling coffee on his jeans.

"Oh, God! Jesus! How—? Who—?"

Evers said, "May we come in, Mister Rosko?"

"Sure, sure." Still numb, he stepped back to let them pass. "Jesus, who would do a thing like that?"

He felt like he'd been dunked in the Copper River. Deep down he'd been hoping that Kaplan was just a paranoid head case. Dear God, someone *was*, as he'd put it, tying up loose ends.

He glanced at his coffee cup and noticed it shaking. He grabbed it with his other hand to steady it. He had to say something . . . but what? Then he knew: Exactly how the average person would react.

"Hey, wait a minute. Why are you coming to me about this?"

"We talked to his staff first thing this morning. They said you had an altercation with him a few days ago."

"I had an argument with him and you think I killed him?"

"We're just checking all possibilities, Mister Rosko."

"Well, you can cross me off your list. I did not kill Doctor Kaplan."

"But you did threaten him."

"Like hell!"

Winters pulled out a tattered notepad, flipped through half a dozen pages until he found what he was looking for.

"According to witnesses you said, 'You're hiding something, Kaplan. I'm going to find out what it is, and when I do, you're through.' " Winters looked up. "That sounds like a threat to me. How about you?"

Did I say that?

He didn't remember. This was looking bad. He felt cornered.

"Yes, I . . . I guess it does sound like a threat but, Jesus, against his reputation, not his life." He had a question of his own, but was almost afraid to hear the answer. "How . . . how did he die?"

"Bludgeoned."

Paul winced. God knew he hadn't liked the man, but beaten to death . . .

"Can I ask with what?"

"That's under investigation." Winters pencil hovered over a fresh page on the pad. "Now, just what was this disagreement about?"

Paul coughed for time. How much should he say?

"A professional matter."

"Care to elaborate?"

He decided to stick close to the truth—a version of it.

"It had to do with a cancer treatment developed by his company. My son received the treatment and lately I've developed some concerns."

Winters scribbled, then said, "Such as?"

"I prefer not to get into that. It's . . . it's personal."

"There's nothing personal in a homicide investigation." His pencil remained poised over his notepad. "When was the last time you saw Doctor Kaplan?"

Here it was. The big question: Come clean or not?

If he said last night he'd become their number-one suspect. And that meant they'd do a background check if they hadn't already. And once they did . . . they'd never believe he was innocent.

A thought struck him like a blow. Did the killer know the truth about him and set it up so he'd be a suspect?

The smart thing to do right now was clam up and call a lawyer. But that would send Winters's suspicions soaring.

"That morning at his office."

"No contact with him since?"

"None."

"Any contact before?"

Again: truth or lie? His fingerprints had to be in Kaplan's home. If he denied any other contact and they found the prints . . .

Go with the truth.

"Once. It was—last week. Doctor Takamura and I had an impromptu meeting with him at his house."

"What about?"

"The same subject: my son."

Winters stared at him for a long, uncomfortable time. Then he let out a breath that puffed his already ample cheeks.

"Okay, Mister Rosko. One last question: Where were you between five and eight P.M. last night?"

Paul felt as if he'd wandered into an episode of _Law and Order._ He saw no choice but to lie again.

"Well, earlier I was with Doctor Takamura—in her office. Later I was home here with my son. And in between I was on my way home."

"Spell the doctor's name for me please."

As Winters began questioning him about precise times, Paul felt himself beginning to sweat. He said he'd left Sheila around six. It had been more like four. Did he dare ask her to cover for him?

As to what time he arrived here—

"Wait," he said. "Let me check my cell phone."

He retrieved it from his bedroom and keyed his way to the "Calls Received" list. There—the last call had been from Coog.

"My son called me at six-seventeen while I was in transit. I was three minutes away then. That would mean that I've been here since six-twenty last night."

No way he could have been to Marblehead and back in that time—_if_ they bought his half-true story.

Sheila was the weak link. If they asked her what time he'd left—

and he was pretty sure they would—and she told them the truth, he'd be cooked. He had to talk to her first.

"Okay, Mister Rosko," Winters said. "I think that's all for now. Sorry to bother you and thanks for your cooperation."

Evers gave Paul a friendly nod. "Have a nice day."

And then they were gone. Paul leaned against the door he'd closed behind them and gasped for air.

This can't be happening, he thought. It *can't* be.

PAUL

Paul felt like a heel asking Sheila to meet him outside in his car, but he couldn't risk walking into Tethys today. Who knew who was watching? Being seen together might not be safe for either of them.

He wished he could waltz in there with a dozen roses, *two* dozen, and tell her how much yesterday meant to him. Instead, he called her on his cell phone.

"*I've been trying to get hold of you all morning,*" she said.

He could hear the hurt in her voice.

"I couldn't take the calls. Believe me, if I could have I would have. We need to talk."

"*I don't like the sound of that.*"

"Not about us. And not in your office."

"What?"

"Look, I hate to go all cloak and dagger on you, but can you meet me outside? It's important."

"*Come on. What happened last night? What did Kap—*"

"Don't say his name. I know that sounds a little crazy, but just don't."

A pause, then, "*You're worrying me, Paul.*"

She's worried, he thought. I'm scared half to death.

She sighed. "*Okay. We'll play it your way: What did our friend say?*"

"Just come outside, okay?"

"*Give me ten minutes. Where are you?*"

"Parked behind the Admin building. I'll pick you up in front.

Bring your umbrella. It's a mess out here."

Ten minutes felt like forever as he waited, watching all the doors and windows for anyone suspicious. He didn't know what he was going to say but he had to tell Sheila something. Even if they dropped the whole thing and ran away to start a new life, Paul wasn't sure he'd ever feel safe. That had been Kaplan's plan and look what happened to him.

The best and worst idea was probably to act as if he knew less than he did and cool it with Sheila. Best because it would protect her. Worst because it meant not seeing her. Hurting her. She'd probably feel used. Keeping his distance might be the hardest thing he'd ever done, but he saw no other way.

He also had to put the brakes on her inquiries into VG723. But how?

"Damn it!" He punched the steering wheel. "How am I going to do this?"

He looked up and had to smile as she stepped out the front door. What a beauty.

She ran full speed through the rain to reach his truck. Her hair swirled about and clung to her face. She swatted at it with one hand while she wrapped the other tightly around her coat to keep it closed.

He sighed. She looked so small and frail in the wind and rain. She could barely make it to him without being blown away. How could she stand up to a corporation that killed people as easily as deleting line items off a budget?

He opened the door for her and she jumped in.

"Made it. Whew! That wind is something else. My hair must be all over the place."

"It's fine."

Of its own accord his hand started to reach out to her, to smooth a few strands back in place. He stopped it. What he really wanted to do was cup a hand around the back of her neck, pull her closer, and kiss her. A lingering kiss. How he wanted her.

"Sorry to drag you out here. A minute ago it was only rain."

"That's all right. So, what's the big secret? What did Kaplan say?"

Now to begin the lies. God, he hated this.

"Nothing. Said I wasn't a doctor so he refused to talk to me."

Sheila's face reddened. "But the list—I gave you the list of what to ask. Did you show him?"

"I tried. I told him what you said and dangled the note in front of him but he wouldn't talk. Wouldn't even call you. Wouldn't say a damn thing. I'm sorry."

"Well, we'll just go see him together. Tonight. We'll get the story. What a jerk. I'm sorry you went all the way there for nothing."

"So am I. But for a different reason."

His eyes must have given something away, for she clutched his arm and stared at him.

He said, "Kaplan is dead."

SHEILA

Sheila gasped. "*What?* Are you serious?"

He nodded.

"But how?" She thought of Tanesha. "Heart?"

"Bludgeoned to death in his home."

Sheila felt a wave of nausea. It made no sense . . . her mind wouldn't register it. They'd seen him just a few days ago.

Then a question worked its way through her confusion.

"How come you know and I haven't heard a thing?"

"The cops told me."

"Cops? Paul, what's going on! Why were the police—?"

"Seems he was murdered not too long after I left."

"They can't suspect you!"

"Oh yes, they can. Someone told them about our little contretemps the other morning."

Head spinning, Sheila leaned back in the seat. What was going on in her life? Patients dying, doctors dying—

She bolted upright—

"I don't believe you about Kaplan."

She saw Paul stiffen. "I didn't kill him, Sheila."

"I know. I didn't mean that. I meant that I think he told you something and you're afraid of what I'll do with the information.

You're afraid I'll get killed. But whatever he told you doesn't matter. There's already been an attempt on my life. How much more dangerous could it get?"

Paul looked away for a minute, tapped his fingers on the steering wheel. He glanced back at her. "You're right, okay. There's a lot to tell but not right now. Suffice to say, Kaplan doesn't think the deaths of your two patients were accidental."

Sheila bowed her head. "Hal Silberman died today."

Paul grimaced. "That means four people dead who could cause problems for VG-seven-twenty-three. Kaplan was terrified because he knew too much. He was taking off. Hiding. He said if we didn't drop the investigation, then most likely Coogan and I would be added to that list. He said whoever it is isn't playing around and we should just look the other way."

"Coogan?"

"Kaplan says he's evidence."

"I'm sorry, Paul. I'm so sorry I got you two involved."

"I got *you* involved, asking for that test."

Oh God, the test.

"I found out the lab samples were switched. Bill was seen around the lab. I think he took Coog's samples from before he had the KB-twenty-six and substituted it. This sounds crazy but I think the therapy changed his DNA."

"It's not crazy. You're right. It changed him."

"What?"

Paul looked frightened suddenly. "Look up there." He didn't point but jutted his chin in the direction of the building. "Is that Bill's window?"

She looked and saw two figures, watching them. She couldn't see their faces but they were facing their way.

"Listen Sheila, all our lives are in danger. Kaplan told me everything he knows but I can't tell you now. I need you to go back in there and pretend we're fighting or something. I'll bet dollars to doughnuts the police are fingering me for Kaplan's murder."

"What did they think about you being there last night?"

He looked away again. "I didn't tell them."

Sheila closed her eyes. "Oh, no. Don't tell me you lied to them."

"I was most likely the next-to-last person to see him alive and I panicked."

"Next to last?"

"Well, figure his killer was the last."

Oh, right. Of course.

"But if they find out you were there when you said you weren't, you'll be their number-one suspect."

"I know." It sounded like a moan.

"You've got to tell them, Paul. Call them and tell them just what you told me: You had a contentious history with the guy and he was killed shortly after you left him, so you panicked. Now you're coming clean."

"I can't, Sheila."

"You've got to! It'll look a lot better if they learn it from you than if they find out on their own. We should tell the police everything. All we've found out."

He shook his head. "We can't prove anything. And with me behind bars, you and Coogan won't be safe."

She stared at him. "What happened yesterday—"

"Sheila, I'm crazy about you. And what happened yesterday was incredible. I'm sick that instead of taking you to a nice restaurant or filling your house with flowers, I'm in a car in the rain asking you to lie for me. But I swear to you we'll get through this together and I'll spend the rest of my life, our lives, making it up to you."

She looked back up at the window. Bill and someone else were still watching. She couldn't hug Paul without being seen, so she squeezed his hands.

"Tell me what you want me to do."

BILL

"Do you think they suspect something?" Bill said as he and Shen stood at his office window and watched Rosko's car.

Shen had come to Bill after overhearing the call from Rosko about meeting in his car.

"Four deaths . . ." His piercing eyes riveted Bill. "Only a fool would not suspect."

Only a fool would not suspect. Condescending creep. Bill liked Shen a lot better when he was subservient. Ever since he had given him the money the tables had been switched. He was at Shen's mercy and they both knew it. So much for respect.

Bill glanced at him. "Three: The Slade woman, Tanesha Green, and then Kaplan."

"Doctor Silberman died this morning. Four deaths." The wolverine tone and that omnipotent stare.

Bill had given the man the tickets and money he'd demanded. Just this morning he'd wired the other fifty thousand into his account for Kaplan. What did he want now? Shen kept watching him. Bill could feel goosebumps on his arms under his shirt. This was not someone he wanted as an enemy. Whatever it was, he could have it. Bill didn't want Shen angry with him.

"Fine, four deaths. But it should have been three. If Kaplan had kept to himself and left well enough alone we wouldn't even be having this conversation."

Bill had spent last night in a state of sweaty nausea. He still had a conscience. But sometimes conscience had to surrender to a higher purpose.

And the nausea would pass.

"I *meant* does she suspect that she's bugged?"

"I cannot know."

Bill had to smile. Of course Shen could not know.

The major disappointment was that Rosko had called Sheila. Bill had hoped the police would have placed him at the scene of the crime by now, looked up his record, and slapped on the cuffs.

Rosko's passenger door opened. Sheila stepped out and rushed back through the rain. Her head was down, her shoulders slumped, her usual bouncing stride was gone.

Had they had a fight?

"Here she comes. Get back to the monitoring room and stay on her. I want to know every word she says to anyone."

"Yessir."

"And if you need to call me, use my cell. I'll be out of town this afternoon."

Shen nodded, then headed for the door.

Bill turned back to the window and watched Sheila approach.

Tramp. He'd tried to expunge the images from his memory but they kept recurring . . . the same scenes flashing again and again across the screen of his brain like some foul porn loop . . .

No, not fair. He couldn't bring himself to hate her. After the initial shock and revulsion had worn off, he realized, hell, she was human. She had needs. He might fantasize about her when he was with Elise, but at least he found his release.

No, he didn't hate her. But he was very, very disappointed.

She needed to know the truth about her boyfriend. But Bill wouldn't be the one to tell her. He'd let the cops give her the bad news.

But to do that they'd have to know about Rosko themselves.

As Rosko drove away, Bill wrote down his license plate number.

_____ ▪▪▪ _____

Where have all the phone booths gone? Bill wondered as he cruised what appeared to be Marblehead's main drag. Cell phones had put them on the endangered species list.

He wanted no chance that his call would be traced, and figured it would carry more weight if it came from Kaplan's own town.

Finally he spotted a booth and pulled into the curb half a block past it. He opened his umbrella and hurried through the downpour.

When he reached it he pulled out the memo slip with the police number, plunked in a couple of coins, and dialed. Once connected, he asked to speak to the detective in charge of the Kaplan murder. Seconds later a soft voice came on the line.

"*Detective Winters.*"

"Yes, detective. I just heard the terrible news about Doctor Kaplan and I just had to call."

"*What is it, Mister . . .?*"

"I-I'd rather not give my name. I don't want to get involved, but I think you should know about the strange car parked in Doctor Kaplan's driveway last night."

"*Strange how?*"

"Well, Gerald isn't a social man and never—well, almost never—has company."

"*Really.*" The detective's tone shifted from bored to interested. "*Can you give me any details?*"

"Not many, I'm afraid. I know it was an SUV—an Explorer, I think. And it was a dark color. As to whether it was black or dark blue, I'm afraid I can't say."

"*Did you happen to notice the plates?*"

"Yes. I'd first thought maybe a relative was visiting from out of state, but then I saw it was a Massachusetts plate."

"*Can you remember anything, anything at all about the number?*"

"Well, I have a near-photographic memory, but I wasn't paying all that much attention. The best I can recall it started with 789 and ended—I think—with something like L-V-E."

Rosko's plate actually began with 739, but Bill didn't want his recall to seem too prefect.

"*This might prove very helpful,*" the detective said. "*Where can I reach you if I have any further questions?*"

Bill hung up and walked back to his car. Once inside and back in traffic he laughed aloud.

Everything was working so perfectly. Like the string-puller Supreme, he was the Piper who'd chosen the tune and now everyone was dancing to it, whether they liked it or not—whether they heard it or not. He was back in control.

PAUL

"Want some more fries?" Coog said, extending the bag across the Explorer's center console.

Paul hadn't been able to sit around the house any longer, so he and Coog had taken in a movie—the Rock's latest puncher-upper—and stopped at a Wendy's. Coog had brought along his leftover fries for the ride home.

"Just a couple."

Paul snagged three and stuffed them in his mouth.

At least something was good.

He had long since given up hope that this would all go away. He'd left Kaplan's with a pit on his stomach. But also a sense of relief. He *had* fathered this child. And like Kaplan said, he was alive and healthy with his memory unchanged, so what else really mattered? But the rest of the world might not feel the same way. Certainly Sheila wouldn't. What Kaplan's therapy had done to the patients was unintentional. But not VecGen or Tethys. They knew the therapy would change the patients' DNA and didn't bother to tell them. Didn't they think the public would figure it out eventually?

If Kaplan hadn't been killed, Paul might have tried to talk Sheila into running off with him, to a new state, to swear off looking into Tethys and VecGen and just pretend it never happened. Turn a blind eye to all the patients. But if he ran, he'd look guilty. And Sheila would never let this go.

So what was his plan? Besides continuing to look for evidence against VecGen and IV and trying not to get killed . . . hoping Sheila could play it cool at work . . .

"Dad!" Coog pointed though the windshield. "Cops!"

The words jolted Paul back to the here and now. He looked where Coog was pointing, blinked, looked again.

Through the rain he could see two black and whites plus an unmarked car at the curb in front of his house.

His chest tightened.

Coog was still pointing. "Hey! They've got the garage door open! You think someone tried to break in again?"

Paul tried to speak but words wouldn't come. Good thing Coog was babbling and didn't notice.

"Looks like they're all over the house. Don't they have to have a search warrant or something?"

"I'll bet they do," Paul croaked.

This could only mean they'd placed him at Kaplan's last night. After looking up his record, a search warrant was inevitable.

At least they wouldn't find anything. But now Coog would learn about his past. Paul had been planning to wait until he was sixteen. Now it would all come out under the worst circumstances.

Damn them!

He tightened his grip on the wheel and kept his speed even as he approached.

"Hey, Dad! Aren't we going in?"

"Not yet."

Maybe not at all. He couldn't stand the thought of Coog watching when they slapped the cuffs on. He'd lied—obstruction of justice. It would all be straightened out eventually, but the sight of him being led away in handcuffs would scar the boy.

He'd find a place for Coog to stay—maybe his friend Jimmy's— and then walk into the police station and say he'd heard they were looking for him.

He drove by, turned the corner, and pulled into the curb before the Simons' house. They'd left for Florida and, as usual, had asked Paul to keep an eye on the place. Since the rear corner of their property abutted a rear corner of Paul's, all he had to do was hop a low fence and maybe he could get an idea of what they were looking for . . . what they thought they'd find in his garage.

"Stay here," he told Coog as he opened his door.

"Where are you going?"

"Just taking a quick look. I'll be back in a minute."

"I'm coming."

"No." He put steel into the word. "You wait."

He leaped out and ran through the rain and across the Simons' darkened side yard to the right rear corner of their lot. He stopped at the fence and stared at his house. All the lights were on. The garage was closest—no more than fifty feet away.

Across a muddy yard.

He'd leave a trail of footprints. But he saw that the mud had already been kicked up. Probably from the cops searching for whatever they were after. Good chance that no one would notice with all the water, but should he risk it?

Yeah, he should.

He hopped the fence and ran in a crouch to the garage window. A quick peek showed Evers and Winters poking though the pile of junk that over the years had usurped the unused half of his double garage. Both wore latex gloves.

Faint traces of their chatter trailed out the open doors and around to Paul.

"Not finding it doesn't get him off the hook," Winters was saying.

"I know, but finding it will put the last nail in his coffin."

Find what? What were they looking for?

"We've got his fingerprints at the scene, on that chair he smashed into the wall, but if we could just find the weapon."

The chair—it showed his propensity toward violence . . .

Evers moved toward the rear while Winters hung around the middle.

Paul felt exposed out here. He'd seen enough. Heard enough too. That nail-in-his-coffin remark had set his nerves on edge.

Even so, he didn't see any alternative to turning himself in—but not here, not now.

He was just about to head back to Coog when he heard Evers say, "Jesus!"

Paul's gut twisted as he glued himself to the window.

Evers stepped into view holding a baseball bat by the knob with his thumb and index finger.

"Do you believe this?" he said.

Even from where he was Paul recognized his Louisville Slugger. He didn't recognize the reddish brown stains near the bat's business end. He felt his chest tighten. Blood.

Winters bent for a closer look.

"If that matches Kaplan's, we're in business." He straightened. "Pardon the pun, but I'm long overdue for a pop fly."

Paul could barely breathe as he stumbled away.

This morning he'd idly wondered if someone might be framing him. Now he knew. He was in a nightmare.

He went back over the fence and ran back toward the car.

There had to be a way out of this. He needed a place to hide, to cool his jets and calm down so he could think straight.

"What's wrong, Dad?" Coog said as Paul hopped into the car and slammed it into DRIVE.

"We're not going home."

Coog turned to face him. "W-why not?"

Paul was cold, wet, and scared. His brain wasn't on track. What could he say? Best tell him the truth—not all, not yet, but enough for him to appreciate what was going on.

"I'm being framed for murder."

Coog laughed. "Yeah, right."

"I'm not kidding, Coog. Just before you called last night I was visiting a man named Gerald Kaplan. Shortly after I left him he was murdered."

Coog's voice rose half an octave. "Shit! Really?"

Paul let the four-letter word pass.

"Someone beat him to death with a baseball bat—*our* baseball bat. Which the cops just discovered in our garage, bloodstains and all."

"Dad, you *gotta* be kidding me." An edge of hysteria had crept into Coog's voice. "*Please* tell me you're kidding!"

"I wish I were."

"But why you?"

"Someone wanted Kaplan dead. They must have known I was visiting him last night and thought I'd make a convenient fall guy."

"That noise I heard in the garage last night!"

"Yeah. Someone borrowing the bat."

"But you didn't kill him. They can prove that! You'll be ex . . . ex . . ."

"Exonerated? Not easily. My bat in my garage with my fingerprints and Kaplan's blood. Pretty damning. If you were a cop and I told you I was being framed, would you believe me?"

Coog didn't answer, just stared ahead through the windshield.

"And I can't prove I didn't do it because I was *there*."

"I'm scared, Dad."

"You and me both. But I'm more worried about you."

"Me?"

"Where can I stash you so you'll be safe?"

"Stash me? Where are *you* going?"

"I need to find a quiet place to stay where I can figure this out."

"I'm going with you."

"No, you're—"

"Yes, I am and there's no way you can stop me. You're my father and I'm staying with you."

Paul sensed the finality in Coog's voice. Though he wanted him out of harm's way, he knew he couldn't leave him someplace if he refused to be left.

You're my father and I'm staying with you.

His heart swelled and his throat constricted. Why had he had to question his paternity? Freakin' pride. Curiosity killed the cat. And Kaplan.

"All right," he said after a moment. "Any ideas?"

"How about a motel?"

Paul shook his head. "I don't have enough cash. My credit card can be traced if I use it."

"How about a beach house somewhere. Must be lots of deserted places. We can break in and . . ."

Deserted . . . the word echoed through Paul's brain. And then it hit him.

"I know just the place."

But first . . .

He pulled a U turn.

"Where are we going?"

"To the gas station. I need to use their bathroom."

———■■■———

Paul drove around the back of Rudy's gas station and walked into the men's room. He'd used it before and knew they never locked it. He popped open his cell phone. He didn't want Coog to hear the phone calls he had to make so pretended to need to hit the john. His phone was poised in his hand as he hesitated.

Paul was leery about confessing everything to Sheila but had to tell her *something*. She'd be home now, so he called her office. When he reached her voicemail he spoke in a low tone.

"Sheila, this is Paul. My situation has deteriorated beyond imagining. I'm being framed for Kaplan's murder and the police are buying it. Right now I'm in a safe place until I can figure out what to do. I care about you, Sheila, and I care about what you think of me. That's why I need to warn you that you're going to hear . . ." This was the hard part. "You're going to hear things about me. Bad things, presented in the worst possible light. But know this: I did not kill Kaplan, Sheila. I did *not* kill Kaplan. Sometime I hope you'll give me a chance to explain what you'll be hearing. Trust me, okay? That means the world to me. I don't know what else to tell you. Just . . . have faith, that's all I ask."

He broke the connection and took a deep breath. Whatever relationship may have formed between them was probably shattered, gone. He knew that, but couldn't handle Sheila's thinking it was *all* lie.

One more call.

A plan had been forming. To make it happen he had to get in touch with Lee Swann—or whoever pretended to be Swann.

Information gave him VecGen's number. He knew no one was there but he needed to leave a message. The receptionist had called "legal" when he'd been there. Was that because Paul was acting crazy or because they knew exactly who Swann was?

He went through VecGen's voicemail maze until he heard, "If you wish to speak to our legal department, press six now."

He did and was given another set of options: names and extension numbers. He picked one at random.

"This is Paul Rosko. I'm sure your receptionist will remember me. I want you to get this message to Mister Lee T. Swann. Tell him this: Paul Rosko wants to make a deal." He left his cell number.

"Tell him to call me at six o'clock tomorrow night. I'll put my cell phone on for ten minutes. I think we can come to an agreement that is to our mutual benefit."

He wasn't quite sure what he had to offer, but he'd do anything to ensure Coog and Sheila's safety.

He turned off his phone. The police would soon go to his cell carrier with a court order to locate him. He didn't have to be making a call, just have his phone turned on. They could triangulate his signal between a number of the area's ubiquitous towers and locate him within a hundred-yard radius. But not if his phone was off.

Being a cable installer hadn't been his life's ambition—far from it—but working with electronics day in and day out had its perks.

———▪▪▪———

"We're really breaking in?" Coog said. He sounded astonished.

With good reason, Paul thought. He was watching his father trying to slip the latch on the front door of a small office building. Staying at the Simons' would have been more convenient and more legal, but it was too close to home.

"Trying."

He was pretty sure he could do it. He kept an array of tools in the back of the Explorer, parked on a nearby dead end street. Thank God for the flooding—no one was on the road. He'd picked out a spackling spatula and was now working its flexible blade around the door's spring bolt. He'd be doing a better job if he didn't feel the need to look over his shoulder every half minute. He felt naked out here silhouetted in the light from the vestibule.

Almost had it . . . another quarter inch . . .

The latch moved.

"Got it."

Now what? He hadn't noticed an alarm system on his only other visit. Years at his job had familiarized him with every kind of wiring and he'd developed an instinctive eye for it. But he'd been preoccupied that day.

Well, if it went off they could run. Couldn't get in much more trouble than he was already.

He levered back the latch, pushed the door open, and waited for the howler. Nothing. He stepped inside and checked the doorframe for silent alarm contacts. None.

"Let's go." He held the door for Coog and pointed toward the stairs. "Down there."

The Innovation Ventures door was a snap. As he'd figured, no alarm there either. Why alarm an empty office?

"What is this place?" Coog said as he stepped into the darkened room. "And where's the light switch?"

"No lights, Coog. Can't risk it. We've got to make do with whatever leaks in from the parking lot."

"Hey, where do we sleep?"

"There's no chairs so I guess on the floor."

"Aw, maaaan."

Paul gave him a light tap on the shoulder.

"Still want to stay? We can drive over to Jimmy's right now and you can stay with him."

"Uh-uh. We're in this together, Dad."

For the second time tonight Paul felt a lump build in his throat.

Coog *was* his son, no matter what his DNA said.

He looked round. Nothing to do now but begin exploring this dark office with his son.

__TWELVE__

SHEILA

She sat at a back-corner table in the caf and rubbed her temples. A nasty headache. Most likely tension. She was certainly stressed enough.

She sipped her coffee. Burnt. Awful. And it tasted funny. Well, why should her coffee be any different from everything else? She sniffed it. That same medicinal scent as her sandwich the other day. She looked over the counter. No way someone would poison a whole pot of coffee in the hopes of her drinking a single cup. Most likely no one the caf had poisoned her sandwich either but she didn't trust anyone anymore. Maybe an energy drink instead. She needed caffeine and wasn't going to inject anything unsealed from Tethys until this was over.

A fresh cup of coffee slipped under her chin. She recognized the hand that pushed it to her. Bill's. No way in hell she was drinking that.

He put a hand on her shoulder and she flinched. *Please don't hurt me.* Her heart pounded and her face flushed.

"You okay?"

She tried not to recoil. The ghost of that switched blood sample and so much else hovered between them.

"You don't look okay." Maybe he *did* still trust her.

"H-had a fight with the new boyfriend. Should have known

better." She hoped she sounded sincere.

"Really?" His smile formed.

This might work. "Just doesn't have that spark, you know?"

Before Bill could respond, a man with a gaunt face and gray hair approached her. He wore a trenchcoat over a faded suit, and had an apologetic look in his eyes. Something was wrong.

"Dr. Sheila Taykayama?"

"It's Takamura," Bill said. "Doctor Takamura. Can I help you?"

"Detective Winters. Marblehead police."

Sheila froze, remembering the last time police had come looking for her at work . . .

Oh God, not Paul. Don't let Paul be dead.

Her heart slammed in her chest.

Winters stared at her. "*Are* you Dr. Takamura?"

Sheila nodded.

"I have some questions for you about a Paul Rosko. The hospital records indicate he's a volunteer here."

"What of it?" Bill said. "I'm CEO and COO of Tethys Medical Center. Any questions about Rosko can be directed to me."

The detective gave Bill a cold look. "I'd like to speak with Doctor Takamura, if you don't mind." He turned to Sheila. "Ma'am do you know Paul Rosko?"

"Is he hurt?"

"Not that I know of. I'm looking for him to ask some questions. So, you do know him?"

"Of course. Everyone here knows him. Why?"

"He's wanted in connection with the murder of Doctor Gerald Kaplan."

Paul's words rushed back: *I'm being framed for Kaplan's murder and the police are buying it* . . .

"Murder?" She shook her head. "Not Paul."

"How well do you know him, Ma'am?"

"How well do we know anyone, officer?" She couldn't think of anything else to say. Her mind seemed frozen.

"We pulled his phone records and see a lot of calls back and forth from him to you."

"We've become friends, I guess." She tried to steady the quaver in her voice. "But I don't know him all that well." She had to pretend disinterest to fool Bill and to keep from being implicated. "I know him from here. His son has had problems and we've been doing some research together."

"What *can* you tell us?"

She watched Bill stiffen. There's so much she could tell them, and how much she'd like to watch Bill squirm as she rattled down all her suspicions.

"That's about it. He's a good person. Ask anyone. He volunteers here all the time. Reads to patients . . . he couldn't possibly have done anything to Kaplan."

"You know Kaplan too?" Winters said.

Her first instinct was to deny, but that had gotten Paul into hot water.

"I've met him twice. But Paul couldn't be involved. He's a kind man."

She was eager to offer Paul an alibi for that night, but had to wait until they asked.

"Ma'am, Doctor Kaplan was bludgeoned with a baseball bat. A bat with Kaplan's blood was found in Mister Rosko's garage. His prints were on that bat. His prints were also on an overturned chair ion Doctor Kaplan's house." He paused and locked eyes with her. "*Now* can you think of anything to tell me?"

Mother of God, the evidence against him . . .

How well did she know him really? No matter how devious, someone couldn't plant fingerprints could they?

"You must be mistaken." God, she *hoped* he was mistaken.

"A few nights ago, Mister Rosko was seen carrying a baseball bat in his yard, allegedly looking for a prowler. He implied to the officer on the scene that he planned to use it if he found the prowler."

"Well," Sheila said, "if he was in his yard looking for someone, that's just self defense. He can't be your man. He wouldn't hurt anyone."

Sheila recognized her robotic denial of the facts—the same, *No, no, no!* she'd screamed out when they told her Dek was dead.

"Ma'am, here's something you may not know about him. A

background check revealed that Mister Rosko has a history of violence."

Was he baiting her? Hoping she'd divulge something he'd told her? No such luck. She didn't know a damn think about Paul Rosko's past.

"He's been in jail, Doctor Takayama."

Sheila's breath caught in her throat as the words took hold. "Wait. *Jail?*" She pulled away from Bill and the detective. "What do you mean, jail?"

All eyes in the caf turned her way. She didn't care.

Bill reached for her but she stepped back farther.

"What's this about jail?" Bill asked Winters.

Winters cleared his throat again. That familiar *ahem*. Like her folks, his lungs were probably caked with nicotine. She could smell it on him.

"He killed a man about fifteen years ago. Second-degree manslaughter. Beat the guy to death. No bat that time, just his fists. He confessed and served a year in prison."

His matter-of-fact eyes didn't flinch.

What to think, what to do? In the short time she'd known Paul she'd seen the temper flares. The man who'd run down Coogan had felt his wrath, and the way he had shouted at Kaplan, the rage in his eyes . . . God, how had she missed the red flags?

No. Screw the flags. Her instincts were not wrong. Couldn't be. Getting angry was one thing. Beating someone to death with a bat? No way.

But logic gnawed at her. Detective Winters said Paul had confessed to killing someone. Had gone away for it.

"I don't need to hear this." She glared at all of them. "I don't need to hear any of this."

She turned and hurried from the caf, down the hall, and outside. No one stopped her.

———■■■———

Sheila wandered through the rain not knowing where she was going or what to do. Couldn't think.

She walked to the big tree by the swollen river and leaned against it. The ground was sodden beneath her. Her shoes sank in the mud. Her silk blouse was no doubt see-through. She had no gloves or coat and she watched the wet goosebumps on her forearms rise. Her keys and purse were inside the hospital, so driving home, or anywhere, wasn't an option.

She glanced at the wet, gray world around her, the rain river-dancing on the puddle that had overtaken the parking lot, and knew she was sliding into that surreal place her mind led her when too much happened at once.

She picked up a clump of wet leaves with fingers that didn't seem to belong to her. Couldn't feel it. Disassociation, someone had once said. She slipped into that mode sometimes to get herself through. A way to cope, one psych book said. A form of depression, said another. Whatever, she was there now.

Leaning against the tree, silky blouse sticking to the wet bark, tears freezing to her face. All she could do was stare at the Tethys hospital and repeat what she needed to be the truth.

They're wrong! I know what I felt. I have to trust Paul on this.

A few minutes later, or maybe many minutes—she couldn't tell—Bill walked out and offered her his coat. She pushed it away.

"Come on, Sheila, it's okay. You didn't know. People like Paul—well, they take advantage. But it's okay. I cleared it up with the police. You won't be implicated in any of this."

Bill . . . trying to take care of her. Had she been wrong about both of them? Could she ever trust her judgment again? Bill was out here, trying to comfort. Protect her from a man with a shady past, a background—

Sheila stopped short and dug her heels into the mud as her strength rushed back.

Wait. The background check. Bill had told her he'd run that years ago.

So he'd said.

"Why did you let him volunteer here if he had a record?"

He looked stunned. "I-I didn't know. Just found out. Like you."

Right. If he *had* known, he'd never have allowed an ex-con free access to the campus. No background check years ago as he claimed. He knew about Paul's and Rose's past some other way.

Like overhearing the conversation she'd had with Paul about Rose in her office.

She felt her vision blur as blood pounded through her head. A bug? Bill. Watching, listening. It explained how he knew so much. Had he heard every conversation she'd had with Paul? Did he know they'd gone to see Kaplan?

A sick feeling filled her. Had he heard her have sex with Paul? Did he know all about it right now and was just placating her? Giving her the false sense of trust *she* was supposed to be doling out?

Gently she pulled away from the tree. Her blouse snagged but then released.

"Bill, I'd like to go home. Absorb all this. Thank you so much for talking to the cops. I'm just glad I'm done with that Rosko. I had no idea."

"Yeah, good thing."

Did he believe her? She had no way of telling. But she had to get away from Bill.

"I need the rest of the day off. My keys and coat are inside, I'll just go—"

Bill put his hand up. "Do you have a set of spare house keys? I can drive you home. You may not want to go back in there now."

She nodded and took his coat.

"You wait here while I go get my car." She stood there, numb from the cold and the circumstances.

Paul didn't kill Kaplan. She was sure of it. Well, pretty sure. She didn't know who she could trust anymore but Bill wasn't on the list. One wrong move and he might kill her.

As she waited for Bill's car to roll up, she prayed to every Catholic saint she could remember that her instincts about Paul were right.

————■■■————

PAUL

"Dad, what's gonna happen if you get caught?"

More like *when* I get caught, Paul thought.

They sat on the office's dusty floor, leaning against the inside wall. Wan light filtered through the blinds. He felt terrible. He'd tried but hadn't been able to get much sleep on the floor. He ached in places he'd never ached before.

"I'll be arrested and thrown in jail."

"But just for a day, right? Everybody gets bailed out."

"Yeah, usually."

But not me. A capital crime by someone who'd already tried to avoid capture . . . uh-uh. No bail for that guy.

But again, no point in making Coog more afraid than he already was.

"So we just wait for the guy at IV to call back?"

Paul nodded. "In the meantime, make sure you keep away from the windows. And no lights. At night we can go in the bathroom to read or in that closet over there, but make sure you don't put any lights on out here where there are windows. And we have to talk softly during work hours, until the other tenants leave for the day."

"I know, Dad." Coogan reached over and punched Paul on the shoulder. "I'm kind of glad this is happening."

"I'm being framed for murder, we're hiding out in an abandoned office with nowhere to sit or sleep, we can't talk above a whisper, and you're glad?"

"The last few weeks you've been acting funny. I know you said you weren't, but you were. You were, like, weird. Now I feel like you're my good ol' Dad again."

Paul smiled. "That I am, Coog. That I am."

But for how long?

He slapped his thighs. "Let's go out and grab something to eat. Has to be someplace with a drive-thru. We'll bring it back here. We can leave through the back window if we stand on that chair. Just woods back there. No one will see."

He wanted to spend the absolute minimum on the street.

He led Coog to the window, unlocked it as quietly as he could, and steadied him on the swivel chair.

He motioned to Coog. "All clear. Let's—"

The phone started ringing. "Get off the chair for a sec." He closed the window and ran to the machine.

After four rings and a beep, a man began speaking. Paul's heart skipped a beat when he heard the first words.

"Mr. Swann? I never received a response to my last message but I'll assume this is still a working number. This is Jason Fredericks again from legal at VecGen. We had a call from Paul Rosko—that's the man I told you about who'd caused a stir. He left a message for you and I quote . . . "

He read off Paul's message, including his cell phone number.

"If you want us to address this matter, please let us know. I'm at extension two-two-three if you need to get back to me."

Paul stood frozen. Here was the last link in the chain: the shadow man Lee T. Swann _was_ part of Innovation Ventures. Not just a front as Kaplan suggested. Perhaps he _was_ IV. This must have been his old office. He'd moved out but left an answering machine. That meant he called in for messages—and soon he'd be calling in for this one.

"We've got to get to Radio Shack."

Coog looked baffled. "Why?"

"To get an ID reader. And then we just pray the phone service is equipped with caller ID. We'll know who's calling, or at least where from."

"Why go to all that trouble? Just dial star-sixty-nine after the call."

Paul stared at his son. So simple. Why hadn't he thought of that? He threw an arm around Coog's shoulders.

"You know, I'm really glad you insisted on coming along."

SHEILA

Sheila waited by the window until Bill's car left her driveway and wound its way back toward the Admin building. The rain was even heavier now, pelting the driveway. The water was halfway up her front step. She dreaded seeing her basement. Her sump pump had been running continually for days but it could do only so much with the ground water level so high. She was glad to be safe inside her house.

As if the word *safe* meant anything anymore. She checked her phones but the cordless models didn't have anywhere she could see to place a bug. Good. Later, when she calmed down, she'd call the groundskeeper and ask for a ride to her rental car so she could get it home to use tomorrow.

Now she wanted a hot soak, to sink to her chin in the tub and forget about the chaos raging around her. But she realized she needed something else more.

She flipped on her computer. She recalled how nervous Paul had become that night when she'd joked about looking him up on the crime website.

She'd start the easy way and narrow it down. She typed in *Paul Rosko, charge, Massachusetts* on Yahoo.

The only hits were Amazon and eBay ads for "Books about Paul Rosko." She typed in *Paul Rosko criminal,* sure it would yield similar useless stuff.

The first hit was for NetDetective. Yeah, I know, I can find out anything in the privacy of my own home for a small fee. She scanned down two or three irrelevant hits and then gasped.

Paul Rosko charged in murder of local. Town up in arms against bookworm gone berserk.

Oh Jesus, Sheila thought.

She paused, her hand numb on the mouse. Finally she forced herself to click the link. She had to know.

She came up with Henry "Hank" Sammer, a laborer at the local paper mill, killed in a barroom brawl at the Last Call. Details of his life—high school football star and such—and funeral arrangements followed, but no details about what had happened that night. A fight in a bar? Was it a one-time thing?

Sheila bit her lip. One time or not, Paul had killed a man . . . got so angry he'd killed someone. What more did she need to know?

She continued searching the more restrictive websites. After an hour she knew little more than she had at first. The details were all the same: some kind of fistfight, Paul killed a local, and spent a year in jail for second-degree manslaughter.

Sheila shut off her computer.

True, he had anger issues, but were they that bad? She'd felt so safe around him. She didn't get it. She wanted—*needed*—more information.

She called Paul's cell phone but he didn't pick up, so she left a message to call her, and then built a fire. She got out a blanket and huddled under it on the couch. The logs burned hot but couldn't warm her.

PAUL

Paul and Coogan were finishing off their Whoppers in their basement hideaway of Innovation Ventures.

Thank God for whoever had dreamed up the drive-thru. Paul had stopped to buy a paper at a newspaper lock box and had seen his face on page one. He'd skipped the paper and hurried back to the car. By now everyone in town must know. Standing in line at a burger place would have been tantamount to turning himself in.

The phone rang and the light on the attached answering machine flashed.

He and Coog stopped in mid-bite to listen.

Swann. It couldn't be anyone else. Paul fought a fierce urge to pick up and start in on him. Here was the guy who'd killed four people and framed him. He wanted to hear the creep's voice, tell him what he'd like to do to him—*would* do if he ever caught up to him.

But he didn't move. Picking up now would give away his location.

Two rings, then the machine clicked on. Half a minute later it clicked off.

Paul put down his burger, and leapt to the receiver. "Coog, I'll repeat the numbers as I get them. Remember them."

He dialed *-6-9. Seconds later an electronic voice said, "The number of the party is 978-333-1222."

Paul gave Coogan the number and then hung up.

"So now what? You gonna call it?"

"No. Whoever it is could have caller ID and recognize this number. We'll call information and see if we can get the address."

Paul dialed 4-1-1 then waited until someone live came on.

"No problem, sir. The address for the phone number is two-nine-three Kingsbury Way. Is there anything else I can help you with?"

"No, that's all. Thanks." Paul stood there stunned, the receiver cold and heavy in his hand.

"What's wrong, Dad? Don't tell me they couldn't give you the address."

"They gave it to me."

He felt hollow. He knew that address: Tethys Medical Center.

He had to get to Sheila.

BILL

As he hung up the phone, Bill felt a spasm of fear. The unexpected message had shocked him. Rosko wasn't on the run. On the defensive, yes, but not running.

He wanted to talk a deal.

Which was out of the question. Too big a chance that Rosko would recognize his voice. He couldn't have a man with a history of violence—of murder, no less—come looking for him.

But Bill now had his cell phone number. Would that be of any use?

He called the Bradfield PD and asked for Lieutenant Zacks. Zacks had been a Tethys patient. VG723 had cured his lung cancer. He'd said he'd be eternally grateful. Time to see if he meant it.

After pleasantries and a little catching up, Bill came to the point.

"What's the status of the Rosko case? He was a volunteer here and frankly he's an embarrassment."

"We've got the usual all points out on him, pictures all over the papers. We'll get him."

"I have his cell phone number. Will that—?"

"We've got it too. Unfortunately he's turned it off. His last two calls were about six o'clock last night to a small company named VecGen and to your place."

"Tethys? Do you know what extension?"

"Sorry, no. He called the main number, probably got transferred."

The question had been for show. Shen had played him the message Rosko left for Sheila. Pathetic.

When Sheila confronted him about knowing Paul had killed someone, he'd frozen up. He had wanted to tell her about Paul's criminal record as soon as he found out, but then logic hit. If he had known before, he couldn't have let him volunteer. He thought he managed to look pretty surprised to learn about Paul's prison time from the detective though, and was relieved she bought it.

"But if he turns on his phone again you'll get him?"

"If he's still in the area. But getting blanket coverage of the region isn't going to happen. For a terrorist, yeah, but not a simple homicide."

"Let's hope he's still in the area, then."

"You sound like you're pretty sure he's going to turn on his phone."

"I believe it's inevitable."

"Yeah, so do I. He's not the brightest bulb in the box."

"Why do you say that?"

"Well, I mean, leaving the murder weapon in his garage. Christ, all he had to do was make a fire and throw it on. Whoosh, all the evidence up in smoke."

"Obviously not a deep thinker. Oops, got to take another call. Thanks for your help, Lieutenant."

Bill smiled as he hung up. He felt sure Rosko was still in the area, hoping to meet with Swann to "come to an agreement that is to our mutual benefit."

I think not, Mr. Rosko. When you turn on your phone at six o'clock, it will all be over for you.

——————•••——————

SHEILA

Sheila heard a noise at her back patio door and jumped. She'd fallen asleep and the day had turned dark. She checked her watch: barely five o'clock. Night fell early this time of year. She looked out her front window. The rain was falling heavier than ever.

There it was again—knocking. She walked around the house, squinting as she turned on light after light. She picked up her phone, ready to dial the police as she stole into her kitchen and peered outside. She flipped up the patio light. Two figures stood there, one man-size, one teen-size.

Her heart leaped. Paul and Coog, dripping and shivering. She hesitated only a second before opening the door.

"My God, come in! You must be freezing!"

They kicked off their boots upon entering. Paul looked ashamed, hesitant as he guided Coog ahead of him.

"I didn't know if you'd let me in. I'm not sure what they told you."

"They told me a lot and I found out some things on my own."

She watched him, hoping he would reveal more about those stories, come out and say it was all lies.

"I'm going to tell you everything. I brought Coog along because it's time he knew too."

"Knew what?" the boy said, confusion written on his face.

"About me—*all* about me. I wanted to wait till you were older, but that decision's been taken out of my hands."

Sheila had never been so confused. Emotions pulled her in all directions and she wondered if this is what it felt like to be bipolar.

"I know you didn't kill Kaplan—don't ask me how I know, I just do. But this other thing . . . "

"What other thing?" Coog said.

Paul reached over and hit the kitchen lights. "We need to shut these off. Anyone driving by can see in. Let's go sit down somewhere where we can't be seen," he said. "I'll tell you both the whole story."

Sheila shut off the lights as she led them down the hall, avoiding the windows. They entered her dark home office. Too dark. She turned on the closet light and opened the door a hair.

A sliver of light framed a rectangle on Paul's face.

"Before I say anything else, I want to tell you how sorry I am that our relationship was waylaid by all this. It seemed wonderful, brimming with potential, and now . . . now I don't know where it is."

"Neither do I," she told him. Might as well be honest.

"You may give up on me when I'm through, but it's time for truth. Long past time."

Coogan leaned closer to his father, eager to hear. Poor kid had been through enough, and now this.

"The novel I'm writing, *The Four Walls of Jim Grisbe*, is about a guy who went to prison for killing someone."

"I don't care about your book right now. Tell me about you," Sheila said.

He stared through her and she understood. "It's about me. My life. That's why I didn't tell you the plot. I was afraid you'd figure it out."

Coogan looked at them in shock. "You went to jail?" Tears welled up in his eyes and he wiped away.

"'Fraid so. But let me explain. It's important for you, for both of you to understand. I really was sensitive kid, like I told you, Sheila, and my dad hated me for it. I was a wrestler in school. All that was true. I got my English degree and then my Masters."

"You have a Masters in English?" she said, stunned.

But in an instant she realized it explained so many things. His love of books, his vocabulary . . . his novel.

"Yes. All set to be a teacher. Everything going just the way I wanted. I'd landed a job at Saint John's prep right here in Massachusetts. I was the happiest I'd ever been."

Sheila looked at him and understood. Just how she'd felt right before Dek died. A primo fellowship, a wonderful husband, a baby on the way—life couldn't get any better. She knew a tragedy was coming in Paul's story. As she looked to Coog she knew he was bracing for bad news. She put her arm around him and he leaned into her. Poor kid needed a mother.

"About a week after graduation my dad came out to see me. Said he came to make up with me, to apologize. My brother and he took me out for a few beers at the local VFW hall. I was excited. It was the first time he'd been civil to me since I started college and now he'd come all the way from Albany to apologize. Except that's not what happened. Dad and my brother had a few too many and started making fun of me. How I must be gay to want to teach English to a bunch of prep school sissy boys. *'What's wrong with you? Can't be a real man? Wants to play with little boys all day?'* "

"Oh, man!" Coog whispered. "Grandpa said that?"

Paul nodded. "That's why you see him only once in a blue moon."

Sheila wanted to protect him from the memory but saw no way to do it.

"Bad enough the two of them giving me the business, but then Dad enlisted some of the other vets in the room. They were all laying into me. *'Faggot, faggot, faggot.'* " He shook his head. "I lost it. I completely lost it. I picked up my dad and slammed him into a wall. Learned later I'd broken his collarbone. Then I ran out, got in my car, and sped off. I stopped at the nearest bar. Some dive filled with a pack of locals who'd just finished a shift at the mill."

Sheila remembered that detail from the Internet accounts. The dead man had worked in a paper mill.

"I went there just to unwind, but one of them started in on me about giving him my bar stool. Not a big deal. I should have just moved over, but I was ready to explode and wasn't about to give an inch to anybody. So I ignored him. Well, he'd made a point of getting my seat and all his buddies were watching. He couldn't back down so he shoved me. Not hard, but enough. All I heard were my father's words over the years: Loser, faggot . . . "

Knowing what came next, Sheila wanted to close her ears. She pulled Coogan closer.

"I laid into the guy. Knocked him down. He should have stayed down. But with his buddies around he had to come back at me. He wound up on the receiving end of twenty-five years of pent-up anger. I pounded him, broke his nose and he fell back, hitting his head on the edge of a table. He never woke up."

Silence in her office. Not even the sound of breathing. Sheila stole a look at Coog. She'd expected to see horror, revulsion. Instead she saw wonder.

"Good thing someone had already called the cops because the rest of his friends jumped me. I hurt a number of them as well but would have ended beaten to a bloody pulp if the cops hadn't broken it up."

"But Dad, it was self defense!"

Paul shook his head. "Not according to his buddies. They said I was drunk and looking for a fight. Said I sucker punched the guy." He looked from Coog to Sheila with pleading eyes. "But I didn't have to sucker him. I was too full of rage for anything but a head-on frontal assault. Didn't matter what I said, though. The evidence was overwhelming—just like now in this Kaplan thing—and so my lawyer worked a plea bargain and I went off to jail for a year."

Sheila rubbed his arm. "Paul, I'm so sorry. That must have been horrible."

"What? The jail part? Yeah, it was bad but it paled in comparison to the rest: Living with the guilt that I'd killed someone; my mom never speaking to me again—going to her grave being ashamed of me; or maybe worst of all, my dad finally being proud of me."

He sighed and for a moment looked like a lost little boy.

"No, that wasn't the worst. Not even the fact that no one would ever let a manslaughter felon be a teacher, or that from that day on my future wasn't bright anymore because one senseless act had forever derailed the life I'd planned. No, worst is the lingering memory of the fierce dark joy I took in pummeling that poor bastard."

Another silent pause. Then Paul cleared his throat.

"An MA in English and I wound up a cable installer. And glad to be one." He turned to Coogan.

The boy said nothing, simply got up and threw his arms around Paul and hugged him.

In the faint light Sheila could see the glitter of tears in Paul's eyes. Her own vision blurred.

They held that tableau for a full minute, then Paul spoke in a thick voice,

"Thank you, Coog. You can't know how much you mean to me. If I ever lost you . . ."

"Hey, you're my dad."

Another embrace, then Paul said, "Why don't you go out by the fire. Make sure the blinds are drawn. I have some things to talk over with Sheila."

Coog grinned. "Lovey-dovey things?"

"Yeah."

As soon as the boy was gone, Paul moved closer to Sheila and lowered his voice.

"I need to tell you what Kaplan said. There's definitely a correlation between KB-twenty-six, VG-seven-twenty-three, Innovation Ventures or Lee Swann or whoever is trying to erase all the evidence. Kaplan told me all about Coog. And the same with other KB-twenty-six kids: O-negative blood and an eventual usurpation by the donor DNA. That's why Kaplan stopped the trials. The kids were all becoming their donors. IV knocked him into bankruptcy then their guy Lee Swann bought the assets for VecGen."

"Swann works for IV?"

Paul nodded. "When Coogan and I were hiding out at IV, a guy called in from VecGen's legal department for a Mister Swann. Swann's not a front man. He *is* IV. It's just a shell office. Swann, on behalf of IV, funded Kaplan then shut him down when he refused to use the therapy he'd discovered. Then Swann bought the assets in bankruptcy and used them at the newly IV-funded VecGen. And then *they* started using the same therapy with a new moniker, marketing it as VG-seven-twenty-three."

"Administered by Tethys," Sheila said.

"Just like KB-twenty-six."

"I overheard Bill yelling at someone on the phone one day. Knowing all this, I'm pretty sure it was Swann. Bill said something like, 'You're the boss.' I think Bill is just a puppet for Swann."

"Interesting. Because after the VecGen message, someone called to retrieve it. I used Star sixty-nine to get the number and then called the operator for the address. Swann called from Tethys."

The news rocked Sheila. Every path led back to Tethys.

"But who?"

"I don't know. Abra?"

"No. No way she's the boss. She's too passive. Whoever Bill talked with, he was kowtowing to. At one point he said something like, 'sorry that was disrespectful.'"

"I think he's in love with you, Sheila—or whatever approximates love in someone like him. He'll kill you if he has to, but I think he'll first do whatever he can to try to divert you from the truth. I don't know who's in charge of all this, but Gilchrist must have enough pull to keep you safe. At least for now."

"He said he didn't want to do something but would if he had to. Mentioned something about *she* being tenacious but *she* was under control. I know he meant me. God, I wish I could remember everything he said. But you may be right. It seems killing me is a last resort. What's the number from that IV/Tethys call? Maybe I'll recognize the extension."

When he showed her, she shook her head. "No idea. I'll call it and hang up if anyone answers."

"No, Sheila. What if they have caller ID?"

"My number's unlisted and unpublished. Won't show up."

She dialed the number and waited as it rang a few times. She heard it pick up, hoping to get an answering machine or voicemail with a name on it. Instead she heard a high-pitched screech.

"It's a fax line." She hung up. "No help there."

Paul said, "Bill has probably done what he can to keep you safe. But if he finds out how much we know, I don't see a way to turn back."

"I think my office is bugged."

She explained why and Paul agreed. Then part of the phone conversation she'd overheard rushed back at her.

"Bill said 'All of Proteus hinges on this' or something like that. Any idea what that means?"

Paul frowned. "Proteus? You're sure that's what he said?"

"Positive."

"It's got to mean something." Paul closed his eyes. "Proteus . . . Proteus . . . Pro—" His eyes snapped open as he turned to her with a shocked stare. "Jesus Christ! Proteus was the Greek god who could change his shape at will!"

Sheila understood in a flash. "The new DNA . . . changing people."

Paul was shaking his head. "Proteus's father was the god Poseidon. But his mother was one of the Titans. Care to guess her name?"

Sheila struggled to remember high school Greek mythology. "You're going to tell me her name was Tethys, right?"

"Right."

"But this means that the genetic makeover—or maybe *takeover* is a better term—is intentional. They're not trying to cover up an unwanted side effect. They *want* to replace DNA. Why on earth—?"

"What are they up to? What can they be thinking?" He paused. "If Bill Gilchrist is arguing about Proteus, he's not innocently administering it to patients, being guided by VecGen. He knows exactly what it's doing. He ever give you a clue as to what he might think he's getting out of it?"

Sheila shivered in the darkness. "No, never. It's not as if he needs the money. And he's always been devoted to curing people. I can't believe he'd be involved in knowingly replacing his patients' DNA without their consent."

"You're absolutely sure about that?"

"Well, no. First thing in the morning I'm calling the FDA and blowing the whistle—tell them VG-seven-twenty-three is replacing recipients' DNA without their consent. They'll have to investigate. Once JCAHO finds out what Tethys and Innovation—"

Sheila felt a rush and her vision started to dim. She felt dizzy and sick. Paul's arm wrapped around her.

"Dek," she mumbled.

"What? Who?"

"My husband Dek." She looked up at Paul, snuggled closer. Her speech felt slurred. "He worked for JCAHO."

"So?"

"He was working on a big case, he said. Something that would make his career. He said he was waiting to show his boss his files until he had all the facts but he said he was close. Impropriety with a cancer hospital. Something about collusion. But all his cases were like that so I didn't—I mean that was his job, finding out the bad stuff."

"What are you saying Sheila?"

"If Dek was about to uncover what we're uncovering now—his motorcycle skidded on the road and he died. While I was still in a fog, trying to get over his death, I got a call out of the blue from Tethys. Interviewed with Bill, the head of the whole hospital. Even though I was an emotional train wreck he hired me on the spot. The other residents were jealous and I was incredulous. A golden opportunity just handed to me."

"Jesus," Paul said, leaning his head all the way back on the couch. "Sheila, he hired you to watch you, to make sure your husband hadn't told you anything. Then kept you on and watched you all these years."

She nodded. "After a while, I was just another staff oncologist. I befriended Abra and Bill grew convinced I knew nothing. And everything would have gone on fine, until Kelly Slade walked into my office."

"I don't want you going back there, Sheila. It's not safe."

"That *bastard* killed my husband! I was pregnant, Paul. I was pregnant and had a miscarriage when Dek died. Then Bill set me up and hired me under false pretenses. I'm not going to rest until Bill Gilchrist and Lee Swann are in jail and Innovation Ventures and Tethys are a pile of rubble."

She had never been this angry. Never, and it scared her. If Bill were in front of her, she'd kill him without hesitation. She had a new appreciation for Paul's situation.

"I'll help you put them away, Sheila, but we have to use the right channels. You call the FDA, the AMA and every other government acronym you can think of. Tell them everything. And I'll work on proving I didn't kill Kaplan. We're going to beat this, Sheila. From now on, I tell you everything. No secrets."

"All right." She took a deep breath. "All right. We'll do it together. So what's our next step? I mean, after I blow the whistle—anonymously, of course."

"I get you two out of here. Fly you somewhere safe while I sort this out."

"It's safe here. Bill's gone to Switzerland for a couple of days on business."

"But what about Swann? The one calling all the shots?"

"From what I heard, Bill is the action man. The one "doing" everything. With him gone, I'll be safe."

"I don't know, Sheila."

"Trust me. Swann is the head man but he's not going to get his hands dirty."

"I hope you're right. Okay, Bill's being gone can work in our favor. See what you can learn while he's gone. See if there's anything that will link him and Swann. And me—I'll stay out of sight. I'm supposed to turn on my phone about now for a call from Swann but I've decided not to. I'll hide in his old office and—" He snapped his fingers.

"What?"

"Can you do an Internet search on the building where IV's office is?"

"I think so. Why?"

"Let's see who owns it."

It didn't take long but the answer was a stunner: Tethys Corporation.

It all fit. Tethys *was* Innovation Ventures. They funded Kaplan Biologicals and VecGen. They administered both the KB26 and VG723. And they killed everyone who made the connection.

Paul glanced at his watch. "I've stayed too long. Can I ask a huge favor?"

"Anything."

"Keep Coog for me? I don't trust him with anyone else and I'll feel a lot better knowing he's safe while I'm trying to stay under the radar."

"Say no more. I'd love to have him."

"Great. Now I have to convince him to stay."

Sheila walked into the living room and drew her blinds, then called Paul in. They sat on the floor in front of the fire, facing Coogan.

"You okay?" Paul asked him.

Coog nodded. "Yeah. It's a lot to take in, but yeah." He sat up straight. "So what's next?"

Paul shook his head. "Next is that I have to do some risky stuff and you have to stay here with Sheila."

"No, Dad, I have to come with you. I can handle anything you can."

Sheila could see the hurt and fear in his eyes. Paul looked at Sheila and then at his son.

"Yes, you can handle anything. You're a strong, smart boy. But I need to do this alone; if I have to keep looking over my shoulder to make sure you're okay, it'll slow me down. Might even get me in hot water."

Coogan's eyes teared up. "I'll be in the way?"

"I didn't mean it like that. I want you with me, but I can't take you. Not now. It's not safe. I'll be able to handle this better knowing you're here with Sheila."

Sheila reached over to Coog, wondering what to say. Sorry, your dad just confessed to killing someone, but now he has to evade the police to do some more illegal things to prove he didn't kill someone else?

"Coog," she said, "I don't feel safe here and I'd sleep a lot better if you stayed with me. I'm in the middle of all this too."

"The middle of what?" he asked.

Paul chewed his lip. "We'll tell you later when we have the answers. Right now what you need to know is that someone is doing something bad and Sheila and I, and you, are working together to stop him. The best place you can be is here, hiding out. The best place Sheila can be is here, or at work, pretending everything's okay. And me? I'll be underground trying to straighten things out. You have to trust me on this, Coog."

"Okay. But Dad, please be careful. You're all I have."

"You're all I have too." He hugged his son. "Sheila, can I talk to you in the kitchen for a minute?"

They walked together to the other room, out of earshot of Coogan. Sheila went into caretaker mode.

"I know this is the last thing on your mind right now, but let me pack you some food and drinks. You can't risk going into a store; and you have to eat."

"Food would be great, thanks." He then drew her away from the counter. "But, listen, this is more important."

He pulled her close, pressed his body against her. She could feel her heart speed up as he whispered in her ear.

"I don't know if I'll be able to come back. You don't want to hear this, but I might end up like Kaplan. And if I don't, I might go to jail. Rose is out of the picture and the rest of my family represents everything I'm against. This is a lot to ask but, please, if anything happens to me, will you take care of Coogan?"

She pulled away. Sheila felt tears streaming down her face. Take care of his son? The responsibility didn't rattle her. It was that he had asked. She meant that much to him that he'd entrust her to raise his son if something happened. God, she hoped nothing did, but—

She hugged him and sobbed on his shoulder.

"Hey, it's okay," he murmured. "I'll be back, I just need to know he'll be taken care of, just in case."

She broke the embrace, wiped her eyes, mascara smearing the backs of her hands.

"I'd be honored. But Paul, you have to come back. For both of us. No ifs. You *have* to."

"I will. We'll get through this, okay? And then we'll figure out you and me. After all the stuff I told you, I'll understand if you back away."

She nodded. "We'll work it out."

She packed him a couple of sandwiches and a box of Wheat Thins while he hugged Coogan goodbye again. And then she watched Paul walk out the back door into the rain.

Would they really get through this? And what would become of Tethys and all the people it had saved?

—THIRTEEN—

SHEILA

Sheila awoke to a pounding noise. She sat up in bed. Wan light filtered through the windows. That noise . . . from above her. After a moment, she realized it was rain pounding against her bedroom skylight like a heavy-metal drummer on speed. A cascade of water ran down the skylight and, as she looked to the window, down the side of the house as well.

Like being inside a waterfall. She hit the clicker on the TV. Every channel was broadcasting the flood conditions in Northern Massachusetts. The governor declared a state of emergency. The National Guard was being called in. She hadn't realized it was *that* bad. Enough about the weather, she thought. She had larger concerns: like the Paul situation.

Paul!

She suddenly remembered that Coogan was in her guest room. She glanced at the clock: not quite seven. Too early to call the FDA. And way too early for any self-respecting teenager to be awake, but she needed caffeine.

A jug of strong coffee was her norm for breakfast, but a thirteen-year old would need real food. With her car still in the Tethys lot, plus all this rain and melting snow, no way she could get to the doughnut shop or the grocery store. She'd have to make him something.

She got out of bed and started to walk into the kitchen in her T-shirt and underwear but stopped. Needed more clothes than this. Having a boy stay with her would take some adjusting. She added baggy sweatpants and the outfit was complete.

Sheila ground and brewed some Starbucks and then fished through the cabinet for something Coogan might like. The only cereal she had was shredded wheat. The fridge yielded skim milk, fat free yogurt, some cold cuts, shrimp. She had eggs, so maybe an omelet? When she spied a few brown bananas on her counter she recalled her mother's staple—banana bread.

The old paperback *Better Homes and Gardens* cookbook with its red-and-white plaid cover was worn and stained, but a corner was folded to page 166. *Banana nut bread.* She scanned the recipe and smiled when she saw she had everything she needed except the nuts, which she always omitted anyway.

Buoyed at having someone to cook for, she got to work mixing. She didn't bother separating the wet and dry ingredients so it was a messy venture, but fifty minutes later, just as Coogan came down the stairs, the golden-brown loaf was done.

"What's that smell?" he asked, smiling.

She noticed he was wearing the same T-shirt and jeans as yesterday. Not that he had much choice. Poor kid needed a change of clothes.

"You like it?"

"Smells so good it woke me up.

"Great. I hope you like banana bread."

"I love it."

Sheila smiled. "Have a seat in here. I've got coffee, but it's kind of strong. I don't know if you'd like it. I've got milk too."

"Milk's great but you don't have to wait on me. I can get stuff myself."

"You're my guest. I'm going to go into work for a while. When I get back we'll see about getting you some new clothes."

Coogan blushed and sniffed his armpit. "Yeah. I guess I can't go home to get anything, huh?"

"Not a good idea. The police might be keeping a watch on your house." With a start she realized they might be watching hers as well. "I don't mean to sound paranoid, Coog, but it might be best if you stay out of the living room, away from the windows. The spare room has a TV and bathroom and it's in the back. I'll give you a T-shirt and some sweats. They'll be too short, I'm sure, but they'll do for now. I'll throw your clothes in the laundry."

"Cool. But I'll do my laundry. Just show me where the machine is. It'll give me something to do."

"Okay. The laundry room is next to the spare room."

"I'm glad you're helping us like this, helping my dad. You like him huh?"

"Yes, I like him."

"*Like* like him?"

She laughed. Some terminology never changed. "Yes, Coogan, I *like* like him."

"And you believe him, right, that he didn't kill that Doctor Kaplan?"

"I believe him. I know he couldn't do something like that."

Coogan dropped his gaze. "But he did kill that other guy."

"But he told us he didn't mean to. He's been living with that secret for so many years. I think he was glad to get it out. Whatever happened, it was a long time ago. The man your father is now is the one who matters. He's the one who raised you and would do anything to keep you safe."

"He's a good guy," he said with that charming Paul Newman smile.

"He *is*. And I have to run. Here's your milk and a plate for the bread."

Coogan said thanks as Sheila headed for the shower.

———···———

Sheila called Tethys security and a guard came to pick her up in one of the medical center's Land Rovers. As they splashed into the nearly-empty flooded parking lot a flash of lightning startled her. Thunder rumbled in the distance.

Sheila shook her head. Maybe it wasn't just a lot of rain.

The driver dropped her off in front of the hospital and she spied her car in the distance, parked there since yesterday, water up to the bottom of the door. She stumbled and almost fell as she hurried over the water-loosened cobblestones.

Once inside, her anxiety grew. She wished she could contact Paul. Hearing his voice would be a tonic. Knowing he was all right would set her at ease. But his cell phone was off.

Thankfully no life-or-death situations on the ward right now. All Tethys required of her today was a body and a pulse, which was good because she couldn't offer much more.

She looked at her watch. Time to call the FDA.

Sheila stepped into the ladies' room and checked to make sure the stalls were empty, and then used her Blackberry to find the number in Washington. What followed were fifteen minutes of frustration. No one had the authority to launch an investigation based on a "hysterical phone call." Could she submit something in writing? Which entity was it exactly she was reporting? The hospital, or the manufacturer? The best anyone could do was assign her to a representative, take her number, and have someone call her back later.

She clicked off and resisted the urge to hurl her phone against a wall.

The stone wall of bureaucratic incompetence made her crazy.

She stalked out to the nurses' station.

"I'm going to my office for a while," she said to the charge nurse. "I have my beeper and cell phone if you need me."

She wanted to find the bug in her office.

The tunnels felt damper than usual. The rain had brought more water than the ground above could absorb so the ceilings and walls were dripping. Water seeped from every available crack. And a building this old had a _lot_ of cracks.

Drip-drip-drip she heard along with the _squeak-squeak-squeak_ of her wet shoes. Some high-tech hospital.

Water pooled along the edges of the floor. Not a lot, but something maintenance should be alerted to. If the rain didn't stop they'd have inches in here by tomorrow.

She made it to her office and turned on the light. Though late morning, the day still had a predawn gloom.

Time to look for that bug.

She glanced around. Probably hidden in something that didn't move. Something bolted in. The heater vent in the ceiling?

She got up and looked. Nope, nothing she could see, even standing on her chair with a penlight.

She stepped down and looked around. She checked along the wall. Pictures, framed diplomas.

She checked the phone. Negative. She looked down at her desk. A lip ran around the edge. She felt along its underside. Nothing. Where could it be?

Her mouth went dry as she looked at her pencil cup. The place she would never look. She peered inside and saw the contact paper had a bulge. She peeled it away and a small circle fell inside to the bottom. A bug.

Mother of God. Her desk . . . sex with Paul. Someone *had* recorded the sounds they'd made. She remembered moaning. Bill had heard it all and then looked her in the eye and said nothing.

Feeling queasy, she shut off the light, slipped on her squeaky shoes, and headed for the hall. If they'd planted a bug, they had to have a monitoring station somewhere.

The first place she checked was Bill's office. With him in Switzerland, this was the perfect time to snoop.

She didn't expect to find anything. Keeping such equipment in his office where Marge could come across it would be stupid. But she needed to cross his office off her list and wanted to poke around and see if she might come across something about Proteus.

Her footsteps echoed along the empty hallway. She wasn't alone here, but close to it. The pounding rain had kept all but the hardiest at home. The hospital never slept but in the office today it was mandatory personnel only.

The outer door to Bill's office was unlocked. People tended to be lax about security. But she had no illusions about his inner sanctum. That would be locked.

And it was.

She went to Marge's desk and checked the top drawer. There: a solitary key on a ring. She tried it on Bill's door and was in.

She stepped into the familiar office and stopped. She'd always felt comfortable here. Now it held a different feel. The dark paneling seemed ominous, the awards and testimonial certificates and photos with celebrities mocked her. But she shook it off and got busy.

The storm had blotted out the sun but she didn't dare turn on the lights for fear of drawing attention.

A quick survey of the cabinets yielded the expected: nothing.

As she approached his desk she jumped when a bolt of lightning lit the sky and the office; the immediate blast of thunder rattled her along with the leaded glass windows.

Too close.

The desk proved as unrewarding as the rest of the office. Except for pens, paper clips, sticky notes, some keys on a changing-the-world-one-person-at-a-time key chain, and other miscellaneous desk stuff, the drawers were virtually empty. One held a large near empty bottle of Jack Daniels. That explained the whiskey breath. The only surprise was a small metal lockbox in the bottom drawer. She lifted it. Heavy. Something metal rattled within. None of the keys on the chain fit the lock and if she tried to pry it open then Bill would know he'd been searched.

She returned the box to its place and sighed. Marge managed the paperwork. Most of the data that concerned Bill would be stored on his computer.

Sheila's gaze snapped to the blank monitor. Bill's all-access computer—why hadn't she thought of that in the first place?

She seated herself in the big leather chair, booted it up. She tried every password she could think of—his wife's name, his childrens', Proteus, Tethys—but couldn't get past the login screen. She wanted to slam her fists against the keyboard. The answers she needed could be just a few keystrokes away. So damn frustrating. In the movies somebody always sussed out the password. But this was no movie.

She turned off the computer, locked the door behind her, and returned Marge's key. She peeked before stepping back into the empty hallway.

Now where? The search seemed hopeless. That bug's receiver could be anywhere—even in some locked room in Bill's basement at home. But she couldn't see Bill spending hours running through the recordings. He didn't have enough time as it—

She heard one of the entry doors close down the hall. Instinctively she stepped back into the shallow well of Bill's doorway. Stupid! If whoever it was walked by and saw her standing here . . .

She heard squeaking footsteps but they were headed away from her. She risked a glance and saw that it was Shen Li. No surprise there. The chief of security seemed devoted to his job and to . . .

. . . Bill.

Mother of God. Had Shen been a part of this the whole time?

A prickle of fear shot up her spine. He'd been so close-by for the break in. And his height . . . Shen. Reliable Shen. "If someone wanted you dead, you'd be dead," he had said. Or something like that. He knew. She was alive because, for now at least, Bill didn't want her dead. Hadn't ordered Shen to kill her.

Sheila watched Shen head for the elevators, but he opened the door to the tunnels instead.

Who more likely to be doing the monitoring and dirty work than Bill's trusted chief of security?

The question was, where was he monitoring from?

Sheila was on the move as soon as Shen stepped out of sight. She hurried to the door, reaching it just before it swung shut. She hurried down the two flights and emerged into the tunnel. The *empty* tunnel.

After a mental coin flip she chose a direction and began to search. No need for subterfuge. She had perfectly good reasons for being here, like going to or returning from one of the wards. No one in their right mind would brave the weather raging above.

She walked softly, cursing her squeaking soles, stopping at each of the half dozen doors she found. She couldn't knock or yank on their knobs, so she pressed her ear against them and listened. No sound from the first three, but the fourth . . . the fourth had a peephole—the only door with one. She pressed her ear against the wood.

A faint voice—a woman's, barely audible. Couldn't tell who she was or what she was saying, but this had to be the place. The elation of a successful hunt mixed with vague nausea at knowing that Shen Li was probably spying on someone else at that very moment. She wanted to bang on the damn door and make him stop.

But she hurried away. Needed to get in there. Maybe it held other secrets—something on Proteus, perhaps? But now she'd have to wait for Shen Li to leave, and then find a way to get past the lock. She'd need a key—

Keys! In Bill's desk.

She ran back upstairs.

ABRA

Abra beamed at the regal, white-haired woman on her computer screen.

"Why didn't we think of this before, Mama?"

"To tell you the truth," Mama said in her thick German accent, "I had no idea it was so easy."

Mama knew all about genetics but not about Skype? Well, perhaps that wasn't such a surprise. She tended to have tunnel vision.

They'd had a lovely, meandering conversation over a wide range of topics.

"And how is *Die Perfekte*?" Mama said, sipping her tea in her office in Geneva.

Abra smiled. "So, Bill told you about that?"

"Of course. He is quite proud of it. And you should be too."

"It's an interesting experiment with no real practical use."

It had been Bill's idea, really: create a stem cell line with a genome as close as possible to flawless. They'd dubbed it *Die Perfekte* in honor of Mama. Of course, no genome could be perfect, but *Die Perfekte* was pretty close. They'd scrutinized its genetic structure for years, scrubbing it of any defects.

Mama laughed. "One could always add it to the water supply."

"That wouldn't work. Chlorination and purification processes would kill the cells before—" She stopped when she saw Mama's expression. "You're having me on, aren't you."

She shrugged. "Perhaps. Would it be so terrible?"

Here we go again, she thought. This sounded like a lead-in to their ongoing argument about expanding the scope of Proteus far beyond Tethys.

"Mama, please. Can you imagine the havoc that would cause?"

"Not so bad, I think."

"Are you serious? First off, *Die Perfekte* is a blond-haired, blue-eyed Caucasian genome."

"You say that as if it is a bad thing."

"I know you're joking, but considering the recent tragedies here—"

"Yes. Bill told me."

Bill told her everything, it seemed. Abra couldn't help but feel a flash of jealousy at their closeness.

"Well, then you can understand why I don't see any humor in it."

Mama stared straight at her. "I wasn't joking, dear."

"What? Considering Grandpapa's background—"

"Must you always bring that up? He has nothing to do with this."

Mama's father had been a member of the Nazi Party during the war. Just a paper shuffler in the Berlin headquarters, but still . . . the taint was there.

"It's not *my* bringing it up we'd have to worry about. If people hear you talk like that and look him up—"

Mama's chin lifted defiantly. "It is not as if he was a death-camp guard. He was a simple clerk and did nothing to be ashamed of. In those days you had to join the party to survive."

"It doesn't matter, Mama. The whole racial purity issue will rear its ugly head and drown out rational discourse."

"This isn't at all about racial purity, although you'll have to concede that race lies at the heart of much of human conflict."

"Race and religion."

"In the end it all comes down to *differences*, yes? We fear the *other*, yes?"

"I suppose."

"And so it stands to reason that if we were all less different, we would have less conflict, yes?"

"I suppose."

"But let us put those issues aside and, just for the sake of intellectual exercise, assume that *Die Perfekte* cells could survive in the water supply. What would the resultant world be like?"

Abra tried to imagine and couldn't help but laugh. "Cataclysm and chaos—*Die Perfekte* is male. The female population would become sterile and begin to develop male characteristics."

Mama waved a hand before the screen. "Let us just assume that we can neutralize the gender effects of the genome."

"I don't think that's possible."

"Oh, it is, my darling. It is."

Something in her tone, her eyes . . .

"What are you saying? Have you—?"

Another laugh. "Oh, no. I am simply saying that with enough will and intelligence, anything is possible. So let us assume that we have neutralized the gender effects of *Die Perfekte* genome and introduced it into water supplies all over the world. What will happen?"

"Well, after a number of years, dark-skinned people will begin to notice a lightening of their pigment, and changes in their hair."

"Yes-yes. That is the first generation. But the next generation and the generation after that?"

"Everyone will begin looking more and more the same."

"All superficial. It is the internal changes that will cause monumental shifts in society."

"You mean diseases . . ."

"Just for starters, yes. All the inheritable forms of cancer and diabetes and heart disease and so many other diseases that have been eradicated from *Die Perfekte* will be absent from its population as well. Spontaneous mutations will still occur, but *Die Perfekte* will attack those tumors aborning and replace them with healthy cells."

"No question that the resulting population will be healthier," Abra said, "but—"

"Not just physically, my dear. So many forms of mental illness—depression, alcoholism, schizophrenia, and so on—are due to inherited aberrations in neurotransmitter levels. *Die Perfekte* will maintain serotonin, norepinephrine, and dopamine at their proper levels without drugs."

"You paint such a rosy picture."

"How can I not? With a healthy, happy populace, *differences* will fade, and along with that decline we will see less crime, less violence, less need for wars . . . what is not to like?"

"You're playing God, Mama."

She made a dismissive sound. "God botched it. *Die Perfekte* would correct His errors. And let us not cast aspersions: What do you think you are doing at Tethys? Do you not think you are playing God?"

"Not at all. People come here of their own volition requesting a cure. I give them a cure."

"And more."

"Yes," Abra conceded. "Much more."

SHEILA

Sheila shook herself as she felt her eyes drifting shut.

Wasn't Shen ever going to leave?

She'd made a return trip to Bill's office and scooped up the keys in his top drawer. They'd been in her pocket for almost an hour now as she sat at her window watching the parking lot. It looked more like a pond.

She yawned. No one had called from the ward. Lucky thing. Left her time to wait on Shen. Tired. Not much sleep last night. But then, who could sleep with what was going on? Things moving too fast. She needed a little breathing room, a little time to—

She straightened in her chair as a figure slogged away through the icy water toward one of the half-dozen cars in the lot. She glimpsed his face as he slipped behind the wheel: Shen Li.

Sheila's fatigue evaporated as she all but leaped from her seat and headed for the hall. She bounded down the flights to the tunnels and made a beeline for the mystery door.

Caution slowed her as she neared it. She peered around to confirm that she was alone and that wet footprints wouldn't give her away. She pressed her ear against the door: all quiet. Just to be sure, she knocked. She had no idea what she'd say if anyone answered, but that would be better than being caught with a key in her hand—*if* she had the key.

When no one answered, she tried the first key. No luck. Too big for the hole. The second fit but wouldn't turn. She took a breath and tried the third.

It turned.

Another look around, then she pushed through. Before closing the door she found a light switch and flipped it. As the overhead fluorescents flickered to life, she closed the door and turned the deadbolt.

She looked around and felt as if she'd wandered into the storage room of a Best Buy. Red and green lights glowed in the faces of black electronic boxes stacked on shelves along the walls. The room was tiny to begin with, but so much equipment made it feel even smaller. She'd never been claustrophobic, but this would be the place to start.

She looked for something recognizable. Two chairs and two cheap pressboard desks sat at right angles. Scattered papers, a pair of black leather gloves, a pair of small video monitors plus a DVD player on each of the desks.

Monitors? What good were they if you were recording audio?

And then it hit her.

Not knowing what she was doing, but unable to stop herself, Sheila stretched a trembling hand toward the nearest monitor and pressed the ON button. The screen flickered to life with an overhead view of an empty office. She couldn't tell whose it was but knew it wasn't hers.

Her mouth went dry.

They weren't just listening, they were watching as well.

Oh-no-oh-no-oh-no . . .

She turned that off and tried the neighboring monitor—and saw just what she prayed she wouldn't.

Her office.

She closed her eyes and leaned against the desktop. Had they been watching when . . .?

A disc protruded from one of the DVD players . . . the one with its wire connected to the monitor showing her office. She pushed it into the slot and waited as the machine accessed it and started playing.

At first she couldn't tell what she was seeing, then gasped as she recognized the two naked figures writhing on the desk.

Her . . . Paul . . . in *flagrante* . . . her legs spread . . . Paul between them . . . the two of them moving . . . moving . . .

Sheila jabbed a fingertip against the EJECT button.

Weak, breathless, she felt her face and the rest of her body burning, perspiring . . . Shen had been spying then and no doubt watching an encore this morning . . .

She suppressed a surge of bile. He'd burned a disc of it. How many times had he watched? And who else had seen it?

Oh, God. Bill.

He must have seen it. That was why he'd seemed so different. He'd said all the right words, made all the right gestures, but always seemed one step removed. Now she knew why.

You filthy bastard.

Her embarrassment mutated to anger. She and Paul in their most intimate, private moment . . . and Bill and Shen making it into a peepshow, a porn movie. She wanted a hammer to shatter every screen, smash every piece of electronics in here.

But she couldn't. Couldn't let them know she'd been here. Had to leave everything as it was. Even the disc.

She stared at it sitting there in its slot, ready for another viewing. She wanted to take it home and throw it on the fire.

Sheila forced herself to turn away and survey the filthy little room to make sure everything was as she'd found it. She had one hand on the deadbolt and the other on the light switch when she heard footsteps in the hall.

Headed here? Shen's replacement?

Even if someone was simply passing by, they might notice light under the door. She flicked the switch and held her breath. The sudden darkness revealed a spot of light from the peephole.

She put her eye to it and began a litany as she listened to the footsteps.

Please don't stop . . . please don't stop . . . please—

But the steps did stop—right outside the door. An Asian face, distorted by the fisheye lens, hove into view.

Shen.

Mother of God, what to do? What to say to explain? Would he kill her?

Hide. But where? The room was so small.

Under one of the desks. It seemed ridiculous even to try but she couldn't just stand here.

As the key slipped into the lock she ducked into the kneehole of the desk on the right and tucked herself into a ball. She couldn't hold this position long. Her only hope was that he'd forgotten something and would stay only a minute.

She heard the door swing open, saw a shadow on the floor framed in a shaft of light from the hall before the overheads came on. She watched as dripping boots stepped into sight and moved past her.

Please don't let him play the disc!

She couldn't sit through that, listening to her moans. She'd jump up and throttle him.

She heard him muttering as he shuffled papers on the neighboring desktop. Then the boots appeared again. She pressed herself back against the wall as they stopped only inches away.

More muttering, more shuffling papers, then a pleased sound followed by a Chinese phrase.

The boots backed away. She heard him slide his hands into his gloves and then saw the bottom half of Shen, papers squeezed tight in his gloved hand.

The lights went out.

The door closed.

The bolt clicked home.

It took her a couple of minutes to muster the nerve to unwind her body and regain her feet. She felt wobbly as she stumbled to the door and peered through the peephole. No one in sight. She turned the deadbolt. Before she stepped out she turned on the lights and took one last look around. What had Shen come back for? Please not that disc.

No. It was in the DVD slot, still partially ejected just as she'd found it. As she stared at the disc it seemed to call to her.

Don't leave me here. Take me . . . take me . . .

Nothing she'd like better, but she couldn't let on that she'd been in here.

Then she thought of Shen watching it again, touching himself as she and Paul touched each other, as they—

She stepped over and snatched the disc from the player. Let Bill and Shen worry about where it had gone. Let them wonder who had been in their nasty little den. So what if they knew.

Her jaw muscles bunched in rage. The disc is gone? Deal with it, you bastards.

Neither of them would ever watch it again.

Fuck 'em.

SHEN

Li Shen stepped into the monitoring room and locked the door behind him. He felt ashamed at coming back here instead of staying home with Jing and Fai, but the disc, the cursed disc had drawn him back.

Dr. Gilchrist was not in Switzerland. His flight had been canceled. He was home and had called Shen, asked questions about Paul Rosko that he could not answer. Shen feared he might come to the monitoring room and find the disc, so he had to retrieve and hide it.

He had ignored a direct order in not erasing the file. But he could not.

He didn't know why it fascinated him so. He'd seen many pornographic films, both here and in China. None of them terribly interesting. One viewing always enough. None had ever stayed with him.

But not so with this one. He couldn't stop thinking about it. Maybe because he was acquainted with both people. Maybe because Doctor Sheila was so beautiful. Perhaps because it was not acted. It was real—real lust, real passion, real—dare he say it?—love. He did not know the reason; all he knew was that he needed to watch it again and again.

He took off his dripping coat and hung it up. But when he sat and reached for the DVD, he found the slot empty. Quickly he glanced at the other player. He always used this one but maybe—

No, that one was empty too.

Sharp-toothed fear gnawed at his heart. Had Dr. Gilchrist already been here? Had he found it? That would be a catastrophe.

Shen rose and began a search, stacking all papers in one spot, examining every videocassette to see if it might be the one he sought. He hadn't labeled it, but he had stuck a round orange sticker on it.

But he could find no disc with an orange sticker. Had it fallen off? If so, it wasn't in sight.

And then Shen realized that if Dr. Gilchrist had found the disc, he would have called immediately to rage at him.

Unease wormed through his skull. Had someone else besides him and the doctor been in here? It seemed impossible.

He flipped the switches to activate the video feed from Sheila's office. Empty. He quick reversed today's recording for an accelerated look at her activities. He watched her quick-step backward into the office; saw her sit at her desk . . .

. . . saw her pulling the bug from her pencil cup.

He shut off the recording. This was bad, terrible. She'd discovered the surveillance and then somehow she'd found her way in here and stolen the disc. He must call Dr. Gilchrist.

But what to say? Shen couldn't tell him that he'd burned a copy of their coupling.

———···———

BILL

Bill's cell phone interrupted an informal meeting with Abra. He couldn't ignore it—couldn't ignore *any* calls now.

"Gilchrist."

"*Oh, Doctor*," said a familiar voice. "*This is Shen Li.*"

Please have good news about something.

"Yes, Mr. Li." He put his hand over the mouthpiece and turned to Abra. "I've had security on extra alert since the Kaplan murder. No telling if that killer might turn up here."

Abra looked startled. "Oh, dear. I never even thought of that."

Bill smiled. "That's why you have me."

Shen was saying, *"I am asking, sir, if you might have been in the monitoring room today."*

"Me? No. Why?"

"*Well, sir*"—was that relief in Shen's voice?—"*I am sorry to report that I fear someone may have been here.*"

Bill felt spicules of ice begin to form in his blood. He faced away from Abra and lowered his voice.

"Impossible. What makes you think so?"

"*I am not sure, sir, but the room looked different, as if items had been moved. And one thing else, sir. Doctor Sheila found one of our bugs.*"

Bill felt the room swaying.

"You're sure?"

"*Yessir. It was recorded.*"

It's unraveling. It's—

Again, that dread that kept him awake nights. This time a vision of his kids being raised by someone else while a father they barely remembered rotted alone in prison.

Prison.

Once the inmates found out what he'd done—or rather their third-grade understanding of the process—he'd probably be stabbed. Or beaten to death with bars of soap wrapped in towels. Not to mention rape. Surely he'd be raped. That went without saying. If they didn't kill him right off, they'd all want to drive their dicks into him . . .

He caught himself. *Don't start. Once you think you're beaten, you are.*

He could salvage this yet. The key was Rosko. He had to find him, silence him. Once he did that, he was sure he'd be able to control Sheila. He'd explain the bug as overzealousness on Shen's part. But if she ever found out about the recording . . . thank God it had been erased.

And where the *hell* was Rosko?

Bill had called him last night from a blocked cell phone at exactly six. No answer. Then again at 6:02, 6:05, 6:10. He never answered.

He'd checked with Lieutenant Zacks to see if they'd been able to trace Rosko's phone, but no—he'd never turned it on.

Damn the man! Where could he be?

Then it hit him: Sheila's?

Bill walked out of Abra's great room and into the hall.

"Can we tap Doctor Takamura's home phone?"

"*Not in this weather,*" Shen said. "*Not without Doctor Sheila knowing. Need light, need time. Would need better equipment.*"

Shit.

"All right then, I want you to watch her house all night."

"*But sir—*"

Bill felt a surge of anger. "No arguments! I'm here with my sister and we are both sure that Rosko won't go out during the day; but he'll feel safer at night. If you see him enter Takamura's house, or spot him through a window, call me. If you see him come out, follow him. Whatever you do, do not call the police. Am I making myself clear?"

"*Yessir.*"

"Excellent. Get to it."

Bill jabbed the OFF button and turned to find Abra staring up at him from her wheelchair.

"Do not call the police about what?"

Oh, Christ.

"I was telling Shen not to call the police about the flooding in the parking lot. I don't want people thinking that Tethys can't take care of its own."

Lame . . . Christ, that was lame.

Abra stared at him. "Really."

He saw questions, doubt in her eyes.

Don't you turn against me too, he thought. I'm doing this all for you. Someday you'll understand the sacrifices I've made for you and your dream—or at least a version of it . . . mine and Mama's.

PAUL

Paul couldn't read in the dark and turning on the light in the bathroom so he could read would also turn on the fan. Hadn't thought of that until Coogan switched on the light the first time and the loud hum filled the room. No one was in the building as far as he knew but he couldn't risk it. Couldn't do anything in the dark but sleep, and that wasn't an option. Until this was over he doubted he'd sleep at all. He felt like a caged animal.

Some father, some protector. So far he'd done nothing but put the two people he cared most about in danger. He'd been sitting here at the IV offices for hours, trying to work out a plan. And coming up empty.

Gilchrist was out of town, which was too bad because Paul was dying to beat the shit out of him. Shake him up, knock him around until he told who Lee Swann was. And once he did, he'd smash his face in for killing Sheila's husband. Paul smiled. Okay, he wouldn't really do that because he was trying to stay out of prison. But God, he'd like to.

On the other hand, Gilchrist was probably the only thing standing between Swann and Sheila. Taking out Gilchrist might doom Sheila.

Not to mention that if Paul showed his face anywhere around Tethys he'd be arrested on the spot.

He needed to talk to Sheila and Coog and assure himself that they were okay, but didn't dare turn on the cell. And he didn't dare risk using the IV phone in case Swann called to check the answering machine and got a busy signal.

He stared out the window at the darkness and listened to the pelting rain. It afforded some cover—not as much as snow would, but better than nothing. He had to get out of here. A basement office was the worst place to be in a flood. Water was seeping in from everywhere and the Berber carpet was spongy and starting to smell like mildew. The stench and cabin fever was fogging his brain; maybe a drive would clear his head.

Maybe he'd drive by Sheila's place. Sneak in the back again. A quick visit and he'd come back here refreshed.

Paul stepped up on the chair and heaved himself out the first floor window, the only exit he trusted now. Water gushed in. He hoisted himself over the soaking, muddy grass line, slipping through the muck. His hands and knees were covered. He looked around. Coast was clear. He slid the window most of the way closed. More water would leak in, but if he shut it too tight, he might get locked out.

He walked down the street to his car and drove to McDonald's. Again he blessed the drive-thru. He was shaking from lack of sleep and worry. Food, especially the high-fat, high-protein variety, would calm him. He bought a grilled chicken meal. The friendly voice coerced him into a fruit yogurt parfait and a few packages of cookies too. That much sugar would surely keep him awake.

He wolfed down the sandwich and fries as he drove. When he coasted up to Sheila's he saw a car parked on the road in clear view of her house. Someone was sitting in it. Watching? Not a police car unless it was unmarked.

He drove by and scanned the streets for a public phone. The one on Main Street was too conspicuous. A mile away he found another near the Catholic Church. A sign?

He glanced around the darkened street. No sign of life. No houses close by. And no one in the church lot. He parked his car sideways to hide his plates. With his hood on, standing in the rain, no one would recognize him.

SHEILA

Sheila couldn't sit still. That disc. Dek's murder. The message Hal Silberman had scrawled on Tanesha's file: *Changing the World One Person at a Time.* Kelly Slade sitting in the examining room, a wispy white woman in a black woman's skin . . .

And Abra—dear little Abra—the last time she'd seen her . . . lying through her teeth. How much did she know?

Hated to even think it, but she couldn't trust Abra.

Sheila sniffed the pot of noodles and beef. Dinner in a box. Not her usual fare but the lasagna wannabe smelled pretty good. Hearty was the only way to describe it. Coogan would like it.

As she called Coog over to the table, the phone rang. She watched the caller ID. "Pay phone."

Paul.

Instead of hello, she said, "Listen, before you say anything, don't tell me where you are. Don't even say your name. I found a bug in my office today."

She heard a deep intake of breath on the other end. Then a reply.

"They're watching from all angles. There's someone parked in front of your house."

She squinted out the window but couldn't see anyone.

"Stay away from the windows. Do you catch my drift? Stay away from the windows unless the curtains are pulled."

Drift? What drift?

Coog! He didn't want to say Coog's name.

She looked around and gasped when she saw the boy standing before the bay window. She'd meant to shut the blinds. How had she forgotten?

She covered the mouthpiece with her palm and waved her free arm.

"Coogan, over here! Quick!"

She motioned him toward the table in the corner.

She stretched the cord into the windowless hall. She couldn't let Coog know she was speaking to his dad. He'd want to say something. And if the line was tapped . . .

But she wanted to stay on the line, needed to talk to Paul, hear his voice.

"How you holding up over there?" Paul asked. "You okay?"

"We—I'm okay. Staying dry and inside."

She wanted to talk in code but her mind was blanking. Even

if she could think, what could she convey? That she was terrified? Wished he was there with her? He knew that.

Inspiration struck.

"That puppy I'm watching for my friend, he's doing great. I thought he'd be afraid in a new house but he's fine." Her eyes welled up. "He's a brave little puppy. He misses his owner I bet, but he's acting fine. "

"That's good to hear." Paul's voice softened. Maybe even choked. "You never know with puppies."

She wished they could really talk.

Paul said, "Gotta go now. Can't stay here too long. Have to get back to work. You be careful."

"I will. You too."

She hung up and took a deep breath.

For the hundredth time she checked the locks on all the doors and windows. She shut every blind and curtain. She was creeped out but knew one thing she could do that might help them—at least until FDA investigators started swarming the campus—and that was to identify Lee Swann.

Paul had written two phone numbers on her kitchen scratch pad. The first was the phone at IV where she could reach him in case of emergency—but _only_ in emergency. The second was the number that had called in to the answering machine—the fax machine with the Tethys address. That was the one that could help them.

Sheila moved close to Coogan and lowered her voice. She didn't want to frighten him but he needed to know.

"Someone is watching the house. Stay away from the windows. They might see your silhouette." Then, limiting how much information she gave him, she added, "I got called into work and have to leave for a little while. Don't answer the phone or the door. Your dad called. He's fine and he loves you. I'll be back soon. Don't worry."

His bit his lip and his eyes teared. "Didn't he want to talk to me?"

"Yes but the phone might be tapped. He doesn't want anyone to know you're here."

If he was shaken, he hid it well. He nodded.

"You be careful," he said.

It touched her. The same words his father had spoken. She hugged him, then started for the closet to bundle up and head down to Tethys.

SHEN

Li Shen started his car again. He would run it just long enough to warm up the interior and clear the fogged windows. He didn't want his exhaust fumes to announce that the car was occupied.

He returned his attention to Dr. Sheila's house and raised his Leica Duovid field glasses. Her picture window swam into view again.

Swam . . . very appropriate. In all his life Shen had never seen rain such as this. So much for so long. Even at 12X he could see little through the downpour. He had spotted Sheila a number of times through the bay window.

He rested his elbows against the door to steady his hands. At this magnification the image tended to wobble. He wondered how long Dr. Gilchrist wanted him out here. All night?

Shen stifled a yawn. He began to lower the glasses to rub his burning eyes when a different figure appeared in the window. Not Dr. Sheila. No, this was a male, but too small for Rosko. A boy? His son, perhaps?

As Shen tried for better focus, the figure ducked out of view. Then the blinds went down. He saw a shadow of the added blockage of curtains falling as well. Jotting down the time and his impressions, he watched a while longer but could see nothing of the inside. From the way the figure had darted from view, Shen assumed the boy had either realized that he was exposed or was told to get away from the window.

He decided to call Dr. Gilchrist. He put down the binoculars and had his finger poised over the speed-dial number when he saw Dr. Sheila's car's reverse lights go on. Troublesome rain! He had missed her exiting the house. Her car backed out the driveway and headed for the road. Shen slammed his car into reverse and backed up until he was around a bend and not visible from her driveway. If she drove his way, she'd see him. He prayed she would turn the other way.

He waited but no car came around the bend. Leaving his lights off, he put his car into motion. Ahead, down the slope, he spotted Dr. Sheila's taillights and followed her.

Was she going to meet Paul Rosko? He hoped so. To end this once and for all would be a relief. He could call the police and they could take him. Then *Jiù-zhù-zhě* and Dr. Gilchrist would finally stop asking him for special projects.

It didn't take long to realize that she was heading for Tethys. Most likely she'd received a call from the hospital and was going in to see a patient. Despite his disappointment, he continued following. Maybe she was meeting Rosko at the medical center. A bold move, and unlikely, but people sometimes surprised him.

He hung back as her wheels plowed through the hubcap-deep water in the parking lot. He noted with interest that she did not go to the hospital lot but parked instead near the Admin building.

She splashed through the rain to the main entrance. Once she was inside he parked at the other end of the lot and hurried after her. Despite his water-resistant jacket, he was soaked by the time he reached the entrance.

The main hall was dimly lit—after-hours lighting consisted of widely placed sconces near the ceiling.

There. Down the hall. Dr. Sheila walked slowly with her cell phone in her hand. She appeared to be pressing buttons but not speaking.

What could she be doing?

SHEILA

Sheila held down the *SEND* button on her cell phone then listened—not to the phone but to the nearby office doorway.

She'd entered the Lee Swann number. It might be a colossal waste of time, but she needed proof of a direct a connection between Swann and Tethys.

The fax would pick up after the third ring. If she heard three rings from Bill's office, she'd know.

And now, somewhere beyond Bill's door, a phone began to ring.

One . . . two . . . three . . . then it stopped.

She hit *REDIAL* with the same result.

With a sick-sour feeling in her gut she opened the door and stepped into the reception area. She stood by Marge's desk and hit *REDIAL* once more. A phone rang three times inside Bill's inner office.

She knew the source: the fax machine in the corner near the desk.

Her chest felt as if it were about to burst.

Bill, how could you?

Sheila leaned back against Marge's desk and sobbed.

BILL

Bill sat in his home office looking at his quarterly investment statement. Then next one would be shy a hundred and fifty thousand dollars. He hoped Elise never found out. He'd already changed his contact information online so there'd never be a statement sent home again. Now if he could just keep her from looking at their tax returns next year.

He looked out the window at the rain. What a mess. He was damn glad they lived at the top of a hill. No flood damage for them. They should be able to escape this whole deluge unscathed. Too bad the same couldn't be said about the Proteus situation. The damage was done but hopefully the worst was behind them. Next week, sunny skies and a normal life. He hoped. April was at a sleepover at a friend's house and Robbie was in his room playing video games or doing whatever he did on a rainy night. Elise was racking up the most recent Netflix DVD for Bill and her. "Let's do *something* together tonight," she'd said. He never had time for movies but she liked the classics. The current disk was an old Hitchcock film: *The Man Who Knew Too Much.*

The title had startled him. Perfect description of Paul Rosko.

What was he going to do about that man? Well, he couldn't hide forever. Whether the police or Bill found him first, his life would be over. He was the last slice of trouble pie. Sheila wasn't strong enough to carry on this quest of hers with her blue-collar lover in the slammer, or dead.

Most likely she'd have a breakdown, like last time. No one would believe her story. She didn't even have all the pieces. She'd tell what little she did know, then fade into obscurity never to be heard from again. Sad, but true.

His cell phone rang. It could only be one person. He snatched it up.

"Did you find him?"

"No, sir. But I follow Doctor Sheila to Admin building."

Shen then went on to relate a confusing story about Sheila wandering the hall with her cell phone but not talking to anyone.

"Is she still there?"

"No, she home now. But was in your outer office, sir."

A stab of panic straightened Bill in his chair. God, his computer— if she ever got to it and figured out the access code . . .

"What was she doing there? Did she get into the back office?"

"No, sir. I hear strange noise. I go to peek and see her sitting on secretary's desk. She was crying."

"Crying?"

What the hell was going on?

"Yessir. Then she go home."

"And you're sure Rosko's not there?"

"No, sir. Cannot be sure. But a boy is staying with Doctor Sheila."

The Rosko kid—had to be! Bill pumped his fist. *Got him!*

"Thank you Shen. You go home and rest. I'll call you in the morning."

Bill hung up, his mind racing. If he couldn't find Rosko, he could use his kid to flush him out.

FOURTEEN

The gusting wind and pounding rain threatened to collapse Shen's umbrella as he approached Dr. Sheila's front door. Per Dr. Gilchrist's instructions, he had dressed in a full Tethys security uniform, including a cap. As he raised his hand to knock, he hesitated. He didn't want to be here, did not want to do this.

He did not want to kill this boy.

But Dr. Gilchrist had told him that the child was the most serious threat to *Jiù-zhù-zhě's* dream and had to be removed. He also offered him another hundred thousand dollars. Already Shen had one hundred and fifty thousand dollars in an account. After this last job, he planned to take Jing and Fai away. He would have someone sell his home and the profit would be sent to him in Jamaica or whatever island they chose. And the three would live a happy, wealthy life in a new country.

After this one last job. He swore on the life of Fai that this was the last time.

Shen forced his hand forward and rapped on one of the glass panes.

As expected, no response. Shen knew that Dr. Sheila had braved the flooded streets this morning and made it to the hospital. Certainly she would have told the boy not to answer the door.

Shen knocked again. He could have broken a pane, reached

through, and unlocked the door, but he preferred to talk his way in. Forced entry would raise questions. The boy's death must look like an accident.

When no one responded Shen put down his umbrella.

"Coogan Rosko!" he shouted. "I come from Tethys hospital. Doctor Takamura is hurt. She ask for you."

Still no response.

"She told me to come get you. She need to tell you something. She say is very important."

He saw a shadow move toward the door, then a boy's worried face appeared, peering at him through the glass. A handsome boy with wide, innocent blue eyes.

Shen flipped open his identification wallet and held it up to the glass.

"I am chief of Tethys Security. You must come with me."

The boy made no move to open the door.

"Is she hurt bad?" he said, his voice barely audible through the glass.

He cupped his hand to his ear.

"Too much wind. I cannot hear you. You must come see her. She ask for you."

Shen saw the boy look past him at the Land Rover with *Tethys M.C. Security* emblazoned on its side. He heard the latch snap back. The boy opened the door a crack.

"Is she hurt?"

Shen nodded. "Very bad. Her car turn over in flood. She has two broken legs. You must come. I drive you."

The boy's features reflected his inner struggle. He had surely been warned not to leave the house, but he was worried for Dr. Sheila.

"Okay," he said finally, "but I have to make a call first."

He went to shut the door but Shen stuck his foot in the way. A look of alarm flashed across the boy's face.

"Be quick," Shen said. "I wait here."

As the boy turned and hurried toward the rear of the house, Shen stepped inside and pulled a Ziploc bag from his pocket. He whispered across the living room, opening the bag as he moved. The smell of chloroform wafted around him.

The boy stood at the kitchen counter, holding a slip of paper as he dialed the phone. Panic widened his eyes when he looked up to see Shen padding toward him. The struggle was brief. The boy had no chance. The chloroformed rag over his nose and mouth stilled his flailings.

As Shen lifted him into his arms he noticed the slip on the counter next to the phone. It read "IV" and then a scribbled phone number. The name meant nothing to Shen, but Dr. Gilchrist was looking for the boy's father. He might be at this number so Shen pocketed the slip.

Minutes later he was driving the unconscious boy down the slope toward Tethys. The unrelenting torrential rain had caused the river to overflow its banks during the night. The low-lying areas of the town were flooded and, unfortunately, the Tethys Compound was in one of those areas. The hospital seemed safe on its rise near the rear of the campus but the river had taken charge of the parking lots and was lapping at the steps to the Admin.

Before reaching the flooded area Shen slowed and looked around. Only a few cars. The rain and the flood and the state of emergency from the governor had limited traffic to rare brave souls who simply *had* to be here. He turned left into the brush. When he was out of sight of the road he stopped and sat with the engine idling.

Finally he forced himself to move, to step out of the car into the downpour. Through the naked trees he heard another, deeper sound above the clatter of the rain. The roar of a swollen river. He opened the rear door and pulled the boy from the back seat. Keeping his eyes straight ahead so that he wouldn't have to look at his burden, he carried him toward the river.

Dr. Gilchrist had instructed him to see that the boy drowned in the raging water. His death would be just one more tragic fatality associated with the flood.

When Shen reached the bank he stopped and stared in awe. What used to be a low, clear, gently flowing stream had become a high, mad, foaming, mud-colored torrent. He would not have to hold the boy under. All he need do was step to the edge of the bank and drop his arms. Even fully conscious, the boy would have no chance. But unconscious . . .

As he took that final step toward the edge he glanced down at the boy. And stopped. He saw his rosy cheeks, his unblemished, rain-beaded skin, his long-lashed eyes closed in sleep. A picture of innocence. As innocent as his own little Fai.

Shen stepped back. No. He could not do this. No amount of money was worth killing an innocent child. He should never have agreed. He had enough money now to leave with his family. Plenty in the offshore account. He would go home and tell Jing to pack and they would leave tonight.

The wonderful *Jiǔ-zhù-zhě* . . . she would not want this. Dr. Gilchrist must have misunderstood.

He turned and carried the boy back to the car. He drove him down to Tethys and made his way through the muddy pond that once had been the parking lot. He drove slowly, carefully, so as not to stall. He parked on the walk near the Admin steps and took the boy again in his arms. He was stirring as Shen carried him inside.

———■■■———

Bill sat at his desk and held the bottle of whiskey upside down over his paper cup but it was empty. He dropped the bottle in the metal trashcan and stared into the cup. Dry. Damn. Well that was all right. He didn't really need it. He'd just erased all mention of Coogan Rosko from the Tethys computers. As far as the system knew, the boy didn't exist.

Bill knew that somewhere out by the river the digital nonexistence of the Rosko boy was becoming physical nonexistence as well.

Any moment now the phone would ring with word from Shen that the deed had been done. An awful, unthinkable deed.

Well, such a thing *used* to be unthinkable.

He rubbed his eyes and wondered what he'd become. Killing a thirteen-year-old boy . . .

He sighed. No sense in dwelling on it. It had to be done. The stakes were far too high to let sentiment or moral dilemmas get in the way of Proteus. He kept telling himself that a couple more lives—no more beyond the boy and his father, he hoped—meant nothing when weighed against the betterment of millions and eventually *billions* of lives all over the world.

He kept telling himself that . . . over and over . . . and praying that someday he'd believe it.

The boy's death would remove him from the equation. He might never be found. Wouldn't that be wonderful? Then, even if the police reached the father before Shen did, what could he say? He'd sound like a madman. If the boy's body never showed up, Rosko, with his history, would be the prime suspect. And if it did wash up, a dead body made a poor witness.

He heard a squishing sound and looked up. Shen, looking like a drowned rat, stood dripping in the doorway.

With the boy!

Bill shot to his feet with a cry. "Shen, have you lost your mind? You were supposed to—"

"I know, sir, and I will if I must, but not until I hear it from *Jiù-zhù-zhě* herself."

"How dare you!" Bill shouted in a sudden blaze of fury. "Are you calling me a liar?"

Shen pinned him with his violent, all-commanding stare. Bill felt his bowels clench. He should know better than to lose his cool with Shen. Had to remember who was in control. Not Bill. Not anymore.

Shen remained impassive. Bill wished to God he could read that face, those black eyes. Was he going to strike?

"I do not wish to harm a child. But I will do so if *Jiù-zhù-zhě herself* tells me it is necessary."

Pigs will fly and the damned will be having snowball fights in hell before that happens, Bill thought.

But if he challenged Shen, then he'd be the one floating dead in the river.

Very well, then, he'd pussyfoot around Shen and then deal with the kid himself.

"I'll call her later. She hasn't been well recently and I don't want to wake her."

Shen nodded, then carried the boy across the office and laid him on the settee. Bill opened his mouth to say the water would ruin the fabric, but shut it. A water-stained couch was the least of his worries.

Instead he pointed to Coogan. "It's too dangerous to keep him here."

Shen ignored the protest and pulled a slip of paper from his pocket as he approached Bill. He dropped in on the desktop.

"Boy was calling this number when I took him. Is important?"

Bill looked at the slip. His jaw dropped. He knew that number. The answering machine at the IV office! Was that where Rosko had been hiding?

He shook his head. You almost had to admire the man. Not only had he found a warm, dry, rent-free hiding place, but the choice was a way of thumbing his nose at Bill—or rather at his alter ego, Lee Swann.

Bill had planned to use the boy's disappearance to flush Rosko out of hiding and bring him to Tethys. But now that Bill knew where he was, he could simply call him.

A slight variation on the original plan, but one that would work just as well.

He could dispose of both Roskos at once.

———···———

Paul sat on the desk of the IV office. The floor was under three inches of water, and it stank. Water dribbled in from all sides and made continuous ripples. It kept getting deeper. He wondered what Sheila and Coog were up to. He felt trapped—helpless, useless, sequestered from Coog and Sheila and the rest of the world in this Godforsaken, four-walled cage. Might as well be in prison.

He stood and balled his fists. But damn it, this time he hadn't done anything. This time *he* was the victim.

He recognized the rage surge and tried the 10-9-8 breathing, but it didn't work. He felt his blood pressure rising fast and he started pacing the cell—the office. Just like fucking prison.

Paul swung a fist at the wall and smashed through the sheet rock. His hand hurt but the rest of him felt a little better. He flexed his fingers. Blood. What the hell? He looked up and saw a three-foot gaping section of wallboard torn open, demolished. How did that happen? He remembered one punch. Only one. But there must have been more.

He was losing it. An anger blackout. The first in a long, long time. He shuddered. All those years of anger management, of rage control, all the lessons, the techniques were slipping away. If he didn't—

The phone rang, startling him back to reality. He stared at it, listening for the message.

A man's voice. *"Pick up, Rosko. I know you're there."*

How the hell did he know? Paul walked closer, his anger rising again.

"Rosko, it's Lee Swann. Pick up."

He grabbed the receiver but it bounced out of his shaking hand onto the floor. He scrabbled to retrieve it from the water.

"I want to meet with you," the voice said. *"Maybe we can work something out."*

Right, like that would happen. A meeting with Swann was an invitation to a setup. The police were probably beside this guy right now. No way was Paul going to—

"Rosko, I've got your son. I think you'd better speak up."

Coog?

"I'm here," he managed to say, fear doubling the already high adrenaline from his anger. "I'm here."

"I figured that would get your attention."

Slimy bastard. Paul clenched his bloody fist.

"Meet me in a half hour."

"Where?"

"The Tethys Administration building, first floor."

Gilchrist's office was on that floor. The last piece of the puzzle clicked into place. But Paul decided to keep calling him Swann for now.

"Tethys. Why am I not surprised?"

"You wanted to make a deal, well, it's deal time. Come alone or your son goes for a swim—in the river. I don't know if you've seen the river today. Quite a sight. No matter how good a swimmer he is, your boy will be coming out of that water horizontally."

Paul took deep breaths, counted backward . . . nothing was working.

"Let me speak to him."

"No."

The flat, matter-of-fact refusal jolted him.

"Then how do I know you really have him?"

"How do you think I found out where you're hiding? But if you still doubt me, call your girlfriend's house. See if he answers Let me save you the trouble: He won't. And besides, even if I wanted to let you speak to him, I can't. He's unconscious."

Paul stood frozen. He felt the heat of rage drain away as an icy calm took over. Had Bill beaten Coog? Unconscious . . . or dead?

No. Paul couldn't accept that. In danger of death, yes, but still alive.

He had to *do* something. He couldn't walk into Swann's—Gilchrist's—setup. That would mean the end of Coog and him.

He needed time, needed to throw Gilchrist off balance. Put him on the defensive. But how?

Then Paul had it. A counterpunch. A shocker.

"Yeah, well, so you've got Coogan. Big deal. Think that's going to make me come running? We both know, thanks to you and Kaplan, he's no longer my son. I know all about Proteus, and I know it turned him into someone else's kid. So what's he to me? Do whatever the hell you want, Swann. Why should I care what you do to some lab rat genetic freak?"

And then he hung up.

Didn't expect that, did you, you shit.

Paul's heart thrashed against the wall of his chest like a wounded animal. He'd just taken a monumental gamble.

Whatever Gilchrist had planned hinged on Paul's caring about his son. But if Paul didn't care, then it became a whole new game.

Gilchrist would have to rethink, regroup, and that would give Paul
time to get to Tethys.

As he grabbed his coat, a small bag of McDonald's cookies fell
out. He was starving and if his blood sugar got any lower, no telling
where his moods might go. As he snatched them up and ran for the
door, the phone began to ring.

———■■■———

Bill stood in speechless shock. Rosko hadn't waited for a
response.

"Rosko?"

A dial tone.

He hung up on me! What the hell—?

What kind of man hangs up on someone holding his son? All
right, technically not his son anymore, but a boy he's raised for
thirteen years. What kind of cold-hearted bastard was he dealing
with?

Bill glanced at the kid, saw his eyes flutter open, then close
again. He was coming out of it. Shen still stood by him. Fucking
lioness protecting her cub.

And what had Rosko said about Proteus? Where had he heard
that name? Even if Kaplan had spilled the beans about the process,
no one but the family ever called it Proteus. Not even Sheila
knew.

He ran his fingers through his hair, hard, pulling at it. How
could he know?

"How!" he screamed.

Shen was looking at him as if he'd lost his mind.

"Doctor Gilchrist, you are all right?"

Some assassin he'd turned out to be.

"Fine. I'm fine. Rosko's phone must have cut out. I'd better call
him back."

As Bill redialed he tried to think of a way to save face with Shen
and regain the upper hand. He looked from Shen and the kid to
the leaded window. Rain. Heavy rain eroding the Tethys campus
drop by drop.

Rosko answered on the second ring.

He sighed. *"You again, Swann? What now?"*

Again Bill was taken aback. How could this joker act like this? He had his boy for God's sake! This was not a time to be acting the wise-ass tough guy.

Acting . . . yes, maybe it was all an act.

"Don't hang up on me. Rosko. If you do, I will kill the boy."

Wait . . . what was that sound? Crunching? Chewing? Was this guy eating? Was it *that* small an issue to him that he could be snacking while his son's life hung in the balance?

Bill banged his pen on the desk. Christ!

"Try to bluff me again and he's gone. If that doesn't matter to you, then let me know."

Nothing. At least the chewing stopped.

"Say something, Rosko."

"It matters. What is it you want, Swann? My silence? Is that it? You want me to stop looking into Proteus?"

Bill didn't have an answer for him.

What do I want?

He wanted Rosko to come here so he could kill him. Not the right response though. What to say, what to say . . .

"You keep throwing out the name Proteus. I don't know where you heard it, but trust me, it encompasses so much more than the sliver of what you know. It's an important therapy that will save millions of lives. It shouldn't be stopped. The future of mankind is at stake here. I don't want to hurt anyone. I don't want to hurt you or your son. Hurting is not what I'm about. I took an oath."

"Yeah, I know. First, do no harm right?"

"Yes, exactly. Do no harm. I don't want to hurt anyone."

"But you did. You killed the Green woman and Kaplan and probably Silberman, then you framed me. Why the hell should I trust you?"

Good point.

Bill felt a buzz in his breast pocket and nearly jumped off his chair. The cell phone vibrated always startled him. He pulled it out and looked at it.

Abra—home.

Third time she'd called this morning. He didn't have time for her right now. He hit the ignore button and replaced the cell in his pocket.

"You have to trust me because I have your son. You don't have a choice."

"So you're admitting that you killed those people?"

Stupid question. He knew damn well—

The phone! He realized that the whole conversation was being recorded on IV's answering machine. God, what an idiot he was. Bill pulled the phone cord tight, wrapping it around his fingertips as he tried to recall everything he'd said since Rosko picked up. Had he admitted anything? Jesus! Of course he had. Said he'd kidnapped his son and was going to kill him, and he'd given his location. If Rosko took that to the police . . .

Had to bring him in, then Bill could call back and use the machine's "erase-all-messages" option.

Someone shoved his shoulder. He looked up to see Shen, pulling the cord off Bill's finger.

"You are all right, Doctor Gilchrist?"

Bill nodded, glad for the jolt back to reality. He stared down at his purple fingertip. It burned as blood flow returned.

He needed to shake up Rosko—gamble on his paternal instinct.

"You want to know if I have him? You want to know if he's still alive? You want to hear his voice? How about hearing that voice scream in pain?" Bill snapped his fingers to Shen. "Wake the kid and break his arm."

But Shen shook his head. "No sir. No, I cannot do that."

Shocked, Bill jammed his hand over the receiver's mouthpiece. "What?"

"I cannot do that. I am sorry, sir. No disrespect but I will not hurt the boy in any way before I talk to *Jiù-zhù-zhě.*"

Shen looked away and stood in front of the kid. A barrier.

Oh for Christ's sake, *Jiù-zhù-zhě, Jiù-zhù-zhě.*

As Bill glared at Shen he remembered Rosko. He put the receiver to his ear in time to hear him begging.

"Please, please don't hurt him! I'm begging you! I'll come in."

Bill had to smile. "So, you *do* care."

"Yes. I do." Rosko's tone turned cold, menacing. *"If you've hurt him I'll—"*

Bill laughed. "You'll what?"

"I know who you are, Gilchrist, and if you've got kids of your own . . . a little Biblical justice will be in order. And in case you don't know what that means, the phrase an eye for an eye should ring a bell."

Bill swallowed. How long had he known his identity? Did Sheila know? Robbie . . . April . . . dear God.

No! He couldn't let Rosko turn the tables.

"Half an hour, Rosko, or the kid goes swimming."

He hung up and turned to find Shen dissecting him with his eyes, scrutinizing every move.

Bill reached into his drawer, pulled out his lockbox. A key from his ring opened it and he removed a small .32 caliber revolver— loaded. He slipped it into his coat pocket. The instant Rosko stepped through that door—*blam!*—he was dead.

Then what? Kill the boy? Might even have to kill Shen. This was out of control with no one to rely on but himself.

His life's work was not going to fall apart because of some ex-con cable installer and that overzealous slut Sheila.

"Get the kid into the tunnels! Lock him in the monitoring room. Then we'll go talk to my sister."

Shen looked at him, analyzing him. Probably thought he'd lost it. But Bill didn't care. He hadn't gone nuts, but someone had to get things under control. Let Shen Li judge all he wanted. He wasn't long for his world. But for now Bill needed him. If nothing else, he knew the man would protect him.

Shen lifted the unconscious boy into his arms and walked down the hall toward the elevators.

The cell phone buzzed again and Bill flinched. He reached in and hit IGNORE. He didn't have to look to know it was Abra. What did she *want?* He had no intention of taking Shen to see her.

Abra relied on him to take care of things and that was exactly what he was doing. When it was all fixed, he'd call her back.

———···———

Paul ran through the deluge in blind panic. If only he'd been able to hold up his bluff. But how, when someone invited you to listen while your son's arm was snapped? And worse, he *still* didn't know for sure if Coog was alive, if Coog's light was still out there, still burning.

One thing he did know was that he had to get to Tethys before Gilchrist could harm Coog.

Paul's anger was focused now, and just as cold as before.

He looked at his watch. He was due at 8:50.

I'll be there in fifteen, Gilchrist. And then you and I will have a nice little chat.

He jumped into his Explorer and turned the key, but it didn't start. It whined but wouldn't catch. Wet wires. Had to be.

He began to shake. Oh, no. Not now. Not *now*!

He kept trying, and on the fourth go round the engine caught and roared to life. Paul rested his forehead on the steering wheel and allowed himself one sob.

When the engine had warmed, he threw it into gear and headed for Tethys.

He'd known about the rain, of course, but lack of a TV or radio had left him unprepared for the flood. The streets were churning streams of water, running clear when he started out but turning muddier and muddier the closer he got to Tethys. The water forced him to cut his speed. Couldn't afford to drown his engine now.

Sheila!

He'd been so focused on Coog he'd all but forgotten about her. If Gilchrist had abducted Coog, what had he done to Sheila?

He pulled out his cell phone and turned it on. Fuck the police. Fuck giving his position away. The last thing he needed was to be stopped by the cops and hauled off to jail, but he bet they now had their hands full with flood-related problems.

He speed-dialed her cell number and waited.

"Paul?"

Relief poured though him like sunlight.

"Sheila! You're okay? Where are you?"

"At the hospital. It's crazy here. Most of the staff can't get in. We're keeping things going with a skeleton crew. But shouldn't you be calling from a land line?"

How did she know he—? Oh, right. Her caller ID.

"I'm past caring about that now. Gilchrist has Coog."

"What?"

"He's Swann."

"Yes, I know."

"You know? Then why didn't—?"

"I wanted to tell you last night but I couldn't risk it."

Paul sighed. "Wouldn't have made any difference. But he called the IV line this morning. He's kidnapped Coogan and wants to meet with me."

"It's got to be a trap, Paul! Don't go!"

"Don't have much choice. He said if I don't show up he'd kill him."

"Wh-where are you meeting him?"

Paul opened his mouth to reply, then quickly shut it. If he told her the Admin building, she wouldn't be able to stay away. She'd run through the tunnels and do something crazy, like confronting Gilchrist to talk some sense into him.

But Gilchrist was out of control. No talking sense into that man now.

"At a motel."

"Which one?"

Think fast. He chose a cheap trysting spot on the edge of town.

"The Starlight."

"The Starlight? Why on—?"

"I don't know. But don't go doing something foolish like rushing out there. This is my fight. I'll take care of it. You stay there where you're needed."

"But Paul—"

"Can't talk now. I'm running into deep water. Bye."

No lie about the water. He'd entered a particularly deep intersection. He heard the water sloshing in his wheel wells.

The engine coughed . . .

. . . sputtered . . .

. . . died.

———■■■———

As the elevator descended to the tunnels, Shen wished he had refused this mission and had already left. But he would do that soon, in a few hours.

Dr. Gilchrist had promised to take him to *Jiù-zhù-zhě* so that he could hear the boy's fate from the woman herself. But Shen knew he had been lying. He could see from his reaction that she knew nothing about it. Shen had been a *fool. Jiù-zhù-zhě* knew nothing of *any* of the murders. All along this had been the doctor's fight, his plan to eliminate threats to Tethys. And he had used Shen's devotion to his sister to carry it out.

Shen gritted his teeth. No one makes a fool of Li Shen.

He looked down at the boy, a fallen angel.

But as the elevator doors began to slide open this angel became a writhing, kicking, biting, screaming demon who twisted from his grasp. He landed on his feet and turned to run. Shen grabbed his shoulder but the wet fabric of the shirt slipped from his grasp. The child whirled and kicked at him. Shen lurched backward with pain blazing through his right knee as the boy ran down the tunnel crying for help.

Shen leaped in pursuit but his injured knee slowed him, his limp making him unsteady on the puddled floor. As he rounded the first turn he stuttered to a halt. An empty tunnel stretched before him. Impossible. The boy could not have run that fast.

Shen looked around. He had to be hiding, but—

Then he spied a doorway labeled *Authorized Personnel Only.* Shen smiled. He had to be in there. The boy had probably never been down here. And since the passages weren't labeled, he would have no way of knowing which way to the hospital—might not even know he could reach the hospital from here. So he'd done what Shen would have done: Got out of sight as soon as possible.

Too bad for him that he chose that door. It dead-ended down toward the river. He was headed *away* from all possible help.

Shen opened the door but did not immediately step through—in case the boy was waiting with another kick. But he found no one. He listened and heard splashes echoing from somewhere ahead—the boy, running away. He followed them along the dim corridor.

This tunnel ran slightly downward and curved to the left. Since it led nowhere useful, it had not been renovated. Dark mold and mildew coated its stone walls; lighting consisted of naked incandescent bulbs widely spaced along the ceiling.

The splashing grew louder, but this was not the sound of footsteps. More like a small waterfall into a pond. Shen picked up his pace, but slowed again when he rounded the bend and saw the water.

A shiny dark pool reflected the overhead lights, stretching away to where a stream gushed through the ceiling and fed it. Shen felt his chest clench. The overflowing river had broken through the ceiling. A small break, but who knew how long it would stay small? If the ceiling should collapse many people could be killed.

Where was Coogan? Though Shen could not see past the waterfall, he knew that was where he had to be hiding. Cold and frightened, no doubt. Soon he would start to make his way back. Shen could wait until he reappeared and grab him then, but that might take a long time. He had to warn Dr. Gilchrist of the leak.

He took a step into the water, then snatched his foot back. *Cold!* No more than a few degrees above freezing. Clenching his teeth he stepped in again and kept going. The cold penetrated to and through his bones. His ankles felt as if someone were driving dull spikes into them. His calf muscles began to cramp.

How had the boy done it? Fear must have given him a will of iron. Shen would lose great face if his resolve proved to be less than that of a teenage boy.

The water deepened, reaching almost to his knees as he approached the waterfall. The stream seemed larger and louder than when he'd first seen it. No doubt because he was closer now. He hoped.

He angled to his left to skirt the icy cataract. The boy had to be just beyond it. Shen hadn't been in this shaft in a while but his memory told him that it ended not too far ahead. As soon as he got past—

Movement to his left, a flash of something slashing toward his head. As Shen raised his arm to ward off the blow he saw the boy's terrified face as he swung a length of two-by-four like a baseball bat. It struck Shen's forearm and shattered into a cloud of splinters and sawdust.

Termites.

The boy hesitated for a heartbeat, then turned to run. Shen grabbed him by the shoulder and this time his grip held.

"You have twice caused me pain, Coogan Rosko." He began dragging him back toward the dry area of the tunnel. "A third time and I will cause you pain. I am not here to hurt you."

"Yes, you are!" His voice shook and his eyes puddled with tears. "You're supposed to kill me. I heard Doctor Gilchrist say so."

Shen smiled again. "How long were you playing as the possum?"

He had spunk, this boy. He had not curled into a ball and awaited his fate. He had fought back. Shen liked that. He hoped Fai would grow up to be as spirited.

"Long enough!"

"Did you hear him tell me to break your arm?"

The boy nodded.

"And is your arm broken?"

The boy shook his head.

At last they reached dry floor, yet the deep ache in Shen's legs eased slowly.

"Then you must trust me to keep you safe until I take care of things."

As they began to round the bend, Shen glanced back and saw that the water level in the tunnel had risen. The waterfall seemed wider . . . and louder.

Sheila was furious. Why wasn't Paul answering her calls?

She started to pace, rubbing her upper arms. She had a wool sweater under her white coat but still she felt cold.

Tethys . . . the once idyllic medical center had become a hellhole.

Because of Bill Gilchrist, of all people. But how could she stop him? She'd never get out to the Starlight through all the flooding.

And then a thought struck. The Starlight . . . Paul had hesitated before saying that was where he was meeting Bill. Why? Because he hadn't wanted her to know? Or because the meeting place was closer?

No way it would be Bill's house. That left his office. Tethys was his home turf, and virtually deserted today.

Without a word to anyone, she left the lounge and headed for the elevators. The wards were quiet.

The tunnels. They'd give her quick, discreet access to the Admin. If Bill wasn't there, she'd return to pacing the doctors' lounge. But if he was . . .

Maybe she could help.

———···———

The goddamn car wouldn't restart. Paul had bloody fingers from turning the key so hard and so often. He had exhausted every four-, ten-, and twelve-letter word he knew in every possible combination he could imagine.

And while the car sat quite literally dead in the water, the clock kept ticking.

His phone began to ring—again. He checked the ID: Sheila—again. He couldn't talk to her now, couldn't risk giving away anything about where he was or where he was going.

He needed more time. He punched in the Swann number and held his breath until Gilchrist answered.

A low, affected voice said, "*I don't suppose I have to ask who's calling.*"

"Gilchrist, I'm stalled out at Pine and Holmwood. The intersection's flooded. I'll need more time."

"Sorry. We agreed on thirty minutes and you've used almost half that."

"Give me another thirty minutes. I'll get there. I'll swim there if I have to."

"Sorry, no. I—"

Paul squeezed his phone, then eased up. Breaking it would only screw things up worse.

"Well, then, if that's the case I'll skip going to your office and head straight for your home."

A pause, then, *"You're bluffing, Rosko."*

Of course he was. Too many innocent lives had already been lost. But he had to keep up a front.

"You're sure of that? You know my record. You know what happens when I'm pushed too far."

"All right, Rosko. Another fifteen minutes and that's it. Because if you can't get here you can't get anywhere else."

Paul cut the connection.

Fifteen minutes . . . what good was that? In fact, what good was an hour, *two* hours if he couldn't move past this intersection?

He hit the switch to lower the window but it didn't move. Dead. He wiped off the condensation and looked around. None of the other cars he saw within the limited view the deluge allowed were moving. He climbed over the console and wiped the passenger window. This side faced the river where the deeper water made the chances of finding a working car even less. He spotted one vehicle—an empty Hummer. Christ, if a Hummer couldn't get through, what hope had an Explorer?

He noticed something white and red bobbing in the water past the Hummer. He wiped again and squinted. Looked like a boat, a dinghy.

Of course. Baxter's boat dock was down that way. They rented rowboats and putt-putts to people who wanted to cruise the river. The river than ran right through Tethys.

The dinghy lay upside down, but still afloat.

What good was that?

Then again, what other option did he have?

Paul pushed open the door. It moved two or three inches before the flowing water caught it and ripped it from his grasp. The car canted as ice-cold muddy water rushed in. He gasped when it ran over his feet and ankles. In a whine of tortured metal the current broke the door's hinges and bent it back to where it bounced against the front fender. Not a fast flow, but enormous force behind it. Paul didn't know if he could fight it, but he didn't see any choice.

He grabbed his baseball cap, tucked his cell phone under it, and put it on as he slid out of the car into the rain and flood.

A shudder ran through him as frigid water swirled to mid-thigh level. He forced himself forward, one step at a time. It was like walking through icy Jell-O. The water kept pushing him to his left and it took all his strength to fight it and stay on a perpendicular course from his car. He'd aimed himself at a spot upstream from the boat.

But the closer he moved to the river, the deeper the water and the stronger the current.

Still he fought forward. The water had risen to his waist and Paul sensed himself losing ground. He couldn't feel his legs; his muscles seemed to be turning to rubber. But he was the only hope Coog had, so he gritted his teeth and soldiered on.

He glanced back and saw that his intended ninety-degree angle from the car had been eroded to forty-five. Losing it. Not going to make it. Just a question of which got him first—the water or hypothermia.

The water had reached the bottom of his rib cage when he lost his footing and was swept into the current. He knew he'd never regain his feet so he started swimming. He stroked crosscurrent, trying to stay upstream from the boat just a little longer.

As he neared it he realized he was going to miss it unless he could goose a little more force from his frozen arms and legs. He pushed them like he'd never pushed them before.

Closer . . . closer . . . he lunged and caught the edge of the stern with one hand. The water fought to tear him free but he forced his fingers to keep their grip. He pulled himself to the boat and eased along its side. It was aluminum, maybe ten or twelve feet long.

He felt something bang against his knees. Another boat. The overturned dinghy was resting atop one of its sunken brothers. Both were still tied to a piling.

Paul positioned his feet on the drowned boat, grabbed the gunwale of the dinghy, and pushed up with all the force he could muster. The boat resisted until the gunwale broke the surface. The wind caught it, and with its help Paul righted the boat, but not before it took on four or five inches of water.

He jumped in. The rain was cold but still warmer than the river. He spotted a pair of aluminum oars fastened to the inside of the port hull. He fitted them into the oarlocks, untied the bow, and began to row.

The water the dinghy had taken on made the boat sluggish but Paul had no way and no time to bail.

He put his back into the rowing. The activity warmed his body, got the blood flowing, loosening his cramped muscles. Thank God for all those hours with the weights and the heavy bag.

He checked his watch. He was going to make the time limit—beat it, in fact.

And that gave him an idea.

———···———

"Hold your head still!" Shen said.

He had found it difficult to tie the struggling boy into one of the chairs in the monitoring room. The child had winced every time Shen had touched his chest. Had he injured his ribs? No matter. He now was fighting Shen about taping his mouth.

"Help!" the boy screamed. *"Help!"*

"Hush. There is no one to hear you."

"Hel—!"

Shen slapped the duct tape over his mouth, then wrapped a second, longer piece around his head as an added precaution.

That done, he opened the door and checked up and down the tunnel. No one to hear him now, but who could tell the future? Someone might step into one of the tunnels and hear his cries.

Something glistened on the floor beyond the elevator.

Water.

Shen closed the door and tried not to listen to the frightened sounds the boy made through the gag, tried not to see Fai in the boy's frightened eyes. He grabbed the phone and tapped in Dr. Gilchrist's extension.

"*What is it?*" He sounded angry.

"Water, sir. A hole in the ceiling of one of the unused tunnels. Water is pouring in. I fear the ceiling may fall through and the tunnels will flood."

"*What are you doing in the unused shafts? I told you to watch that boy.*"

"I am, sir. He is here beside me. But the tunnels—"

"*They'll be fine.*"

"I am not sure. Back in China—"

"*I don't have time for this, Shen. I gave you a job to do, now do it. Just stay down there with the kid. I'll call you later.*"

Dr. Gilchrist hung up. What disrespect. Now that Shen was not his killing machine, he treated him like a dog.

Shen had seen this before in leaders. Too much pressure and even the best men cracked. Forgot who the real enemy was. The boy was innocent. Perhaps his father too.

But Coogan was safe with Shen for now. He would not hurt him but releasing him might cause him more danger. Dr. Gilchrist might kill the boy himself if he found him.

As for the water, maybe the tunnel ceiling would hold until the river receded. Shen hoped so.

He turned to the boy. His gut tightened as he saw him flinch.

"You shall not be harmed. Do you believe me?"

The boy shook his head and looked away.

"On my honor . . ."

Shen paused, weighing what he was about to say, knowing that once the words passed his lips, he could not take them back, even if *Jiù-zhù-zhě* ordered him.

"On my word and on the life of my son, I will not hurt you."

The boy looked at him with changed eyes.

"Do you believe me now?"

He nodded. And seemed to relax.

"But this is the safest place for you now."

Shen patted his shoulder and turned away.

———···———

Abra sat among her terraria and thought about the events of the past two weeks.

Three people had posed a threat to Proteus. All three were dead. Kelly Slade, an accident; Tanesha Green, a cardiac arrest; Gerald Kaplan, bludgeoned. No pattern there, but all so . . . convenient.

Too convenient. It had started a nagging suspicion. She'd managed to keep it at bay so far, but her conversations with Billy the last few days had set off an alarm.

Something about his attitude, his distraction . . . those terrible suspicions persisted.

Could her Billy have anything to do with this?

She bowed her head. Her Billy. How well did she really know him? Obsessed with the Proteus Cure, as he called it. But only during the last decade had the dream became an attainable goal.

After Billy's departure yesterday she'd contacted the funeral home and obtained the name and phone number of Gerald Kaplan's sister, Robin Dillon, his only known kin. Abra had called her. The ensuing conversation confirmed what Billy had said.

Kaplan had never forgiven Innovation Ventures.

From their talk, Abra realized that Robin had cared very much about her younger brother, doted on him and worried about him. Abra knew how that was.

"*The company that funded him dumped him like yesterday's garbage. And just recently he learned they bought his research and started using it under another name,*" she had said.

Abra had felt her stomach flop. Kaplan had known about the KB26-VG723 link. Who else had he told?

"That's terrible, Ms. Dillon," Abra had said. "When did he learn this?"

"*A few days ago.*"

"The poor man. He must have been furious. Did he contact the company and ask for compensation?"

"*He wasn't looking for a payout. Nothing like that. It wasn't the money. He said it was the principle. During his last call he said he was going to tell someone everything—whatever everything was—and he was leaving with a clear conscience. Going somewhere warm. He'd only called to say goodbye. And later that night he was murdered.*"

The woman's sobs had torn at Abra's heart.

But now, in the cold light of day, she wondered to whom Kaplan had told "everything?" Certainly not Bill. Bill already knew.

Someone else.

Sheila? Paul Rosko? In danger now, if not dead. Tears fell. Would Abra be reading about another unusual death in the paper tomorrow? Or another "car accident" perhaps? Would Billy be cavalier about that one too?

Abra's heart sank.

Billy. She couldn't see him actually killing anyone, but she could envision him paying to keep the blood off his hands. And better still if that murder could be pinned on Paul Rosko, the only other person, save Sheila, who posed a threat.

Billy, Billy, Billy, what have you done?

Abra banged her hands on her chair. Stupid blind fool! Why didn't you stop this? Your fault! You refused to see what went on under your own eyes!

She had to talk to her little brother. Now! Confront him. Make him stop.

She called his house. Elise said he was at work.

"*Where else would he be during a flood?*" she asked, her voice spiked with sarcasm.

Abra tried his office phone several times. No answer. She tried his cell phone. No answer. No reason to leave a message. He'd see her missed calls.

A sick feeling enveloped her, prickling her skin.

Kill for Proteus . . . she found it unfathomable, unconscionable, unspeakable. To end lives in order to protect the secrets of something designed to save lives. Sacrilege. Or sacrifice.

So much like Mama, her Billy. Too much, perhaps.

She dialed Henry's number. Felt bad about bringing him out in this weather, but she needed him to drive her to the campus. If Billy wasn't in Admin, he'd be at the hospital.

But Henry couldn't come.

"The street outside my house looks like a river, ma'am. No one will be doing any driving around my way any time soon. I'm awfully sorry."

So was Abra. She turned to the window and stared at the Admin Building. Her house sat on the perimeter of the campus. Between it and Admin lay a field of muck. A New England bayou.

She'd chosen this particular site because of its proximity to the buildings. She'd had one of the tunnels extended so that it terminated in her basement.

Well, as much as she disliked the tunnels, she had no choice. She'd take her elevator—she'd made that a must when she'd designed her house—down from her main floor to the basement and unlock the door to the tunnel. When she reached Admin she'd take another elevator up.

Simple.

She pushed the toggle that wheeled her into the elevator. As the doors pincered closed she heard her phone begin to ring. Bill, no doubt, returning her calls. Well, she'd be seeing him soon enough.

————■■■————

The amount of water in the tunnels alarmed Sheila. It seeped into her shoes as she splashed through it. Where was it all coming from?

A sound made her stop as she heard a sound. A voice? Calling?

She waited but didn't hear it again. She resumed her hurried pace toward Admin.

Creepy down here. So deserted.

But that didn't bother her nearly as much as figuring out what she'd do when she got to Bill's office. What if she found Coog tied up on the floor with Bill standing over him?

She slowed her pace. This wasn't smart. She hadn't thought this thing through. Going to him alone didn't make sense. She needed an ally . . .

And who better than his own sister?

Sheila pulled out her cell phone and dialed Abra's number.

Abra had to know about Proteus. Sheila could see how someone with a genetic defect like hers would be interested in gene therapy. That meant she'd been lying to the patients as well, changing their genomes without their knowledge or consent.

Sheila couldn't imagine Abra involved in something so heinous. But then, she'd once considered Bill above all that he'd been doing.

But Abra wouldn't kill to protect Proteus.

And if she knew Bill had gone this far, she'd step in to help.

The phone rang four times before Abra's voicemail picked up. Sheila tried again with the same result. Where was she? She had to be home. She couldn't go out on a day like this.

And then an awful thought struck like a blow.

What if Bill had killed Abra too?

She hurried on to Bill's office.

———···———

Bill slammed the phone onto its cradle. Shen defying him, now leaks in the tunnels . . . he didn't *need* this. With everything else going on, the last thing he needed now was a nervous Nellie.

He gnashed his teeth. Face it: If Shen was complaining about a leak, it was probably serious.

But he had to wait for Rosko. The tunnels would hold. They'd been here a long time. They'd be fine. Shen was overreacting.

He sat again and positioned himself at his desk with his pistol ready. He fingered the cold metal as he reviewed his plan.

First and foremost, he'd shoot Rosko as he stepped through the door. No preamble, no last minute explanations, no time to plead or ask about his son. *Boom.* Dead. No more interfering with Tethys or with Sheila.

I hope you enjoyed her while you could, Rosko.

Bill felt a glitter of glee and relief as he thought of that man's brains sprayed across his wall.

Once Rosko was dead Bill would throw some stuff around and tip over a chair or two to make it look as if there had been a struggle. He'd tell the cops that Rosko came in screaming about stem-cell therapy being "unholy" and how he'd kill him just like he'd killed Kaplan. The violence in Rosko's history and the "unholy" bit would provide a motive for his killing Kaplan.

Not bad, he thought. In fact, a beautiful plan. A perfect example of grace under pressure.

Tragically, he'd tell them, Rosko also killed his son because he had received the "unholy" therapy.

He jumped as the fax rang again. He picked up the receiver.

"What now, Rosko?"

"I'm going to be late."

"How sad."

"Listen, I just found a boat and I can row over there but it's going to take a half hour."

"I'll add another fifteen minutes—no more."

And then Rosko was gone.

He'd count the seconds until he could blow this guy's brains out.

Bill glanced at his watch. He had time to check on Shen and the alleged tunnel problem. He'd have Shen do the kid now. No more waiting. And if that yellow bastard said, *I must hear it from Jiù-zhù-zhĕ,* even once, he'd blow a hole in him and do the kid himself.

"Where is he, Bill? Where's Coogan"

He recognized the voice immediately but still felt an explosion of shock when he looked up and saw who stood in his doorway.

"Sheila!"

He barely recognized her. Her softness had been replaced by a steely gaze and a hard-set jaw. Her eyes flashed.

Thank God he'd had Shen remove the boy. If she'd found him unconscious on the couch . . .

The eyes that had looked at him with such respect and admiration now held nothing but contempt. Disgust. He had to face it: Sheila was lost to Abra and him. She knew too much. The plan to bring her into their circle had become an impossible dream. She had to go.

She spoke again, this time through a snarl.

"*Where?*"

———···———

Paul closed his cell phone and looked up at the Tethys sign just ten feet ahead.

Gilchrist had bought it. Thought he was fifteen minutes away.

The current had helped, but his back and shoulder muscles had done most of the work. They weren't sore. They'd *liked* the workout. They hungered for more.

If—when—Paul got his hands on Gilchrist they'd get a different kind of workout.

All the way over he'd wrestled with the problem of what to do if Gilchrist had a gun. Surprise . . . surprise might give him an edge.

As he started to row the last hundred yards through the flooded parking lot, Paul felt his rage bloom. The closer he got, the hotter it ran. Adrenaline seemed to steam from his pores. This was how he'd felt all those years ago in that barroom. All his anger management courses and techniques and training were burning away in the flare of his rage.

Paul knew he was out of control, and he reveled in it.

———···———

Sheila glanced around Bill's office. No one else here. But she did notice a wet stain on the settee.

Shaking inside she forced herself to take another step toward him. She couldn't let him see how frightened she was. But if he'd hurt that little boy . . .

He put on a perplexed expression. "What on Earth are you talking about?"

"I know what you've done. You've lied, you've killed, you've even tried to have me killed. And now you've sunk to kidnapping and threatening a child! Where is he?"

He flinched.

"Have you gone mad?" he said. "Where did this insanity come from—that madman Rosko?"

"No. I put it together myself—Mister Swann. And I know you're trying to lure Paul here by threatening his son." She shook her head. "How could you have sunk so low?"

"I haven't the faintest idea what you're—"

"Where is he? Stop this madness and take me to him. Don't add a child's death to your list of crimes. Take me to him, let me take him home, and then turn yourself in."

He shook his head. "I can't do that."

"If not for me, do it for Abra. Or is she as guilty as you?"

His eyes flashed. "Don't you dare insult my sister! She knows nothing but the good parts. I've shielded her from the rest."

Thank God. She was safe. And not the monster that Bill was.

At least he'd stopped the denials.

"You need help, Bill. Please. Before it's too late."

Bill grabbed something off his desktop and pointed it at her.

A gun.

Sheila's already dry mouth turned to sand. She'd never dreamed she'd live to see a gun pointed at her, and by Bill Gilchrist of all people.

"It's already too late."

She took an involuntary step back. "You wouldn't."

"You haven't left me much choice." He waggled the barrel toward the door. "Let's go for a little walk, shall we?"

Sheila could sense what was coming. Coog was probably already dead and she was next. But she put on a brave face.

"No. You won't shoot me here."

"Why not? The building's empty."

"Well, then . . ." Her voice choked off. "Go ahead. Do it here. Now. You're going to do it anyway. You can't let me live, so get it over with."

"I'm not going to kill you, Sheila."

She didn't believe that for a nanosecond, but he seemed anxious to get her out of his office. Why? Was Paul nearby?

When she didn't move he added, "But if you don't turn around and walk, I *will* shoot you. In the knees. And then I'll have to carry you out. I don't feel up to that, so let's not play games. *Walk!*"

Sheila twisted her lips into a snarl. "You're despicable."

And so she turned—

And ran.

———···———

Paul reached the building and hopped out of the dinghy.

Cold . . . God, the water was cold. He sloshed toward the Admin's front door, reached for the handle, then stopped. Water puddled against its lower edge. If he opened the door, it would cascade in along with him.

He backed up and looked around the side of the building. The area above the small rise hadn't flooded yet. He ran around to the other entrance and opened the door as quietly as possible. He eased inside and padded to the edge of the vestibule where he peeked into the hallway—

—and saw Gilchrist disappearing into the door to the stairwell. Gotcha.

———···———

Bill dashed into the tunnel and looked around. Sheila's flight had taken him so by surprise that he'd lost precious time. He caught sight of her splashing around the corner. He took two quick steps after her but stopped when he heard the elevator whine.

Oh, hell. Who could that be?

Who else would come to the Admin tunnels today of all days?

Rosko? Had he arrived early?

He raised the pistol and flattened himself against the wall. As soon as Rosko stepped out . . .

Come on. Let's get this over with.

But when the doors opened, no one stepped out. Pistol at the ready, he stepped away from the wall for a look inside.

"No tricks, Rosko. I'm ready for you."

But the car was empty.

"What the—?"

He sensed movement behind him, the door from the stairwell swinging open. Before he could turn and bring his pistol to bear, a mass of human fury hit him like a Mack truck

Rosko!

Bill was slammed against the wall. He heard a bone crack as a blaze of pain shot through his shoulder—his clavicle.

Rosko was on him, a raging bull, pummeling him with fierce crushing blows. He tried to raise the pistol but Rosko knocked his arm down.

"Shen! Help me! *Shen!*"

Please let him hear me.

And then Rosko grabbed the gun. He began twisting it from Bill's hand.

No! That was the only hope he had against this maniac. Fear sent shock waves through his body, giving him a surge of strength that allowed him to wrest the pistol partially free. He snaked his finger onto the trigger. All he needed was to angle the muzzle a few more inches.

Out of the corner of his eye he saw Shen step into the tunnel, take one look, then break into a run. Thank God.

"Shen! Stop him!"

Bill smiled. He had Rosko now. Shen was almost upon them. He'd distract him enough so that Bill could—

Rosko banged against his finger, depressing the trigger. The gun went off, the report deafening.

Shen stopped, clutching his chest, a look of pain and shock on his wide-eyed face as he crumpled to the floor and lay still.

Oh God. I shot him!

Rosko's grip slackened for a second—he had to be as surprised as Bill—and Bill saw his opportunity. He angled the barrel and—

A fist slammed against his nose, flattening it with a loud *crunch.* Dazed, he loosened his grip on the pistol and felt it wrenched from his hand.

Metal smashed against his head. He gasped with the excruciating pain. Rosko was screaming like an animal but the words didn't penetrate. Something about *Where's my son? Where's my boy?*

Bill would tell him—tell him anything to make him stop—but the madman wouldn't wait for an answer.

Another blow to his head. This time the pain didn't register quite so much.

Another blow and he barely felt it as consciousness slipped away. Bill seemed outside himself.

He's killing me, he thought with a strange detachment. Make him stop. Someone please make him stop.

————···————

Sheila heard angry voices echoing behind her, then a shot. She'd been fleeing toward the hospital to get help from the few security men who had made it in, but the sound stopped her in her tracks.

Paul?

She turned and ran back, expecting to find him lying in a heap.

On the way she made out his voice, a strangled angry cry.

"Where's my son?" His rage and anguish echoed down the hall. "Where's my boy?"

When she finally arrived she saw Paul on top of Bill, bashing his head with a pistol.

Oh my God, he'll kill him!

"Stop it! Paul, stop!"

She dove for him and grabbed his arm. She saw a maniacal look on his when he spotted her, but only for a second, then recognition drove it from his eyes. He relaxed enough for her to take the bloody gun from his hand and drop it on the floor.

She softened her voice. "Stop it, okay? He's had enough."

Paul stared up at her, the rage draining from his face. He looked grateful to be stopped. He wrapped his arms around her and buried his face in her shoulder.

"Sheila, you're all right?"

She stroked his hair, thankful she'd come back. Bill wasn't moving but was breathing. He wasn't dead. She started as she saw another body crumpled on the floor beyond them. Shen Li?

She tugged on Paul's arm. "Come on. Get off him. He's not going anywhere."

"Where's my son?" he asked Bill again.

But Bill wasn't going to be saying anything for a while.

Paul held his arm firmly around her, protecting her. Sheila was relieved that he wasn't one of the figures on the floor.

Just then the familiar figure of a wizened woman with withered legs rolled down the tunnel in a wheelchair.

"What's going on here, Sheila? What's happened to my brother?" She moved over to Bill, leaning over to touch his blood-soaked head. "Dear God, what have to done to my Billy?"

"I'm sorry, Abra," Sheila said, partly out of reflex, partly out of grief for what Bill had allowed himself to become.

"Who's this?" Paul said.

"Doctor Abra Gilchrist. She's the other half of Tethys. Bill's sister." She pointed to Paul. "Abra, this is Paul Rosko."

Abra's hand shot to her mouth. "The man accused of killing Doctor Kaplan. What have you done to Billy?" Abra looked back and forth between Paul and Sheila. "And why?"

"I think you know why." It broke Sheila's heart to have to say those words.

The little women bowed her head and sobbed. "I fear I do."

"Then in God's name why didn't you stop him?"

"I didn't know! I only put it together this morning!" She glared at Paul. Her China-blue eyes were rimmed with red. "But you had no right to beat him half to death!"

Before either responded Abra picked up her cell phone and started to dial.

"Don't you move. I'm calling the police."

"Good," Paul said. "Then they can take you away for murder and kidnapping too."

Her finger poised above the number pad.

"Me? Kidnapping? What are you talking about?" She looked genuinely shocked. "I said, *what* are you talking about?"

Sheila rubbed Paul's arm to calm him. Looking at Abra now, so confused . . . Sheila had no doubt that Bill had kept her in the dark about his deadly activities.

But that didn't get her off the hook for the genetic crimes of Proteus.

———···———

Abra stared at these two people and tried to grasp the situation. Her brother Billy, the person she loved more than life, lay on the floor, his head a bloody lump.

She recognized the other body as Shen Li, their head of security. A stream of blood leaked out of his chest.

She noticed a pistol a few inches from her brother's twitching hands. Who had shot Shen—Billy or this puffing bull of a man, red-faced and crazed?

If she could have, she would have leapt upon him and beaten him the way he'd beaten Billy. But she knew too well her limitations.

Rosko gestured to Billy on the floor. "Your brother kidnapped my son. Used him to lure me here so he could kill me like the others."

She'd suspected the worst of Billy and now this confirmed it.

She looked up at him. "What do you want?"

"I want my son, what do you think? Your precious Billy kidnapped him from Sheila's house. Threatened to kill him. Where is he?"

"I have no idea."

He started for her but Sheila grabbed him.

"Stop. I doubt she knows anything. Look at her. She's been out of the loop in all of this."

"Thank you, Sheila."

She had hoped to salvage some of her relationship with Sheila, but with all that had happened . . . things could never be the same.

"How *could* she be?" Rosko yelled. "She heads up Tethys. She knows *something*." He stepped toward her, shrugging off Sheila's hold. "My boy! Where is he? If he's been hurt—"

Abra's hand's clenched her chair. What was he going to do to her? He sounded like a broken record. Did he think repeating the question would help?

"I don't know! If I did I'd tell you!"

Shen moaned before Paul reached her.

Abra turned to him, now lying on his side down the hall, his blood puddle spreading. She had forgotten all about poor Shen. He reached up and pointed to an open doorway.

"Boy in there."

Just then Abra heard a boom like a cannon shot, followed by a gurgling roar. She looked back down the tunnel and saw a foaming wall of water rushing toward them.

It could only mean that one of the tunnels had collapsed. God save her, the river was rushing in.

Abra tried to reverse her wheelchair but the icy water surged over her, covering her, shorting it out.

The shock of cold was almost as numbing as the realization that she was going to die. Terrified, grief stricken about Billy, she closed her eyes.

Better perhaps to die, she thought. Maybe better now to let go and not face the truth of what Billy had become.

Then she felt a hand grab her wrist.

———···———

Sheila fought the rushing water and pulled Abra from her chair—her body was so light, like a child's. In the old woman's eyes she saw fear and heartbreak. Sheila felt it too. Seeing everything she'd worked for and believed in washed away.

Couldn't let her die here. She managed to pull her up onto the steps. As soon as Sheila was sure she wouldn't tumble back in, she ran back to the torrent. No sign of Bill or Shen Li. Gone, washed away. Where was Paul?

"Paul!" she shouted. "*Paul!*"

"In here!"

She looked up and down the tunnel. In where? Then she heard him again, off to her right.

"In here!" His voice sounded strained. "I need help!"

She spotted the door that Shen had indicated. He had to be

there. She jumped into the frigid surge and stroked toward the monitoring room. A renewed sense of disgust toward Bill and Shen filled her when she recalled the last time she was in this room.

As she entered she saw Paul struggling with a chair. What was he doing?

Then she saw Coog—gagged and bound to it. Paul was fighting to keep Coog's head above water.

Sheila stood frozen, shocked, trying to ignore the aching numbness in her legs as she searched for a way to help.

Paul grunted. "The chair's too heavy to move and I can't hold him up and untie the knots at the same time! Can you get to them?"

She could try. Her brain rebelled but she took a breath and forced herself to duck underwater. Pain from the cold blasted through her head like a hammer blow. Couldn't give into it . . . Coog's only hope . . .

Sheila could barely see. Had to go by touch. She found a rope and followed it to a knot. Her frozen fingers felt thick and clumsy. Like bratwursts. She forced them to work at the knots. So hard. Damn fingers weren't cooperating.

She started getting dizzy, felt the world closing in around her. Needed air, needed warmth, but she couldn't stop now. Almost there . . . she felt a loop come free. She pulled on it, felt the knot fall apart, and then she was pushing her head out of the water to gasp some air.

"Got one!"

"Great!" He rotated Coog and the chair a hundred-eighty degrees. "There's another on this side!"

Coogan freed one of his arms and pulled off the tape gag.

"Dad, I'm so cold!" His voice sounded weak. "Get me out of here! Please get me out of here!"

Sheila ducked under again, found the other knot and began working on it. Suddenly she felt other fingers tugging on it— Coog's free hand. Together they loosened it enough for Coog to pull his arm free, and then he was rising out of the chair.

When Sheila surfaced Coogan was in his father's arms.

"Come on, Coog," Paul was saying. "We're getting you out of

here." He looked at Sheila and she saw love shining in his eyes. "Thanks to Sheila."

He carried Coog through the door and into the current, weaker now but running higher—chest high. The stairs were upstream.

She saw Paul stagger against the current. Coog was causing extra water resistance. The boy looked shocky. If they were going to get through this, he couldn't give into it. He had to stay alert.

"Coogan!" she yelled. He opened his eyes and stared at her. "You have to stay with us. You'll be out of this soon. Just hang on."

She positioned herself behind Paul and pushed.

Struggling as a team, they made it to the stairs where they crawled above the waterline and huddled in a gasping knot.

Up on the landing, tiny Abra sat and shivered.

Sheila looked back into the tunnel.

"No sign of Bill," she said. "He's gone."

Paul squinted into the dim passage. "Good riddance."

Sheila was glad to be free of the threat Bill had posed, but not happy he was dead. He had been special to her for so long. She'd hoped he would have said something, anything to redeem himself. Now they'd never know the whole truth.

Paul pointed. "Who's that? Is that him?"

Someone struggled against the far wall, clinging to a standpipe. Surfacing and sinking, surfacing and sinking . . .

"It's Shen," she said.

"Leave him," Paul said.

"No!" Coogan shouted from two steps above. "Save him, Dad! He helped me!"

———···———

Shen had no strength left. Much of his blood had drained and washed away, and still the wound in his chest bled. He tried to keep his head above water, but could not. He did not want to die, did not want to surrender to the water, but his body could give no more.

Then he heard a voice—the boy's voice.

"Dad, please! He protected me! Please, don't let him die! I'd be dead if it wasn't for him!"

The boy, the wonderful brave boy was pleading for him. Oh, to have such a son. He sobbed and gulped water. He would not see Fai grow up. And Jing . . . poor Jing? What would she do for money when he was gone? He hadn't told her about the money in the Jamaica account. No one would ever claim it now.

He stole one last breath, then stopped struggling and let the water take him. He closed his eyes and called up images of his beautiful Jing and Fai. For all the lives he had taken, he begged forgiveness from any god who could grant it. The faces of all of his victims flashed before his eyes.

It is time to die. I am sorry. I am so sorry to all I have hurt.

Suddenly strong arms slipped under his shoulders and pulled his head above water. Mr. Rosko.

Shen stared at him. "You are saving me?"

"Not my idea," he said as he hauled Shen through the torrent. "My son said we owe you."

"I could not hurt boy," he gasped. "I have son too. I could not follow my orders."

"What did Gilchrist tell you to do?"

Shen no longer cared about betraying Dr. Gilchrist. He was a liar and had used Shen to kill for his personal reasons. Used his trust and devotion to _Jiù-zhù-zhĕ_. When he'd heard Bill scream and saw Mr. Rosko beating him, he had run toward them to shoot Dr. Gilchrist. He deserved to die and Shen wanted the honor.

"He tell me to throw Coogan in river."

Mr. Rosko got him to the steps where Dr. Sheila and the wonderful boy helped pull him out of the water. Shen looked up and saw _Jiù-zhù-zhĕ_ staring at him.

Her face told him she did not know. All this time, she did not know.

———···———

Sheila snapped her phone closed and turned to the wet, disheveled human farrago clustered in Bill's office. Paul had carried Shen Li while she and Coog had carried Abra. Then Paul found the thermostat and cranked up the heat. He'd also ignited the gas logs in the fireplace. They didn't offer much warmth, but anything helped. Sheila couldn't stop shivering. She was surprised the police had been able to understand her through her chattering teeth.

She raised her voice. "The police say they'll get here as soon as they can, but they don't know when that will be. They've got people stranded in cars and on roofs who get priority."

Shen slumped on the settee. Blood had soaked through the front of his windbreaker. She stepped closer.

"Was it you who drove me off the road that night?"

Shen nodded, and coughed quietly. "A misunderstanding. I thought it order from *Jiù*—from Doctor Bill Gilchrist."

"It wasn't?"

He shook his head. "No. Doctor Gilchrist very angry I almost killed you. He said you were not to be hurt."

Imagine that. So Bill hadn't ordered the hits after all. "The other women, Kelly Slade and Tanesha, were those misunderstandings too?"

She knelt next to him, examining him as best she could, trying to staunch the bleeding with some paper towels form the kitchenette down the hall.

Shen winced as he tried to get comfortable. "No. Doctor Gilchrist killed Kelly Slade. I take care of Tanesha Green." He paused and then, "Also he make me poison Doctor Silberman."

Sheila should have known Silberman's death wasn't from natural causes.

"What about my husband?"

Shen cast his eyes down and she had her answer. Another order from his boss.

"He made me. I am sorry. I did not want to hurt anyone."

So much for absolution, Bill. She couldn't hate Shen. He was just a pawn. Used by Bill just as she had been.

"We need to get you over to the hospital."

He looked up at her. "I wish not to go."

She reached out to pull back the coat. "Shen, you have a chest wound and—"

He pushed her hand away. "It is not so bad." The weakness in his voice said otherwise. "I will be fine, Doctor Sheila. I will stay until the police come."

Sheila would have argued further but it was a moot point. The hospital didn't have any spare orderlies to wheel a gurney over for him. Maybe the cops would be able to carry him.

"My Billy," Sheila heard a voice say. "My dear little Billy."

Abra sat at Bill's desk, looking as cold and wet as everyone else, but far more miserable. She seemed lost to the world as she stared at the crystal pen set on the desktop, given to Bill by some civic organization, no doubt. Tears rolled down her cheeks.

Paul stepped away from the fireplace. "I wish I could say I'm sorry, but it wouldn't be true. Not after what he did—what you both did."

Abra looked up at him. "And just what is it you think I've done?"

"How about murdering innocent people for starters."

She lowered her eyes. "I had nothing to do with that. I never would have countenanced . . ."

Her voice drifted off. Though Abra seemed heartbroken, Sheila had questions only she could answer.

"Are you also going to tell us you know nothing about the genetic side effects of VG-seven-twenty-three?"

Abra's small mouth curved into a brief smile. "They aren't side effects."

It took a moment for that to sink in. Paul recovered first.

"You mean . . ." His voice was hoarse. "You mean you _wanted_ those changes? _Intended_ them?"

She nodded.

Paul's voice dropped to a sputtering whisper. "But-but-but you gave my son KB-twenty-six and now he's got completely different DNA."

"The DNA he was born with was flawed. He would have died."

Sheila glanced over at Coog, alarmed at what he was about to hear, but the shivering boy lay in a fetal position next to Shen. He seemed oblivious, dazed.

"He's a different person!" Bill continued. "How many others came to you looking to be cured and were . . . *replaced* instead?"

Fire flashed in Abra's strange eyes. "Your child was cured, yes? He no longer has leukemia, true? No traces of his former disease?"

"No traces of his former anything—and no trace of me left in him."

"Only in the genetic sense. Do not confuse parenthood with paternity or maternity. He's still your child. His memories of growing up will not be changed—his memories of growing up or the values you've instilled will not be altered in the slightest. No one erased his past or his dreams of the future, only his pain. I gave him *back* his future."

Paul moved toward the woman but Sheila put a hand on his arm.

"Easy, Paul." Sheila looked at her. "Why, Abra?"

Sheila had to know. Betrayal was a cold lump in her stomach. She'd been part of this, administering it, never knowing the changes she'd been causing.

Abra sighed and leaned back. "It all started with me." She spread her arms, displaying her undersized, twisted body. "Because of my osteogenesis imperfecta, I suffered more than a hundred fractures in my first ten years. That was my childhood. My bones snapped like matchsticks. My parents were research biologists, yet they could not do a thing to make me better. But they tried. I joined their quest after college. And then Bill joined us. The four of us worked night and day to find a way. There was no hope for me, but maybe hope for others. Papa died and still we searched. And then Kaplan discovered the key. When he abandoned his research and we discovered why, we were thrilled. We bought the patent, created a new corporation—"

"VecGen," Sheila said.

Abra nodded. "And Tethys administered their VG-seven-twenty-three. We secretly called it the Proteus Cure."

"After the Greek god," Sheila said.

Another fleeting smile. "The stem-cell therapy not only allows us to cure disease, but it replaces defective genomes with superior DNA—DNA with no ticking bombs of defective genes. My dream could now be realized."

"Dream?" Paul said as if the word tasted bad. "Remaking people into members of some new genetic race is your *dream?*"

She gave him a cold look. "What do you know about me? You stand there six-foot tall with strong arms and legs and you judge me? I've had a lifetime of pain and isolation. I wanted to see to it that no one else would have to suffer as I had. Tell me, Mister Rosko. If your son had been born with O-I, and"—she gestured to her shrunken, twisted body—"you knew that *this* lay ahead for him, what would you say to an offer to save him from that? Even if the offer meant changing his genome to someone else's? What would you say?"

Paul stood silent a moment, then nodded. "I'd have said go ahead. But I wasn't given that choice with Coog."

"That was because no one knew of KB-twenty-six's Proteus effect at that time."

"What about the current patients?"

She shrugged. "I wanted to tell them, but Billy and Mama said no. The FDA would never have approved clinical trials if they had known. Mama's wish was to give it to even more patients without their knowing. Hospitals all over the world. But I said no. We fought but eventually Mama and Bill agreed to keep the therapy at Tethys for now, keep records of all the patients, track their progress. She opened an unrelated company in Switzerland and Billy and me operate sub rosa from here."

"That's why he always goes to Switzerland? Because of your mother?"

So she was the mastermind. The one Bill had cowered before on the phone.

Abra nodded. "This last trip was rained out. That's why he's home. Logan was closed because of the weather."

"But how long did you think you could get away with it? Especially when you had people like Coog Rosko undergoing radical changes in appearance?"

"Those changes were limited to KB-twenty-six recipients, before we knew better. And so far Mister Rosko is the only one to complain. Our solution was never again to use the stem-cell therapy on children. Never."

"What about Kelly Slade and Tanesha Green?"

Abra shook her head. "I felt terrible for them. We had so many safeguards against that sort of thing. It's why we take detailed pictures of all our recipients and check their DNA—so we can match up their appearances with the donors'. Adults show far fewer and less noticeable changes. They receive clean genomes, so that after they're cured and go on to have children, their offspring will be far, far less at risk of inherited diseases." Her eyes lit up with excitement. "Eventually we can wipe out a plethora of inherited diseases, and treat spontaneous mutations like O-I whenever they occur. Think of it—perfect cures for heart disease, diabetes, muscular dystrophy, familial cancers, cystic fibrosis, hemophilia, no osteogenesis imperfecta! The list goes on and on."

"I see a replay of what Hitler wanted," Paul said. "Eugenics. A perfect race based on his view of perfect."

The woman's eyes blazed. "How dare you compare us to Hitler! He wiped out lives. We wipe out only pain and suffering. He destroyed futures. We restore them!"

Sheila said, "But where do you get the cells? Who do you get them from?" And then she knew. "The fertility clinics!"

Abra nodded. "We do deep background screenings on the family history of each applicant—male and female. We map the DNA on those with the best histories and every so often find someone with a nearly flawless genome. We take some of their blood stem cells, modify them and, *voila*, we can provide a healthier genome."

"So, in the end, Abra," Sheila began, "if this all played out and you were able to cure all genetic diseases—"

"Not limited to genetic," she said. "You know, I am sure, that some people, despite multiple exposures to HIV, don't get AIDS. And you know that the rare gene that protects them has been identified. We have sequenced that gene into our stem cells. Think what this will mean to Africa."

Sheila shook her head. It sounded promising on the surface, but . . .

"If it's all so wonderful," Paul said, "why haven't *you* taken VG-seven-twenty-three?"

She smiled up at him. "Oh, but I have."

Paul blinked, obviously as surprised as Sheila at that answer. "But it . . . you . . ."

"Haven't changed? Not externally. Not in any way you can see. My skeleton stopped growing when I was a child. Thanks to seven-twenty-three I no longer have O-I, but stem cells cannot change my twisted spine, nor my short and bowed limbs. The change has been inside. The defective gene that kept me from producing sufficient collagen has gradually been eliminated. My body is now able to replace the old fragile bone with new, hard, tough bone. I still look like I should be in a sideshow, but at least my bones no longer break like saltines."

That made sense to Sheila. She had wondered how Abra made it through the flood in one piece. Unlike a child, bone shape and size would not be affected by changing an adult's genome, but defective bone *architecture* could be corrected without external signs.

"I'm glad for you," Sheila said. "But it's playing God. I can't see what you planned to do with this . . . this Proteus. You said yourself the FDA would never—"

"Ah, but we have that covered. Given a few more years of research and clinical trials to perfect our technique and allow us to expand our genome library at VecGen, we would inform the FDA that we are shocked—*shocked!*—to learn that our seven-twenty-three, though one of the most successful cancer therapies in history, causes irreversible genetic changes. The FDA will call for an immediate withdrawal."

Sheila shook her head. "I still don't—"

"Don't you see?" The light grew in her eyes. "We can cure cancer! We can cure AIDS! We can prevent a host of inheritable diseases! Do you think the public will allow the FDA to stand in the way of something like that? The government will *have* to let us make it available."

Paul said, "But what about the people you've been using as guinea pigs? I don't think they'll be so happy."

Abra's eyebrow rose. "Really? You said yourself you would have approved of the treatment knowing it would save your son's life."

Sheila felt as if she'd fallen down an ethical rabbit hole. On one hand she found Proteus and the way it had been handled morally, ethically, legally odious. But then she thought of all the hopeless cases brought into Tethys on stretchers who had walked out with a cure.

Where was right and wrong here?

"We will open clinics all over the globe. We will transform humanity, make the world a better place, one person at a time."

Sheila comprehended the magnitude of this phrase.

A harsh, hoarse voice spoke from the doorway.

"Except it wouldn't have worked that way."

Sheila whirled to see Bill Gilchrist slouched against the doorframe, his face swollen, bruised, and bloody from the beating Paul had given him.

He was holding a pistol.

———···———

"Billy!" he heard Abra cry. "You're alive!"

Bill winced at the bolts of pain shooting through his head and his broken clavicle. His left arm was useless. Maybe his shoulder was broken too. Hard to say. His nose throbbed and his right eye was swollen shut. Blood oozed from who knew how many lacerations on his skin. Rocky Balboa after the big fight.

"Just barely."

Rosko started for him. "You son of a—"

Bill lifted his pistol and pointed it at the big man's midsection. "Not so fast, asshole."

It took a supreme effort not to gut-shoot the fuck. The only thing that made restraint possible was the knowledge that he'd soon have the pleasure of doing just that. Very soon. Along with Sheila and the brat, who looked zoned out—hadn't even looked up when Bill had come in. Shen looked like he was half gone already.

Might simply let nature take its course in his case, even though the guy did get shot trying to save him.

All the players in one room. Perfect. What he needed now was to figure out how to orchestrate the carnage so that all the blame came to rest on Rosko.

"Billy! Put that down!"

Bill glanced at his sister. "You've got to be kidding, Abra." His tongue snagged on a sharp tooth when he spoke. Three of his front teeth were chipped and one was missing. Another reason to blow Rosko's head off. "This jerk almost killed me. You want me to give him a second chance?"

The icy water had revived him enough to break the surface and catch some air, but his clothes had weighed him down and his knees had been too weak to keep him upright. He'd thought he was going to die, but then found the strength to stand.

His first instinct had been flight, but he realized he could go nowhere in the flood. Then his foot had stepped on something small and hard. His pistol. With that in hand he knew what he had to do.

"Bill, please," Sheila said. "It's over. The police are on their way. Don't make matters worse."

Worse? How could they get any worse? His luck had bottomed out. He had nowhere to go but up.

He had a vague memory of Sheila pulling Rosko off him. She'd probably saved his life, and he owed her for that, but not enough to let her walk out of here. She knew about Slade, Green, and Kaplan and probably Silberman, and would never be able to keep her mouth shut.

He waved the pistol at Rosko and Sheila.

"Back up. Both of you. Over by the settee."

Right. Get all four of them in a tight little cluster where he could watch them.

He stepped over to his desk and sat on a corner. Christ, he was dizzy. And cold. He couldn't remember when he'd felt this cold.

"Rosko, if you hadn't been so conceited, none of us would be here now." Bill wiped his bleeding lip with a wet cuff. "You were so disturbed that your son, the boy your wife gave birth to right before your eyes, wasn't really yours." He looked at the boy. "What do you think of that, kid? Your old man causing all this because his precious redneck DNA's not in you anymore."

The kid looked at him dully, then closed his eyes. Bill knew the signs: shock—physical and emotional.

"Shut up, Gilchrist." Rosko seethed. "If it were your child you'd—"

"I'd what?" Maybe it was the cold, or the pain, or the complete arrogance of this thick-necked blue-collar felon, but Bill smiled. "If it were my kid? That what you're asking?" Then it wasn't funny anymore. "If it were my kid, I'd take my pride out of the equation and save her life."

He looked over to Abra who was slowly shaking her head.

"No, Abra. I'm not keeping it secret anymore. Who're they gonna tell?" Bill felt drunk with power. Couldn't wait to finally tell Rosko, show him what a complete dick he'd been. "My daughter, my beautiful little girl was born with cystic fibrosis."

He looked to Sheila who showed the right response: shock.

"No," she mouthed.

Under other circumstances, this is where she would have hugged him and said, *I'm so sorry, Bill.* But those days were gone.

"We found out in vitro and Abra and I decided we weren't gonna let it happen. Never told Elise. Never told anyone. Matched her skin and hair with a stem line and gave her the therapy right after birth. She's been healthy ever since. And you think I give a damn whose DNA she has? Shit no. A real parent wouldn't care." He pointed the gun at Paul's devastated face. "Go to your grave with *that* thought."

"Billy, you could have handled all this another way," Abra said.

"Yes, I could have," he said without turning. "I wish to God I had. But I panicked when Sheila started in on me about the Slade woman. And once I'd started on that slippery slope . . ."

Exposure would have ruined his other plans—his and Mama's. She'd fallen out with Abra about providing the public with full disclosure; she'd been dead set against Abra's go-slow approach. Bill agreed with Mama that his sister was wrong, but had stayed on with Abra. Worked with only limited numbers of patients, tracked all their data . . . so small compared to what he and Mama wanted but it kept Abra under control. Created the façade for her and the public of following protocol and gave them access to the stem cells from her fertility clinic.

"You could have come to me and we'd have worked it out together. Instead, you arranged all these 'accidents.' "

"Remember what you said when I told you? Your first reaction was, 'Maybe God is telling us to go public now.' You've always had a blind spot there, Abra. The government would shut us down— " he snapped his fingers "—like *that*, and people would *not* be clamoring for seven-twenty-three. Every organized religion in the world would be up in arms, screaming that it goes against God and nature. We'd have the entire ideological spectrum, right, left, and middle, condemning us as Nazis. We'd be tarred and feathered. It *must* be kept secret. Your problem, Abra, is you've always thought small. 'One person at a time'? Sentimental crap! The human genome is going down the tubes. Humanity needs help and it's getting that help in spite of itself."

"What-what do you mean?" Abra said.

"Mama and I took matters into our own hands years ago, and we've been doing just that."

Abra gasped. "How—?"

"We can discuss this later. Right now, we've got some nasty business to attend to."

Could he do this? He'd have no qualms about shooting Rosko. But the kid? And Sheila?

He'd have to. Otherwise his whole life, and Abra's and Mama's, would have been for nothing.

He raised the pistol and pointed it at Rosko's chest.

———···———

Shen knew as soon as Dr. Gilchrist stepped into the room what was on his mind. He'd seen it in his eyes: Kill everyone except *Jiù-*

zhù-zhě and blame it on Mister Rosko, the man wrongly accused of murdering Doctor Kaplan.

Kill the brave boy and the man who had saved his life? Kill the woman whose husband and baby he had stolen away? Shen Li always paid his debts.

He slipped his hand inside his jacket and found the handle of his 9mm semi-automatic. He was glad that he always kept a cartridge in the chamber, for he doubted he had the strength to work the slide now. He slid it free of the shoulder holster, clicked off the safety, and cocked the hammer. But when he tried to raise it in the doctor's direction, his hand shook so that he could not aim it.

Someone else would have to do it. The boy was closest, but Shen could not give it to him. Rosko was too far away.

That left Dr. Sheila.

———···———

Sheila felt something nudge her calf. She glanced down and saw Shen holding something out to her in his wavering hand. It looked like—

Mother of God, a gun!

At first she thought he was pointing it at her, then realized he was holding it by the barrel.

Offering it to her.

For what? Protection against Bill? How? She'd never held a gun, let alone fired one. She might do more harm than good. Maybe Bill could be reasoned with. Violence was always a last resort.

She heard Abra cry out, and turned to see Bill pointing his pistol at Paul.

"You're first, Rosko. I think I'm going to enjoy this."

Without thinking, Sheila grabbed the gun and pointed it at Bill. She hadn't found the trigger yet when she shouted.

"Don't, Bill! Don't make me shoot you!"

His eyes widened as he glanced her way and saw the pistol.

"Where the hell—?" Then he looked at Shen Li. "You've really disappointed the shit out of me, Shen. I'll deal with you later. Right now . . ." He redirected his gaze at Sheila and smiled. "We both know you're not going to fire that, Sheila, so why don't you—?"

"I will!" She hooked her index finger over the trigger. "I swear I will! And it won't be in the knees!"

She told herself that was true, but she was it?

Bill was still smiling that cocksure smile she'd once found so endearing. Wasn't he aware that his new face was little more than tattered, blood-caked flesh around splintered teeth? He looked like he'd been ravaged by rats. He took a step closer.

"You know you won't. It's not in you. Besides, this is me, Bill, the guy who pulled you out of a career-ending funk." Another step. "You owe me too much. You were an emotional basket case and I took a chance on you." Another step. He was only three feet away now. His left arm hung at a funny angle. Mutilated scarecrow. "Think about it: Where would you be without me? What—?"

Where *would* she be? Dek? Bill had killed Dek and brought her here to spy on her.

"Don't let him get too close!" Paul cried.

Bill began to swing his revolver toward Paul. "That does it! I've had all—"

"This is for murdering my husband." Sheila's pistol fired with a deafening report. She didn't remember pulling the trigger but the gun jumped in her hand. She saw a bright brass casing arc through the air as Bill grabbed his left breast. He stumbled back, blood leaking between his fingers, eyes wide with shock and disbelief.

He turned and fell face first across his desk where his sister stared at him in open-mouthed horror. The pistol slipped from his fingers as he slid to the floor, leaving a red smear across the desktop.

He gasped twice, then lay still.

Sheila dropped the pistol and began to cry. Paul rushed over and threw his arms around her.

The shot seemed to have shocked Coog out of his daze. He was up and hugging her and his Dad. Out of the corner of her eye she saw Shen Li smiling up at her.

———···———

Sobbing, Abra rose and pulled herself out of her chair to crawl around the desk to where her Billy lay. She touched his throat to feel his carotid pulse—still there, but weak and slow. Her little brother, the darling of her life, was dying

But what had happened to him to lead him to this fate?

Human nature.

He'd been wrong about many things, but she saw now that he'd been right about the dangers of enlightening the public.

. . . *the entire ideological spectrum, right, left, and middle, condemning us as Nazis.*

Nazis. She gagged at the idea of being lumped with those beasts. Mama had fought so hard to erase the stigma of being the daughter of a party member. Married a nice Englishman to get his name and flush out the German image. Told Bill and Abra they were different. But the public would disagree. Today, tomorrow at the latest, their dream, the Proteus Cure, would be dragged out into the open. She could see—see clearly for the first time—what would follow.

Public excoriation in all the media . . . saying her mind was as twisted as her body . . . comparisons to Mengele . . . effigy burnings . . . hurled rocks, perhaps hurled bombs . . . her name dragged through the scientific mud . . .

When all she'd wanted to do was help.

No one would understand—no one would be *allowed* to understand.

It would all come down, and she could do nothing to stop it.

She looked up and spied Bill's gun lying on the desktop. She glanced over to where the Sheila, Paul and Coogan were hugging each other and crying. All together while she was alone . . .

"Your dream . . ."

She gasped. Bill's voice, barely audible. She leaned closer, her ear nearly touching his lips.

"What?"

"It's coming true . . ."

———•••———

Sheila glanced over and saw Abra leaning over Bill. His lips were moving. Still plotting? But no . . . the growing look of horror on Abra's face said otherwise.

She straightened. "No! Oh, no!"

Bill's slack mouth and open glazed eyes confirmed the inescapable truth—he was dead. But that didn't seem to be the reason for her horrified reaction. What had he told her?

Abra grabbed Bill's pistol, pressed the muzzle against her carotid artery, and pulled the trigger.

FIFTEEN

"I still can't believe I killed someone," Sheila said as she pushed a floweret back and forth through the juice leftover from her broccoli and garlic sauce.

She couldn't believe Abra had killed herself either. Like losing her mother all over again. The grief would hit her, and hard. But for now she was safe from emotion, in that special place in her mind that allowed her to wade through her trauma and still function.

Numb, exhausted, she sat at her kitchen table with Paul. Coog had migrated to the TV in the front room to watch the news stories about the three of them. Thank God he didn't remember what had been said about him yesterday. The afternoon was all a blur for him.

"You're going to have to tell him soon," she said.

He nodded. "Very soon. I'll give things a few days to settle down, then ease him into it. I just hope it doesn't hit the airwaves first."

The TV seemed to be carrying only one story. The rain had stopped and the river was starting to recede so now they concentrated on what was being called the "Tethys Tragedy." The nature of Proteus hadn't broken yet, but it was only a matter of time.

The way she felt, cooking had been out of the question, as had eating in public. So they'd ordered Chinese takeout.

Paul reached over and gripped her hand.

"I'm so sorry you had to do that, but you had no choice."

"I just wish I felt bad about killing him."

That single finger twitch on the trigger had saved four lives. Still, it had been her finger, and she wasn't about killing, she was about life. And she couldn't help feeling good that she had stopped Bill from going any further.

She sighed and closed her eyes. It was over. After a day and a half of hell, it was finally over. Or so she hoped.

The cops had arrived sometime in the afternoon. She'd bet Bradfield's finest had never seen anything like the scene in Bill's blood-bathed office: two dead, one wounded, and three wet, bedraggled survivors.

It had taken the rest of the day to remove the bodies, cart Shen Li to the hospital, and sort things out with officialdom. By night she and Coog had been allowed to go home, but Paul—to Sheila and Coogan's horror—had been led off in handcuffs and jailed. Sheila had searched frantically for a lawyer, but trying to find one willing to take a murder case during a flood had proved impossible.

And then this afternoon, miracle of miracles, Paul had been released. Shen Li had made a deathbed confession, taking blame for Tanesha and Hal, and describing how he'd stolen the bat from Paul's garage and returned it after he'd killed Kaplan.

Deathbed confessions apparently carry a lot of weight, and Paul was freed.

All Bradfield was in shock—both from the flood and the deaths—and Tethys Medical Center was in chaos. The Feds had shut the place down and the patients were being moved to other hospitals. Nobody knew who was in charge.

But at least it was over.

Or was it?

Alone in her bed last night, Sheila had cried for Abra. How could such a good person go so wrong? Her bloody death had been a horror—Sheila had pulled Coog against her so he wouldn't see the red spray from the poor woman's neck.

And now she was gone, leaving another hole in Sheila's life.

But mourning for Abra wasn't the only thing that had kept Sheila awake. Something Bill said had bothered her. Bothered her still.

She turned to Paul. "Do you remember what Bill said before he died?"

Paul shrugged and smiled. "I don't think I was paying attention. I was just a wee bit distracted by that gun he was pointing at us. What I can't figure out is Shen Li. He was a cold-blooded murderer, but he wouldn't—or couldn't—kill Coog. Why did he give you the gun? Why confess?"

"Maybe because you saved his life. He sensed he was dying and decided to do the right thing. But Bill said something to Abra . . . something like 'Humanity needs help and it's getting that help in spite of itself.' What did he mean by that?"

"Megalomaniacal raving."

"Let's hope so. What bothers me is that he sounded so smug about it."

Paul squeezed her hand. "He was crazy, Sheila."

"But he said, 'Mama and I took matters into our own hands years ago, and we've been doing just that.' What's that mean? That VG-seven-twenty-three is being used somewhere else?"

"There's a scary thought."

Sheila nodded. "The thing is, neither he nor Abra ever mentioned his mother before. I didn't even know she was alive."

"Let's just hope she's not as crazy as he was."

"Amen. And then there's what Bill said to Abra before she killed herself. Whatever it was, it seemed to horrify her."

"You're sure the horror wasn't simply seeing the life go out of her beloved 'Billy?'"

"Could be, but I sensed it was something else."

Paul sighed. "Well, we'll never know, will we."

That's for sure, she thought as she reached for a fortune cookie.

She cracked it open and pulled out the narrow slip. Along the bottom ran a string of six lucky numbers, but the fortune gave her a chill.

Nothing is as sure as change

Her insides twisted as she handed it to Paul. He took it with a grin, but the smile faded as he read it. He looked up at her.

"It's just a coincidence, Sheila. I mean, you can't really believe a fortune cookie's got anything to do with reality."

No, she didn't.

But still . . .

__EPILOGUE__

Anna Gilchrist squirmed in her first-class seat.

Lufthansa did everything possible to provide a comfortable flight but, considering her advanced age and where she was bound, how could one be comfortable?

No parent should have to face the tragedy of outliving a child, but burying two of them—both Abra and Billy, gone at once—was almost too much to bear.

Their legacy, however—hers and the children's—would live on.

Changing the world . . .

But not one life at a time as dear, romantic Abra had believed—*millions* at a time.

Her company, Schelling Pharma, had joined the vaccine business—flu and pediatric types such as DPT, MMR, and so on. Last year Schelling had shipped one-hundred-million doses of Viron-P, its flu vaccine. Fifty million of those to America. This year the USA sale had reached seventy million. And why not? Since profit was not her motive, she was selling it for a little above cost.

Viron-P was as good against influenza as any of its competitors, but each dose also contained a helping of *Die Perfekte* stem cells. Only a few were needed to begin the job. She and Billy, working together, had neutralized its gender effect years ago. Already it was at work in last year's vaccine recipients. And seeing as children as young as six months were in the recommended vaccine population, it would already be having an impact.

A hundred million doses last year, a hundred-fifty million this year—many donated to Third World countries—and even more next. And on and on. Not as good as adding it to the water supply—Abra had been right about the unfeasibility of that—but a close second.

Billy had told her about Tanesha Green. More Tanesha Greens would be appearing. And so it was inevitable that, in a few years, the world would realize that something was amiss. But it would take them many more years to pinpoint the Schelling vaccines as the cause, and by then she would be gone and nearly a billion doses would have been dispensed. And the good will have been done.

No, not done—*begun.*

Stopping the vaccines would not stop their Protean benefits, because those benefits wouldn't be limited to the recipients. With vertical transmission to their children, and even horizontal transmission through blood banks, Proteus would keep spreading.

Anna smiled. Yes, a New World was in the making—a smarter, healthier, more peaceful world. Her legacy—hers and Abra's and Billy's. She only wished she were younger, so that she could witness it, glory in being a part of it.

THE AUTHORS

TRACY L. CARBONE is a Massachusetts native who sets most of her work in the fictional town of Bradfield. She was nominated for the Bram Stoker Award for her editing work on Epitaphs: A Journal of the New England Horror Writers. The PROTEUS CURE is her fourth published book, with previous titles including a Young Adult science fiction novel, a suspense thriller, and a collection of horror and literary dark stories. Her short stories have been published in several magazines and anthologies in the U.S. and Canada. Her medical thriller HOPE HOUSE will be released by Shadowridge Press the summer of 2013.

www.tracylcarbone.com

F. PAUL WILSON is the award-winning, NY Times bestselling author of nearly fifty books and many short stories spanning horror, adventure, medical thrillers, science fiction, and virtually everything between. More than nine million copies of his books are in print in the US and his work has been translated into twenty-four foreign languages. He also has written for the stage, screen, and interactive media. His latest thrillers, NIGHTWORLD and COLD CITY, feature his urban mercenary, Repairman Jack. Paul resides at the REAL Jersey Shore.

www.repairmanjack.com

www.shadowridgepress.com

CPSIA information can be obtained at www.ICGtesting.com
Printed in the USA
LVOW13s1458161013

357225LV00003B/587/P